D0605355

AFTER THE KISS

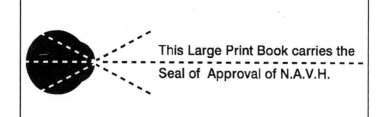

This Large Print Book carries the
Seal of Approval of N.A.V.H.

AFTER THE KISS

SUZANNE ENOCH

WHEELER PUBLISHING
A part of Gale, Cengage Learning

WASHINGTON COUNTY
COOPERATIVE LIBRARY SERVICES
HILLSBORO OR 97124-3036

GALE
CENGAGE Learning™

Detroit • New York • San Francisco • New Haven, Conn • Waterville, Maine • London

GALE
CENGAGE Learning

Copyright © 2008 by Suzanne Enoch.
Wheeler Publishing, a part of Gale, Cengage Learning.

ALL RIGHTS RESERVED
This is a work of fiction. Names, characters, places, and incidents either are the product of the author's imagination or are used fictitiously and are not to be construed as real. Any resemblance to actual events, locales, organizations, persons, living or dead, is entirely coincidental.
Wheeler Publishing Large Print Hardcover.
The text of this Large Print edition is unabridged.
Other aspects of the book may vary from the original edition.
Set in 16 pt. Plantin.
Printed on permanent paper.

LIBRARY OF CONGRESS CATALOGING-IN-PUBLICATION DATA

Enoch, Suzanne.
  After the kiss / by Suzanne Enoch.
    p. cm. — (The notorious gentlemen)
  ISBN-13: 978-1-59722-878-7 (alk. paper)
  ISBN-10: 1-59722-878-8 (alk. paper)
    1. Inheritance and succession—Fiction. 2. Art thefts—Fiction.
  3. Aristocracy (Social class)—Fiction. 4. England—Fiction. 5.
  Large type books. I. Title.
  PS3555.N655A69 2009
  813'.54—dc22   2008039341

Published in 2009 by arrangement with Avon Books, an imprint of HarperCollins Publishers.

Printed in the United States of America
1 2 3 4 5 6 7 12 11 10 09 08

For Esi Sogah —
who thought this story needed
a masquerade ball.
Thanks, Esi!
You were right.

PROLOGUE

The First Royal Dragoons
Maguilla, Spain
June 11, 1812

Captain Sullivan James Waring ducked low along his mount's neck just as a rifle ball whistled past his head. The French continued their retreat, but they weren't making the English advance an easy one. Guiding his chestnut gelding, Salty, with his knees, Sullivan reloaded his pistol as he and nearly seven hundred members of the combined First Royal Dragoons and the Third Dragoon Guards pounded across the rolling Spanish plain.

"Sullivan! What the devil is Slade doing?" the rider just to his right shouted.

"Advancing seven miles past any assistance," Sullivan replied grimly, not certain Captain Phineas Bromley could even hear him over the gunfire and pounding hooves. He sent a glance back over his shoulder at the men and horses under his command. The line was ragged, and the horses tiring. And General Slade continued to gallop along in front of them.

The six hundred French mounts ahead of *him* were tiring, as well, but it was hardly a compensation. Seven miles behind them they'd left a hundred or so French captives with a handful of dragoons to watch them — a victory and a damned fine bounty by anyone's measure. Continuing this pursuit so far beyond any reinforcements was mad. With the village of Maguilla and the broken ground of a riverbed coming into view ahead of them, it was beginning to look suicidal.

"Close ranks!" he bellowed.

Another rider angled toward him. "At this pace," Major Lord Bramwell Lowry Johns contributed breathlessly, "in three days we'll reach the coast and then be able to swim home to Dover."

"We'll never live that long," Sullivan returned, blinking dust from his eyes. "That's Maguilla up ahead. You outrank Phin and me, Bram. If you can catch General Slade, you might remind him that the bulk of the French cavalry is out here somewhere."

The major began to reply, then flinched

sideways as his black watering cap flew back off his head. "They've shot my bloody hat off, the bastards!" Bram took aim, fired his pistol, and dropped one of the French cavalrymen ahead of them. "Take that, you brigands!"

The French might be brigands, but the Royal Dragoons had their own troubles. A hundred feet ahead of them General Slade waved his saber in the air, yelling as he had been for the past ten minutes. "Haste, haste! Gallop, damn you!" The black horse hairs on his hat trailed behind him like a bloody parade streamer.

"That man is the worst officer I've ever seen," Sullivan grunted, beginning to see why they'd had to make it a punishable offense to shoot one's own commanding officer.

They pounded over a low rise, twelve hundred French and English cavalry stretched out over nearly a quarter mile. Ahead the ramshackle town of Maguilla looked deserted, as did the broken, tree-dotted riverbank beyond.

"This is not good," Phin shouted, echoing Sullivan's own assessment.

"Take the right flank," Bram ordered Phin, abruptly serious as he signaled for his men to fall to the left.

9

Spread out as they were, flanking maneuvers at best would keep them from being surprised from behind. Waving an arm forward, Sullivan kept his own men pounding up the middle behind the general. "Idiot," he muttered. At least Slade hadn't stopped the charge to adjust his stirrups this time, like he'd done last month at Corunna, but the current insanity didn't seem to be much of an improvement.

The French dragoons slowed as they reached the outskirts of the town. Sullivan lifted his pistol, accelerating as Slade stopped, the dimwit probably surprised that the chase was ending. "*Arrêtez!*" he yelled, focusing his attention on the nearest of the green-coated officers.

At the same moment he heard Phin's distinctive bellow. "Fall back! Fall back, for God's sake!"

He looked to the right just as a barrage of pistol and rifle fire nearly took off his head. Charging over the lip of the riverbank looked to be an entire regiment of green-jacketed dragoons, all of them firing into the mass of British cavalry. *Christ.* The French Seventeenth had been waiting for them.

"Covering fire!" He aimed beyond Phin's retreating dragoons and fired off his pistol.

10

One of the Frogs hit the ground, but he barely took the time to note it. The right flank, made up of two hundred of the First Royal Dragoons, was disintegrating.

He wheeled Salty to see that most of the left flank was leading the way back in the direction they'd come. Bram waded his bay against the current, rejoining him. "I knew I should have stayed in bed this morning," the Duke of Levonzy's second son panted, shoving his pistol into his waistband and pulling his saber.

"Maybe we'll find your hat on the way back," Sullivan grunted. A dismounted greencoat grabbed for Salty's bridle. Sullivan kicked him in the face, and the Frog flew backward to the ground, where he stayed. "Where's Phin?"

Wheeling again, he spotted Viscount Quence's younger brother. The captain was on the ground, his bay floundering half on top of him, with the French dragoons cutting a swath toward him through the fleeing English. Without thinking, Sullivan spurred Salty. The chestnut charged forward, right into the French line. Sullivan sliced out with his saber, feeling the wrench and tug as steel met flesh.

"Phin!"

Phineas Bromley staggered to his feet as

Sullivan reached him. Kicking a boot out of his stirrup to provide a foothold, he reached down a hand, grabbed Phin's wrist, and hauled backward. The captain swung up behind him. Salty stumbled sideways as he adjusted to the additional weight, and then they were off back the way they'd come, Bram flanking them and yelling obscenities in French as General Slade passed by them, still yelling.

"Fifty pounds to any man who'll stand and fight with me! Fifty pounds!"

Bram muttered something that sounded like, "Bloody stupid muggins," but Sullivan couldn't be certain.

"My thanks, Sully!" Phin shouted in his ear.

"No need. My mother wants to paint your portrait, remember? You can't get killed before you're immortalized."

Something burned hot and wet into his left shoulder. Sullivan slammed backward, nearly knocking Phin off of Salty's back behind him.

"Sully? Sullivan!"

His vision blurred. The last thing he remembered was Phin reaching around him for the reins, and Bram moving in to grab his left shoulder and keep him upright. And then everything went dark.

CHAPTER 1

London
One year later

It was moments like this that Sullivan Waring was struck by what a difference a year had made in his life. Whatever the circumstances that had brought him to this point, being shot in the shoulder now seemed to have been the best of it.

Sullivan tied the black half-mask across his eyes and sank into the shadows at the base of the house, squatting between the white wall and a low stand of thorny shrubs. He knew how the clocks and calendars of the London aristocracy ran, and so he'd waited until well past midnight to come calling. Tonight was about revenge. And it had the added benefit of being dangerous.

The last light went out upstairs, but he remained motionless for another ten minutes. He had time, and the more soundly the residents slept, the better for him.

Finally, as Mayfair's scattered church bells chimed three times in ragged unison, he stirred.

The information Lord Bramwell Johns had given him was inevitably reliable, though he had to question the motives of a man who sold out his own kind for no better reason than boredom. Still, he and Bram owed their lives to one another many times over, and he trusted the Duke of Levonzy's son. Bram had never betrayed him. He couldn't say the same for his own so-called father, the Marquis of Dunston.

Of course, the marquis probably had his own complaints lately. With a grim smile Sullivan stood. Tomorrow Dunston would find he had even more about which to be privately ashamed, and that was the point of the evening. Sullivan hefted the shoeing hammer in his right hand and jammed the narrower end between the window frame and its sill beside him. With one hard wrench the two separated. He dropped the hammer onto the ground and shoved the window open far enough for him to slip inside.

He'd passed by the Mayfair, London, home of the Marquis of Darshear at least once a week both before his sojourn to the Peninsula and in the six months since his return. As he made his way silently around the tasteful furniture of the morning room, he smiled again. He was inside Lord Darshear's house, now, but he doubted he would ever enter through the front door. Nor would he ever care to. He didn't approve of the marquis' taste in friends. One friend in particular.

It was one thing to be a bastard, he reflected, and quite another to be treated like one, and by his own sire. Well, he could dole out as good as he got. Better, even. And the best part of his nocturnal sojourn was that while no one else knew what was going on, the Marquis of Dunston did. He was fairly certain Dunston's pretty, legitimate progeny did, as well, or he would hope the marquis had been forced into confessing it to his eldest son by now. And there wasn't a bloody thing Dunston or the precious Viscount Tilden could do about it. Well, they could read the local newspapers and be alarmed at what they'd unleashed on their unsuspecting peers, but nothing more than that.

Sullivan tucked an ugly porcelain dove figurine into one of his voluminous pockets and made his way to the door that opened from the sitting room into the main foyer. There he paused again, listening.

Nothing stirred, but then Bram had informed him that the Chalsey family had spent the evening at the Garring soiree. Even the servants would be fast asleep by now.

Crossing through the foyer, he turned down the main hallway, which would open onto the breakfast room, with probably an office or another sitting room and then the kitchen beyond. He didn't need to go that far. Just opposite the breakfast room doorway, he found what he'd come for.

"There you are," he murmured, his heart beating faster as he ran a finger along the gold-leaf frame. An original Francesca W. Perris painting, done back just after she'd married William Perris and left behind her maiden name of Waring. Back when she'd raised him in a small house just outside of London, back when she'd promised him that even though his father might not be able to acknowledge him legally, he still had a heritage — hers.

Except that Francesca Waring Perris had died at about the same time he'd been wounded in Spain, though he hadn't learned that news until weeks later. And then he had returned home a handful of months ago to find that while he'd been good enough to fight for Britain as an officer, in the eyes of the law he had no standing at all. Not when George Sullivan, the Marquis of Dunston, claimed that all of Francesca Perris's property belonged to him. She had, after all, been his tenant for the past thirty years.

Sullivan clenched his fist, then shook his hands loose again. Memories, revenge fantasies, could all wait. At the moment he was in the home of someone who'd probably never met his mother, but who had bought or accepted one of her paintings from Dunston's hand. He didn't care whether it had been a purchase or a gift. All he cared was that by sunrise it would be his again. His heritage, his inheritance. His. And Dunston would hear about this latest theft and pray that no one else made the connection.

He grabbed a second small painting from some other obscure artist off the wall for good measure, then stripped the lace table runner from the hall table and wrapped both paintings in it. A small crystal bowl and the silver salver from the same table went into his pockets as well. Then he tucked the paintings under his arm and turned back toward the front of the house. And stopped dead.

A woman stood between him and the morning room. At first he thought he'd fallen asleep outside the house and was dreaming — her long blonde hair, blue-tipped by moonlight, fell around her shoulders like water. Her slender, still figure was silhouetted in the dim light from the front window, her white night rail shimmering and nearly transparent. She might as well have been nude.

If he'd been dreaming, though, she *would* have been naked. Half expecting her to melt away into the moonlight, Sullivan remained motionless. In the thick shadows beneath the stairs he had to be nearly invisible. If she hadn't seen him, then —

"What are you doing in my house?" she asked. Her voice shook; she was mortal after all.

If he said the wrong thing or moved too abruptly, she would scream. And then he would have a fight on his hands. While he didn't mind that, it might prevent him from leaving with the painting — and that was his major goal. Except that she still looked . . . ethereal in the darkness, and he couldn't shake the sensation that he was caught in a luminous waking dream. "I'm here for a kiss," he said.

She looked from his masked face to the bundle beneath his arm. "Then you have very bad eyesight, because that is not a kiss."

Grudgingly, despite being occupied with figuring a way to leave with both his skin and the painting, he had to admit that she had her wits about her. Even in the dark, alone, and faced with a masked stranger. "Perhaps I'll have both, then."

"You'll have neither. Put that back and leave, and I shan't call for assistance."

He took a slow step toward her. "You shouldn't warn me of your intentions," he returned, keeping his voice low, uncertain why he bothered to banter with her. "I could be on you before you draw another breath."

Her step backward matched his second one forward. "Now who's warning whom?" she asked. "Get out."

"Very well." He gestured for her to move aside, quelling the baser part of him that wanted her to remove that flimsy, useless night rail from her body so he could run his hands across her soft skin.

"Without the paintings."

"No."

"They aren't yours. Put them back."

One of them *was* his, but Sullivan wasn't about to say that aloud. "No. Be glad I'm willing to leave without the kiss, and step aside."

Actually, the idea of kissing her was begin-

19

ning to seem less mad than it had at first. Perhaps it was the moonlight, or the late hour, or the buried excitement he always felt at being somewhere in secret, of doing something that a year ago he would never even have contemplated, or the fact that he'd never seen a mouth as tempting as hers.

"Then I'm sorry. I gave you a chance." She drew a breath.

Moving fast, Sullivan closed the distance between them. Grabbing her shoulder with his free hand, he yanked her up against him, then leaned down and covered her mouth with his.

She tasted like surprise and warm chocolate. He'd expected the surprise, counted on it to stop her from yelling. But the shiver running down his spine at the touch of her soft lips to his stunned him. So did the way her hands rose to touch his face in return. Sullivan broke away, offering her a jaunty grin and trying to hide the way he was abruptly out of breath. "I seem to have gotten everything I came for after all," he murmured, and brushed past her to unlatch and open the front door.

Outside, he collected his hammer and then hurried down the street to where his horse waited. Closing the paintings into the flat leather pouch he'd brought for the purpose, he swung into the saddle. "Let's go, Achilles," he said, and the big black stallion broke into a trot.

After ten thefts, he'd become an expert in anticipating just about anything. That was the first time, though, that he'd stolen a kiss. Belatedly he reached up to remove his mask. It was gone.

His blood froze. That kiss — that blasted kiss — had distracted him more than he'd realized. And now someone had seen his face. "Damnation."

"And what would I do at home, Phillip?" Lady Isabel Chalsey asked her older brother as they descended from the family's coach. "Cower beneath my bed?"

Phillip, Earl Chalsey, frowned at her, tugging at his sleeves as he always did when he was distracted. "You came face-to-face with a burglar, Tibby. The Mayfair Marauder, no doubt. That is not an everyday occurrence."

"Precisely. I can't wait to tell absolutely everyone about it. Which is why you should be taking me to Bond Street and not to look at silly horses. None of my friends will be here, because they are shopping."

"When you jumped into the coach you knew I was going to Tattersall's. You didn't have to join me."

"Yes, I did, because I think Mama wants to send me to a nunnery now for my own safety."

"You've being overly dramatic again. And I wonder if you would be so flippant if it was *your* things that went missing instead of Mother and Father's."

For a moment she considered informing him that her virtue had nearly gone missing, but she didn't want a reputation for kissing intruders. Or Marauders, rather. "Hardly anything went missing at all. And truthfully, I'm not a bit upset that that silly dove of Mama's is gone. But I'm not being flippant. Or dramatic."

"Do tell. Next you'll be saying that the Marauder had you at swordpoint or something."

"Ooh, that does sound terrifying, doesn't it?"

"Tibby."

Isabel took Phillip's arm as they entered the grounds of Tattersall's. Ordinarily she would have preferred to remain home rather than attend the horse auctions, but after hours of listening to her mother bemoaning the loss of her various trinkets and growing faint every time she thought about the danger her daughter had been in, Isabel had had enough. Thank goodness she *hadn't* mentioned that the thief had kissed her, or she wouldn't have to imagine her fate. Her parents would have sent her back home to Burling in Cornwall for her own safety — or her virtue — and she would miss the rest of the Season.

She should have felt terrorized, she supposed, and she had been frightened half out of her wits when she'd slipped downstairs for an apple and he'd been standing there in the middle of the hallway. In that dark coat and black half-mask he'd looked like a demon — but he'd sounded like something else entirely. Not a ruffian, certainly. And his eyes had glittered green in the moonlight. His face when she'd removed his mask . . . No, not a demon at all.

"I'm not being dramatic," she said again, when she realized her brother was expecting her to feel chastised. "Not terribly so. I know I might have been injured. But I wasn't, and if I wish to talk about it with my friends and if it makes me feel braver to make it into an adventure, then I suppose I have that right."

"Yes, I suppose you do," he conceded grudgingly. "I only wish something more useful than a topic of conversation had come from this calamity. If you'd seen his face, Bow Street might finally be able to stop these thefts," Lord Chalsey commented. "You know we're at least the tenth house in Mayfair to be robbed over the past six weeks. The Marauder has everyone panicked."

Men. "Now you want me to have seen his face?" she returned. "I thought I was supposed to close my eyes or faint."

Phillip slowed, bringing her to a stop beside him. "I do not understand you, Tibby," he grumbled, his brown eyes somber. "This was serious. Confronting a thief in your own home —"

"It made me angry," she interrupted, beginning to wish that he would change the subject, after all. "If I'd been a man, I would have shot him or something, I'm sure. But since I wasn't armed, all I can do now is turn it into an amusing tale and pretend it didn't bother me. It's over, anyway. Crying now seems like a waste of time."

Her older brother patted her hand where it lay over his arm. "You're correct. And you're safe, while we've lost nothing but a pair of paintings and a few trinkets, however much Mother may claim to cherish them. If you hadn't awakened when you did, we might have lost more. So if you want to go to Bond Street to gossip this afternoon, I will escort you. But I only say that now that you're safe."

Safe and a little befuddled. No, her thief hadn't spoken or looked like a ruffian, nor had he kissed like one — not that she'd kissed any ruffians before. And there had been something else, as well. The way he'd so carefully wrapped one of those paintings, as though it were a Rubens and not a minor work of a minor artist. As though it were precious to him.

"Ah, there he is," Phillip said with a smile, increasing his pace. "He's absolutely champion."

Isabel shook herself and looked out at the teeming crowd of horses, breeders, trainers, grooms, and hopeful buyers and spectators. "Who is?"

"Not a person who. A horse who." Phillip pointed. "Over there. The bay. Sullivan Waring's stable. Bram Johns is there. Oh, by Jupiter. He's standing with Waring himself."

She spotted Lord Bramwell; in his typical stark black attire with his coal-black hair and eyes, the Duke of Levonzy's second son would stand out anywhere. He was now looking over a small paddock, an equally tall, lean man beside him and several horses, including a very fine-looking bay stallion, beyond. "He's huge, Phillip," she exclaimed.

25

"I think he may be carnivorous."

"I am," Lord Bram returned with a lazy smile, turning around to take her hand, "but never fear. I don't bite unless asked."

"Mind your manners, Bram," her brother said a little abruptly. "My sister had a scare last evening."

"Did she, now?" Lord Bramwell said, straightening. "Do tell."

"We were burgled. Isabel came across the brigand in the middle of his pilfering. We're certain it was the Mayfair Marauder. She might have been killed."

So much for her telling the story. She was *not* letting Phillip take her to Bond Street.

The second man, the one beside Lord Bramwell, stirred. "I hope you're well, then, my lady," he said.

She looked over to find ice-green eyes gazing at her, the left one obscured by a stray lock of brown hair interlaced with strands of gold. Good heavens, he was handsome. And . . . familiar. Her jaw dropped, and all the blood left her face. *Him.* "You —"

"Apologies, Lady Isabel," Lord Bramwell began at the same time. "Have you met Sullivan Waring? Sully, Lady Isabel Chalsey. You know her brother Lord Chalsey, I believe."

Before Isabel could draw a breath to

shriek or to protest that this man was the brigand who'd kissed her and stolen their things, her brother stepped in to shake Waring's hand. "Mr. Waring. Last time we met I didn't have the chance to welcome you home. I'm pleased to see you've returned safely from the Peninsula, sir."

"So am I."

Phillip grinned. "That's the bay I've heard about, isn't it? By Jupiter, he's grand."

Waring turned his gaze from Isabel to look over the paddock fence. "Yes, that's Ulysses," he said, a note of pride entering his voice. "He just turned three."

"Is he broken to saddle?"

"He is." Waring gave a low, two-toned whistle, and the thoroughbred tossed his head and trotted to the fence. "And despite appearances he's actually a good-tempered fellow," he continued, sending Isabel another glance before he produced a slice of apple for the bay.

He handed the rest of the apple to Phillip and moved back from the fence. Lord Bramwell and her brother began a conversation about the rarity of good-tempered stallions, while Isabel kept her gaze on Waring as he stopped beside her.

"I suggest you hold your tongue, my lady," he murmured.

27

"You already attempted that on my behalf, I believe," she said stiffly. "And do not threaten me. You are a common thief, and I will see you arrested."

"Common, am I?" he murmured. "I'll see you ruined if you speak a word about me. I could tell such tales about us, Isabel. You and a *common* thief." With a slow smile that didn't touch his ice-green eyes, he returned to the conversation about horses.

Isabel clenched her fists. How dare he threaten her? She'd spoken nothing but the truth. He was handsome, yes, but he was also a burglar. She spent a moment considering whether she would have been so . . . discreet if he hadn't looked like a tall, lean Greek god, or if he hadn't kissed as sinfully as the devil himself.

Her brother had said that she liked to overdramatize events, and she would agree with that. There was nothing wrong with giving happenings a certain flare to make them seem more interesting in the retelling. And she definitely, emphatically didn't like being told what to do, or being threatened when she'd done nothing wrong. And Mr. Waring had befuddled her, when she didn't like feeling confused. She'd concealed parts of the truth on his behalf — and hers — and now he threatened her?

28

"So you wish to buy Ulysses, then, I assume?" she asked her brother, wrapping her hand around his arm.

"I'll offer you fifty quid for him right now," Phillip said with a nod, "if it will save me the bother of having to bid for him."

Waring gave another cool smile. "Make it one hundred, and I'll be more amenable."

"A hundred pounds? That's —"

"What about that mare?" Isabel interrupted, pointing at the pretty gray in the adjoining corral.

"She's not saddle-broken," Waring said, not looking at her, and apparently confident that his threat had cowed her. "I'll sell her for brood."

"I want her." *Ha.* She didn't cow easily.

"Tibby," Phillip said in a lower voice. "Firstly, declaring you want a horse is hardly the way to get the best price. And secondly, an unbroken mare? For *you?* If you want to learn to r —"

"I want that one. I'm certain if you give him the hundred pounds, Mr. Waring would be happy to throw in the mare."

Mr. Waring pulled in a breath, then gave a short nod, his gaze still on Phillip. "I would agree to that."

"But —"

"*And,*" she continued, as though her

29

brother hadn't begun speaking, "I'm equally certain Mr. Waring would be willing to saddle-train her for me."

"No."

This time he looked directly at her. Apparently he didn't like being dictated to, either. But he was the sinner; not she. He merely needed to be reminded who had the advantage here today. She took a step closer. "A hundred pounds, Mr. Waring," she said with a smile. "Surely for that you can break one mare to the sidesaddle, especially if she's pure-blooded enough to be bred."

He gazed at her evenly. "Very well. I'll have her delivered to you in three weeks."

"Oh, no. I want her now. You may train her at our stable."

"Tibby," Phillip broke in with a frown, "Mr. Waring is a very sought-after breeder. He doesn't have time to —"

"A hundred and twenty pounds, then. Surely twenty pounds would compensate you for your time." Isabel deepened her smile. "Then you wouldn't have to go marauding about Mayfair looking for buyers."

His jaw worked, fury in the straight line of his spine. Every instinct for self-preservation she possessed screamed at her to back away at once and tell her brother precisely what had transpired last night. Just as strong, though, was the wish to turn this to her advantage. She'd never had her hands on a secret of this magnitude before, and it excited her enough that she didn't want to let it go. Not until she could show him she would not be intimidated because of a kiss and a threat.

"Sully?" Lord Bramwell drawled, and Mr. Waring visibly shook himself.

"I'll bring the pair to Chalsey House this afternoon," he grated. "Pray give me your address."

As if he needed that. With another smile she waved her fingers at her brother. "Phillip will see to that. Does my mare have a name?"

"Zephyr," Mr. Waring returned, his voice curt. "But I call her Brat."

Humph. He would regret that. "Well, as you will be working for me, from now on you shall call her Zephyr. Phillip, when you've paid Mr. Waring, please help me purchase an appropriate saddle."

"You don't ride?" Waring asked, lifting an eyebrow.

"Well, I do now. Or I will, when you've finished your work."

Deliberately turning her back on him, she walked over to take a look at her new horse from the safety of the other side of the wooden rails enclosing her. Whether she learned to ride or not, at least she would know where Mr. Sullivan Waring was spending his days until she could decide what to do about him. And to think, she'd wanted to go and tell her friends about last night's excitement. She'd never reckoned that that would only be the beginning of the tale.

CHAPTER 2

"You might have mentioned that someone saw you." Bram opened his monogrammed handkerchief and spread it over a loose bale of hay before he took a seat.

Sullivan didn't want to sit. Pacing seemed to be the only thing that would take the edge off his frustration. "I never expected to set eyes on her again," he growled. "How the bloody hell was I supposed to know that her brother would be here today?"

Bram twirled a stalk of hay in his fingers. "She didn't have you arrested. That does make one curious."

It made Sullivan curious, as well. "I threatened her."

"Apparently she realized that you have more at stake in this than she does. Because you, my friend, would now seem to be her slave."

"Nonsense. I'm delivering a pair of horses."

"And helping your pretty miss learn to ride." He gave a lazy smile. "That's usually a metaphor."

"Not this time." Sullivan bent down to pick up a clod of dirt to hurl it against the wooden side of a watering trough. It exploded into dust. "Damnation."

Bram lifted an eyebrow. "You might leave London for a time."

"I have four more paintings to recover."

"If she carries your tale, Sully, they'll hang you at Tyburn Hill for stealing from aristocrats."

Sullivan shrugged. "If I was arrested, Dunston would probably see to it that I was transported. A hanging in the family tree is a bit messy."

"You're not in his family tree. Not according to his . . . well, his family."

"Do you really think I need to be reminded of that?"

Bram sighed. "No. But I didn't think you needed to be reminded not to be seen, either. Wear a mask from now on, for Lucifer's sake."

"I do wear a mask."

"Then how did Lady Isabel recognize you?"

Yes, how had that happened? Oh, yes. He remembered. "I don't know," he muttered aloud, turning as one of his groomsmen appeared. "Samuel, take Zephyr out of the paddock. She's already been purchased. And have Halliwell take the mare and Ulysses off the docket."

"Aye, Mr. Waring."

Sullivan pulled out his pocket watch. The other four mares he'd brought today would be going up for auction in fifteen minutes or so; he needed to be there. "I'll see you at Jezebel's tonight, yes?" he asked, glancing at Bram as he retrieved his paperwork.

"No. I have plans to seduce a pretty young thing tonight."

"Ah. And who is it this time?"

Bramwell stood, pitching the stalk of hay onto the ground and heading to where he'd left his own horse standing. "I haven't decided yet."

With a quickly covered frown, Sullivan glanced at his friend and then away again. "I kissed her," he said shortly.

He felt rather than saw Bram pause. "Beg pardon?"

"I kissed her, and she took my mask off before I'd realized it. That's how she recognized me." Sullivan kept his back to his friend, but it didn't help. He didn't need to see Bram eyeing him to know that he'd been an idiot. "I never expected her to appear at

Tattersall's, and it's not as though we'd ever meet at Almack's."

"What? Apologies. I'm still at the part of the conversation where you said *you kissed her.*"

"She stumbled across me."

"And onto your mouth?"

"I couldn't think of anything else to do to keep her from screaming."

"You were distracting her, then."

Sullivan shook out his shoulders, trying to relieve the tension in his muscles. "Yes. I was distracting her."

Bram approached him again. "Having distracted several women myself," he said, placing an arm across Sullivan's shoulders, "all I can say is that you, Sullivan, are a complete nodcock."

With a glare, Sullivan broke free of the embrace. "I'm aware of that." Very aware. Not only had he accosted the virtue of a lady who outranked him socially, but he'd put himself, his freedom, into her hands. And from what he'd seen this morning, she was nothing but a spoiled, headstrong chit who liked to play games.

"What are you going to do about it, since you won't listen to me and leave London?"

Sullivan looked at his friend. "I'll find out what it will take to convince her to keep her pretty mouth shut, and then I'll finish what I began."

"Ah. With the kiss, or with the thefts?"

"The thefts, Bram." Sullivan stalked over to the wagon where he kept his equipment and tack, and climbed up to look for his longeing whip. "I don't give a damn about the kiss."

Thankfully Bram had enough wit to refrain from replying to that, and instead he rode off in the direction of Pall Mall. Good. Sullivan didn't feel like continuing the discussion of his missteps and errors in judgment today. Not when he still couldn't shake the odd, foggy sensation that had dogged him since he'd turned around to see Lady Isabel Chalsey standing in her foyer this morning.

He blew out his breath. If he'd threatened her rather than kissed her, if he'd stayed back rather than let her pull off his mask, then even if they had come face-to-face today, even if they'd spoken, she never would have known. He would have been Sullivan James Waring, the most sought-after horse breeder and trainer in the south of England. He never would have tasted her sweet mouth, and she would not have any cause to blackmail him into playing her bloody game, whatever it might be.

"Mr. Waring?"

He jumped down from the wagon as a large, well-dressed man with close-set eyes and a weak chin approached. "Lord Massey," he said, lowering his head briefly and dusting off his trousers. "What can I do for you this morning?"

"I heard some gossip flying about that you brought Ulysses with you today."

"I did, but for a private sale, I'm afraid." Something else he never would have done if not for that damned chit.

The viscount's left eye twitched. "I'd hoped to acquire him, you know."

"You and several others, my lord. Unfortunately, the gentleman to whom I'd given first right of refusal decided to take him."

"Reconsider. I'll give you a hundred pounds for him, if you'll say *I* had the prior claim."

"That's very generous, but a deal is a deal."

"Two hundred pounds."

Sullivan kept his expression cool and sympathetic. "Once again, I cannot, my lord. Ulysses is sold."

"I won't take no for —"

"What I *can* do, however," Sullivan cut in, wondering if Massey had any idea how little he liked being bullied or pressured, "is give you first run at Ulysses' brother, Spartan. I'll be bringing him in for auction early next month."

"Spartan, eh? The sire is Hector?"

"Yes."

"Who's the dam?"

"Lilac Pleasure. The sister of Ulysses' dam, Lavender Pleasure."

"I insist on seeing this Spartan before I commit to anything."

"Come by my stables at your convenience. Someone will put him through his paces for you."

"Very well. The next time you intend to sell one of your prime animals, Waring, I expect to be the first buyer you inform."

Sullivan clenched his jaw. The only thing keeping him from demonstrating his own displeasure with Lord Massey was the knowledge that a fortnight ago the viscount's London house had suffered a break-in. "As Spartan is my next prime animal to be offered for sale, you *have* been informed before anyone else. Now, if you'll excuse me, my lord, I have some matters to attend to."

The viscount glared at him for a moment. Apparently his desire for a prime blood-horse and for the opportunity to bid on future animals, however, outweighed his anger, because with a curt nod he turned on his heel and headed back to the main auction arena.

Bloody self-important aristocratic pudding-bag. As though Massey's parents wearing wedding bands made the viscount less of a bastard than someone whose parents had succumbed to something baser. Sullivan went to find his men to give them instructions for the remainder of the day. If Lady Isabel Chalsey thought he would fall meekly into her little game, she was about to be in for a rather nasty surprise.

"You purchased a horse?" Lord Douglas Chalsey said skeptically. "You, Tibby?"

Isabel favored her younger brother with what she hoped was a disdainful glare. "Yes, I purchased a horse, Douglas. Young ladies of quality do ride, you know."

The sixteen-year-old circled her again. "Yes, I know. But those chits ain't frightened of horses. You are."

"I am not! And stop prancing around me; you're making me ill. For your information, Douglas, I'm cautious around large animals, as anyone with any sense should be. I am not afraid of them. I'm not afraid of any-thing."

Douglas made a rude sound. With his

40

usual impeccable timing their father Harry, the Marquis of Darshear, appeared at the top of the front steps and descended to cuff his youngest offspring on the back of the head.

"Having manners means toward everyone, Douglas," he intoned, and kissed Isabel on the cheek. "Even your sister."

"For someone who's not afraid of anything, she screamed loud enough at that bit of burlap in her bed."

"You made it look like a snake," she protested, wishing the men in her family would make themselves scarce until after her horse arrived. She wanted a moment to speak with Mr. Sullivan Waring in private about who could threaten whom. "You even painted eyes on it."

Her younger brother laughed. "You're such a girl." Sometime over the winter he'd surpassed her in height, and he apparently thought that made him invincible, silly boy. "And you were the one who tried to cow me first," he continued, "when you said you were going to write a book about how to commit a murder."

She'd forgotten about that. It might have come in handy today. "You said reptiles were going to devour me."

"Children, please. If you'll recall, Douglas," her father said, checking the time on his pocket watch, "while you were fast asleep last night your sister frightened away a thief. I hardly call that a demonstration of cowardice."

"Yes, well, if *I'd* come across the Mayfair Marauder, I would have put a ball in him or run him through." Douglas assumed a boxing pose.

Isabel doubted that. Mr. Waring had several inches even on Phillip, and he seemed supremely . . . capable. Looking from one brother down the drive to the other, for a moment she was glad that she'd been the one to stumble across the thief, giving him the option of delivering a kiss rather than a ball.

"Our brave girl did precisely the right thing," the marquis countered, "and I'll not hear otherwise. Now tell me again why your brother is pacing the street like a hound waiting for his master."

She mustered a smile. "He's smitten with his new stallion. We're expecting a delivery at any moment now."

"Ah, your brother and his cattle. I should have known."

Phillip obviously heard them talking, because the earl returned up the head of the short drive to join them. "He's not just any horse, Father," he said, grinning as he had been for the past two hours.

"That's right," Douglas piped up. "He's a thoroughbred."

"What stable?" the marquis asked.

"Sullivan Waring's."

Her father looked impressed. "You must have paid a pretty penny, then."

"A hundred and twenty quid for the two animals *and* training for Tibby's mare." He leaned closer. "Training from Waring himself. Our Isabel's quite the negotiator."

Douglas grabbed her arm, making her jump. "You never said!" he exclaimed. "Sullivan Waring's coming here?"

She shook herself free. "For heaven's sake, Douglas. Yes, a horse breeder's coming here to deliver the horses we purchased from him."

"I thought chits knew all the good gossip," her younger brother said with a grin. "Sullivan Waring ain't just a horse breeder, though he's a lion at that. He's supposedly the by-blow of —"

"Quiet. He's here," Phillip interrupted, sprinting for the entrance of the drive again.

Mr. Waring clattered up the drive, riding a spectacular black stallion, Ulysses and Zephyr in tow. In her admittedly unschooled opinion, Isabel thought Phillip had purchased the second-best stallion in Waring's stable. Beautiful as the horses were, though, her gaze drifted to Sullivan Waring, his chestnut hair shot with gold, his easy, confident seat in the saddle, and the expression in his ice-green eyes as they flicked across her face and traveled on to her father.

"Lord Darshear," he said, giving a brief nod as he dismounted.

"Mr. Waring. What splendid animals."

"Thank you." Waring glanced at Isabel again. "I do ask that you speak with your daughter, my lord. Zephyr is a fine mare, but not fit for a novice."

Shaking herself, Isabel stepped forward. "It's your task to make her so, I believe. That *is* what I paid you for."

"Isabel," her father chastised sharply, surprising her. "Mr. Waring, is Zephyr a dangerous animal?"

All she needed was for her father to release Sullivan Waring from his obligation to remain close by; then the thief could vanish to God knew where, robbing willy-nilly. Even worse, she wouldn't know why. Because while she adored a good mystery or a good secret, she hated when one was kept from her. Especially one that had kissed her.

"No, Zephyr is fairly levelheaded," the horse breeder interrupted, as though she hadn't been speaking. "She's been raised for breeding, however. I've never done more than put her on a lead."

With a frown her father looked over at Isabel. "I have to agree with Mr. Waring, then, Tibby. For your first mount, you should have an older, more gently bred mare who's well experienced at carrying a novice rider."

Isabel lifted her chin. "I want Zephyr," she said, using the same tone she'd favored when she'd been twelve and had wanted a particular new hat. But damnation, she seemed to be the only one who knew what this fellow was doing, and she had apparently developed an obsession to find out how and why. That silly craving she had for drama and excitement again. He looked to provide a great deal of it for her.

"Tibby," Phillip seconded, grimacing at her, "be reasonable."

"I am being reasonable," she said. "You've all three been bragging about Mr. Waring's skill with horses. I'm certain he will sufficiently train Zephyr so that I will be perfectly safe riding her." She deliberately turned to gaze at Waring. "Isn't that so, Mr. Waring?"

He gave a stiff nod. "Of course, Lady Isabel."

She smiled brightly. "Because if anything

should happen to me, you would be blamed for it."

Well, that had perhaps been a bit straightforward, but she didn't know how else to convince him to stay close by until . . . until she'd figured out why he fascinated her so. For heaven's sake, she'd never blackmailed anyone before. It frightened and excited her all at the same time. And that seemed more significant than turning him over to the authorities. At least for now.

Phillip led the group of people and horses around the house to the stable at the back. At six-and-twenty her older brother could at times be almost comically stoic, but today with his flushed cheeks and quick smile he looked more like a boy tasting hard candy for the first time than he did the oldest male offspring of a marquis. As for Douglas, the teen pranced in a circle around Waring with such enthusiasm that if he'd been a puppy he likely would have wet himself.

As they reached the stable she grabbed Douglas's arm and hauled him a short distance from their so-called guest, her admiring family, and the growing crowd of grooms and stableboys. "What were —"

"Fiend seize it, Tibby, let me go," he grumbled.

"What were you saying about Mr. Waring?" she insisted, keeping her voice low and yanking on her brother's sleeve to keep his wandering attention.

"I said he's the primest horse breeder in England. Now let go before I miss something he says."

"No. Not that," she returned, ignoring his protest. "You started to say that he was reputedly someone's by-blow. Whose?"

"I just got clubbed in the head for being impolite. I'm not talking to my own damned sister about bastards."

Stifling a growl, Isabel grabbed his left ear. "Talk!"

Douglas howled and twisted away from her. "Amazon!"

"Coward!"

"Isabel!" her father said sharply. "If you expect me to allow you to ride this animal, you first need to prove that you will devote your time and attention to doing it properly."

With an irritated sigh she stopped pinching Douglas and returned to her father's side. "Apologies," she said stiffly, to him rather than to Waring. "What did I miss?"

"How to saddle a stallion."

"I hardly think that's my concern, then."

"You need to know how to handle an animal."

For a second she couldn't figure out whether her father was referring to Ulysses or to Waring. The men, though, were obviously enraptured, and she was the only one who knew that Waring was anything other than what he claimed. He finished buckling the girth on Ulysses' saddle, then offered his cupped hands to Phillip. "Remember, Lord Chalsey," he said, as her brother swung into the saddle, "he's trained as a hunter, so he's got a sensitive mouth. If you even think about turning, he'll turn."

Since Phillip generally acted as though he knew everything, Isabel was deeply surprised when he only took the reins and nodded. Waring stepped back, ending up directly beside her, while her brother walked Ulysses about the stable yard and said admiring things.

Isabel studied Sullivan Waring's profile as he gazed at the big stallion like a proud papa. She would put him somewhere in his late twenties, a few years older than Phillip. He was built like a born horseman, tall and lean, with strong hands and muscular thighs, his light brown hair disheveled from riding hatless. What was he up to? An obviously well-respected horse breeder who broke into homes and burgled them by night? Aside from the fact that he'd kissed her, this didn't make any sense. Which made for a mystery — something else she enjoyed probably more than she should.

"What are you up to, my lady?" Waring murmured, sending her a brief sideways glance.

"I'll ask the questions, Mr. Waring. And if you wish to remain out of shackles, you'd best do as I say."

"To a point, my lady. Don't push me."

She ignored the warning. Or she pretended to; inside, she was quite a bit less certain. "I'll do as I please," she said aloud. "And you'll do as I please, as well, Mr. Marauder."

Chapter 3

Sullivan Waring leaned over the wooden gate of the box stall and absently fed carrots to his mount. Distraction was never safe, even away from legally declared wars and uniformed enemies, but this evening he couldn't help himself. Achilles nickered as one of the stableboys passed the open doors, a mare in tow. "Sorry, old fellow," Sullivan murmured, rubbing the black's nose, "she's not for you."

"Mr. Waring?"

He shook himself. "Yes, Samuel?"

The groom shuffled his feet. "Sir, I put the sacks of feed up in the loft, and the pasture troughs are full. If you —"

"Off with you, then." Sullivan glanced over his shoulder at the shorter man. "Well done with the mares today. McCray has your pay; you'll find an extra five quid there. And enjoy your holiday in Bristol."

The groom grinned. "Thank you, sir. My

boys are beside themselves to see their grandmum again. I'll be back here bright and early next Tuesday."

"I know you will be. Good night."

"Good night, Mr. Waring." With a half salute, Samuel headed out the back door.

"So now you're giving employees bonuses and time to visit their relations?" Bramwell Johns drawled from the double doors at the front of the large stable. "People will begin to think you're . . . pleasant."

"Only until they come to know me." Declining to admit that he had a soft spot in his heart for families who actually liked one another, Sullivan handed over a last carrot to Achilles and moved away from the stall. "I thought you were going to seduce some chit or other tonight."

"Yes, I already did. Then I got bored. It was lamentably easy, really. Morality these days truly gives me pause."

Sullivan grinned. "No, it doesn't. In fact, I've a suspicion that you're the major cause of Society's decay." Walking past his friend to the main entrance, he pulled the double doors closed and latched them from the inside.

"I certainly hope so. I've put enough effort into it."

"Why are you here, Bram?"

51

"I was worried about you, Sully. How was your afternoon with Phillip Chalsey and the chit you kissed?"

"Say that a bit louder, why don't you?" Sullivan grunted, lifting a lantern off a hook and heading for the back door. With Samuel gone for the next week, Vincent would be sleeping alone in the stable, and he stepped aside as the small man, a former Derby jockey, entered. "You're all set, I presume?"

"Aye, Mr. Waring. Don't worry about a thing."

He couldn't help worrying. Even with two grooms making rounds all night they'd come close to losing stock from time to time — along with the reputation for having the region's finest horses came the risk that someone else would want to possess them. Funny, he supposed, that a thief worried about thieves. "Even so," he said aloud, "I'll take a turn or two about the place tonight. So don't shoot until you're certain it's not me."

Vincent grinned, tugging on his hat. "I'll do my best, sir."

"Does this mean you're not going to Jezebel's with me?" Bram asked, following him across the large stable yard toward his small two-story cottage.

52

"I thought you had a ball or something tonight."

"Almack's," his friend returned, in a tone that said that one word should explain everything.

"Tell me again why you don't have any friends of your own station?" Sullivan asked, stripping off his rough work jacket as they entered the cottage and hanging it on a peg beside the door.

"They're all jealous of my good looks and keen wit. You, however, know the true, inner me."

Sullivan shook his head. "The only inner you I've seen is when you got sliced on the arm. It's red."

"Precisely. As are your innards. You see, we have so much in common."

Obviously Bramwell *was* bored this evening, and just as obviously Sullivan wouldn't have a moment of peace until he gave in. "Buy my dinner, and I'll go with you," he said, dipping his hands into the washbowl and scrubbing off the dirt.

"Done. And then you can tell me what you're going to do about your problem."

His problem. Lady Isabel Chalsey. With a shrug he tossed Bramwell a bottle of whiskey. "She's not much of a problem," he said offhandedly, trudging up the stairs to change into evening attire. "She's had her moment of bravado, so I'll tolerate her for a day or two and meanwhile make it clear that she needs to keep her pretty mouth shut."

"Her 'pretty' mouth?" Lord Bramwell repeated from the ground floor.

Bloody hell. "Yes, her mouth. Her keeping her nose closed wouldn't much benefit me, now, would it?"

"That depends on how much time you've been spending in the stable with the horse shit."

The wisest plan for tonight would probably have been to stay at home and spend the ensuing hours before his morning visit to Chalsey House figuring out what precisely he was going to do about Lady Isabel. Sullivan blew out his breath.

He was popular with ladies of quality, and he'd had his share of lovers. This, though, was different. This was complicated. And despite the kiss and the odd . . . connection he felt with her, he wasn't certain this difficulty was something he could resolve through physical domination or intimidation. What did spoiled, pretty chits fear? What could he offer or threaten that would convince her to keep her silence? She'd kept his secret to this point, but he had no idea why. And he needed to find the answer to that question without delay.

He pulled on a clean shirt and buttoned a waistcoat over it, then shrugged into a jacket. Jezebel's had a very mixed clientele, from merchants to bankers to horse breeders to second sons of dukes, but he would be in Bram's company, and so he would look the part. And to himself he could admit that he didn't want to appear common. Of course, he *wasn't* common. Without his father's acknowledgment, he wasn't anything.

"You look lovely," Bram drawled from a chair by the fire downstairs. "Prettier than me, even. I don't know that I like that."

With a snort, Sullivan pulled on his greatcoat and beaver hat. "You're still the prettiest," he said, calling for his housekeeper and instructing Mrs. Howard to bank the fires and go home for the night.

"As long as we agree about that," Bram continued, leading the way to his coach. "So what do you know about the Chalsey family?"

Sullivan took the opposite seat, and the big black behemoth rocked into motion. "Wealthy, two sons and a daughter. The oldest boy is an earl with a fondness for fine horses, the daughter is a light sleeper, and

they used to own one of my mother's paintings."

"You're beginning to sound cynical."

"I *am* cynical."

Bramwell gazed at him for a moment, his
eyes shadowed in the dark coach. "By some
miracle you're not dead, Sullivan," he finally
said in a quiet voice. "The Chalseys are a
straitlaced lot. And their daughter is one of
polite Society's darlings. Don't take Lady
Isabel's silence for granted. I'd hate for you
to end on the gallows after I went to the
bother of saving your life in Spain."

Sullivan narrowed his eyes. "You're not
actually concerned about me, are you,
Bram? Because I think I was fairly clear
about my intentions when this all began,
and you still agreed to point out the loca-
tions where I might find those paintings
once you spotted them. Nothing's changed."

"Someone saw you. That changes things.
And even if you can persuade her to keep
her knowledge to herself for now, what's
going to happen when you go after the next
painting? Will she stay silent then?"

For a long moment Sullivan gazed through
the coach window at the moonlit evening.
His stable was just outside London, but it
felt far more countrified. Yet within a mile
or two they'd reached the heart of town

again. "The risks are mine, Bram. If you're backing out of our —"

"No, I'm not backing out. Damnation, you're stubborn. Get yourself hanged, then. I'll continue to do my part."

"That's all I ask."

All through dinner he fended off questions from Bramwell about his plans regarding Lady Isabel, and from Molly Cooper about his plans for the rest of the evening. The innkeeper's daughter was a pretty little thing, but it was rumored that her father kept a loaded musket behind the beer kegs, and Sullivan didn't feel like the risk would be worth the reward. Aside from that, he had other things on his mind.

Finally Bram pulled a handful of social invitations from his pocket. "These are the ones I'm undecided about," he said, pushing the stack in front of Sullivan. "Any preferences?"

Sullivan looked through them. They were requests for Bram's presence at various soirees, music recitals, and private dinners; he already would have accepted the invitations to the more interesting and prestigious events. After all, cynical and jaded as he was, Bram did have a duke for a father.

"The Hardings," he said, sending one of the cards back in his friend's direction. "Eugenia Harding already owns two of my mother's paintings legitimately."

"So what should I *not* look for?"

"Two young girls in a flower garden, and Dover at sunset," he said immediately. Even if he hadn't remembered them all, his mother had kept very precise records. That was why when he'd returned home from the Peninsula to find every wall in her home bare of her own dearest paintings, he'd known it hadn't been her idea.

"Are you certain you don't want those back, as well?"

Sullivan shook his head. "She sold them. I only want the ones that were stolen from her, and from me."

"I'm merely saying, as long as you're . . . liberating items from a house and angering Dunston, why stop at the ones to which you have a legitimate claim?"

"Because I have a legitimate claim to them." He handed back another folded card. "This one. Barnett's a collector, and he's greedy."

Bram frowned. "But he has two unmarried daughters."

"And?"

"You know precisely what the 'and' is, Sullivan. The only reason I was invited to their dinner was so one of the chits could trap me into marriage. If I attend, they'll think I'm willing."

"If you weren't willing to go, you shouldn't have handed me the invitation."

"You are hardheaded."

"I'm on a course of vengeance, if you'll recall. It's supposed to be messy." Sullivan took a breath. A good friend probably wouldn't attempt to force his companion to attend something he deemed unpleasant. He knew Bram well enough, though, to have a fair idea that the Duke of Levonzy's son wouldn't do anything he didn't want to, under any circumstances. "Those are the only two that strike a note with me," he continued, handing back the rest of the invitations.

Bram signaled for another glass of port. For a moment he looked as though he wanted to say something, but he finished off the last few bites of his roast duck instead. Good. Sullivan could think of a few choice words for someone who lived the life that Bram did and then handed out advice to others.

Yes, what he'd chosen to do was danger- ous. And yes, he supposed that he'd had the option of making a legal or a public outcry about his missing property. He'd seen the results of such things before, however, and he had a business to protect and employees to support. No, a few thefts were the best way to set things right.

And his burglaries had the added benefit of undoubtedly angering and humiliating the original thief, with the happy knowledge that the Marquis of Dunston could do nothing about it without ruining his own good standing with his fellows. After all, failing to acknowledge an illegitimate son was one thing. Stealing from the poor soul, especially when he was a respected fringe member of Society — well, that would just be shabby. And Dunston and his legitimate brood were never shabby. Thieves, yes. But not shabby ones.

With a breath he set aside his own tankard of bitters. "I'd best be off. I wasn't making up excuses to try to avoid dinner with you, earlier. With Samuel gone, I *do* want another pair of eyes watching my stock." He glanced across the table. "And you have to be at Almack's before long, don't you?"

"I told you, I'm not going."

"Mm-hm. It's not your fault that you're blue-blooded, Lord Bramwell Lowry Johns. I've already forgiven you for that."

Bram sent him a dark smile. "Yes, but there are other offenses on my head."

Before Sullivan could ask what he meant

by that, Bram paid their bill and rose from the table. In the midst of the noise and drinking and wagering and cigar smoke of Jezebel's, private conversation was both easy and almost impossible all at the same time, but business was one thing. For Bram, personal matters were another. And there was nothing new about that.

Sullivan hired a hack to drive him back to his three acres of stables, cottage, and grazing land. It wasn't much by noble standards, he supposed, but at least he'd worked for it and earned it himself. And no one could take it away from him.

Sullivan scowled. No one, that was, except for Lady Isabel Chalsey. Putting him in prison would make his land forfeit. How much of a threat was she, then? Pretty and spoiled, no match for him physically, but she had a mouth on her. Good for kissing, but quite capable of ruining his life. He needed to do something about her. And before his next sojourn through someone's window.

"Mama, I just wanted a horse," Isabel stated for the fiftieth time since Zephyr had arrived. She wasn't any closer to believing it, but she hoped her family was. "Eloise is always going riding, and she says it's wonderful exercise. So I decided to stop being a ninny about it and learn to ride."

Lady Darshear looked at her from across the breakfast table. "Eloise Rampling is a lovely young lady, but you've never felt the need to imitate her daily routine. If anything, the other girls follow *your* lead."

"It's not about aping anyone. I'm nineteen, Mama. Nearly twenty. I'm past being silly, and I would like to be able to do this."

"She certainly couldn't have chosen a better teacher," her father put in as he entered the breakfast room, pausing to kiss his wife and then Isabel on the cheek before he sat at the head of the table. "And as we're something of a family of horse lovers, I'm glad you've decided to give this a go."

Isabel half thought his amenability was because she'd secured the great Sullivan Waring to come to the house for the next fortnight or so, but she didn't say that aloud. She might tend to look for high drama or create her own where none existed, but with her parents — or her mother, at least — expressing concern over her latest project, she'd abruptly begun to realize that she wasn't just keeping a secret. She was lying.

For heaven's sake, if she'd had more time to consider how to proceed, or a bit of advance notice that she'd been about to stumble in broad daylight across the man who'd stolen paintings from the house and a kiss from her, she doubted she would have settled on this solution. It wasn't even a solution, really; it was a stalling tactic to keep Mr. Waring close by until she could . . . what? Decide how to best him for taking liberties with her? Have him arrested? He was a thief, after all. He deserved to be —

"My lord," the butler said, sending a glare at the footman with whom he'd just spoken, "a Mr. Waring is in the stable yard, awaiting Lady Isabel."

"He's here!" Douglas crowed, bouncing into the room. "He rode that big black again. By Jove, he's bang up to the echo."

"Douglas," the marchioness chastised. "A little decorum, if you please. It's not as though the Prince Regent's come calling."

"This is better than Prinny."

"Harry, say something to that boy of yours."

"I'm sorry, my dear, but in this instance I have to agree with Douglas." The marquis pushed away from the table. "I've chatted with Mr. Waring on occasion, but to actually see him work . . . Come along, Tibby. Let's go see what the master horse breeder has planned for today."

Douglas sped out of the room, but Isabel resumed picking at the toasted bread she'd actually finished with five minutes ago. "I'm eating. And he's a horse breeder, for goodness' sake. He can wait."

"Are you certain you aren't delaying because of the horse?" the marquis countered, shaking his graying brown head at her. "I would understand why. Stay here if you wish. I'll send Zephyr home with Mr. Waring."

"I'm not — Oh, bother." Frowning, she stood up. "Very well, then. Let's go say hello to the illustrious Mr. Waring."

She could pretend it was indifference, but the reluctance was very real. It was just that Zephyr wasn't the only reason for it. Luckily Douglas and her father were too occupied chatting about the next Derby races to notice her trepidation. Shaking out her shoulders, Isabel followed along behind them. It was one thing to be uncertain of her ground. Allowing Sullivan Waring to see that would be quite another.

He was seated on the back of her father's phaeton as they exited the house through the kitchen. Today he'd dressed less like a gentleman and more like a stableboy, his coat draped over a post and his shirtsleeves rolled halfway to his elbows. Isabel swallowed. She'd been struck before by his hard handsomeness, but taken altogether, he looked like one of the great Greek heroes about whom Homer had spun his tales.

"Good morning," he said, inclining his head and jumping to the ground. A strand of dark gold hair slanted across one light green eye.

"Mr. Waring," her father said, smiling as he offered his hand. "I see you're a man of your word."

"I thought this might be a bit early," Waring returned, shaking and releasing the marquis' hand, "but it needs to be if I'm to deliver two training sessions each day in addition to my other responsibilities."

"Two?" Isabel blurted. "Each day?"

"That's the recommended routine," Douglas supplied, eyeing Waring's attire as though trying to commit it to memory. "Thirty minutes each, to start with. Isn't that it, sir?"

"It is." Waring nodded, facing Isabel. "Shall we begin, then, my lady?"

"Oh, smashing!"

Wonderful. "No, Douglas," she said forcefully. "I don't want you stomping about and frightening everything on two or four legs."

"But you've —"

"That's a very good point," her father put

in. "You're going to Parliament with me today, anyway."

"But I —"

"Come along." The marquis squeezed Isabel's fingers. "Phipps is about, and what looks like half the grooms and stableboys. You won't be riding today, and Phipps will keep an eye on things."

"I'll be fine. Thank you, Papa." She hoped he believed her, even with her hands shaking. Of course, he expected her to be unsettled around horses, and she was. They also provided a good excuse for nerves of another sort entirely. The game didn't seem quite so much a game with her opponent looking straight at her.

"That was handy," Waring commented as her father and brother returned to the house.

She took a breath, having to look up to meet his gaze. "I'm surprised you waited out here instead of climbing inside through a window or something."

He took a slow step closer, dust rising around his black boots on the bare ground. "Just keep in mind that I *can* climb through a window, anytime I choose."

So that was how they were going to play this game — bluff versus bravado. Except

66

she wasn't entirely certain that he was bluffing.

Neither, though, was she. Or so she hoped. "And you keep in mind, Mr. Waring, that I can clip your wings, anytime *I* choose."

"We'll see about that, my lady."

CHAPTER 4

Isabel followed at a distance as Waring walked into the Chalsey family stable like he owned it. The servants inside all gave him room, apparently under the same misapprehension. That was more than enough of that. "Phipps, please bring my horse out."

Waring ignored her, continuing up to the small stall where Zephyr had already swung her head around to nicker at him. "Hello, girl," he said in a deep, soothing voice that rumbled down Isabel's own spine. He rubbed the mare's nose as he attached a long rope to her halter.

Phipps opened the stall door, and Waring backed Zephyr into the main part of the stable. Her ears flicked back and forth, but she stayed close by the breeder's shoulder.

"Do you want to lead her out?" he asked, offering Isabel the folded length of rope.

She put her hands behind her back, trying

not to gasp. "A completely untrained animal? I think not, Mr. Waring."

He drew even with her, and slowed. "Not as bold as you'd like me to think, are you, my lady?" he said in a low voice. "Be careful; your weaknesses are showing."

Drat. "Well, that's a ridiculous thing to say, unless you intend to put a horse through my window," she retorted in the same tone.

Sullivan Waring laughed. The genuinely amused sound surprised her — and she wasn't the only one. Zephyr lifted on her rear legs in a backward hop. "Whoa, Zephyr," he murmured, keeping her walking forward and actually giving her more slack on the guide rope. "Easy, girl."

Isabel backed away herself as they left the stable for the yard. The animal was obviously unpredictable. Or rather, the animal and the horse were both unpredictable.

She smiled a little at her play on words. She knew this man's character, charming laugh or not. Whether he had everyone else fooled or not. She glanced at Phipps and the other stableboys. They were definitely interested, but far enough away that she could probably manage a private conversation with Mr. Waring. Of course, to do that, she would have to stand closer to him. And to her new, half-wild horse.

"Are you going to stand way over there the entire time?" he asked, echoing her own thoughts.

Reluctantly she returned to his side. However unsettled both he and the horse made her, taking a position of weakness now would never do. Especially not, she sensed, with him. "I believe you owe me an explanation," she said.

Instead of answering, he motioned to one of the stableboys. The fellow came forward immediately, handing over a long-handled whip with a short, tasseled leather on the end. Mr. Waring glanced at her, the end of the whip swaying back and forth, snakelike, in his right hand. "You might want to move to my left," he said, letting out the lead line.

"Are you attempting to threaten me with that?" she grated, beginning to suspect that she might be in over her head. This was not a simple secret, like knowing that someone was infatuated with someone else. This was a large, strong, mobile secret that kissed and threatened and intrigued.

"I'm training your mare, which is what you employed me to do. Back up."

"I will n—"

He clucked his tongue. "Walk on." With that he flicked Zephyr's near back leg, feather-light, with the whip.

Snorting, the mare danced sideways and then began a forward walk in a wide circle around them, as far away as she could get with the lead line. Quickly Isabel took a step back, keeping herself just behind Waring's left shoulder as he pivoted to keep the mare directly in front of him.

"Well, this is impressive," she said after a moment. "In no time I shall be too dizzy to defend myself."

"Whoa." He flicked the whip forward to touch Zephyr's chest, and she stopped. "You do it, then," he said, offering Isabel the rope and the whip.

"That is *your* job. I'm merely wondering why you want me to stand here, spinning."

"Walk on." With another flick the mare walked forward again. "What are your intentions?"

Isabel gazed at his handsome profile, admitting to herself that if he'd been a pock-faced drunkard, he would be in gaol already. "What are *your* intentions?"

"No business of yours."

She took a deep breath, feeling as though she were about to take her first step onto a very rickety bridge strung across a very deep chasm. "I hold your freedom, if not your life, in my hands, Mr. Waring. You will be civil to me, and you will do as I ask — which includes answering any and all questions I put to you. Is that clear?"

He turned his head to look full at her, his green eyes hard and cold as ice. "As you wish, my lady," he half growled. "May I please ask what you intend to do with me, though, when you're finished playing this little game?"

A thrill ran through her. Power. She'd never held anyone's life at her mercy, and had never thought to do so. *Goodness.* "I haven't decided yet."

Slowly he nodded. "You'd best do so, because my patience runs only so deep. And you aren't the only one capable of making plans."

"Are you certain it's wise to give me an ultimatum?" she asked.

"Hm."

" 'Hm'? What is that supposed to mean?"

A muscle in his jaw twitched. "It means that I think you have no idea what you're doing. You saw me, so you feel as though you can't simply walk the other way, but I kissed you and you liked it, so you don't wish to send me to the hangman."

Her cheeks heated, though she wasn't entirely certain whether it was because of embarrassment or frustration. If he contin-ued to understand her that clearly, she didn't stand a chance of keeping him beneath her thumb until she'd wrung all of the excitement out of the situation. "I did not like your kiss," she hissed. "It was such a poor effort that I felt sorry for you. My compassion, however, is swiftly being overwhelmed by —"

"You felt sorry for me?" he repeated. "If you feel sorry for anything, it should be that I was forced to kiss you at all."

Isabel raised her arm, her fist clenched. "You will not —"

"Be cautious, my lady," he murmured. "We do have an audience."

She glanced toward the stable, where half the servants employed there seemed to be gawking at both of them. No, not at both of them, she amended. At him. At the famous Mr. Sullivan Waring. "I think you're the one who has no clue how to proceed," she said in as steady a voice as she could manage. "A true thief and blackguard would have slit my throat. You're training my mare."

"Whoa," he said again, and Zephyr came to a stop. "Just for my edification," he said quietly, something that sounded like humor softening his voice, "are you actually complaining that I didn't kill you night before last?"

This conversation was supposed to be her

method of gaining information about him and his motives. Instead she'd walked into an argument when she couldn't seem to manage even to get the last word. At the same time, she *was* learning some things about him. He didn't talk like a horse breeder, for example. Grooms didn't use words like "edification."

"You may think we're at an impasse," she countered slowly, reflecting that she couldn't even recall the last time a man had challenged anything she'd said, "but you're here this morning, and you'll be back this afternoon. And you'll come here tomorrow and the day after and the day after that, until I say otherwise."

His jaw clenched again. "For now, my lady."

"Keep working Zephyr. I feel the need for a glass of lemonade. I'll return shortly."

"I wait with bated breath, my lady. Zephyr, walk on."

"Yes, do continue." Before she became embroiled in another argument or he could come back with yet another retort, Isabel turned and headed for the house. Having to time her departure around the circling Zephyr left her looking a little less stately than she would have preferred, but she kept her chin up and marched.

Once she made it through the kitchen door she closed the hard oak and leaned back against it, fanning her hand in front of her face. That had gone nothing like she'd imagined. Their encounter was supposed to be harder on him than on her, but he didn't look as though she'd ruffled a single blasted horse-breeding feather. Men smiled at her and agreed with her, barely requiring any mental effort at all on her part. Who did this blasted fellow think he was?

A kitchen maid hurried up, curtsying. "May I fetch you something, my lady?"

"A glass of lemonade, if you please." It was a pity that ladies didn't drink whiskey at nine o'clock in the morning, because she felt in need of some.

Sullivan kept his eyes on the mare, but most of his attention remained on the young lady disappearing into Chalsey House. He hadn't precisely intimidated her into keeping her silence, but he supposed he had an excuse of sorts. Threatening women under any circumstances didn't sit well with him. And he couldn't justify righting the wrongs done to one woman by wronging another. Particularly one who, other than being a member of a family who'd acquired a painting, had nothing to do with this.

Yes, she had a sharp tongue — God, she had a sharp tongue — and she seemed perfectly content to use her knowledge to turn him into little better than her slave. At the same time, he'd begun to think that she had no intention of sharing his secret with anyone, much less the authorities. Why she'd decided to keep her silence, he had no idea, except that she seemed to enjoy holding her knowledge over him. Given that nothing was as changeable as the mind of a female, the wisest thing to do would seem to be to exit her so-called service while he had the chance. If any gossip about his involvement in the thefts began, Bram would hear of it and give him enough time to leave London.

He halted Zephyr again and turned her in the opposite direction. His plan to make himself scarce from Chalsey House meant that he wouldn't be available to continue the mare's training. In itself that was nothing, but all he had these days was his reputation. If he abandoned the training, Phipps or someone would finish it, and probably would do it entirely adequately. But word would get out that he'd been paid for something and he hadn't delivered. A small thing, yes, but he knew better than anyone that small things could add up to very large ones.

"Damnation," he muttered, and Zephyr flicked her ears in his direction. Why in God's name had he kissed Isabel Chalsey in the first place? Idiocy. Pure idiocy. And he needed to leave here before he ended up dangling at the end of a hangman's noose. He motioned for one of the grooms to approach. "That's enough for this morning," he decided, handing the lead line and whip over.

"That's hardly worth twenty pounds," Lady Isabel's cool voice came from behind him.

Sullivan stopped. "You, what's your name?" he asked the groom.

The man actually blushed. "Delvin, Mr. Waring, sir."

"Delvin, hand me the lead back, will you?"

Once he had Zephyr back in hand, he patted the gray mare on the nose and then walked her toward Lady Isabel. "Here," he said, offering her the lead.

She backed away as she had before. "If you're trying to tell me that she's been saddle-trained in twenty minutes, I shall call you a liar to your face," she said, half her attention on the horse.

Though the words sounded defiant enough, Sullivan heard the quaver in her voice. He tilted his head at her. "You *are* afraid of horses, aren't you?" he asked more quietly. "It's not just an affectation."

"I'm wary of them," she countered.

"Given your wariness, then," he continued, wondering what, precisely was driving him to continue, "you chose an odd means of . . . pursuing your suspicions of me. Horses being my profession, after all."

"I couldn't very well hire you to teach me to play the pianoforte, now could I?"

"Whatever your ulterior motives, it's a shame to own such a fine animal and not use her as she was meant to be used."

"You said you were going to sell her for brood."

"She has a very good lineage. Frankly, that's why she's worth more in the pasture than under a saddle."

"She *was* worth more that way," Lady Isabel corrected.

"She still is, if you're not going to ride her." He took a breath. "Let me purchase her back from you, and we'll be rid of one another."

Narrowing her eyes, she took a long, deliberate drink of the glass of lemonade she held in one hand. "You may well wish to be rid of me, Mr. Waring, but you stole from me, and —"

"From your home. Not from you."

"— and you kissed me," she continued, as though he hadn't spoken. "Without my permission. I am not finished with you yet. And so what time will you come by this afternoon for another training session?"

When hell freezes over. "Is three o'clock acceptable?" he said aloud. "I don't wish to interfere with your social calendar."

She nodded briskly. "I expect you to be prompt."

"And I expect that you'll eventually ride this horse." He patted the mare on the nose again.

"That is beside the point. Be here at three o'clock."

His jaw was already clenched so tightly that it ached. He knew precisely what he wanted to say to Lady Isabel Chalsey, and what he wanted to do *with* her, but as long as she held his freedom in her hands, he didn't dare. So instead he swept her a bow. "As you wish."

Turning, he intentionally put Zephyr between them, pretending not to see Lady Isabel back away again. Her fear of horses intrigued him more than he cared to admit. She concealed it fairly well, but from her family's and her own statements it seemed more than a simple girlishness.

He'd long ago learned the perils of curiosity. And yet he already knew he would be stopping by Lord Bramwell Johns's home to see if he could discover more about her. If anyone had any information, it would be Bram. And besides, he had four more paintings to reacquire before he was finished. The more information he had about Isabel Chalsey, the better off he would be. She might own him at the moment, but he could dig his fingers in, as well.

"How the devil should I know?" Bram said, eyeing himself in his dressing mirror.

"You know everything." Sullivan shifted in the deep windowsill of Bramwell's bedchamber. "That's what you keep saying, anyway."

"I'd rather go back to where she commanded you to do as she says. There's a bit of the devil in that chit, I think." He sent Sullivan a dark smile. "Much more interesting than I'd previously thought."

Sullivan frowned. "Oh, no, you don't. Stay away from her."

Bram faced him full on, his expression surprisingly serious. "You like her?"

"I'm more likely to strangle her. I just don't want you cluttering up this mess even further." From the way his heart thudded, the question was more complex than that, but he wasn't about to contemplate the answer in front of Bram. He still needed to explain to himself how he could wish to be rid of someone and want to spar with her and to hear her moans of pleasure all at the same time.

"Then stop asking me questions about her. And *you* stay away from her. Because I do know everything." Bram picked up his riding gloves and headed for the door. "Isabel Chalsey is more . . . complicated than you realize."

That sounded intriguing. Sullivan pushed to his feet and followed Bramwell down the hallway. "Complicated? How? And how is it that you know she's complicated when you didn't know about her Machiavellian bent?"

"No. This is a conversation that can bring about nothing good for me, and I therefore refuse to engage." At the foot of the stairs Bram paused to collect his hat. "I'm going out now. Stay if you wish, but I'm going to see the duke, and I doubt you'll want to be here when I return."

The duke. That meant the Duke of Levonzy, Bram's father. Sullivan eyed his friend. Bram and Levonzy. The least congenial pairing since King Arthur and Mordred. "Do you wish me to be here when you

81

return?"

"I don't need my hand held, Sully." Bram glanced over. "You're going back to the Chalseys' this afternoon?"

"At three o'clock sharp," Sullivan grunted. *That damned chit.*

"I've an obligation tonight, but I should be finished by midnight. If you want to meet at Jezebel's after that, send over a note."

Hm. Why he would need a drink more than Bram, Sullivan had no idea, but he nodded. "I'll let you know. And I still have the sticky feeling that you know something you're not telling me."

"I could fill books with my knowledge."

"But who would publish it? I have nothing to do with your kind unless they're in the market for a horse, Bram. If you know something, tell me."

"No. Some things are better discovered than divulged. For the one with the information *and* the one learning it. Hibble, is my mount saddled?"

The butler nodded. "It is, my lord." He pulled open the front door.

Sullivan stood where he was for a moment, his eyes narrowed as he tried to decide whether it would be worth the frustration of trying to figure out what the devil Bram wasn't telling him. Considering that he had two prospective buyers to meet and sacks of feed to purchase before he returned to Chalsey House, his time would be better spent elsewhere.

He descended the front steps and took Achilles' reins, swinging back up into the saddle. "Don't shoot anyone," he said as Bram headed west and he turned north toward home.

"I'll give you the same advice," Bramwell drawled with a brief grin, tipping his hat as he rode toward Grosvenor Square.

Sullivan's own smile was more grim as he dodged the myriad carts and carriages and wagons north of Mayfair. It disappeared completely as he remembered that he'd neglected to ask Bram whether he'd had any luck tracking down the next painting. So now he had another reason to be wary of Lady Isabel Chalsey, as if he needed one. She was damned distracting.

CHAPTER 5

As the barouche rolled to a stop on Chalsey House's short drive and a footman hurried out the front door to greet it, Isabel took the hand of the young lady seated beside her. "Thank you so much for bringing me home, Barbara. Once Mama sets foot in Mrs. Wrangley's Dress Shop, only a biblical flood could persuade her to leave."

"Nonsense," Lady Barbara Stanley said, her typical smile, together with her blonde ringlets and sky-blue eyes, making her look positively angelic. "You saved me from dancing with that horribly fetid Lord Arnton last week. We aren't even close to being even."

Isabel chuckled. "He does smell of sheep, doesn't he?"

"Very dirty ones." Standing, Barbara accepted the footman's gloved hand as she stepped to the ground. "And as long as I'm here, I want to see this new horse of yours."

Drat. Barbara wanted to see the mare, but given the time of afternoon, that would also very likely mean seeing the trainer. And the best part of a secret was not sharing — well, the best part of *this* secret was keeping those green eyes looking only at her.

Then again, maybe Barbara could tell her something about her new obsession. All her judiciously worded questions to her family had gotten her were more pronouncements of Mr. Waring's genius with horses and some head-shaking. It was as if everyone knew something, and no one meant to tell her what it might be.

As they walked through the house to the stable yard, Barbara wrapped her fingers around Isabel's arm. "You don't think your brother might be about, do you?"

Isabel stifled a sigh. Once Phillip chose a bride and married, she wondered whether she would have half as many female friends as she did now. At least a quarter of the current group seemed to have become acquainted with her merely as a way to gain an introduction to Earl Chalsey, and even the ones of whose friendship she felt assured seemed rather enamored of him. "He's gone out with some of his friends today," she supplied, "unless you're referring to Douglas. I'm certain *he's* about somewhere."

Barbara laughed, so the answer was apparently self-explanatory. Yes, Phillip had another admirer. She'd stopped telling him about his conquests, because it only gave him a big head. A bigger one than he already had.

As they reached the stable yard, she slowed. A stableboy led a large chestnut gelding about the yard while Phipps, a piece of straw clenched in his teeth, watched critically. As he saw her, the head groom straightened and spat out the straw. "My lady," he said, tugging at his forelock. "Mr. Waring ain't arrived yet. Is there anything I can do for you?"

She'd probably seen more of Phipps over the past day than she had in the previous two years. No wonder he didn't know what to make of her. "Lady Barbara wanted to see my new mare," she said.

"I'll have her brought right out for you. Delvin!"

"No, no, that's not necessary," Isabel broke in hurriedly, fighting the urge to turn and run. "She's in her stall?"

"Aye. Fourth one back on the left."

"I remember." Taking a deep breath, Isabel walked into the stable. She only lagged a step or so behind Barbara, but inside she felt miles away from anyone — except for the two dozen horses blowing and nickering around her. *Steady,* she told herself. *You don't have to touch any of them or anything.*

"Oh, Tibby, she's lovely! Might I give her an apple?"

Forcing a smile, Isabel spotted the apple barrel and dug in to hand one over to her friend. "Certainly."

Barbara took it. "Here you go, Zephyr," she cooed, holding it out and then patting the gray on the nose with her free hand as she took the apple. "With that build and a name like Zephyr, she must run fast as the wind," Barbara continued. "Promise me that you'll let me try out her paces once she's broken."

Fast as the wind? Good heavens, what had she gotten herself into? "The — I —"

"I prefer easing a horse into accepting a saddle rather than breaking its spirit," a low voice drawled from directly behind Isabel.

So he'd arrived on time. Isabel turned around to find ice-green eyes regarding her, one of them obscured by the ubiquitous straying lock of light brown hair. "You are very nearly late," she said, unable to conjure anything more witty than that.

"I call it being prompt," he returned. "As you requested . . . my lady."

Barbara made a small choked sound

behind her. Belatedly Isabel stepped aside, annoyed — and not for the first time — that she continually had to look up to meet Mr. Waring's gaze. He had to be at least two inches over six feet.

When Barbara cleared her throat again, she shook herself. *Pay attention, Isabel.* "Mr. Waring, Lady Barbara Stanley."

He inclined his head. "Lady Barbara."

"Mr. Waring. You served with Lord Bramwell Johns on the Peninsula, didn't you?"

Isabel hid an annoyed frown. Obviously she should have asked Barbara her questions about Waring.

"I did."

"I've heard some of the tales he tells. They called the two of you and Phineas Bromley the Musketeers, did they not?"

"Among other things." His tone polite but cool, he shook out the lead line he carried. "If you ladies don't mind, I have some work to do."

"Of course." Isabel pulled Barbara back, and they watched as Mr. Waring attached the lead line to a buckle on Zephyr's halter and led her out of the stall.

As soon as he passed by them, Barbara grabbed her arm. "My goodness he's handsome," she whispered, while they followed him at a hopefully safe distance out to the stable yard. "I nearly fainted dead away when I turned around and saw him standing there."

"What do you know about him?" Isabel asked in the same low tone, ignoring Barbara's fluttering. She fluttered a great deal, generally around Phillip.

"What do you mean, what do I know?"

"About his background, Barbara. Other than the horses."

Barbara eyed her. "You're not seriously mooning after a horse breeder, are you? I mean, yes, he's an Adonis, but he's also practically common."

Practically? Isabel took a deep breath. "It's just that my brothers are mad over him," she said carefully, "and I'd like to know why they think he's such a diamond."

Her friend leaned closer. "All I know is that he's the natural son of some aristocrat or other. The father never acknowledged him, so the rest of us can't very well do so."

Hm. That explained some things. He certainly had a noble bearing about him. And his conversation wasn't that of a poor stableboy, by any means. "You don't know who the father is? Was?"

Barbara shook her head. "If I'd known how handsome he was, I might have listened more closely to the gossip." She giggled again, apparently forgetting that she'd just chastised Isabel for mooning over him — not that she was, for heaven's sake.

Isabel turned her attention back to Mr. Waring. He seemed completely oblivious to them as he once more put Zephyr through the lessons of stopping and going on command. Even to her unschooled, skeptical gaze it seemed the mare was responding much more quickly and with less prompting than she had needed this morning. It was impressive, but not very comforting.

Isabel could describe Mr. Sullivan Waring in much the same way. Yes, he looked very fine, and capable, but she wouldn't wish to turn her back to him. Of course, when he'd kissed her they'd been face-to-face, so she couldn't trust him overly much from that direction, either.

"Your butler said I might find you out here," a male voice drawled from the direction of the drive.

As she started to turn around, she noticed the oddest thing — easy, confident Mr. Waring dropped the lead line. A single heartbeat later he bent and picked it up again as if nothing had happened. Nothing except that his face, the part she could make out with his back half turned, had gone gray. Instinctively she took a step toward him to make certain he was well, but a hand closed over her shoulder before she could take a second step.

"I know you weren't expecting me till seven," Oliver, Lord Tilden, said, smiling as she faced him, "but I couldn't resist the chance to stop by." The viscount's light brown hair, cut and styled in the very latest fashion, glinted almost bronze in the sunlight, his green eyes meeting hers warmly.

His light brown hair and green eyes. And the high cheekbones and patrician jaw. Isabel's heart stopped beating, then thudded into a fierce tattoo. *Oh, no. What had she tangled herself into?* "Oliver Sullivan," she said aloud, unable to keep her voice from quavering over that last bit.

Oliver lifted an eyebrow. "Oliver James Sullivan, if we're being formal," he drawled. "Are we being formal, Lady Isabel Jane Chalsey?"

She forced a chuckle. "Heavens, no. It's just that you did surprise me."

"Tibby was showing me her new mare," Barbara put in with the most wretched timing ever. "Isn't she lovely?"

"Oh, we can ogle Zephyr later," Isabel countered, knowing she was rushing her speech and unable to stop herself. "For now, come inside and tell me about your day, Oliver. Phillip told me that you and your father took breakfast with Prinny."

"We did, yesterday."

As she hauled him by the arm, striding back to the house, scarcely daring to breathe, Oliver glanced over his shoulder. He looked again, then stopped so abruptly that he nearly pulled her to the ground. Pushing her hand off his arm, he walked back toward Zephyr and her trainer.

"Come, Oliver," she said to his broad back. "Shall I have Cook bake us some biscuits?"

He visibly shook himself, stopping again. "Yes. Certainly. Let's go inside. You can't find it pleasant out here amid the stable-boys and the filth in the yard."

Zephyr's lead line flicked up sharply. Abruptly the mare was galloping — and straight at them. Fear stabbing down her spine, Isabel gasped. Oliver hurriedly moved backward, belatedly pulling her with him. A foot short of where they'd been standing, the mare danced to a halt. A second later, Mr. Waring had his hand around one of the straps of her harness.

"You need to learn to control your animal, Waring," Oliver growled. "Apologize."

"That's not necessary," Isabel managed, forcing air into her lungs. As she looked up at Mr. Waring, his gaze was on her.

"I apologize if I frightened you, my lady," he said in his deep voice. "That was not my intention."

Her jaw clenched as hard as her fingers were around Oliver's arm, she nodded. "Let's go in." She needed to get inside, before she became completely hysterical. The charging horse, what she'd just realized about Sullivan Waring, the obvious anger between the two men with her somehow in the middle of it all . . . "Please, let's go inside."

"Of course, my dear." Putting a protective arm around her shoulders, Oliver guided them to the house while Barbara followed behind.

For the second time within forty-eight hours of meeting Mr. Sullivan Waring — or the third time, counting the incident of the kiss — Isabel wanted something very strong to drink. What the devil had she gotten herself into?

Sullivan watched the trio disappear into the house. Oliver fucking Sullivan. In pursuit of sharp-tongued, witty Isabel. "Damnation," he growled. Zephyr shifted uneasily beside him.

So that was what Bram hadn't told him,

that bloody, black-hearted snake. Gradually he became aware again of the noise around him, the bustle of the stable yard, and the muttering and gesturing of the group of servants by the door.

He wasn't one of them. Squaring his shoulders, he loosened his grip on Zephyr and gave her a handful of oats from his pocket. As he returned her to position in the middle of the yard, he glanced over his shoulder at the large house again. He wasn't one of them, either.

If he had been one of them, they never would have dared to rob him blind while he was away at war. At least now he knew why the Chalseys had ended up with one of his mother's paintings. Undoubtedly it had been a gift from dear Oliver.

Where did all of this leave him? From her expression before he'd frightened the daylights out of her, Isabel had realized that Sullivan had significance as a name, and why. He frowned as he started Zephyr around at a walk again. However surprised and annoyed he'd been, he shouldn't have sent the mare charging like that. No matter that he'd had the lead line in hand the entire time. Lady Isabel's fear was obvious and real, and he already knew that. But like the animal Oliver claimed he was, he'd gotten angry and reacted, unmindful of the consequences.

So Oliver Sullivan, Viscount Tilden, was in pursuit of Lady Isabel Chalsey. And yet she hadn't recognized him despite his reputedly close resemblance to his half-brother. And yet even with a beau she'd decided to play this little game of mousetrap with him. And yet when she'd realized who he must be she'd tried to get Oliver into the house rather than sitting back and allowing or encouraging a confrontation as her peers had been known to do.

Hm. So Lady Isabel continued to baffle him, which meant she was still dangerous. But if he'd needed any additional incentive to remain in the employ of Isabel Chalsey, Oliver's appearance had just provided it. Any chance to get in a blow against that arrogant lickspittle was simply too good to pass by. And he'd never been all that successful at resisting temptation, anyway.

He worked Zephyr for another thirty minutes, until he could sense the mare's growing comfort with and confidence in the two commands she'd learned. He could have proceeded more quickly, but Zephyr needed to be as calm and steady and gentle-paced as he could make her. Especially after what he'd done earlier.

95

When they'd finished for the afternoon he put the mare up himself, measuring out her grain and hay and brushing her out as she ate. As he worked, the mare's ears flicked at him and then away. A moment later he scented the light tang of citrus, and something he couldn't put a name to swirled down his spine.

"You're still here," Isabel said without preamble.

He kept brushing. "Do you want me to go?"

"I want you to face me when I'm speaking to you."

Sullivan dropped the brush into its bucket and turned around. "As you wish, my lady," he forced out, folding his arms and knowing it wasn't her fault that he felt scraped raw this afternoon.

"That's better." Her pretty brown eyes gazed at him. "I will be out late tonight, and will be sleeping in. You will therefore be here promptly at ten o'clock in the morning."

"You want me to come back?" Sullivan asked, deeply surprised.

"We have an agreement. And I'm still trying to decide what to do with you." She looked from him to Zephyr, took a breath, and turned on her heel.

"I'm truly sorry I frightened you," he said to her back, half wondering why he felt the need to apologize. Frightening her was probably in his best interest. He'd certainly never prove himself harmless to anyone's — to her — satisfaction.

She slowly faced him again. "Yes. Don't ever do that again. It was unfair."

"It wasn't aimed at you, Isabel," he said quietly. "And I won't. Ever do it again, I mean."

Isabel took another breath, clearly assessing him. What she saw in his face, he had no idea, but her expression finally relaxed a little. "I'll take you at your word, Mr. Waring. Now, if you'll excuse me, I have guests."

Again she didn't say anything about Oliver and their so-called connection. "I'll see you in the morning, then," he said as coolly as he could.

"At ten o'clock."

"Promptly at ten."

He watched her back out the wide stable doors. She'd left Oliver inside the house to come and talk to him. To make certain he'd be there in the morning. Isabel Chalsey liked him, which was bad for all concerned. Even worse, *he* liked *her.*

CHAPTER 6

Though Barbara left to go home and change her clothes for the Edlington soiree, Oliver Sullivan stayed at Chalsey House for dinner and then offered his coach to escort all of them to the party. The five adults squeezed into his carriage while Douglas stood in the drawing room window upstairs and made faces at them. For once she wished she was three years younger so she could avoid attending, as well.

It wasn't that she didn't enjoy the dancing and the music. Generally — until tonight, in fact — she considered them to be the best part of the Season. After today, though, she felt more in need of silence and a very long while to think about what she needed to do next. Tonight, waltzing and smiling seemed a bit of a bother.

From her father's careful queries during dinner about the state of Zephyr's training, clearly he knew that Oliver and Mr. Waring were half-brothers, and also that the relationship was strained, to say the least. Douglas appeared baffled, only rousing from his talk of the latest wagers reportedly going into the book at White's Club when Sullivan Waring's name was mentioned. Phillip just as quickly changed the subject of discussion, so he knew the truth, as well.

Blast it all, why had no one told her? She didn't know that it would have altered what she did, but the knowledge would certainly have saved her at least one of the shocks of the day. And now she couldn't ask any of the additional questions that kept popping into her mind, because Oliver was with them, and he would likely have an apoplexy.

All the same, she wondered what he would say if she informed him that the culprit who had stolen the painting he'd given her family was none other than his own half-brother. She glanced at him from her seat squeezed between him and Phillip. Not once since they'd left the stable yard for the house had he even glanced in its direction. He'd given no sign at all, in fact, that he had any idea his half-brother was just outside. Or that he even had a half-brother.

"You'll have to come stay with us at Burling after the Season," her brother was saying, leaning around her to talk to Oliver. "I can't wait to ride my new hunter after a fox."

Lady Darshear sighed. "Phillip, you talk about that animal more than you do about . . . ladies. I'm going to have to declare you on the shelf if you don't begin courting someone very soon." She sent an exasperated grin at Oliver. "Apparently Mr. Waring breeds very fine horses."

"So I hear," Oliver said, the muscles of his jaw flexing.

Oh, dear. "Barbara was telling me today," Isabel interjected hurriedly, "that Lord Aysling is going to propose to Lady Harriet Reed tonight."

"Tonight?" her mother echoed, sitting forward. "At the Edlington soiree? Harry, we must find a seat close by her mother."

"Yes, dear." Lord Darshear patted her on the hand, then turned his attention to Oliver. "Your house hasn't been burglarized, has it?"

Oliver's expression became very still. "No. Why do you ask?"

"Ours was. Just two nights ago. Tibby here surprised the blackguard and frightened him away."

"But not before he managed to make off with two paintings, a porcelain dove, and a very pretty crystal bowl," Isabel's mother continued. "And one of the paintings was the Francesca Perris you gave to us at the beginning of the Season, I'm sorry to say."

Isabel watched Oliver as closely as she could without being terribly obvious about it. And she realized something else almost immediately. As soon as he'd heard the news, he'd known instantly who'd stolen the painting from them. How and why, she wasn't certain, but he knew it had been Sullivan Waring. Which meant that he knew the identity of the Mayfair Marauder, and he'd done nothing about it.

Given his obvious dislike for Mr. Waring, she had no idea why he hadn't gone to the authorities with his information. Of course, she had the same information and had done nothing about it, but that was different. She wanted to discover his motives. And yes, despite her growing sense that this was more than a game for all concerned, she liked having Mr. Waring at her beck and call. She could always report him later when — if — it came to that. Oliver had no motive for keeping his half-brother's secret that she could see. They hated one another. Another mystery for her to uncover, apparently. They seemed to surround Sullivan Waring on every side.

They were mobbed as soon as they entered the ballroom at the Edlingtons', and it was twenty minutes before Isabel found a space to breathe. As she waved her fan in front of her face, half listening to several of her friends speculating on the impending surprise marriage proposal that apparently everyone knew about, she spied Lord Minster. The earl stood with his usual group of peers, his shock of gray hair standing straight out from his head like a hedgehog's quills.

Glancing over to see her mother occupied with pretending not to congratulate Lady Reed on her daughter's impending betrothal, Isabel slipped away from her friends and approached the earl. "My lord?" she said quietly, when the conversation about war finance slowed for the moment. "Lord Minster?"

"Eh?" He turned around, gray eyes looking about for a moment before they settled on her. "I know you, don't I? Lady Isabel Chalsey."

She curtsied. "Yes, my lord. May I ask you a question?"

"Of course." He looked at his fellows. "Excuse me, gentleman. Someone much more attractive than you wants a word with me."

While the rest of them chuckled, Lord

Minster motioned for Isabel to precede him to a stand of chairs a few feet away. "Thank you," she said, taking a seat. "I know this isn't the most opportune time for any kind of conversation."

"That's why we have the same conversations over and over again at gatherings. After a time everyone knows their parts, even when it's too noisy to hear anyone but oneself. What may I do for you, my lady?"

Isabel mentally squared her shoulders. If no one else wanted to give her answers, she'd find them for herself. "Your townhouse was burgled a few weeks ago, was it not?"

His expression grew more somber. "It was. And I'd give fifty pounds to anyone who handed me the names of those bloody . . ." He cleared his throat, his face reddening. "I beg your pardon, Lady Isabel. My late wife always said I had too much spleen. I heard that Chalsey House was robbed, as well."

She nodded. "Yes. And I was wondering, would you tell me what was taken from you?"

"It's not for a lovely young lady such as yourself to trouble over unpleasant things like that."

Drat. "I ask on my father's behalf," she improvised.

"Ah. I will send him a list in the morning, then."

Forcing a smile, Isabel dipped a shallow curtsy. "Thank you, my lord. I'll tell Papa."

As she turned around, Oliver, two glasses of Madeira in hand, appeared through the crowd. "There you are," he said with a smile. "Minster wasn't trying to wheedle a space on your dance card, was he?"

"No. Just being sociable. Besides, thanks to you my dance card is full." In fact, he'd taken the three best dances for himself.

His smile deepened. "Good."

"Well, that is a shame," another deep voice drawled from beside her. "That'll teach me to get my hopes up, I suppose."

She looked sideways. "Lord Bramwell. If one of my partners breaks a toe, you shall be the first substitute."

He sketched an elegant bow. "Then consider me appeased." He glanced over at Oliver. "Ah, Tilden. Seeing you puts me in mind of something I saw at the British Museum earlier."

Oliver lifted an eyebrow, his stance stiff. "And what might that something be?"

"They had a new pharaoh's mummy on display," Lord Bramwell said smoothly, smiling. "Likeness on the sarcophagus handsome as Adonis."

"Well, thank —"

"And on the inside, sloppily wrapped cotton bandages covering mold and putrified flesh. With the corpse completely hollow of everything but some old straw."

Oliver took a hard step forward. "Apologize," he snarled.

Lord Bramwell Lowry Johns didn't move. Instead his smile deepened, though it didn't touch his black eyes. "I am sorry you haven't been able to stop encouraging people to say such nasty things about you. You really must work on your character." He winked at Isabel. "Remember, any broken bones, and I'll sweep in." With that he strolled back into the crowd.

Isabel had no idea what to say. Obviously she couldn't pretend that she hadn't heard the exchange. What was surprising was that she'd never noticed the animosity between Lord Tilden and Lord Bramwell Johns before. As she thought about it, they'd never socialized that she could recall. Was it because of Sullivan Waring?

It had to be. She'd seen Waring and Bramwell together at the horse auctions, and Barbara had said the two men had served together on the Peninsula. They were friends. And she'd been swirling about so happily in her own little world that she'd never noticed anything. It was beginning to seem that Sullivan Waring had done more than kiss her. He'd . . . opened her eyes to the edges of rooms, to every muttered conversation. Now everywhere were questions, and nothing was what it seemed on the surface. Not even her.

"I'm sorry you witnessed that," Oliver said abruptly, taking her hand and wrapping it around the sleeve of his coat. "Bramwell Johns is a poor reflection of his family's grace and favor, with even worse taste in both humor and friends. I've heard that he and the Duke of Levonzy barely speak."

That wasn't precisely a well-kept secret. "Everyone is entitled to their own opinion," she said carefully. "That doesn't mean it is shared by anyone else."

He lifted her hand again and kissed her fingers. "Well said, my dear. Now let's put this unpleasantness behind us and dance, shall we?"

"By all means."

She still had a great many questions. Oddly enough, though, she felt more comfortable with the idea of asking Mr. Waring than the man who'd been courting her for the past weeks. As for why that might be, well, that was yet another question.

Sullivan was well into his second mug of bitters when Bram finally pushed his way through the noisy, smelly crowd overflowing the main saloon of Jezebel's establishment. He generally liked the place with its ramshackle clientele. Tonight, he didn't like anything.

"I got your note," Bram said, motioning the barman for a glass of his own.

Silently Sullivan pulled a pistol from his pocket and set it on the table between them. "Enjoy your drink," he said, deliberately taking a swallow of his own, "because it's going to be your last. I'm just trying to decide whether to shoot you in the chest or in the head."

"The chest, if you please," Bram said calmly. "I'd like to leave a handsome corpse."

"Why the devil didn't you tell me that Lady Isabel's being pursued by . . ." He paused, reluctant even to say the name. It was like invoking ill luck on purpose. "By Oliver Sullivan?" he finally forced out.

"Firstly, you've been itching to confront one of the Sullivans for weeks, since they seem to be content with cringing in their holes while you rob all of their friends."

"I didn't want a confrontation in a place where I have to watch my tongue!" Sullivan snapped, setting his drink down so hard it sloshed over the pistol. Wonderful. Now the powder was likely wet. "Not in front of —"

"Of a chit you fancy?" Bram broke in.

"I don't fancy her. She's blackmailing me. Which is another reason for me to avoid speaking freely in front of her, by the by." He glared at his friend. "And what the bloody hell does it matter if I fancy her, anyway? She's a marquis' daughter."

"And you're a marquis' son."

Sullivan snorted. "Don't even pretend you believe that signifies."

"It would if he acknowledged you."

"Which he won't. We've had this conversation before." He jabbed a finger at Bramwell. "And you should have told me, you rat."

"Yes, you're right. I should have told you about Tilden. Apologies." Bram leaned his elbows on the table. "I do have a bit of news that might cheer you up, though, Sully."

Immediately Sullivan's attention sharpened. He recognized that tone of voice. "You found another of my paintings."

"I did. And you'll never guess where."

Sullivan eyed him. "You know, I'd give

just about even odds over whether that pistol will fire or not. Shall we give it a go?"

"Very well, let's pretend you've frightened me into revealing my information. But you have to give me your word that you won't interrupt until I'm finished speaking."

"Are you going to be speaking about where you found the painting?" Sullivan asked skeptically.

"Yes."

"Then I give you my word. No interruptions."

Bram nodded graciously. "You know I was summoned for an audience with His Grace this afternoon. Well, I was sitting in his office and he was informing me that I'm a wastrel and on the verge of being cut off both from his money and from the family in general, and my gaze wandered to the wall behind him. And there, my boy, was a large Francesca W. Perris painting of a young lad fishing in a stream. A lad who bore a rather striking resemblance to you."

Sullivan closed his eyes for a moment. "It's called *A Young Fisherman's Dream of Glory*," he said. "She painted it when I was eight."

"Interesting, don't you think, that your father gave my father a gift?"

"One that wasn't his to give." For several

hard beats of his heart he gazed at his friend. Revenge versus loyalty. It was all becoming so complicated. "This is your family, Bram. I won't break into your father's house without your permission."

"By all means, break in. And dispose of that idiotic Burmese fertility statue while you're at it. It's also in his office."

Sullivan grinned, relieved. "Anything else?"

"If those silver-handled dueling pistols he used to threaten me with are still in the billiards room, I certainly wouldn't miss them. There used to be a large inlaid mahogany box of cigars in there, as well. You'll have to share those with me, though."

"I can only carry so much." Sitting back, he finished off the mug of bitters. "Why didn't you tell me that I had a good chance of running across Oliver?" he asked more quietly. "The truth, Bram."

"Are you still tendering your services to Lady Isabel?" Bramwell countered.

"You make it sound sordid. Yes, I'll still be working Zephyr for her. She asked me to stay."

"Did she, now?"

"Stop changing the subject. Why, Bram?"

Lord Bramwell Johns took a deep breath. "Honestly? Because you annoy me."

Sullivan stopped what he'd been about to say. Instead he concentrated on keeping his expression even, determined not to let Bramwell see how much that little statement had hurt. He didn't have many friends, and he counted Bram as the closest among them. Since he'd returned from the Peninsula, Bram and Phin Bromley's family were practically the only members of the peerage he could tolerate. If the —

"Do you have any idea how talented you are?" Bram broke in on his thoughts.

That hadn't been what he'd expected to hear next. "What?"

"Waring Stables. People brag about owning one of your horses, Sullivan. I've seen men come to blows during an auction for one of your hunters."

"They were drunk," Sullivan countered, beginning to realize that Bram's annoyance was something different than he'd thought.

"Beside the point," Bram said dismissively. "If you would just stop examining people's pedigrees before you sell to them, no one would ever need look for another breeder."

Sullivan scowled. "I do not judge people by their —"

"You won't sell to anyone who's known to have a close friendship with the Sullivans. And don't try to convince me otherwise, because I won't believe you. So I didn't tell you about Isabel Chalsey and Oliver Sullivan. And you sold two horses to the family, and you've been having fun with it."

"She saw me inside her house, half-wit. *That's* why I sold them two horses."

"*That's* my point, then, nickninny. You didn't know their connection to Oliver, and I didn't know whether he would make an appearance or not. In the meantime, you've expanded your business and have another satisfied horse owner telling everyone who'll listen to him what a fine animal he received from Waring Stables."

"So you lied for my own benefit."

"I *omitted* for your benefit. Not everyone cares about *your* pedigree, my friend. Your skills speak for themselves."

Sullivan scooped the pistol back into his pocket and stood. "I know you like playing games with people, Bram, but don't play them with me. From now on I expect the entire truth. Not just the convenient bits."

With that he wound his way through the crowd and back outside into the damp, dark streets. So he picked and chose to whom he sold his horses. That was his business. And this mess had only happened because he'd been forced into it. If Dunston and Tilden hadn't stolen his property in the first place, he wouldn't have broken into Chalsey House to get it back, and he never would have seen, much less kissed, Isabel Chalsey. Ultimately it all came back to George Sullivan, the Marquis of Dunston. It always did. It probably always would.

CHAPTER 7

Isabel awoke well before ten o'clock in the morning. Groggy, she managed to don a walking dress with the help of her maid before she made her way downstairs for breakfast. Three hot, strong cups of tea later, and her eyes finally stayed open instead of drooping shut every few seconds.

No one else had risen yet, and considering that they hadn't returned home from the Edlingtons' until after three o'clock, she didn't expect to see anyone for several hours. It would be nice if her family slept until Sullivan Waring had come for the morning's lesson and gone again, but she doubted her luck would hold that long.

Lord Minster probably still slept, as well, but she couldn't risk missing the note he'd promised to send over. If her father saw it, he would have no idea what was going on, and then she would have to explain that she was looking for some common threads in the two robberies. He would then probably send her home to Burling to keep her from getting into trouble. Little did he know it was far too late for that.

As she buttered a fourth slice of toast, though she'd barely begun eating her second piece, she tried to decide how and if she wanted to approach the growing conundrum that was Sullivan Waring. Isabel sighed. She loved puzzles, but this business of Waring and the questions surrounding him had stakes much higher than she generally dealt with. And he interested her much more for that very reason.

The front door knocker rapped, and the butler left the breakfast room. A moment later he reappeared, taking his post at the room's entrance once more.

"Who in the world is calling on us so early?" she asked, doing her best to feign innocent curiosity.

"Lord Minster sent over a letter for Lord Darshear, my lady," Alders answered.

"Oh, he's been expecting that." She pushed to her feet, nearly flipping her plate onto her lap in the process. "I'll take it upstairs to him."

"His valet says he's still to bed, my lady."

"Then I'll take the blame for awakening him." When the butler still didn't move, she lifted an eyebrow. "Please fetch the letter for me, Alders."

A muscle in the butler's gaunt cheek twitched, and he nodded. He left the breakfast room again, then returned a few seconds later with a silver salver in one hand, a single letter resting atop the polished surface.

"Thank you," Isabel intoned, lifting the folded paper free and pocketing it because otherwise she'd be tempted to rip the wax seal open and read it immediately. "And you may clear my breakfast. I'll be in my bedchamber — after I deliver this to Papa."

Alders nodded. "Very good, my lady."

Keeping her hand over her pelisse pocket, Isabel made her way upstairs. She passed by her parents' adjoined bedchambers, pausing there for a moment in case anyone downstairs happened to be listening for her footsteps. After counting to twenty she continued on to her own room and quietly closed the door behind her.

"Now let's see what you're up to," she murmured, walking to the window and fishing the missive from her pocket to break the seal. Her hands shook a little as she unfolded the paper, though she felt more intrigued than nervous. She already knew Sullivan Waring to be a thief, after all. The

Mayfair Marauder, no less. What she wanted to know was what he'd stolen from Lord Minster, and why he'd done it.

She sat in the deep sill to read. The viscount's letter was brief, stating only that according to her father's request as delivered by the delightful Lady Isabel, he'd listed below the items taken several weeks ago from his home. One pair of silver candlesticks, a small jade statue, a painting by Francesca W. Perris, his new boots from Hoby's, and a plain gold ring.

Another painting, and by the same artist. There were robberies all the time in Mayfair. But even if she supposed that two missing paintings made a coincidence rather than a trail, she also remembered the tone of Sullivan's voice when he'd declined to put the painting back. Right before he'd kissed her.

Setting the missive aside, she went over to her wardrobe and dug into the silk bag she'd hidden inside the neckline of her ugliest dress, a brown monstrosity that she'd worn once to please her great-aunt and then had relegated to oblivion at the back of the shelf. Glancing at her closed door, she pulled a black half-mask out of the bag and looked at it. Why those paintings? And why steal them?

She ran her finger along the brow of the mask, then retrieved Lord Minster's letter to stuff it and the disguise back into their hiding place inside the ugly dress. Yes, puzzles were marvelous things. Because she loved finding the answers. And the person who could provide the answers to this particular mystery would be at Chalsey House at ten o'clock. Promptly at ten.

However reluctant he might be to discuss himself or his so-called business, she didn't intend to give him any choice in the matter. He didn't have to know that whatever thoughts she'd had of turning him in were crumbling. In fact, it would be much better — for her, certainly — if he didn't know.

At six minutes before ten o'clock she went downstairs again. Douglas and their mother were in the breakfast room now, but Phillip and her father were apparently still asleep. Good. The fewer gawkers standing about the stable yard this morning, the better.

After a quick greeting to her mother and brother she made her way out the back of the house. She reached the yard just as Mr. Waring rode up on his monstrous black horse. It wouldn't surprise her at all if the beast ate small animals. *Good heavens.* But she still wouldn't be willing to wager over which of the two was more dangerous —

the horse or the rider.

As Sullivan rode into the Chalsey House stable yard, he spied Lady Isabel leaving the house. At the sight of him on Achilles she stopped short, putting her hands behind her back in that endearing, vulnerable manner she had. It seemed so at odds with her sharp tongue. Immediately he dismounted, handing Achilles' reins over to one of the stable-boys. As far as he now stood from being anything resembling a hero, frightening a woman for no good reason simply cut him wrong.

That applied to a woman who was presently blackmailing him, apparently. He took off his jacket and slung it across Achilles' saddle, then rolled up his sleeves as he approached her. "Promptly at ten," he said, pulling on his leather gloves so he wouldn't be tempted by the absurd impulse to take her hand, to touch her skin.

"My congratulations to your nicely wound clock," she returned.

Not quite an insult, but not a compliment, either. He wouldn't mention, then, that he'd been pacing Achilles up and down the next street over for the past twenty minutes. "I'll just get started, shall I?"

"If you don't, your promptness would be

rather pointless, don't you think?"

"You're the one giving the orders, my lady." Sullivan walked toward the stable to meet Phipps, who had Zephyr and a longeing whip already waiting for him. "I'm just doing the work."

"So why are you here, Mr. Waring?"

He cocked an eyebrow at her. So she'd figured out something about him and decided it was time to learn the rest. "I'm training a horse, I believe."

"That's not what I meant," she countered, following behind him. "And I have several other questions to ask, as well."

"Then ask. I seem to be at your disposal for the foreseeable future."

"You'd best keep that in mind, Mr. Waring."

"Thank you, Phipps," he said to the head groom, accepting the lead line. "She seemed a little skittish yesterday. I'd appreciate a bit more room today."

"Of course, Mr. Waring."

As soon as Phipps pulled his people back and then made himself scarce, Lady Isabel cleared her throat. "Don't order my servants about."

"I'm not. I made a request." He faced her. "Before you begin interrogating me, I have a question for you."

She lifted her chin, pretty brown eyes showing almost amber in the sunlight. Immediately he wanted to kiss her upturned mouth again. Sullivan shook himself. *Idiot.* What the devil was wrong with him? "Is Zephyr solely your excuse to keep me under your heel, or do you actually intend to ride her?"

From the way the muscles in her jaw jumped, she hadn't expected the question. Good. He'd long ago learned the benefits of a surprise attack. He waited, Zephyr standing patiently beside him, while she considered her answer.

"Of course I mean to ride her," she finally stated. "Don't be ridiculous."

"Then come here."

She folded her arms across her chest, which drew his attention to her breasts. They seemed just the right size; as Bram had been known to say, anything more than a handful was a waste. "I give the orders," she stated. "Not you."

"Then please come over here, my lady," he revised, reflecting that it was a good thing he'd learned to have patience when faced with willful creatures. He wondered whether she'd realized that he needed to decipher her intentions as much as she seemed to want to determine his.

121

"No."

"If I haven't injured you thus far, Tibby, you can be fairly assured that I won't be doing so. Just hold out your hand."

"No. And my name where you're concerned is Lady Isabel. Or my lady."

Deciding the protest was merely a delaying tactic, he ignored it, looking from her to Zephyr. The mare was a good animal, but no horse did well with a fearful rider. It wasn't fair to either of them. He supposed it would help to know what precisely it was that frightened Isabel, but first things first. If she wouldn't make a single step forward, he would take the horse back and let her find another way to blackmail him until each of them had satisfied their curiosity.

Shifting his grip from the lead line to the harness strap beneath the mare's chin, he took a firm hold. Then he placed his right hand flat on the mare's shoulder. "Stand behind me and put your hand on my shoulder," he said.

"That seems pointless."

"Your right hand on my right shoulder, if you please."

She sighed irritably — or that seemed to be her aim, anyway — then moved directly behind him. Her skirt swished against the backs of his legs, and then warmth touched his shoulder through the rough cotton of his work shirt.

"Happy?"

"I'm becoming so," he returned. Every nerve in his body seemed attuned to that one spot of warmth. Even his breath hesitated. "Now move to my elbow."

"Mr. Waring, this —"

"Please."

Lady Isabel slid her palm down to his elbow, her soft touch like a caress. Arousal spun down his spine. *Good God.*

"Anything else?" she asked, her breath against his shoulder making him shiver. "Perhaps you'd like me to sew on a button, or polish your boots."

He shifted a little to cover his uneasiness, just as she was jabbering to cover hers. She wouldn't let him call her by her name, and he didn't want to continue calling her by her title. "Now my wrist, poppet."

Since he'd rolled up his sleeves halfway to his elbow he wasn't certain she would comply, but with another even less steady breath she shifted right a little bit and ran her hand down his bare arm to the safety of his glove. By now he'd begun to think that she was being deliberately tantalizing, but since she was also obviously nervous, he let it go without comment.

It was a good thing she stood behind him, though, because otherwise he would probably be doing something foolish like smelling the citrus scent of her hair. Since her reach was shorter than his, he'd bent his arm quite a bit. Even so, they were very close to one another. If not for the obvious goal of the horse and their position in the middle of the yard, they would never have gotten away with this.

"Put your hand over the back of mine," he instructed.

"You're not going to trick me and throw me onto her back, are you?"

"No. She's not ready for that." Neither female was, actually. "No tricks."

After a long moment she laid her hand flat over his gloved one. Sullivan wished he'd left the gloves at home, but this way was probably for the best. He held still, aware of her cheek against his shoulder and her left hand gripping the back of his shirt for balance.

"Now what?" she whispered.

"I'm going to move my hand back along her ribs. Stay with me."

Her hand on his trembled a little, but she complied. They repeated the motion twice, and then he paused again with his hand halfway along Zephyr's side.

"Can you feel her breathing?"

"Yes."

"If I stay right here, will you slide your hand next to mine?"

Her breath stopped. "Tomorrow," she whispered unsteadily. "I'll do that tomorrow. If you'll be standing right there."

"I will be." At that moment he felt willing to fight off Bonaparte's entire Seventeenth Regiment single-handedly for the privilege.

The lesson seemed to be over, but she didn't move from her stance against him, her smaller hand over his. He could swear that her cheek rubbed against his shoulder. Every muscle and bone ached from being held so rigidly, when all he wanted to do was turn around and pull her into his arms. He would barely have to move. Just a slight shift of his feet, and —

Zephyr snorted and stomped a hoof. Instantly Isabel gasped and jumped backward. Blinking, Sullivan concentrated on patting the mare's side until he could be reasonably certain that he wouldn't throw himself on Lady Isabel. Then he turned around.

Her older brother, Phillip, Lord Chalsey, stood at the edge of the stable yard. *Damnation.* With a slight nod at him, Sullivan picked up the longeing whip he'd tossed aside. "You did very well, my lady," he said as he led Zephyr to one side of the yard.

She cleared her throat. "Thank you for not teasing me," she said, following him at a safe distance.

He shrugged. "You faced something that troubles you. There's nothing to tease you about." Shaking out the lead line, he sent Zephyr into a walk.

"Who is Francesca Perris to you?"

He froze. *Devil a bit.* It had taken her, what, three days to figure it out? And he'd had the rest of the *ton* — with the exception of Bram and the two people whom he wanted to know — running themselves in circles for the past six weeks. Of course, Isabel Chalsey had the advantage of having seen his face.

"I expect an answer, Mr. Waring."

This was why he should have been cold and distant and threatening toward her from the beginning, instead of kissing the chit and fleeing without his mask. And just five minutes ago he'd sworn he would never harm her. Being the villain of the piece, if that was what he'd become, should have been easier. "Up, Zephyr. Trot." Urging Zephyr into a trot, he pivoted in a circle, Isabel keeping pace behind him.

"I can find out, you know," she continued.

"I imagine Oliver will know who —"

"She's my mother," he bit out. "And don't threaten me with Oliver Sullivan unless you want me to put a knife through him."

"He's your brother!"

"We allegedly share a sire. He's not my brother."

For a moment she kept silent, and he thought perhaps he'd finally managed to frighten her into leaving him be. He waited, but she didn't back away. Well, well. Unless a horse was involved, apparently nothing scared her at all. Even him.

"Your mother is a painter, then," she continued finally.

"*Was* a painter," he corrected. "She died a year ago."

"I'm sorry."

"So am I." He changed the tension on the lead line. "Walk on," he instructed, tickling at the mare's foreleg. With a hopping step she stopped, then continued forward again at a walk. "Good girl," he murmured. Not bad at all for a first attempt.

"And so your father truly is Lord Dunston."

Damnation. She was like a hound with a bone. "Leave it be," he said aloud.

"No. I'm deciphering you."

Sullivan glanced over his shoulder at her.

"I think that would be a great deal of effort for very little reward."

"Are you older or younger than Oliver?"

"Do you ever mind your own business?"

"You are my business. I'm blackmailing you, remember?"

Good God. He sighed, his amusement growing nearly to match his annoyance. "I'm eight months younger."

"You must hate them," she said quietly. "Growing up knowing —"

He snorted. "Until five months ago they barely crossed my mind."

"Why is that? I mean, obviously Lord Dunston hasn't acknowledged you. So —"

"Whoa, Zephyr." Keeping the mare standing and half angry at himself for still not wanting Isabel to be frightened, he stalked up to her. "My secrets for yours," he murmured.

Isabel backed up a step. "What?"

"You heard me."

"I don't have any secrets." She folded her arms. "Except for the one I'm keeping on your behalf."

"And you're enjoying that one, aren't you?"

Her cheeks darkened. "I beg your pardon?"

"People who don't like secrets don't keep

them, and they certainly don't explore them."

"I —"

"If you manage to touch Zephyr tomorrow," he interrupted, knowing he'd already won the point, "I'll tell you something about myself. The more progress you make with her, the more you'll discover about me."

She glared at him, her gaze slipping to the mare and back again. "What if the information, as you said, isn't worth the trouble?"

"That's for you to decide, I suppose."

"I could make you tell me everything right now," she continued, assuming the defiant stance she'd tried with him before.

"Not unless I let you." In most instances he could read people as easily as he did horses. Her, he hadn't quite figured out yet, but he was fairly confident about this. "You could try, of course. But that would mean giving up your hold over me, Isabel. And I think we both know you don't wish to do that."

As she pursed her lips, Sullivan's gaze lowered to her mouth. Abruptly he wondered whether Oliver had ever kissed her. Swift anger and frustration swept up his spine, and he clenched his jaw against it. She was a marquis' daughter. What Oliver had or hadn't done didn't signify, because

Oliver Sullivan was within his rights to pursue her. Sullivan Waring was the one training her horse.

"Get back to your work, then. And it's still *Lady* Isabel," she said, walking over to stand where both of her brothers now watched. Apparently, then, she'd come to the same realization. A well-respected horse breeder he might be, but he was still ankle-deep in horse shit.

Fine. What the devil did he care, anyway, as long as she kept her silence about his nocturnal visit here earlier in the week? "As you wish." With a word and a flick of the whip he started Zephyr forward again. He didn't care. Not one bloody bit. And if she never approached a horse again, he would still have done what he'd been hired to do. Nothing less, and not one damned thing more.

Twenty minutes later he led Zephyr back into the stable. Turning down the multiple offers from the stableboys, he fed and watered the mare himself. At his own stables he had employees to take on mundane tasks like this one, but he'd found that nothing was more conducive to contemplative thought than feeding and brushing down a horse.

"Do you paint?"

He flinched, she was so close behind him. To conceal the motion, he ran the brush through Zephyr's mane again. "Of course I paint," he said, keeping his back to the young woman who should have been his nemesis except for the fact that he liked her — even with her poor taste in beaux. "Every evening between mucking out the stables and mending saddles."

"You don't muck out anything. And I asked you a civil question. Pray give me a civil answer."

Sullivan picked up the bucket and brush and left the stall, latching it behind him. "Is that an order, my lady?"

"If . . . if I were to give you an order, it would be for you to kiss me again."

His heart thudding, he faced her. "What?"

"You heard me, Mr. Waring."

The color in her cheeks had deepened, her breathing fast despite her haughty expression. With a quick glance about to make certain no one else was inside the stable, he dropped the bucket. She jumped at the sound. Sullivan ignored that, instead pulling off his heavy work gloves one by one and tossing them over the bucket's lip.

He'd been wanting to touch her all morning. Striding forward, he placed his palms on her smooth cheeks, tilted her face up,

131

and closed his mouth over hers.

She tasted of tea and toast. Nothing had ever intoxicated him so much in his entire life. Her hands tangled into the front of his shirt, tugging him closer, drowning him in sensation. He teased her lips apart, plunging deeper into her softness and warmth.

Her moan jolted him back to himself. Breathing hard, Sullivan tore his mouth from hers. They were standing in the middle of a bloody stable, for God's sake. Her family's stable. Anyone might have seen them. And then he would discover that there were worse things than being caught stealing from aristocrats. Namely, stealing their daughter's virtues.

Untangling her hands from his shirt, he stepped back. "I hope that met with your satisfaction, my lady," he managed, his voice rough around the edges. All of him felt rough and raw at the edges. He wanted to wipe a hand across his mouth, but he'd have to scrub much harder than that to rid himself of his craving for her.

Isabel cleared her throat. "That was much better than the last time, anyway," she said, her voice as unsteady as his.

The last time had been nothing to sneeze at. He met her gaze. "I'm glad to be of service, my lady."

CHAPTER 8

Isabel expected to see Oliver Sullivan at social gatherings. He was a viscount and the legitimate son and heir apparent of the Marquis of Dunston. Even if he hadn't been in pursuit of her over the past weeks, they traveled in the same circles.

Both he and his family were well liked and well respected, with the Sullivans frequently held up as a fine example of how aristocratic families should conduct themselves. Lord Dunston was heralded for his gentlemanly ways and his perfect devotion to his wife, Margaret.

She liked Oliver, with his charm and deference and confident presence. Goodness knew, though, that she'd been pursued by wife-hunting men since her debut, and honestly she didn't feel any more for him than she did any of the others. In the usual course of events he would probably propose to her in a few weeks, and she would thank him for his kind consideration and tell him she didn't plan to marry until she turned one-and-twenty.

The appearance of Sullivan Waring in her life made everything . . . different. Not only was Mr. Waring unexpected, but his presence made a lie of certain things she'd taken as truths. The Sullivans weren't the perfect portrait they showed the world. And she, who loved and admired her parents and her brothers, could conceal and lie on the behalf of a criminal, imperfect stranger. She could kiss him, and want to kiss him again — even knowing that he brought trouble and chaos with him.

And she'd never enjoyed her life as much as she had in the few days since she'd stumbled across him. But it was more than that. Larger, more significant things were afoot, and even if it was by accident, she felt a part of it. And she liked that, as well. Perhaps that was why she'd begun to want so badly to figure it all out.

"You look very serious, Tibby," her father said as he strolled into the morning room to collect some of his correspondence.

"I was just thinking," she returned, blinking and trying to pull her wandering thoughts back in.

"About anything in particular?"

134

"How well do you know Lord Dunston?"

"Quite well, as you're already aware." He frowned. "Is this about Oliver? Or Mr. Waring? That's something you shouldn't concern yourself with."

"I don't know what it's about, precisely," she admitted. "I'm just trying to reconcile what I thought I knew with what I *do* know now."

"Ah. Well, everyone makes mistakes, I suppose. I've yet to meet anyone who can boast of absolute perfection."

She smiled. "Except me, of course."

"Well, of course. I reckoned that went without saying." Planting a kiss on her forehead, he headed out the door again.

"Papa, why would Lord Dunston not acknowledge that he had another son? It would have made things so much easier on Sullivan. On Mr. Waring, I mean."

"It's more complicated than a matter of ease. There's integrity and family obligation, lines of inheritance . . ." He trailed off. "To be blunt, Dunston is not the first nobleman to produce offspring born on the wrong side of the blanket. He's prided himself on the way he's lived his life. Should he be punished for making one mistake?"

A mistake. She hardly counted fathering a child on the same level as stubbing one's toe. Especially when Dunston held himself up as a paragon of propriety and integrity. She didn't say any of that aloud, though. Her father didn't want to explain it any further, and she suspected that she wouldn't like his answers, anyway. Not when she'd put herself in the middle of a matter of very questionable legality.

Lord Darshear took a step back into the room. "It's the way of the world, my dear. And I hope you are still going driving with Oliver; obviously he's blameless in this, whatever you might think of Dunston at the moment."

"I am going driving with Oliver," she affirmed with another smile, nodding.

"Good. I wouldn't have Mr. Waring here, except that he has an unparalleled reputation with horses and you said you wished to learn to ride. There is no one in England better qualified to perform that task."

"Thank you, Papa."

Once her father left the room again, Isabel resumed her sightless gaze out the window. No, none of this was Oliver's fault. He'd only been eight months old at the time of Sullivan's birth. But neither was it Sullivan's fault. And yet the two of them obviously viewed one another as mortal enemies.

As a fellow member of the aristocracy, she

should be sympathizing with Oliver. But though she wondered why Lord Tilden hadn't arranged for Sullivan's arrest when he obviously knew the identity of the Mayfair Marauder, her curiosity and growing concern were with Sullivan.

But the animosity between the two men meant she probably shouldn't have asked — ordered — Sullivan to kiss her. But she had, and he had, and her heart thudded every time she thought about it. *My goodness.* The first time, she'd been frightened and titillated. That kiss, though, had more than likely been meant merely to surprise her into silence while he escaped into the night. This kiss she'd wanted. She'd been thinking about it for four days. And he hadn't disappointed.

Down the hallway the front door opened, and at the sound of Oliver's voice she stood to summon her maid. A moment later Oliver appeared in the morning room doorway. "Good morning, Isabel," he said, smiling. "You should always wear green; it's very fetching on you."

She curtsied, glad she'd managed to arrange for him to visit while Sullivan was elsewhere. "Thank you, Oliver, though I think after a time I'd begin to feel a bit like moss."

"But you'd look precious as emeralds."

After they went out to the drive and he helped her and then her maid into his curricle, they set off for Hyde Park. Sullivan would be back at three o'clock for Zephyr's afternoon training, but she should be home well before then.

Her father had said she needed to show an active interest in the horse's training if she expected to keep Zephyr, and that provided a good excuse to keep an eye on Mr. Waring. Was that an excuse, though? Because it had begun to seem that keeping an eye on the mare's trainer had less to do with him being the Mayfair Marauder, and more to do with him being interesting and dangerous and . . . different than anyone else she'd ever met. And her very own secret.

"I'd like to ask you a favor," Oliver said, guiding them onto the park's main path.

She shook herself. *Pay attention.* "Of course."

"I know a fellow who trained a winner at the Derby two years ago. Will you accept my counsel and use him to continue your mare's training?"

Abrupt annoyance hit her, but she forced herself to take a moment to consider her answer. She disliked being told what to do, politely or not, but she also knew that she wasn't aware of all the details of Sullivan's life and activities and so needed to tread carefully. "I paid an additional fee for Mr. Waring's services," she said with her usual charming smile. "And my father and brother approve the results thus far."

"Tom Barrett is perfectly competent," Oliver insisted. "And I will see to any additional expenses."

With a breath she shook her head. "I don't wish to ride a race horse." Just the thought made her shudder. "It's a business arrangement, Oliver. Nothing more." Nor did she want to be obligated to Oliver, because that could come back to haunt her later.

But her connection to Sullivan was more than just a business arrangement. She just couldn't tell anyone else about it. Not about the thievery — and certainly not about the kisses. The first would ruin Sullivan Waring, while the second would destroy them both.

"I don't like him hanging about you," Oliver said in the middle of her ruminations.

"He's hanging about the stable; not me."

Oliver pulled the bay team to a halt and faced her. "Don't trust him, Isabel. I'm begging you. He's ruthless and underhanded. And common, whatever he might say."

Her annoyance deepened. "For heaven's

sake, Oliver, Mr. Waring doesn't say anything, except to the horses. You're acting as
though you're jealous or some such thing.
It doesn't become you."

He snorted. "Jealous? Of a bastard horse
breeder? I think not." He clucked to the
team and they started off again. "I merely
pity any proper female who might cross his
path unawares."

She drew a breath. As determined as she
was to decipher Sullivan, Oliver would likely
be a splendid source of information. If she
attempted it, she would have to be careful
to avoid letting the viscount know *she'd* realized that Mr. Waring was the thief who'd
been tormenting the residents of Mayfair. It
wasn't only the need for caution that made
her hesitate, though. Whatever Oliver told
her about Sullivan would be bad. According
to her uncovering-of-mysteries plan, she
needed to hear it. But did she truly want to
know?

"Oliver, since Mr. Waring is in my family's
employ, I would appreciate if you would
elaborate on your concerns about him."

"I should think it obvious," he returned.
"Where does a nobody acquire the funds
necessary to begin a thoroughbred horse-
breeding establishment?"

Through hard work, she immediately

thought, but of course couldn't say that aloud. Some people needed to work for a living, but not nobles. "Do you think he took money from someone?" she asked, careful not to mention Mayfair or marauding.

"I wouldn't put anything past him. What do you expect of someone with whom no one wishes to associate except for business?"

"But his work is well respected by nearly everyone."

"Ha. You'll notice that *I* don't own a horse from Waring Stables."

Hm. She wondered whether that had been his decision, or Sullivan's. "If you suspect him of illegal doings, why haven't you reported him to the authorities?"

He blew out his breath. "There are some things a gentleman doesn't do," he returned with a scowl. "I prefer to think that if given enough rope, a scoundrel will hang himself."

Hang. She'd threatened Sullivan with that, but when Oliver said it, she realized that not only would the viscount be perfectly content to see it happen, but it was a real possibility. Sullivan Waring could hang. Oliver, despite his stated intention to stay back and observe, could easily see that it *would* happen. And if she wanted otherwise, she'd best have a reason.

After all, he'd known Sullivan Waring for a great deal of time longer than she had. If she'd heard Oliver's opinion of Sullivan before she'd stumbled across him burgling her house, she probably would have turned him in to the authorities without hesitation. It would have been foolish not to. Now, however, what had been complicated before was so tangled she could barely see the spider for the web.

She needed to learn more of those secrets kept by Sullivan Waring. And her best chance to do that would be while she trusted him to keep her safe as she put her hands on a horse.

"Samuel, I need you to deliver Hector to Lord Brewster this morning," Sullivan said, as he finished saddling Achilles. "And remind him that he's signed a contract. He has a fortnight. And whether any of his mares produce or not, he owes us a hundred quid."

The groom nodded. "Subtle or straightforward, sir?"

Sullivan grinned. "Subtle. Brewster's never tried to cheat me before. I just don't want any nasty surprises later." Thunder boomed across the meadow, and he glanced through the open stable doors. "Tell him if the weather puts Hector off, we'll give him another day gratis."

"I'll see to it."

"Good. I'll be back in under two hours. Before you leave, have Halliwell bring in the pair of bays for Gilroy. I want them dry and brushed down when he comes to take possession."

"No worries."

There were half a hundred other things he needed to attend to, but as he swung into the saddle and sent Achilles off at a trot toward Mayfair, foremost in his mind was seeing Isabel. Odd, that in such a relatively short time she'd become such a central piece of his life. Of course, much of that was because she insisted on blackmailing him, even though by now they both had a fair idea that she wasn't going to have him carted off to gaol.

Yesterday afternoon she'd kept her distance, but he had the feeling that that was more because of her younger brother's presence than because she didn't want to kiss him again. He definitely wanted to kiss her again. And that wasn't all he wanted of her.

Unfortunately, whatever his feelings toward the aristocracy in general, ruining pretty young things of high birth had never appealed to him — and especially not when this one actually interested him. He'd had his share of ladies of the peerage, ones who had their eyes open and on occasion rings on their fingers, but he'd never found them to be more enticing than any other chit in the world.

It amused him that the ladies and the more horse-wise men of the *ton* practically worshipped his skill with and knowledge of the animals — unless Dunston or Tilden or any of the other Sullivans were about. Then he became invisible. A shame he couldn't take that act to the fair.

Or rather, it had amused him until his return from the Peninsula. Since then it had served only to remind him of the hypocrisy and conceit of the people with whom he did business. There were exceptions — Bram, for example, and Viscount Quence, Phin Bromley's older brother. And Isabel Chalsey.

That last one was probably an illusion on his part, but she'd kissed him twice now. And the second time had been her idea, and it had been after she'd realized that he and Oliver Sullivan were half-brothers.

Thunder boomed again. Achilles hopped sideways, neighing, but Sullivan reined him in, patting him on the neck. "It's only noise, boy," he said soothingly.

The clouds let loose. A gray curtain of cold and wet closed around him. And over him.

"Noise and rain," he amended, pulling his hat lower over his eyes and holding his greatcoat closed with one hand. "Bloody bracing, don't you think, lad?"

When he reached Chalsey House he was soaked to his bones. At least he'd arrived at ten o'clock sharp — prompt once again. The stable yard drained well, but it was still muddy. Ah, well. The horses didn't mind, and the devil knew he'd trudged through worse. For her future rider's sake he wanted Zephyr accustomed to varying terrain, anyway.

"Good morning, Mr. Waring," Phipps said, meeting him at the stable's main doors. "I thought perhaps you'd pass us by today, what with our fine weather."

Grinning, Sullivan shrugged. "It's like as not to rain tomorrow, and I can't get much wetter now."

The groom chuckled. "I do hear that. I'll take care of your Achilles for you."

"My thanks."

Grabbing a spare blanket, he laid it across Zephyr's back and tied it down before he led her outside. She barely batted an ear as she pranced into the rain. Good. Today a blanket, tomorrow a sack of grain, and the next day or so, a saddle.

He let her canter about for a few minutes on the end of the line — she'd been tolerating being closed up in a stable extremely well, and she'd be easier to work with once she'd kicked off her high spirits. The back door of Chalsey House remained firmly closed against the weather, so he supposed he might as well settle down to work, himself. And the disappointment running through his chest? That was just idiocy.

"Mr. Waring?"

A ground-floor window of the house pushed open. As he recalled from his late-night visit, through it was a cozy sitting room. That was beside the point, though, as Lady Isabel, her blonde hair loose around her shoulders like soft spun gold, motioned for him to approach.

"Good morning, my lady," he said, sweeping his wet hat off his wet hair.

Her gaze lowered briefly to his mouth. "You didn't have to come this morning, you know."

"It's just rain. And it's not good for an animal being trained to miss a day of lessons."

"You're very dedicated."

He grinned. "Are you alone in there?"

"Yes."

"Then I'm meeting the terms of my black-mail. But I don't suppose you'll venture out here to do your part regarding that other matter."

" 'Other matter'?"

"The trading of secrets. Or information, since you claim to have none of the other."

"I am not going out in that," she retorted, gesturing at the out-of-doors in exaggerated horror. "I'll catch my death!"

For a moment he wondered whether she worried more about the weather or about patting the horse. Then she looked behind him at where Zephyr danced through a puddle, tossing her head and nickering. Ah. Definitely the horse, then.

"And what's so amusing about me catching cold, Mr. Waring?" she demanded.

He hadn't realized he was smiling. "Apologies. I never expected your resolve to get to the bottom of . . . well, of me, to be damp-ened so easily," he improvised.

"It's not dampened. Only delayed. And I shall be watching you from the window, so don't think you can get away with anything."

Sullivan inclined his head. "I wouldn't dream of misbehaving, poppet. Not without you."

While Isabel sat in the window, warm and

dry and sipping what smelled like peppermint tea, he put Zephyr through her paces, first clockwise, and then the other way around. He did his best to concentrate, but every inch of him knew she was watching. It raised the hairs on his arms and sped his breath.

"When I ride her," she called through the window, "is Zephyr only going to be able to walk in a circle?"

"She can also manage a figure eight," he answered over his shoulder, otherwise trying to ignore her comments. It was easier, though, to ignore the rain.

"How will she learn to take the bridle when you've been pulling her everywhere?"

"Have you been reading up on techniques of horse training?" he asked, torn between annoyance and amusement. He doubted she would have been asking those questions if she'd been standing next to him. If that had been the case, he would have been tempted to throw her on the back of a horse — any horse — and see how she fared.

"Yes, I have been," she returned. "Phillip gave me a book."

"Perhaps you'd like to come out here and put your reading to good use, then."

"Not while it's raining, Mr. Waring. For heaven's sake."

"Whoa, Zephyr." Once the mare stopped, he faced the house again. "Just keep in mind, my lady, that I can reach right through that window."

"Oh, yes, I recall. You're very good at climbing through windows."

"Lucky for you, or you'd be stuck in there with no one to torment."

"Unfortunate for you, because you were so unskilled as to be caught."

That was enough of that. He dropped the lead line and stalked up to the window through the mud. As he reached the window she leaned out with a breathless laugh and pulled it closed, latching it before he could dig his fingers into the frame and open it again. She waved at him from behind the safety of the glass.

He glared at her, then went back to work. Closing that window was the smartest thing she'd done since they'd met. Because foremost in his mind after getting his hands on her was kissing her again. It wasn't her safety he was likely to endanger. It was her virtue.

"Tibby, it's not seemly for you to be staring out the window at strange men."

Isabel actually jumped as her mother, embroidery in hand, walked into the sitting room. "He's not a strange man," she replied, gazing out at Sullivan again as Zephyr circled gracefully around him. "I hired him, and I am making certain he's attending to his duties."

Lady Darshear joined her at the window. "Mr. Sullivan Waring looks very fine in the rain," she said after a moment.

"Mama!"

With a chuckle, her mother sat in the chair by the crackling fireplace. "I was young once," she commented. "I remember what it was like to admire a fine, fit form and earnest blue eyes."

"They're green," Isabel corrected, then flushed as she realized her mother was looking at her. "They're quite distinctive."

"Your father told me who Mr. Waring purportedly is. Last night. I suppose he reckoned that with Mr. Waring about and Lord Tilden calling on you, it would be best if I knew their connection. You're aware of it, too, he said."

Isabel nodded.

"Then you know that for Lord Tilden's sake you need to keep your distance from Mr. Waring. And for your own sake you need to stop staring at him, through windows or otherwise."

"It's not his fault, you know."

"It's the way of the world. And you, my dear, are very close to making a splendid connection. Don't ruin it because you feel sympathy for a common horse breeder with a handsome face."

A horse breeder and thief, and a well-educated and articulate one, at that. And yes, handsome. Perhaps that was it — the only thing "common" about Sullivan Waring was that everyone else used the term to describe him. Everyone else was so easy to decipher, when she'd barely begun to figure him out.

"Isabel?"

"Yes, I know," she said absently. "But I'm not marrying Oliver. I don't love him."

"You might come to, if you would refrain from antagonizing him by continuing to employ Mr. Waring."

"I want to ride a horse. According even to Papa, no one else is as qualified to see to that."

"Very well. Then come away from the window and tend to your embroidery."

With a last look, she reluctantly did so. Obviously she couldn't tell her mother that Sullivan had been the one to steal from them and that she'd taken it as her duty to figure out why, and to keep him from doing further misdeeds. She couldn't say it because it wouldn't be entirely true. He did fascinate her, and the more everyone told her to stay from him, the more intrigued she became.

Even if it meant getting close enough to the horse to touch it, she hoped it wouldn't be raining tomorrow. She had some more questions for Mr. Sullivan Waring. Questions that were fast becoming as important to her as they might be to him.

Oliver Sullivan, Lord Tilden, shook rain off his coat as he climbed the stairs and made his way down the short hallway on the first floor of Sullivan House. As usual the office door was closed, and he rapped his knuckles against the hard wood.

"Who is it?" came the low voice inside.

"Oliver."

"Come in."

Still shedding his gloves, Oliver pushed down the door handle and walked into the austere, candlelit room. While the figure seated behind the desk hunched over a ledger and continued scribbling figures, he dropped into the chair opposite, slapping his gloves against his thigh.

"What is it?"

"I thought you'd like to know that your by-blow is spending better than an hour a day at Chalsey House, training a horse for the chit I'm planning to marry."

The pen hit the paper, a glob of ink dripping from the tip to stain the ledger sheet. Pale, washed-out eyes beneath a shock of gray hair finally lifted to regard him. "I do not have a by-blow," George Sullivan, the Marquis of Dunston, grunted.

"You're the only one who thinks that."

"Nonsense. Nothing of the sort can be proven, and I won't have you speaking of such rumors and lies in this house."

Oliver drew in a breath. He'd never won one of these arguments, but they did gall the old marquis — and generally that was enough to encourage him to continue. "Very well. Mr. *Sullivan* Waring is working for the household we both know he robbed less than a sennight ago. I thought you might be interested in having that information, especially considering that he's managing to strike against your particular friends with impunity." He pushed to his feet. "Good day, Father."

As he closed the office door behind him once more, Oliver had to give Waring a small amount of credit. The bastard had certainly found the most effective way imaginable to aggravate their father — and there wasn't a damned thing the paterfamilias could do about it unless he cared to admit to his own shortcomings first. And all of London knew he'd never do that.

An interesting way of gaining revenge, and one he might have chosen himself if he'd ever been as stupid and trusting as Sullivan Waring had obviously been in giving the protection of his property over to someone else while he traipsed across the Peninsula. But stupid and trusting were two things Oliver would never be. Especially where his possessions were concerned. Lady Isabel Chalsey in particular.

CHAPTER 9

As Isabel walked outside into the breezy morning sunlight, she nearly wished for rain again.

Yes, she had questions for Mr. Waring and a mystery to decipher. Aside from that, no one had been burgled since he'd begun working for her, so perhaps keeping him employed was enough to remove him from further temptation, which would be enough reason for her to continue to blackmail him into remaining. But how she'd ended up promising to make friends with a very large animal, she had no idea. Sullivan Waring was clearly a devious fellow.

"Do you wish it had continued to rain?" he said, appearing from the direction of the stable, Zephyr on the lead line behind him.

That had to be a guess. He couldn't possibly know her that well already. And she was supposed to be making the observations. Not him. "Nonsense. And please run

Zephyr about a little before you approach me with her."

He nodded. "As you wish."

From his amused expression, she realized he'd intended to do that anyway, but it couldn't hurt to remind him that she made the rules in this game and that he'd best play along. Shivering, she closed her eyes for a moment. She didn't have to do it. She could go back inside the house or deny that she'd ever mentioned approaching that horse.

They would both know that she was lying, though, and if she'd lied about that, she might have lied about being willing to have Mr. Waring arrested. And then she could expect disaster. She — her knowledge — might very well be his only incentive to stay out of people's houses, after all.

And so she kept her hands clasped hard behind her back and watched Zephyr gallop and hop about and toss her head while Sullivan stood calmly at the other end of the lead line, keeping it free of tangles and letting her do as she pleased. Finally he drew her in and patted her on the withers, then whispered something in her ear and led her across the stable yard to where Isabel made her feet remain in place and not hurry her away to safety.

"What did you tell her?" Isabel asked, seeking for anything to keep her mind off what she was about to do. "To kick me?"

Sullivan shifted his grip from the rope to the harness, as he'd done the other day. "I told her to behave herself."

Isabel forced a smile. "You're a very unusual thief."

"And you are a very unusual blackmailer."

"Have you known many with which to compare me?"

His lips curved. "Not one. And you?"

"Not one." Isabel shook herself. "So do you think Zephyr will listen to you?"

"Yes. Even if she doesn't, I promise that you will be perfectly safe."

That seemed a bold statement, but since she badly wanted it to be true, she didn't dispute it. "Very well."

"Stand behind me."

"I don't need —"

"I am apparently your slave," he interrupted, grinning in a way that touched his ice-green eyes and made her heart skitter, "but I know horses better than you do. Stand behind me."

"Oh, very well," she grumbled. Actually, having his tall, lean body between her and the horse seemed a fairly good idea.

Moving behind him as she had the other

day, she grabbed a handful of his shirt to keep him from escaping.

"Can you put your hand over mine again, just as before?"

"Yes." *Oh dear, oh dear.* She should be asking him questions and demanding answers, but all she could see was the large gray flank in front of her.

"Do it, then."

"I will. In a minute."

"I was in Spain, wounded, when I received word that my mother had died of a fever," he said unexpectedly, his voice low and intimate. "I'd already missed her funeral, so I remained with my unit. She had several good friends who'd promised to look after her concerns, and when she became ill she'd also arranged for them to take over supervision of mine, so there didn't seem to be any reason for me to return to England immediately."

As he spoke, he reached back with his free hand and took hers. She knew he was only trying to distract her, but listening to him finally giving her some of the answers she'd wanted was certainly easier than thinking about the horse just in front of her. "But you did return to England, obviously."

"Yes. Six months ago. As I said, I took a French ball in the shoulder a year ago, but I managed to talk my commanding officer into letting me stay in the field. Then I was wounded again, in the same shoulder. When I next opened my eyes, I was on a ship halfway back to Dover. Bram arranged to sell out my commission — and his — in order to escort me home."

"Bram. Lord Bramwell Johns?" She laid her hand on his larger one as he stroked Zephyr's withers.

He nodded. "When I could get about, I went to my mother's cottage to pack up her paintings and bring them to my home. They were gone. All of them. Apparently the property's owner had decided that since she'd died, all of her things belonged to him. No matter what her last wishes were."

As he spoke, his voice became harder and colder. "I think I can guess," she said carefully, her cheek against his shoulder, "but who owned the property?"

"Dunston. I have no idea why she continued to live there, but she said she liked the light in the house. If your next question was why she painted as Francesca Perris, she married William Perris when I was three. He died two years after that."

"Do you think she retained an affection for the marquis? Perhaps that was why she st—"

"No," he returned sharply. "I think it's more likely she wanted to remind him of his shortcomings at every opportunity. Hence my name."

"That seems crueler to you than to your father, if that was her goal."

"She had her own opinion of things, I'll give you that." He paused. "And look at you," he continued, his voice softer again.

Her hand rested beside his on Zephyr's flank. Isabel's breath caught. It was the closest she'd been to a horse in eleven years, since she'd been eight. "Goodness," she breathed, suddenly afraid to move.

"You can feel the muscles shift under her skin," he said in the same soothing tone, "and her ribs moving as she breathes."

She didn't know how he understood so well what she felt and what she needed to hear, the small, mundane things that told her this was normal, and simple, and she could do it. But at the moment she felt enormously grateful. Still nervous as anything, but grateful. And proud of herself.

Slowly she lifted her hand and set it back again. The muscles moved beneath her palm, the fur coarser than she'd thought it would be. She patted Zephyr again.

"Well done, Tibby," Sullivan murmured. "See her ears flick? She's listening for your voice. Say something to her."

"Hello, Zephyr," she ventured, managing to keep her voice steady. "You're a pretty thing, aren't you?"

The mare blew air out of her nose and tossed her head. Isabel jumped, but Sullivan covered her hand with his.

"She's saying hello back to you," he said calmly. "She didn't try to move away from you, and her ears are up and angled in your direction. She likes you."

"Are you certain?"

"I do know something about horses," he said, his tone easy.

So she'd done it. No sense pushing things further and undoing her so-called triumph. Isabel pulled her hand out from under his. "I think that's good for today," she said, releasing his shirt and backing away.

"Do you want to hold the lead line?"

"No." She cleared her throat. "Not yet."

"Will you stand with me while I send her walking?"

She nodded. She could do that. At the moment she nearly felt as though she could do anything. With a grin that probably looked as silly as it felt, she followed him into the middle of the stable yard. "Thank you," she said belatedly.

"You're welcome. Walk on, Zephyr."

Gazing at his profile, it occurred to her that he'd never teased her about her hesitation around Zephyr. Neither did her own family, ever, but she'd certainly been teased about it by nearly everyone else who approached her on horseback or in a carriage. And yet this man, who was probably more comfortable with horses than anyone else she'd yet encountered, had said nothing.

"What?" he asked after a moment, glancing sideways at her.

"Nothing."

"No questions about bridles or saddles or the length of lead lines today?"

"No."

She took a breath, wondering why she felt compelled to continue. This was supposed to be about him. But he'd told her some things — some important things — without being asked. It felt like trust, and she wanted to reciprocate.

"My friend Mary and I were walking along the lane at Burling — that's our family estate — when a man riding by in his phaeton lost the reins. The right-hand horse hit me in the side and knocked me into the ditch. Mary got tangled up with the horses. They . . . dragged her, kicking and screaming, halfway around the bend. She died."

"Whoa, Zephyr." Sullivan faced her, his

face serious and his gaze full of an unexpected compassion. "How old were you?"

"Eight."

"I'm sorry."

She shrugged, abruptly uncomfortable. "Thank you. It was a long time ago."

"Some things are never very far away."

Isabel felt her lips curve again. "You're very wise for a horse breeder."

"You are the first to say so."

He continued to look at her. Warmth crept up her cheeks. They were standing so close to one another. . . . Her gaze lowered to his very capable mouth. An illegitimate son of a nobleman. A thief. A man who worked with his hands. Everything a proper young lady was supposed to avoid. And she wanted him to kiss her again.

"Tibby?" he murmured.

She shook herself. For goodness' sake, he'd been calling her by her familiar name yet again despite her demands to the contrary, and now she was nearly *touching* him. And his half-brother was courting her. Everyone knew that. Including him. "Get back to work, if you please."

His smile darkened. "No, some things never are very far away, are they? Walk on, Zephyr."

"Don't try to fault me for merely doing

163

what's proper, Mr. Waring."

"I fault you for choosing to be proper only when it suits you, Lady Isabel," he retorted, turning his back to her. "Get up, girl." Zephyr moved into a trot.

So much for their momentary alliance. "You're the one who feels wronged by one man and does wrong to dozens of others as a consequence."

"I'm getting back what's mine," he snapped, no amusement at all remaining in his expression now.

"By stealing from perfectly innocent people."

"No one is perfectly innocent. And don't think your little games are keeping me from anything. Keep your ear to the wind, poppet. You'll be hearing something soon."

"Pray you don't hear the iron bars of the gaol locking you away, then, Mr. Waring. And yes, that is a warning." Before he could respond, she turned on her heel and, avoiding Zephyr, strode back to the house.

What was she doing, keeping her silence about what she knew? He had a compassionate side, certainly, but his selfish, vengeful side clearly surrounded and nearly suffocated the rest of him. And he'd just *told* her that he meant to rob again.

"Stupid, stupid," she muttered, stalking

through the kitchen into the main part of the house.

"What's stupid?" Douglas asked, leaning over the stair railing to look down at her.

"Nothing."

"Do you think Mr. Waring would let me assist him in training your mare?" he continued, hopping down to the foyer.

"He doesn't want you hanging about."

"You hang about."

"She's my horse."

Her younger brother made a face. "That's not fair. I'll just go ask him myself."

As he passed her, Isabel grabbed his arm. "Wait a moment."

"Tibby, don't be so selfish. Don't you know how famous he is among horse people?"

"No."

"Very, very famous. A complete hand. A great gun. All-accompli—"

"I think you've made your point."

"Phillip nearly wept when Mr. Waring went off to the Peninsula, and he did it just because Levonzy made Lord Bramwell join the army. Did you know Waring sent letters to his stable weekly, instructing them about feed and breeding? If he'd been killed, the entire stock of English blood-horses might have been doomed to oblivion."

"Don't be ridiculous."

"I am not being ridiculous." He shrugged free of her grip. "And I'm going to learn all that I can while I can. Perhaps I'll set up my own stable someday."

She turned and watched him head down the hallway. Oh, she was going mad. Protecting Sullivan Waring, accusing him, *kissing him* — she needed advice. From someone she could trust to remain silent. "Douglas?"

He slowed. "What? He'll only be here for another thirty minutes."

"I need to talk to you about something."

"Later, Tibby."

"No. Now. Come with me."

Reluctantly he turned around and followed her into the morning room. "You're not going to make me try on hats for you again, are you? Because I ain't going to —"

"No hats," she interrupted, closing and latching the door behind him.

"Oh. Good, then."

"I can trust you, can't I, Douglas? Truly trust you?"

He stopped his pacing and jabbering to face her. "Of course you can. I'm your brother."

Douglas had proven trustworthy before, but that had been when she'd temporarily misplaced their mother's ear bobs and when she'd decided to go ice-skating and had nearly fallen through the frozen surface of Burling's pond. This was much, much more serious. But she couldn't tell any of her friends, and informing her parents or Phillip about what she knew was just out of the question. They would take it all away from her control, and she refused to let that happen.

"You must promise that this will remain between us. No one else can know, Douglas."

"Zooks. You didn't murder anyone, did you?"

"Promise me," she insisted.

"Fine, fine. I promise."

"Truly promise."

"God's blood, Tibby, do you want me to stab my eye with a needle? I promise."

"Very well." Isabel blew out her breath. Plunking herself down on the overstuffed couch, she mentally crossed her fingers. Sullivan had threatened to take action again, and so she had to, as well. "I saw the face of the man who broke into the house," she said.

"*What?*" Obviously she'd captured Douglas's notoriously unreliable attention. "You said he wore a mask!"

"He did."

"Then how did you —"

"I took it from him."

Douglas frowned, his brows lowering. "You fought him? Tibby —"

"Will you shut up and let me tell you?"

He dropped into the chair opposite her and folded his arms across his chest. "Tell me, then. I won't utter a peep."

She doubted that. "I surprised him, as I said, but he didn't turn and run. He . . . he kissed me."

Douglas lurched forward. "He —" With a quick breath he sat back again. His face turning bright red, he gestured for her to continue.

That was why she couldn't tell any of the adults in the household. She'd be halfway home to Burling, wrapped in nun's robes, before she finished speaking. And that wasn't just her being dramatic. "He just did it to surprise me, to keep me quiet while he escaped. I didn't know who he was until I caught sight of him the next day at Tattersall's."

Now Douglas looked as though he was choking on a bug, but other than uttering a few strangled sounds, he kept his silence.

"It was Sullivan Waring."

This time her brother shot to his feet. "Oh, no no no! If you've changed your mind about having a horse, that's well and good. But to ruin a man's reputation just because —"

"He's taking back paintings done by his mother. She was a very talented artist. Lord Dunston took them after she died. That's the reason for his thievery. That's what Mr. Waring claims, anyway."

"But Dunston is . . ."

"His father. I know."

"And you and Tilden are . . ." He flung his arms up in the air. "You're going to give me an apoplexy before I've ever kissed a chit, you know."

"It might help if you stopped referring to all the young ladies you know as 'chits,' " she said dryly. "And Oliver has absolutely nothing to do with this."

"What?" he said incredulously. "Are you mad? Maybe he's not part of this as far as you're concerned, but I'd wager you a hundred quid that neither he nor Waring would say that."

Isabel looked at the sixteen-year-old for a long moment as he resumed pacing aimlessly about the room. She truly hadn't known about Oliver and Sullivan's relationship until well after the break-in. But Oliver knew they'd been robbed. In all likelihood he'd known by then not only who'd done it, but that Chalsey House would be at risk of a break-in before it happened. As for Sullivan's actions, her social connections weren't precisely a secret. Had he known when he'd kissed her that Oliver was courting her?

"I think I must be missing something," Douglas was saying. "You hired Waring knowing — *knowing* — that he'd broken in here and kissed you?"

"I wanted to be able to keep an eye on him," she admitted, "until I decided what to do." It had begun as a bit of a game of mystery and revenge for that kiss, but it was turning into something more important than that. In fact, her original excuses seemed a bit silly, now.

" 'What to do,' " he repeated. "Has he kissed you since then?"

"No!" she lied. "Not that it's any of your affair."

"Well, I'll tell you what to do. Tell Father."

"I can't very well do that now, Douglas. Be serious."

"Why can't you?"

"Because I've hired him. Papa will be convinced that I'm . . . infatuated with him or something. There will be bloodshed, I'm certain."

"*I'm* infatuated with him, and I still say we

170

should hand him over to the authorities."

"What if he had good reason to do what he did?"

"Are we still talking about him kissing you?"

Isabel growled. "We're talking about how something was stolen from him, and how he's attempting to recover it."

"By stealing."

For goodness' sake, this sounded like the same argument she'd just had with Sullivan. Except that now she seemed to be taking his side. "When Oliver gave us that painting, all he said was that it was a gift from his family to ours. Did you have any reason to think differently? Because I didn't."

"No, but —"

"If some horse breeder knocked on the front door, would you let him inside the house?"

"If it was Sullivan Waring, yes, I would have."

"Would you have given him the painting?"

"I . . ." He trailed off. "Well, can he prove that it belonged to him?"

"I doubt it."

Douglas paced to the window and back again. "You have to tell him not to steal anything else. If he were to be caught, and people were to realize that he was the one who stole from us and then you hired him, well, that would be very ugly."

"That's why I'm telling you; he *has* threatened to steal something else."

"Then if you can't turn him over to Bow Street, you have to send him on his way." He scowled darkly. "And I can't believe I'm saying that."

"Oliver did suggest someone else who might complete Zephyr's training," she offered reluctantly. Perhaps Lord Tilden had been correct about Sullivan's character, after all.

"Who?"

"I'm not certain. Barnett? Something close to that."

"Was it Tom Barrett?"

"Yes, that's the name."

Douglas shook his head. "He's a plug. Can make a horse run like the wind, but the animal's just as likely to drop dead afterward as to win another race. He don't know anything slower than a gallop."

"That's awful. Why would Oliver recommend him?"

"You really are a very silly chit," her brother observed. "Barrett's not Waring. *That's* why. Of course, he probably don't know about your fright around horses, but I'd never have Barrett train a lady's mount anyway."

"So you still trust Waring more, even though you know what I know." Well, not everything, but close enough. "You see? That's where I am, as well."

"I . . . I trust him with your Zephyr, I suppose. But that's horses, and he does know horses. As for the rest, you have to give me more than a minute to think about it, Tibby."

"Fair enough. He'll be back this afternoon."

"Oh, yes. I should have everything figured out by then." He sent her another incredulous look. "I take it back," Douglas continued, sinking down into the chair again. "This may take an entire day. You're certain I can't tell anyone else?"

"I'm very certain."

"A day should do it, then. Definitely."

She knew her brother was being sarcastic, but part of her hoped that he would have an answer or two that she could live with. Because when she wasn't angry and frustrated with Sullivan Waring, she still could think of little else but kissing him again. And nothing good could come of that.

CHAPTER 10

" 'And that is a warning,' " Sullivan sneered as he swung down from Achilles and handed the reins off to one of the Bromley House grooms. "Her kettle's black. She should leave mine be."

The front door opened as he reached it. "Welcome, Mr. Waring," a stout, white-haired man in blue and black livery said, inclining his head.

"Graves. Is Lord Bramwell here yet?"

"His lordship sent word that he would be late, if he was able to attend at all."

Just as well. Bram was far too observant and cynical. Tonight he wanted some bloody space to breathe. "Thank you," he said belatedly.

The butler nodded. "Lord Quence is in the drawing room, sir."

Handing over his greatcoat, he trotted up the curving staircase to the first floor. He tried to tell himself that it didn't feel odd, walking into a grand house through the front door, but it did. Generally the only occasion for him to use the main entry was in the middle of the night when the household was asleep and he wore a mask. Not here, though.

"Ah, Sully," a warm male voice said as he walked through the drawing room door. "You heard that Bramwell had another obligation."

Sullivan nodded. "His father's in Town."

"So I gathered. Elizabeth is here, however, so at least we'll have something pretty to look at."

With such precise timing that she must have been listening behind the door, Quence's younger sister swished into the drawing room. "Mr. Waring, I'm so pleased you could join us this evening," she chirped, her ginger curls bobbing as she curtsied.

"Miss Bromley," he returned, smiling. "I hadn't realized that you'd come to London." And her presence definitely explained Bram's absence. The girl was like a moth to his candlelight.

"I fled East Sussex," she said brightly, her hazel eyes dancing as she swooped over to kiss her older brother on one pale cheek. "Talking to myself all the time is tiring."

"Can't imagine why," Lord Quence intoned dryly. He pulled a folded piece of paper from his pocket. "Here. Give your letter to Sullivan. It's nearly a month old; apparently the weather in Spain has been abominable."

"It's from Phin, then?" Sullivan asked, masking his impatience as the seventeen-year-old, letter in hand, strolled over to him. The missive was addressed to Elizabeth Bromley; as far as he knew, Phin never wrote his brother.

"It is," she answered before her brother could, finally handing the missive over. "He asks after you."

"He can read that in the letter, Beth. Please inquire with Graves if dinner is ready, will you?"

She wrinkled her nose. "You might just ask me to leave you in peace for a few minutes. There's nothing wrong with being direct. In fact, *I* think —"

"Beth, please go away for a few minutes and leave us in peace," the viscount interrupted.

"Oh, very well." With a last, brilliant smile she swirled out of the room.

"Good God, I dread her debut next Season," Quence muttered. He motioned at the footman standing behind him, and the fellow pushed his wheeled chair away from the hearth. "I'll leave you to read the letter."

"Nonsense," Sullivan countered, lowering himself onto the couch and trying to look at ease with the motion. "I have a question for you anyway, William, that I'd rather not ask . . . well, with —"

"With the magpie anywhere about?" Quence finished. "Ask away, then. I doubt she'll stay absent for long."

"I'm training a mare for Lord Darshear's daughter," Sullivan began, watching the other man's expression carefully as he spoke. And there it was, the flinch of gaunt cheek muscles, quickly disguised. Quence knew of her, then. Or of who had been in pursuit of her, at least. "How long has Tilden been courting her?"

"Shouldn't you be asking Bramwell? He's certainly more intimate with London social machinations than I am."

"Bram always suspects ulterior motives and asks too many questions."

"Hm. Which questions don't you wish asked?"

Sullivan shifted. "Never mind that. I'm asking purely to avoid any . . . unpleasantness," he lied, "since I am obligated to spend time in Darshear's stable yard for at least the next fortnight."

The viscount nodded. "Tilden's been calling on her since just after the beginning of the Season, as far as I know. Last year it was Lord Mayhew and Clark Winstead and some other fellow, so I have no idea whether this pursuit is serious or not."

Sullivan wasn't surprised to hear how sought-after Tibby was. But at least three beaux last year and only one this year. . . . "Do you think he'll offer for her?" As he asked the question his jaw clenched, the last word coming out as a growl. Lucifer's balls, it couldn't be jealousy. Not after two kisses and thrice that many conversations. Arguments, more like.

"I think he might," Quence said. "Dunston has no reason to disapprove the match, and I can't think that her family does, either." He tilted his head, the early gray at his temples showing silver in the firelight. "Does that help with your avoidance of any unpleasantness?"

With a small, grim smile, Sullivan nodded. "She seems fairly agreeable; I suppose I can't help a bit of astonishment when I encounter anyone contemplating a voluntary association with Dunston and his oldest whelp."

"Ah. I thought so. It's only my legs that

don't work, Sully. My mind's still fairly spry yet."

"You still ask fewer and less annoying questions than Bram."

"I'll take that as a compliment. Read Phineas's letter, and Andrews here will fetch us some claret."

While Quence sat in his wheeled chair by the window and silently contemplated the deepening dusk outside, Sullivan unfolded Phin Bromley's letter. Phin was the reason he'd been invited to walk through the front door of Bromley House in the first place; apparently the family was desperate enough for news of the captain — no, major now, according to the letter — that they would welcome anyone. He certainly couldn't think of another reason Quence would allow a rake of Bram Johns's reputation in the same room with his younger sister, whoever seemed terrified of whom. Aside from that, he thought Quence was trying to reel Phin back into civilization by degrees. Friends first, then the man himself.

But despite the ulterior motives and the oddness of him being invited to dine with a viscount and his family, he was glad of it. William Bromley and his younger brother Phineas were very much alike in their intelligence and wit, and he'd come to feel nearly as much affection toward the family's crippled patriarch as he did for both Phin and Bram. Brothers-in-arms, they'd called themselves, and so they were. He certainly felt closer to them than he did to his actual half-brother. Reputed half-brother, since no one had bothered to claim him in any legally significant manner.

He shook himself. Reminiscing had never been something of which he was overly fond. Too often it left a bitter taste in his mouth. The present suited him much better. And peculiarly enough, that was even when it included Isabel Chalsey and her associated complications.

Sullivan sat bolt upright. Downstairs the high squeak of his front door opening had stopped, but he knew he hadn't imagined it. He'd left the squeak for a reason — old soldiers' habits died hard.

As he rolled off the bed and silently pulled on his trousers, he glanced toward the curtained window. Only the dimmest sliver of light showed along one side of the heavy blue material. Barely dawn. Too early for his housekeeper, and none of his other employees would ever enter the house without knocking.

He pulled a pistol from his bedstand. As

footsteps ascended his staircase, he settled his back against the wall right beside the bedchamber door. His heartbeat held fast and steady as he ran through the list of who his visitor might be. At the top of the list was Isabel. Somewhere in the middle would be a thief, with extra points for the irony of that, and down at the bottom were the members of his own so-called family.

His door rattled and eased open. Sullivan leveled the pistol against the intruder's ear. "Do not move a muscle," he murmured.

The fellow shrieked and jumped backward. Lunging forward, Sullivan slammed his head into the wall with his free hand and shoved him to the floor.

"For God's sake! Don't murder me, Waring!"

Sullivan stopped his foot midkick. "Douglas Chalsey?"

The boy covered his head with both hands. "Yes!"

"Sweet Lucifer," he muttered, setting the pistol on the bed and reaching down to haul the boy to his feet. "What the devil are you doing here?"

"I wanted to speak with you." Douglas gingerly touched his nose. "You've disfigured me!"

"It's not broken," Sullivan muttered

grudgingly, eyeing it critically. "Go down to the sitting room. I'll be there in a moment." He tossed the boy a clean cloth from his small dressing table.

Once Douglas returned downstairs, Sullivan dressed quickly. He didn't want the young lord wandering about the cottage and finding the small, concealed room off the kitchen — especially since several items previously belonging to the Chalsey family were inside.

What the devil was the boy doing here? Logically he could come up with three reasons for the predawn visit: Douglas knew Sullivan had kissed Isabel; he knew about the thefts; or he wanted some horse advice. He hoped it was the third one. If it was either of the first two, the lad should have brought someone larger and more menacing along for company.

Yanking on his work boots, he clomped down the narrow stairs. His guest, holding the cloth to his nose, sat on the front edge of a chair. "What are you doing here?" Sullivan snapped, squatting before the hearth to stir the coals and set in some fresh tinder. "I'll be at your residence in . . ." He lifted his head to look at the mantel clock. "In three and a half hours."

"I wanted to speak with you," Lord Douglas said nasally, his nose pinched shut. "In private."

So it probably wasn't horse advice the boy was after. *Bloody wonderful.* Sullivan stood again. "What is it, then?"

Douglas eyed him. "First, are you going to hit me again?"

"No promises. But I didn't hit you; I encouraged you into the wall."

"That ain't much of an assurance."

"You broke into my house."

"Then we're even."

Thanks to years of hard discipline, Sullivan held on to the mildly annoyed expression he'd put on upstairs. "Beg pardon?"

"Don't pretend innocence, Waring. Tibby told me everything."

The muscles across Sullivan's back tightened. Taking a breath, he lowered himself into the chair opposite the boy's. "Have you considered that breaking into the home of someone you believe to be a criminal might not be the wisest course of action? Particularly when you're alone, and when you haven't informed anyone else of your whereabouts?"

Lord Douglas paled, then forced a laugh. "Never been accused of being brilliant. But I didn't come here to see you arrested. I ain't a shab rag."

"And you apparently have balls, if not brains," Sullivan admitted. "What did you want to speak to me about?"

"I wanted to tell you to leave my sister be. Tibby thinks you're mysterious or danger-ous or some such thing, and that she's clever enough to deal with you." He lowered the cloth to examine the blotch of red on it. "She's only three years older than I am, you know, and I can see that she's going to get herself into trouble."

She thought he was mysterious. Much better than ordinary or beneath notice. For a moment Sullivan dwelled on that, ignor-ing the remainder of Douglas's prattling. *Mysterious.* To him that implied one thing over any other consideration — she was interested in him. That second kiss . . . He wasn't a fool, and he'd seen hints, but it still surprised him to hear it said aloud. Catching the boy's suspicious expression, he snorted. "I don't know whether to be flattered that you consider me a threat, or insulted that a schoolboy's come to ballyrag me."

"I'm not threatening you," Douglas said shakily. "God's sake."

"Yes, you are. More politely than most, I'll give you that, but it's still a threat." He stood. "So should I gullet you and bury you beneath the floorboards? Or perhaps I'll have a horse kick you in the head and leave you to be found in the stable."

"Look here, Waring," Douglas countered, shooting to his feet and drawing himself up to his full height — which was about to Sullivan's nose. "Just train Zephyr as we've paid you to do, and leave us be. You keep your mama's painting and those other bits and bobs. But Tibby ain't for you."

She actually had told her brother everything. Shoving his growing annoyance and the knowledge that the boy made a good argument back into his chest, he eyed the young man. "Lord Douglas," he said deliberately, keeping his voice even and quiet, "I am not going to ruin my own reputation with your kind by mucking about with one of Society's precious gems. Believe you me, I know how the world — your world — works."

"Oh. Very good, then."

"Mm-hm. Anything else?"

"Since you asked . . . don't burgle anyone. Once we know your intentions and we keep quiet about it, we're bad as you."

"Then turn me in." That was beginning to seem like the only way he could be assured of getting Dunston's attention, anyway.

"Don't want to."

Obviously this was going nowhere. "Then I declare a stalemate. Now, don't you think you should trot yourself back home before someone misses you?"

The boy's face flushed bright red. "Actually, I was wondering if I might give you a hand with your stock this morning."

Sullivan lifted an eyebrow. "Beg pardon?"

"Well, it's just that you're quite famous, you know, and the other lads at university will turn cabbage-green when they find out I've been getting pointers from Sullivan Waring himself."

So they could learn from him, as long as he stayed away from their sisters and daughters. He shook himself. He'd learned that lesson a very long time ago. Still, the young fellow did have courage. And he could provide some leverage against Isabel, which might turn out to be useful. Sullivan shrugged.

"Leave your coat here. You might wish to work in a stable for a morning, but I doubt you'll want to look — or smell — like it."

Douglas grinned. "Oh, that's splendid, old trout."

It was more trouble; that's what it was. Sullivan knew it. And as he'd done since he'd first set eyes on Isabel Chalsey, he decided to walk straight into it. At least things were more interesting, these days.

"Oliver, it's very thoughtful and generous of you to offer," Isabel said, taking another lump of sugar for her tea, "but I don't wish to leave London during the Season."

"Not even for the amusements of Brighton?" Lord Tilden persisted. "Ask anyone along you like. My father's given permission for me to hold a house party there for as long as the next fortnight."

"I'd much rather stay here," she returned, risking a glance out the sitting room window only when Oliver dropped a spoon and bent down to retrieve it.

She couldn't see anything that might be transpiring in the stable yard. For the past three days she'd barely caught a glimpse of Zephyr, much less her trainer. Obviously Oliver had figured out Sullivan's schedule, because he called every morning just before Mr. Waring was due to arrive, stayed until his departure, and then dragged her out to some diversion or other which would last until Zephyr's afternoon training had begun and ended.

Whatever her own feelings on that circumstance, she considered it pure luck that Sullivan hadn't robbed anyone in the interim. She wasn't certain why, since he hadn't seemed to take her threat very seriously.

"Any particular reason that London is suddenly so dear to you?" Oliver asked offhandedly. "When I mentioned an excursion with our friends a few weeks ago you seemed delighted by the idea."

"Well, now that the Season has begun, I'm having such a splendid time that I've changed my mind." When he opened his mouth again she held up a hand. "Please, Oliver. I know perfectly well why you wish me elsewhere, and I assure you that there is no need. And I don't wish to speak of it again."

He shoved to his feet, setting his cup and saucer aside with a clatter. "He's here every day."

So are you, she thought. "That's what we hired him for," she said aloud. "I'm sorry if you don't deal well together, but I hired him without knowing of your animosity."

"And yet now that you do know, you still haven't sent him away. Even when I've recommended a perfectly suitable replacement."

Phillip had objected to Oliver's suggestion of Tom Barrett and his services even more strongly than Douglas had. Carefully she set her own cup on the serving tray. "If you're going to persist in this . . . obsession,

Oliver, I'm going to have to ask you t—"

"Did you see it?" Douglas burst into the room, flinging open the sitting room door and nearly knocking the maid who sat behind it to the floor. "Oh, I say. Apologies, there."

"See what?" Isabel asked, smiling at his obvious excitement. "And what in heaven's name is all over your boots?"

"Horse shit, of course. Or mud. Don't know for certain." With a wide grin he swiped his hand across his face, leaving another streak of the stuff there. "Come and see."

At least she had an excuse now to venture into the stable yard. Her father had nearly ordered her to do so, of course, but not even he could insist that she spend time with a horse rather than with a beau. Stifling her amusement because Oliver was clearly annoyed, she took his proffered arm and followed Douglas back through the kitchen.

"You know, he's been letting me assist him," her younger brother was chattering, happy as a cat with a box of mice. "It's fascinating, the way he works. Don't even own spurs. And the whip's like a tickle, just to remind the animal what he wants."

"I'd like to remind him of some things," Oliver murmured very quietly.

189

"Beg pardon?" Isabel asked, even though she'd heard him quite clearly.

"Nothing, my lady." He smiled. "It's good that Mr. Waring has some skill with horses. Otherwise he might be mucking out the stalls or delivering vegetables or whatever it is that commoners do for money."

That hadn't been very subtle. As if she needed to be reminded who stood where in Society. "Do you ever wonder where you would be if your parents had been unmarried?"

Oliver slowed, turning his head to look her directly in the eye. "No, I don't. I was born for a purpose, as were you. I was not the product of some heated exchange in a coatroom."

Douglas turned around as he pushed open the kitchen door. "I say, Tilden. That's hardly fit conversation in front of my sis."

In all fairness, she'd begun it, but she wasn't above sending her brother a grateful nod. Whether Oliver had a point or not, it simply seemed ill-mannered for a viscount to demean someone below his station — whatever their much-rumored connection.

"Of course you're correct, Douglas," Oliver said easily. "I shouldn't allow my sense of propriety to get the best of me. Do you forgive me, Isabel?"

She smiled, most of her attention already on the tall, lean man halfway across the stable yard. "You know I do."

Douglas led the way to the center of the yard. Once she'd told her brother the circumstances surrounding Sullivan's presence, she'd worried that he would behave so hostilely toward Mr. Waring that he would find himself bruised and bloodied. Instead, her brother looked like a puppy prancing about its master. What the devil had happened between them, she had no idea. To herself, though, she could admit that she was glad she wasn't the only one who continued to enjoy Mr. Waring's company despite knowing of his background and recent illicit behavior. It certainly removed some of the guilt she felt at their continued association.

Isabel held on to it for a moment, the feeling of anticipation before she turned to look full at Sullivan Waring. It felt like Christmas, just before she opened her first present. It was silly, of course, and no one knew that better than she. Sullivan was interesting, and different, but certainly no one she could be . . . romantic about. Should be romantic about. Even so, she supposed *thinking* about kissing him couldn't do any harm.

"See?" Douglas crowed. "Look, Tibby!"

She looked.

Zephyr trotted in a wide circle around Sullivan, her head up and her ears perked in his direction. On her back she wore the saddle Isabel and Phillip had purchased, and the lead line was now attached to a bridle rather than to her halter, which she also wore.

"Stunning," Oliver said dryly. "A saddle horse that can carry a saddle."

A wave of nervousness ran through her bones. If Zephyr carried a saddle, then sooner rather than later she would be expected to ride. *Oh, dear.*

"Well, what do you think, Tibby?"

She shook herself, looking from Douglas's happy expression to Sullivan's much-harder-to-read one. "That's brilliant," she said aloud. "You've made amazing progress."

"Zephyr's a quick study," Mr. Waring noted, bringing the mare to an easy stop. As far as she could tell, he hadn't even glanced at Lord Tilden.

"So I assume that means you'll be finished here soon, Waring." Oliver kept his tone cool and low, but Isabel could hear the disdain and anger in it.

"You have to decide, Lady Isabel," Sullivan went on, as though his half-brother hadn't spoken, "whether or not you wish to practice your seat on an old, staid horse before you take on a fresh mare."

Another shiver ran down her spine. Why hadn't she hired Mr. Waring to find a horse for Douglas or something? No, she'd had to say she wanted a horse for herself. To ride, dash it all. When she realized all three men were looking at her, she nodded. "I'll consider it," she managed.

"I have an old mare that might do," he went on. "I'll bring her by tomorrow so you can see if you get along."

"With a horse?" Oliver countered. "Yes, and perhaps they can go out for tea and biscuits afterward."

"Oliver," she chastised. "Yes, Mr. Waring, I think that would be a fine idea."

Lord Tilden took her hand. "Come, Isabel. I want to take you for a drive in Hyde Park. It's far too fine a day to be standing about in the mud."

For the first time Sullivan's ice-green eyes flicked in Oliver's direction. And then, as he looked back at her, he smiled. "Have a pleasant day, Lady Isabel. I'll see you tomorrow."

Oh, goodness. She drew a short breath as she returned to the house with Oliver. It made no sense; she was in the company of a very pleasant, handsome man, about to go for a pleasant, amusing outing. And all she could think of, even knowing she'd probably be expected to pet another horse, was that tomorrow she'd be able to spend thirty minutes with Sullivan Waring.

CHAPTER 11

Sullivan glanced toward the street. At this time of night only the very inebriated elite roamed the streets of Mayfair. The coat of arms on the passing coach confirmed that — the Marquis of St. Aubyn was actually returning home early; Sullivan had seen the marquis on several occasions still in his evening clothes well into the next morning.

All that concerned him at the moment, though, was that the coach continued past him. Once it was gone, he ducked around the picturesque stand of elm trees that clustered at the north corner of the Duke of Levonzy's main London property. He tied on his black bandit's mask, then one by one checked the windows on the ground floor of Johns House. No luck. All of them were secured. Levonzy had always been a cautious fellow, and naturally that translated to his household staff.

With a silent curse, he circled around

again to the south side of the house. The trellis for the climbing roses seemed steady enough, so he pulled on his heavy work gloves and began to climb. He couldn't avoid crushing a few of the white blossoms, and their spicy sweet scent hung heavily in the air around him.

This would have been a little easier if the duke had been away from home, but not by much. With the presence of his substantial staff, any house breaking attempt had its drawbacks. At least he'd been able to convince Bram not to join him, though with the list of items his friend had given him to liberate, he almost felt like he was embarking on a shopping excursion rather than a burglary.

Halfway up he stretched out sideways and pushed up on the nearest window with his fingertips. The glass lifted a fraction. He opened it another few inches, then grabbed hold of the ledge with his leather-covered fingers and kicked away from the trellis. For a long moment he hung suspended in midair, the abrupt ache in his left shoulder reminding him that he'd taken two balls there within the past year. With a breath he pulled himself up and then in through the window.

That had been a one-way trip; once he

had a painting with him he'd have to leave through another exit, preferably on the ground floor. He stood in the billiards room for a moment while he ran his mind through the floor plans with which Bram had provided him. It was unfortunate that he couldn't go into a house immediately after Bram had been there and both of their recollections were fresh, but he damned well didn't want suspicion falling on his friend for his own so-called misdeeds.

The door into the hallway stood open, but he couldn't detect any lights at all inside the house. As a soldier going into battle he'd always felt a hard excitement coupled with a sharpening of his senses. He'd expected to feel the same way as a thief going into someone else's territory, but mostly what he felt was anger. Not anger toward the house's residents, but toward Dunston. It hadn't been enough to deny him a birthright; the marquis had attempted to deny him his inheritance. The one heritage that had been left to him — his mother's.

But he could only reclaim it as long as he didn't pit himself against any of these aristocrats legally. If he brought charges against any of them for having his property, Dunston would find a way to tie it all up neatly, to make certain that the Sullivan family had done nothing improper, and that Sullivan Waring never even existed, much less deserved his mother's paintings. Bloody nobility. If he couldn't take their money by daylight or in darkness, they wouldn't be worth anything.

Except that he couldn't make those sweeping statements any longer. One of those aristocrats didn't precisely make him angry. Neither did her family. And he hadn't been prepared for that, for feeling some sort of affection for them. For her.

In a few hours he would be at their home again. Or in their stable, rather. Two of them knew how he spent some of his nights, and though they didn't like or understand it, neither seemed inclined to turn him in. It wasn't just that, though. He couldn't quite put his finger on what it was he felt around them, but he knew the wisest course of action would be simply to disappear for a few months. Especially with Oliver Sullivan involved.

What the devil did Isabel see in that fool, anyway? Other than wealth, power, rank, and a handsome face, of course. And there *he* was, raised and educated to be a gentleman, with no expectation of becoming one.

Somewhere in the large house a clock chimed, and he shook himself. Now was not the time or the place to be distracted, for Lucifer's sake.

Half the items Bram had wanted liberated seemed to be in this room, so he walked over to the weapons display on the far wall. A very nice pair of silver-handled dueling pistols were bracketed one on top of the other, and it only took a minute for him to pry them loose and dump them into his pockets. The cigars took another few seconds. He left the carved mahogany box there, but emptied the contents into his inner coat pocket. If Bram wanted a share of them, he was going to have to find the location of those last three Francesca W. Perris paintings first.

Finished with the billiards room, Sullivan padded silently down the wide, winding staircase. A pair of stone griffins guarded the bottom of the banister, but since he'd come in from above they seemed fairly useless. He clinked one of them on the head with a knuckle.

The duke's office was exactly where Bram had said it would be. He paused for a moment after he slipped inside. *A Young Fisherman's Dream of Glory* hung at eye level behind His Grace's desk, a slanted corner of moonlight illuminating it dimly. "There you are," he murmured.

It was too large for his carrying pouch, but he pulled off the blanket he'd slung across one shoulder and bound it carefully. For good measure he pocketed the silver inkwell on the desk, then caught sight of the hated Burmese fertility statue Bram had mentioned.

Good God. Its cock was nearly a foot long, and given that the figure stood barely twice that high, the fellow looked distinctly front-heavy. There was no way in hell he was going to carry that anywhere, so with a quick prayer that he wasn't about to call bad luck upon himself, he reached over and snapped the fellow off at the root. With a wince he dropped the penis into his last free pocket. "Sorry, old boy, but we can't have you being pasted back together."

He tucked the painting under his arm and made his way back out to the hallway. The front door was bolted and locked — as a man who evidently considered his possessions at risk, Levonzy needed only take more care with his upper-story windows to make his mansion a bloody fortress.

The morning room windows were also latched, but thankfully didn't require a key to open them. Sullivan set the painting aside and shoved at the window overlooking the garden at the side of the house. Nothing.

"Damnation," he muttered.

In the dark it took a moment to make out the thick layer of paint sealing the ground-floor window closed. Given Bram's dislike of his own father, Sullivan had never been particularly fond of the fellow, himself. Now, however, "not fond of" was swiftly sliding toward "damned annoyed with."

He pulled the knife from his boot and dug it along the bottom of the window. The wood parted from the paint reluctantly, and with a whining moan the window raised a few inches. *Damnation.* He did not like lingering in a house after he'd recovered his property. Not all households sported residents as enchanting and sweet-tasting as Lady Isabel Chalsey.

Working as quickly and efficiently as he could in the near-dark, he slipped the painting out through the narrow opening and then went to work with the knife again. It gave a half inch with every hard shove. Levonzy needed to hire a carpenter to repair his damned windows. The man had more money than Croesus, so he could bloody well afford a better paint job.

A bright flash lit the room. Instinctively Sullivan ducked sideways as the boom of a weapon followed. A ball whizzed past his ear and shattered the window.

"You damned thief!" the Duke of Levonzy bellowed. "I'll see you stretched on the gallows!"

At the sound of another pistol being cocked, Sullivan did the only thing he could. He dove out the window. Broken shards of glass showered around him as he landed hard in a bed of daisies. Whipping back to his feet, he scrambled against the wall for the painting — just as the duke reached the window.

Sullivan dodged around the corner of the house as another shot exploded from the window. The tree trunk beside him erupted into splinters, and something slammed into his thigh, making him stumble. Clenching his jaw, he gripped the painting, sheltering it with his body, and ran for it.

"Why didn't you wake me earlier?" Isabel snapped at her maid, shoving aside bedsheets and scrambling to her feet.

Penny produced a blue sprig muslin from the wardrobe. "Apologies, my lady, but you didn't specify. And you were out so late last night, I —"

"No mind," she interrupted, slipping out of her night rail and hurrying into the gown. "I just don't want to hear from Mr. Waring when he's prompt and I'm late out to the stable yard."

The maid sent her a quick glance in the dressing table mirror.

"What?" Isabel asked, scowling.

"Nothing, my lady."

"Penny, I do recognize that look."

"Very well, my lady," the maid said, taking a brush to Isabel's tangled hair. "You said that you don't want to hear from Mr. Waring, but he works for you. I can't imagine he would say anything unbecoming while you —"

"Yes, yes, of course. It was a figure of speech. I said I would be available at ten o'clock, and I didn't wish to be late. It's a matter of my own pride." That didn't explain why she was blushing, or that she knew full well she and Sullivan *would* have words — or that she was looking forward to it.

As soon as she finished dressing, she hurried downstairs. Alders stood halfway between the foyer and the breakfast room, clearly ready to move in whichever direction he was most needed. "Alders," she greeted, "I'll be outside with Zephyr and Mr. Waring."

"Mr. Waring hasn't yet arrived this morning, my lady," the butler intoned.

She stopped. "He hasn't? But it's fifteen

after ten."

"Yes, it is, my lady. Perhaps you wish some breakfast? I'll inform you as soon as he arrives."

"Oh. Yes, of course."

As she made her way into the breakfast room, a footman joined the butler behind her. She heard them muttering, and she made out the word "burglary."

Her heart lurched. Isabel turned around, nearly stumbling in her haste. "What was that you said?"

Alders shoved the footman back toward the servants' quarters. "Nothing you need trouble yourself about, my lady. Just below-stairs gossip."

"About what?" she persisted. "I insist that you tell me, Alders."

The butler motioned her into the breakfast room. "Very well," he said, holding out her chair for her. "Stevens heard from Cook, who heard from the milk peddler, who heard from the Duke of Levonzy's cook, that His Grace's home was burgled early this morning. By the Mayfair Marauder, yet."

Her heart accelerated even further. "Oh, my," she said, swallowing hard as she took her seat. He'd done it again. She'd warned him, and blast it all, he hadn't listened. "Did anyone say what was taken?"

"My information is obviously not very reliable, my l—"

"I understand that, Alders. What did you hear?"

"Gossip has it that several things were broken, and some silver, a painting, and a handful of cigars went missing. The old duke apparently got several shots off at the scoundrel, so never fear. They'll probably find him in an alleyway dead. I hear His Grace is a crack shot."

She'd heard the same thing. *Oh no, oh no.* Shaking, she pushed to her feet so hastily she nearly tipped her chair backward. "Oh, dear, I've forgotten I'm to meet Barbara this morning. Is Douglas risen yet?"

"I don't believe so, my lady."

"Please see to it. He promised to escort me."

"Right away."

As Alders hurried out of the room, Isabel paced to the window and back. She couldn't see the stable yard from there, so she went down the hallway to the sitting room. What if the duke actually had shot Sullivan? What if he was . . .

She took a breath. He was a thief; she'd caught him in the act. And she'd warned him, damn it all. So why in heaven's name was she so worried that something might have happened to him?

But she was worried. Very worried. For a bare second she contemplated running out to the stables and commandeering a horse. The thought terrified her, though, and even if she had drummed up both the courage and the skill, she had no idea where he lived.

"What the devil is it?" Douglas asked, stumbling into the sitting room behind her. He was only half dressed, his waistcoat unbuttoned and only one boot on.

"Close the door."

Scowling, he did so, then flopped onto a chair to pull on his second boot. "I was up until nearly dawn playing whist with Phillip, you know."

"The Duke of Levonzy's house was burgled by the Mayfair Marauder last night," she managed, her words coming out in a breathless rush. "The duke took several shots at the thief. And now it's after ten o'clock, and Sullivan isn't here."

Her brother sat bolt upright. "St. George's buttonholes. Levonzy's a crack shot."

"I know that, blast it all. Take me to see Sullivan."

"What? Why do —"

"Who else can help him if he's injured?" she insisted, striding over to pull him to his

206

feet. "And I don't know how to get there."

"Maybe I should go by myself, Tibby. It ain't seem—"

"Don't you dare tell me it's not seemly, Douglas Raymond Chalsey," she snapped. "Go have the curricle made ready."

He stood up, sighing irritably. "You're heading us into trouble, Tibby. I hope you realize that."

"I know." She took a breath. Logic would suit her better than panic. Especially when she couldn't decide why she felt so anxious. If logic ruled, however, she would be deciding how best to contact the authorities so that Mr. Waring could be arrested — if Levonzy hadn't killed him. Obviously this wasn't about logic. And it wasn't about any kind of mysteries or secrets, either. "Thank you for assisting me."

"Don't thank me yet. And you don't need to use my full blasted name. Meet me outside in five minutes."

He stumbled off, calling for Alders and coffee, while she went back to pacing. She'd already dressed for going out-of-doors, so all she could do was wait. And the longer she waited, the more anxious she became.

If something had happened to Sullivan Waring, everyone would probably say he deserved it. He broke into people's homes, after all. He was the blasted Mayfair Marauder. Keeping his secret was one thing, but now he'd gone too far. What was she supposed to do?

As for her worry, she could tell herself it was just a natural concern for a fellow human being. Yes, that was it. As soon as she saw the stableboys moving the pair of bays into position at the front of the curricle, she snatched up her wrap and hurried for the door.

"My lady, shall I tell Lord and Lady Darshear how long you and Lord Douglas will be gone?" the butler called after her.

"I'm not certain, but it won't be long."

She didn't wait for a reply. Outside, Phipps handed her up beside Douglas, and her brother clucked to the team.

"Thank you for not complaining that this would have been faster on horseback," she said after a moment, mostly to take her mind off the fact that they were traveling quite swiftly through some rather crowded streets.

"Horseback ain't an option," Douglas returned shortly, then whistled at a rag-and-bone man to get his cart out of the way. "And I suppose I needed to come downstairs in the next two or three hours, anyway."

"Very funny. You're the one panting after Mr. Waring. I expected you to be awake and waiting for him."

"You're anxious enough for both of us." Douglas glanced at her as he maneuvered through the crowds. "And you'd best stop it."

"Stop what? Being concerned that someone with whom I'm acquainted might be injured?"

"He ain't a servant or anything, but he ain't exactly someone you should be mooning after, either."

Isabel clubbed him on the shoulder.

"Ow! I'm driving, damn it all!"

"For your information, Douglas," she said stiffly, refusing to consider anything but her precise words, "I am not mooning after Mr. Waring. He's a horse breeder. Just because we've kissed a few times doesn't mean —"

" *'A few times'?*" he repeated. "You said he kissed you once, so he could escape!"

Dash it all. "Oh, what does it matter?" she retorted. Hopefully volume and violence would overcome logic. "He's . . . he's rather like a . . . a friend. Aren't you worried about him?"

"Maybe. A little. I told him to stop his thieving before he put us all into something sticky."

"You did?"

"I did. And you didn't need to hit me."

"Oh, heavens, Douglas. You have so much padding on your shoulders you probably didn't even feel it."

He stiffened. "I'll have you know that this is all the fashion. I'd wager that Tilden pads his shoulders."

She had no idea whether he did or not. Sullivan didn't. "How much farther? Where does he live, anyway?"

"He's got a huge stable, and about three acres. Another mile or so."

So he'd been riding three miles twice each day to train Zephyr. That seemed significant, whether he'd been paid to do the work or not. Of course, she'd blackmailed him into it, but from what she'd seen he didn't seem to do much that he didn't truly wish to.

And at this moment, *she* truly wished that no one had shot him last night. She wished that very much.

CHAPTER 12

Sullivan winced as he pulled on his boots. The bandage around his thigh held this time, but it was going to play havoc with any riding he did today. And he would be doing a great deal of that, naturally. And that would be after he explained his tardiness to Lady Isabel, though he actually looked forward to that — which was why he'd declined to send one of his men over with a note when he'd realized he would be late.

Hm. Him, looking forward to a dressing down by an aristocrat. Things had changed over the past few weeks. But it wasn't necessarily the dressing down he looked forward to; it was seeing her again. She'd been nervous yesterday when he'd suggested that she attempt to ride a more mature horse before she mounted Zephyr, but her reluctance made sense. As did teaching her to ride on a more experienced, sedate animal.

Teaching *her* wasn't strictly a part of their agreement, but nothing much was, now.

Of course, if it were up to him, he would still be practicing the trot and walk with the mare, and Zephyr would be nowhere close to ridable. Even Isabel's younger brother had realized that Zephyr's progress had been . . . methodical. That was the word Sullivan had used to explain it to Douglas, anyway. Admitting that he'd been stalling in order to have more days with Isabel — that could be fatal to both their reputations.

He limped downstairs to see whether the water he'd hung over the fire had begun boiling yet. Unused as he was to rising so late, he knew a hot cup of American coffee might not help his leg mend more quickly, but it would soothe his temper. His housekeeper, Mrs. Howard, would be in at any moment, and he preferred to have himself and his limp gone by the time she arrived for the day.

Someone rapped on his door. "Mr. Waring? It's Halliwell."

"Come in," he called, nearly burning his finger as he poured the water into a pot. Perhaps he should have waited for Mrs. Howard after all.

"You have a customer, sir. He wanted to know if he could meet you in here."

212

Damnation. He was already going to be nearly an hour late to Chalsey House. But he wasn't nearly well off enough to pass up on meeting a customer. "Send him in, Halliwell. And make certain Achilles is saddled, will you? And Molly, with a sidesaddle." Molly was a companion mare for his sick or nervous animals — the steadiest, calmest animal he owned. She would be a good first ride for Isabel.

"I'll see to it." Halliwell stepped back from the doorway and motioned whoever stood behind him to enter. "This way, my lord."

Despite being shot at last evening, Sullivan had begun feeling a bit more charitable toward his supposed betters. They could all thank Isabel Chalsey for more reasonable prices from his stable, though none of them could ever know that. He turned around. "Good morning, my —" His blood froze. "Get out of my home."

George Sullivan, the Marquis of Dunston, closed the door with the tip of his walking stick. He was probably worried over catching a commoner's infection if he touched anything. He'd be lucky if he didn't catch a commoner's knife blade in his gut. "I'm interested in one of your hunters," the marquis said, taking off his hat but keeping hold of it and his stick.

"I'm bloody well not selling you anything, and I'm not playing any of your bloody games. Now get out before I toss you out on your damned arse."

"I only ask that we have a civil discussion, Mr. Waring."

"Mr. . . . it's just the two of us here. Why bother with the pretense?"

Sullivan was surprised that his voice sounded steady. Every muscle clenched, and he held himself still to keep from striking the man — the only man in London who refused to admit that Sullivan Waring was his son. It had been nearly six months since they'd last seen one another, and while he would have liked to say that the old man looked older, or at least remorseful that he'd stolen his own son's inheritance, Dunston looked as fit and arrogant as he always had.

The marquis didn't respond, so Sullivan took a reluctant step closer to him. "Get out of my house. I'm not going to say it again."

"I'm not here for banter, Mr. Waring," the marquis said in a low voice, still not moving, and still looking ready for a confrontation.

Sullivan glared at him. Over the years he'd set eyes on the marquis a handful of times, mostly when Sullivan had still lived with his mother and well before he'd decided to fight on the Peninsula. George Sullivan had been a handsome man, though the years had now rounded his gut, and constant disapproval or fear of it had pinched his cheeks and narrowed and shortened his mouth.

"You will stop this thievery at once," Dunston went on. "I heard that Levonzy shot at you last evening. There's no logic in risking your life for this . . . nonsense."

"Nonsense, is it?" Sullivan returned, resuming the task of making himself some coffee mainly because it enabled him to turn his back on the marquis.

"Yes. It's absolute nonsense."

"Not to me, you high-handed arrogant snake. Your kettle is blacker than mine, Marquis."

As Sullivan faced Dunston again, the marquis' fair skin had paled even further. "How dare you? You, a bastard horse breeder, calling me —"

"*You* made me a bastard," Sullivan broke in. "That was none of my doing."

"This idiotic thievery *is* your doing. And you will cease it at once."

"I could debate over whose doing it is, since you robbed me while I was fighting in Spain to preserve the kingdom, but I'm more interested in what you think you can possibly do to stop me from reclaiming what's mine." He took a sip of the coffee. It was too hot, and too strong, but he scarely noticed. "Have me arrested, Dunston. Please. I'll shout from the prison towers about how you've taken from me, and driven me to a life of crime. Papa."

Dunston clutched his walking stick so hard his knuckles showed white. "You go too far, boy. Your mother granted my family name no favors when she gave it to you. As if she expected me to give it to you."

Sullivan narrowed his eyes, his own temper closer to breaking than it had been since he'd first returned to England to find his mother's cottage ransacked and his so-called father bestowing the artworks on his friends and acquaintances. "My guess would be that she didn't expect you to give me anything; she merely wanted to remind you of your hypocrisy and failed responsibility."

"You were a mistake. And I will not compromise my family's standing because your mother decided to name her bastard after me in hopes that I would, what, raise you as my own? Grant you lands? Make you my heir? It's ridiculous."

"Tell yourself whatever enables you to sleep at night," Sullivan shot back. "Just do it elsewhere."

"First give me your word that you'll stop thieving. And that you'll stop hanging about Chalsey House and bothering my son."

"So Oliver tattled on me, did he?" Sullivan forced a smile, wondering if Dunston realized how close he was to getting hot coffee thrown in his face. "The family hired me. Unlike some, I fulfill my obligations."

"Then promise me that you won't try to embarrass my son or my name by bandying about your theory of your parentage. Or by disrupting the lives of my peers, my friends, with your housebreaking."

Sullivan stalked past Dunston to the front door. "Surely Lord Tilden can fend for himself against a bastard horse breeder," he retorted. Of course, the marquis hadn't warned him to stay clear of Isabel; it was ridiculous to consider that he might make a play for her in the first place, with or without noble competition.

"I don't want to hear the talk. I get enough of the stupidity every time you sell someone a damned horse. I have no idea why your mother didn't drown you at birth."

"So I could make your life as miserable as possible right now, I suppose." He yanked open the door. "I'll be happy to put a boot to your arse, Marquis."

"Bah. Keep clear of me and mine, Waring. Mind your damned place before someone does shoot you. I won't be claiming the corpse for burial." With a last sniff and a disdainful glare, George Sullivan turned on his heel and left.

Sullivan slammed the door. The satisfying thud reverberated through the house. The soft sound that directly followed it, though, stopped him cold. He whipped around.

Isabel Chalsey stood in the front room doorway, one hand over her mouth and the other over her heart. "Hello, poppet," he murmured, the heat in his chest traveling downward. "You've strayed a bit, haven't you?"

"I heard a rumor that a thief was shot last night," she said, her voice breathy. Worry or uncertainty, he wasn't certain, but he liked the sound.

"You were worried about me?" He left the front door to approach her.

"You were late arriving. The —"

He grabbed her shoulders, pressing her back against the doorframe, and lowered his mouth over hers. Since they'd met he'd made excuses for being around her, for kissing her. Now, though, he had to admit what he couldn't even conceal — he wanted her. Badly.

Her fingers tangled into his shirt, pulling him closer as she kissed him back hungrily. She sighed against his mouth, her tongue flicking against his, then pushed him back. "We're not alone," she managed shakily.

Sullivan took a step backward just as another form came up the hallway behind them. "Sprout," he grunted, nodding at Douglas Chalsey, then turned his back and strode again into the front room. All the boy needed to do was get a look at the present cut of the jib in his trousers, and the fight would be on.

"You ain't dead, eh?" Douglas commented. "Saw Dunston's carriage in the yard, so we went around back."

With a stiff nod, Sullivan went to grab his coat and pull it on. Of course Isabel wouldn't have come alone; she didn't even ride. He should have realized. *Idiot.* "Apologies for being late. It won't happen again."

"You are wounded," Isabel announced.

As Sullivan faced the two Chalseys again, Tibby's brown eyes were gazing at him critically, her expression halfway between dazed and worried. "I caught a splinter," he said. A seven-inch splinter buried halfway into his left thigh, but he'd spare them the details. "Let's be off, shall we?"

"Douglas, would you bring the curricle

219

around to the front?" Isabel asked, her gaze still on Sullivan.

"But I just —"

"Give us a moment, sprout," Sullivan cut in.

"Well, you might have just said that to begin with," Douglas grumbled, turning back down the short hallway again.

"Do you often call on your employees at their homes when they're" — he glanced at the small clock on the mantel — "fifty-two minutes late?"

"I warned you to cease your . . . nefarious activities, Mr. Waring."

"And I told you that I wouldn't. I suggest, therefore, that you have me arrested. Because I'm informing you that I will do it again."

She gazed at him. "And I do understand why. But —"

"You understand," he repeated. "You."

"Yes, me. I overheard your conversation with Lord Dunston," she said. "Part of it, anyway."

Damnation. "Then we can add eavesdropping to your list of accomplishments. And house breaking. You're steadily becoming . . . me, I suppose."

She cocked her head at him. "I wasn't planning on a robbery. I thought you'd been hurt. I was . . . I was worried."

He held himself still. "What makes you think it was me who burgled Levonzy's home, anyway? His son is my closest friend. It would mean I had no positive qualities at all."

"A painting was taken." She took a breath. "Of course I know it was you. I don't understand why you feel the need to dissemble with me. I certainly know enough to cause you harm even without this latest expedition of yours."

That was true enough. Slowly Sullivan nodded. "He missed me. Except for the splinter when he blew apart an elm tree."

"Do you need a physician? I can —"

"I've been wounded much worse than this," he interrupted. "It's no matter." Aware that her brother could stomp back in at any moment, he took a step closer to her again. "I appreciate that you came all this way just to make certain I wasn't dead."

"I do have twenty pounds invested in you."

"Now who's dissembling?"

Isabel took a glance about the small room. "Why don't you speak like a horse breeder?"

"Because I was raised to be a gentleman. Tutors, school, and of course Continental travel on Bonaparte's heels."

"Did your mother expect that Lord Dunston would acknowledge you?"

Obviously she *hadn't* heard all of the conversation he'd had with Dunston. If he hadn't wanted to kiss her again, he would have been considerably less willing to answer. "He made it very clear from the beginning that he would never acknowledge me," he said quietly. "She wanted me to have the education to do whatever I wished. I'm the one who had no desire to be a parson or a solicitor or bookkeeper."

"No, I can't imagine you being sedentary," she returned thoughtfully. "And I can tell that you enjoy what you're doing now. And you are quite good at it."

"Thank you, not that I need your approval."

She frowned, her fine eyebrows lowering. "You may know about horses, but it's becoming obvious that I confound you."

He took another step closer, near enough to touch her, to kiss her, again. Then what she'd said dawned on him. "Beg pardon?"

"You kiss me, and then you insult me. You have no idea what you want, do you?"

He grabbed her upper arms again, tugging her up against him. "I know quite well what I want, Isabel. Just be glad that I haven't taken it, so far."

She looked up at his face, meeting his gaze

squarely. "You still don't frighten me."

"I'm not trying to frighten you," he whispered. "I'm trying to warn you."

"Because you're not a gentleman?"

Sullivan shook his head. He wanted her so badly he could taste it. "Not in the least. And I'm happy not to be one."

"I'm beginning to think that's what I like about you."

While he stood as still as he could with her so close to him, she ran her hands up his shoulders and into his hair. Then she pulled his face down to hers and pressed her lips softly against his.

With a moan he deepened their embrace, lifting her in his arms so their faces were level. His heart pounded against his ribs, and he swore he could feel her fast pulse beneath his fingers. God, this was dangerous, for both of them. Maybe that was part of why being with her was so intoxicating. But even without the difference in their stations she would have mesmerized him. Sweet and cynical, strong and timid, witty and naive, all at the same time.

His front door rattled, and he set Isabel down so quickly she stumbled. With a curse he put out a hand to steady her as the door opened. "Let's go, Lady Isabel," he said, turning the caress into a gentlemanly offer of assistance. "Unless you wish me to forgo today's instruction."

She swallowed, the skin of her cheeks rosy. "You said it would set Zephyr back to miss a day. So yes, please, let's be going. I don't make a habit of tracking down tardy employees, whatever you may think."

"Or kissing them," he whispered into her hair as she passed by him.

Isabel wanted him about. So whatever Dunston might warn about staying away from Chalsey House and stepping back from Oliver's . . . whatever it was, he would stay, until he either came to his senses or someone did manage to put a ball through him.

Isabel looked over her shoulder again as Douglas turned the curricle onto the Chalsey House drive. A few yards behind them Sullivan rode on his monstrous stallion, another horse in tow. The chestnut mare would be the one he'd decided she needed to ride. And at the moment she felt as apprehensive about speaking with him again as she did about actually sitting on a horse.

When she was with her friends, or dancing at one of the hundred balls scheduled for the Season, she knew how ridiculous it was to even think about kissing the unacknowledged, natural son of the Marquis of Dunston. In his presence, though, she could think of nothing else.

As a child she'd been the one to jump into the lake first, and she'd climbed more trees than either brother, mostly because they'd told her not to. She always got what she wanted, from dresses to beaux. Was that it? Sullivan Waring was something she wasn't supposed to have? Was that what attracted her?

She glanced back at him again. He swung down from his mount, handing off the reins of both horses to Phipps. Very well, the forbidden fruit aspect was part of the attraction. As was the mystery of him. After seeing him with Lord Dunston, though, she nearly had his puzzle pieced together. And he attracted her even more now than he had before.

He had a better education than some of the men who courted her, or at least he had a better understanding of what he'd learned than a great many others. He spoke his mind, even though their social rankings said that he shouldn't. And he . . . understood her fears and her determination as well as her own family.

He looked over at her, and a slight smile touched his sensuous mouth. Her heart beat faster in response. As her father and Phillip emerged from the house, she set the haughty expression back on her face. After all, he was still in her employ. And now he'd stolen from a duke. And as long as she wanted him to continue kissing her, she had no choice but to keep that a secret, as well.

"There you are," her father said, coming forward to help her down from the carriage. "Whatever you and Barbara found so urgent, I would appreciate more information than 'I'm leaving for a bit.' "

"Apologies, Papa." Isabel said, leaning up to kiss him on the cheek.

"I did go along," Douglas said offhandedly. "I think I could manage to protect Tibby's virtue."

Phillip snorted. "You couldn't even protect your own virtue."

"I say! That is not —"

"Enough, children. I am off to do my accounts. Pray behave yourselves."

The viscount returned to the house. Phillip was chatting about something with Sullivan, while Douglas joined them to hang on every word.

"Are you going to ride today, Tibby?" her older brother asked, motioning at the chestnut mare.

Swallowing hard, her hands beginning to

shake, she shrugged. "I haven't decided yet."

"May I fetch Zephyr for you, Mr. Waring?" Douglas interjected.

"If you can be calm about it," Sullivan returned.

"I'm always calm."

Phillip laughed. "You're frightening *me* at the moment. But be quick about it, will you? You'll make us late for our appointment at Hoby's."

"Zooks! I forgot." Douglas hurried off to the stable, Phillip trailing behind him.

"So are you, poppet?"

Isabel turned to face Sullivan. "Am I what?"

"Going to ride today."

"Oh." She shrugged, clasping her hands behind her back so he wouldn't see them tremble.

He crossed his arms over his chest. "Have you ever sat in a saddle?"

"No."

"Well, let's begin with that, shall we?" Sullivan started for the stable and motioned for her to join him.

"I'm still giving the orders, you know," she stated. As distracted as she felt by his mere presence, it wouldn't do for him to think he could now order her about just because they'd kissed several times.

He stopped. "What shall we do now, then, Lady Isabel?"

Isabel lifted her chin. "Take me to the stable, so I might learn about sitting on a horse."

"As you wish."

CHAPTER 13

"What's to keep it from rolling over on me?" Isabel asked skeptically, nudging the tipped-over barrel with one toe.

"I will." Sullivan squatted in front of it, a knee on either side. "It's perfectly safe."

He'd placed her sidesaddle over the barrel and cinched it securely to the rotund middle, but however strong and capable he appeared, she had her doubts that he'd be able to keep her from landing on her back-side the moment she sat down. Isabel eyed him again. "This looks very silly."

"But it's low to the ground, and it won't walk off with you." He tilted his head, that gold-shot strand of hair obscuring one green eye. "Why are you protesting? It's a hollow hunk of wood and metal. And no one else is going to say anything."

She grimaced. "Very well. You have a point." Gathering her skirts, she sidled up to the barrel and awkwardly sat, looping one knee around the saddle's cantle. "I'm not precisely dressed for this."

"You did it well, though."

"Oh, please. As you pointed out, it's a hunk of wood."

A quick smile softened his mouth as he crouched, gazing up at her. Goodness, she wanted to kiss him. Phipps and several of the other stableboys continued to meander about the stable, though, so she didn't dare. And not being able to made her want to even more.

"Do you feel secure?"

"You're not going to spin me about, are you?"

"No."

"Then yes, I feel fairly secure."

"Good." He looked away. "Phipps, hand me a bridle, will you?" The head groom brought one over, and using a free hand Sullivan draped it over his own shoulders and then handed her the reins. "The height's a bit off, but it's fairly close. You hold them in whichever hand you're more comfortable, and without wrapping them around anything, run the ends through your other hand, in case you lose them."

" 'Lose them'?" she repeated, shivering.

"It's not likely to happen, but I don't want you to be surprised if it does."

With a tight nod she held the reins as he instructed, loosening her fists a little when he pointed out that the cow the bridle had been made from was already deceased. She knew he was trying to set her at ease, and she appreciated it, but they both knew that sitting on a barrel was an ocean apart from sitting on a horse.

Using a surprising amount of patience and understanding, he showed her how to turn an animal, how to hold on if things became rough, and how to exert her will on a stubborn mount. All the while he had a bridle draped over his head, demonstrating as he spoke. Her heart did several odd flip-flops. She couldn't imagine anyone else in her acquaintance, employee or not, being as patient or thorough, or willing to look so silly for her benefit.

"May I ask you a question?"

Sullivan stopped tugging against the reins. "You seem to, whether I want you to or not."

"I know I asked you before, but do you paint?"

He blew out his breath. "I used to sketch sometimes. Not for years, though."

"Why not?"

"Because I'm not skilled enough to be able to make a living at it, and I can't afford to be idle." He shifted, a quick grimace crossing his lean face. "I think it's either time for you to attempt riding an actual horse, or for me to take Zephyr out for some work."

Grabbing on to his shoulder, she carefully stood again. Even crouching as he was, he felt solid as a rock beneath her fingers. No padding there; just hard, well-earned muscle. She swallowed, reluctantly releasing him. "Perhaps I could mount while the horse is in its stall," she suggested.

Pulling off the bridle, he straightened, looming over her. "No," he returned, carefully stretching out his left leg. "If she fidgets, you could end with a crushed leg. And then you wouldn't be able to dance."

That sounded almost like an insult, but she wasn't about to argue the point. Instead she watched as he flexed his knee again. "Is that where you received your splinter?"

Sullivan nodded. "The bandage is holding, so I won't trouble about it. So you or Zephyr, poppet?"

She liked when he called her poppet. He placed it where someone of her own rank might use her familiar name, when he wasn't supposed to. And it kept him from calling her Lady Isabel every moment. "What's the other horse's name?" she asked, her voice shaking at the edges.

"Molly. She's fifteen, and a companion mare for fidgety animals. I've never seen her make a false step, and she doesn't like to trot, much less gallop."

"Are you saying I'm fidgety?"

His mouth curved up at the edges again. "A bit high-strung, perhaps."

Isabel took a deep breath, holding it for a long moment. A thousand excuses ran through her mind, along with the thought that if she refused to ride today, her father would probably have Sullivan take Zephyr away and she wouldn't have an excuse to see him any longer. And that now seeing him had less to do with knowing what he might be up to, and more to do with her . . . liking having him about.

"Will you hold Molly?"

"Absolutely. You have my word."

"Then I shall ride a horse."

He hadn't expected her to agree. Isabel Chalsey had more backbone than he might have previously given her credit for. As she hurried into the house to change into a riding dress, he put the training bridle back on its hook and answered the usual questions about breeding and grooming and training put to him by the stableboys.

Even as he did that and then led Molly around the stable yard a few times to familiarize her with the footing, he was considering Isabel. She still ordered him about, but more as an amusement or an afterthought than because he frightened her. It seemed to be meant to distract him, and everyone else, from realizing . . . what? That she liked him?

If she'd been some married, bored, worldly lady, he would have simply bedded her once or twice and then gone on his way. He used her kind for amusement and a bit of revenge for being left out of the inner circle, he supposed. Some of the chits were amusing, and he wouldn't say he hated them, but everyone involved took it for what it was — a night or two's fun, with nothing more wanted or expected.

Isabel Chalsey was more complicated. If she'd been some parson's daughter, or even a baron's youngest or some such thing, a union between them would have been possible, if not popular. But she was the only daughter of a marquis.

Sullivan shook himself. *Union?* Where the devil had that come from? It had been several delicious kisses, a handful of enjoyable conversations, and some heated thoughts. And whatever images his mind might conjure, her lineage and the circumstances of his birth would never change.

She emerged from the house, and his breathing stilled. He hadn't known she even owned a riding outfit, but by God she did — and she looked . . . edible in it. Hunter-green and black, it hugged her figure in all the right places, the skirt flaring out over her black riding boots. Sullivan attempted to conjure thoughts of mud and harsh, cold winds, but with her swaying hips and bright, nervous gaze she melted them all away. *Christ.*

"Well, let's get on with it before I lose my nerve," she said, eyeing Molly at his shoulder.

Right. Now was not the time for compliments or drooling or other distractions. Especially as he glanced toward the house to see her parents standing in front of the sitting room window, watching. They looked at least as nervous as Isabel did. Understandable, but with Isabel it could be a problem.

"The worst thing that could possibly happen to you is that you'll lose your seat and fall in the mud," he said, leading the mare over to the raised stone mounting block.

"I actually don't want to hear that, Mr. Waring."

"I know, but you need to understand that a possibly muddy dress is all you're facing. And I won't let even that happen."

"You have a great deal of confidence in yourself." She favored him with a smile that was obviously forced. "Not that I wish you to be wrong."

"I'm not wrong." He held out his right hand, his left holding Molly by the bridle.

After another hesitation Isabel stepped up onto the block. Steadying herself with his hand, she hopped up into the saddle. The fair skin of her face had paled to an alarming degree, but she stayed where she was. Only her coloring and her fierce grip on his fingers gave away the fact that she was terrified.

Molly's ears flicked back and forward. "Say something nice to her," Sullivan instructed. "She's worried that you don't like her."

"*She's* worried?" Isabel visibly shook herself. "Good girl, Molly. You're such a good horse."

Sullivan continued to be more and more impressed. To most people it would seem like nothing, but he understood fear. And he understood how much courage it took to overcome it. "Very nice," he said soothingly. "Hold the reins as you practiced, and I'll walk her about the yard."

With a tight nod, Isabel took the reins. He doubted a cannonball could blow her hold loose, but since he was doing the guiding, he didn't comment. Instead, with a slow breath and a quick prayer that everything would proceed precisely as he intended, he led Molly out into the middle of the yard.

Clearly he'd chosen the right horse for her. Used to fearful animals, Molly probably considered Isabel to be just another skittish foal. "How do you feel?" he ventured aloud.

"Good," Isabel answered tentatively. "It's very rolly."

He chuckled. "You should attempt riding a camel. I nearly became ill."

"You've ridden a camel?"

"A Spaniard had several on his land. Interesting animals. They spit, you know. Quite accurately. But you'd have to ask Bram Johns about that."

Out of the corner of his eye he caught sight of her patting Molly's neck with one hand, but he pretended not to notice. Inside, though, he was cheering. Whatever mess she'd caused and could cause for him, these past weeks had been worthwhile ones.

And considering that he'd nearly been shot last night, and not even taking into account his general feelings toward the aristocracy, that was something he'd never expected to admit, even to himself.

"Well done, Tibby," Lord Darshear called, grinning as he and his wife came outside through the kitchen door.

The marchioness clapped. "You look quite the horsewoman, my dear."

Sullivan smiled; he couldn't help it. He'd begun the day late, was going to spend far more than his usual thirty minutes at Chalsey House, and was likely to miss an appointment with Lord Massey as a result. It didn't matter.

After three complete circles around the yard, he could see her relaxing a little, her back straightening, and her hold on the reins becoming looser. "Do you want to guide her to the step?" he asked.

"How far away are you going to be?"

"Three inches."

Isabel gathered up the reins again, testing her hold. "Very well. No more than three inches."

"My aim shall be two."

He let go of the bridle, falling back half a step to stay even with Isabel in case he needed to pull her from the sidesaddle. She clucked, tugging the reins to the right. Amateurish and tentative, but Molly veered to the right. *Good horse.*

Once they reached the stone mounting block, he took the reins and looped them through the hitching post ring. Then he lifted his arms and Isabel practically leapt onto his chest, hugging him tightly. "I did it," she whispered fiercely. "Thank you. Thank you, thank you, thank you!"

For the space of a heartbeat he hugged her slender form, then made a show of setting her feet onto the ground. "I only provided the horses. The courage is yours. Congratulations, poppet."

As she headed over to her parents, Sullivan caught sight of movement by the carriage drive. Oliver stood there, his expression grim enough to rust nails. Sullivan allowed himself a moment of satisfaction before he shifted his attention to Tilden's companions. Isabel's friend Lady Barbara and another chit stood there with Oliver. As he watched, the two girls whispered to one another and then glanced at him. A cold breeze went up his spine.

Had they seen her embrace him? He had to assume so. And while Oliver wasn't likely to risk making a row, he had no idea of the loyalty of the chits to Isabel. And he'd never put much faith in the kindness of the aristocracy. *Bloody hell.*

"Lady Isabel?" he called. "Do you wish me to put up Molly and take Zephyr out for her exercise?"

Surprised, Isabel looked over at Sullivan. He'd never asked her permission for anything before. Then she caught his glance toward the side of the house and followed his gaze. *Oh, dear.* "Yes, please do," she returned, leaving her parents in order to go greet her friends.

"That's not your new mare, is it?" Eloise Rampling asked. "She's ancient!"

"I haven't ridden much," Isabel said defensively. "I wanted a bit more practice before I took on a newly broken animal."

"But Mr. Waring says he doesn't break horses," Barbara put in with an amused smile. "He *tames* them."

"He seems to have tamed someone," Eloise noted.

"Oh, please." Isabel forced a grin. "Do come inside so I can change. Will you wait, Oliver?"

Lord Tilden stirred. "Yes, of course. If you still wish to go shopping today."

"I have never passed by an opportunity to go shopping."

"And neither have I," Barbara added. "You looked very fine in the saddle, Tibby."

She sent her friend a grateful smile. "Then

come along," she said aloud. "Cook's been baking biscuits all morning." Cook always baked biscuits in the morning, but it sounded like a good distraction. Obviously they'd all seen her hug Sullivan, and the more quickly they forgot about it, the better. *Stupid, stupid, stupid.*

On the other hand, she'd thanked a man because he'd helped her with something. She hadn't hugged him because he'd kissed her and she'd enjoyed it. But she still felt as though she'd done something wrong. She snuck a glance back at Sullivan to see him look quickly away from her. This was so much more complicated than her trying to keep an eye on a burglar. It had probably always been more complicated than that.

CHAPTER 14

Sullivan sat heavily in his overstuffed chair. His damned leg ached, and as soon as Mrs. Howard had set out the platter of ham and potatoes, he'd sent her home. He'd left his snifter of brandy on the mantel, but wasn't inclined to get up and retrieve it. The fire burning in the hearth made his small front room look cheery. That was not how he felt.

His front door opened. "I came by with two coins for you to give Charon," Bram drawled, slipping inside and closing the door behind him, "since I assumed you to be dead and ready to cross the River Styx."

"Why is it that no one ever knocks at my door?" Sullivan asked. "I'm beginning to think I'm surrounded by housebreakers."

"Birds of a feather. Where's the brandy?"

"On the end table. And hand over mine, will you?" He gestured at the fireplace.

"You may work for a living, my friend, but you do have good taste in liquor," Bram

242

said approvingly, lifting the bottle.

"Thank you."

"So did he shoot you?" Bramwell poured himself a generous amount of the amber liquid, retrieved and handed over Sullivan's snifter, then dropped into the chair opposite. "He told half of White's Club that he did. And apparently there was blood."

"He shot his tree. I caught a splinter."

Black eyes looked over the rim of the snifter at him. "I know several discreet physicians, if you require mending."

"No. And thank you for taking eighteen hours to come see whether I was still breathing."

"I came by this morning."

Sullivan stiffened a little, taking a sip of brandy to cover it. "Did you?" he said aloud. "I generally notice when you're present. You being the talkative sort."

"I saw Dunston's coach in the yard, and Chalsey's curricle circling around the back. It all frightened me, so I fled."

"Ah. It had nothing to do with your dislike of sticky personal entanglements, then?"

"What did Dunston want?" Ignoring the last comment, Bram stretched his boots out toward the fire. It was early yet for him, and he was dressed for an evening out, but if he wasn't in a hurry, neither was Sullivan. His leg hurt, but other things troubled him even more.

He realized Bram expected an answer, and shook himself. "He ordered me to stop the thievery nonsense and stay clear of Oliver and his marriage prospects."

"Was that why Darshear came by, as well? That's a bit brutish of them to double up like that."

Sullivan hesitated. He trusted Bram, but his friend also had a cynical streak a mile wide. "It wasn't Darshear. It was his off-spring."

Bram sat forward. "All of them?"

"Douglas and Isabel. They'd heard the rumor that your father had murdered a thief, and wanted to know if it was me."

" 'They'?" his friend repeated.

"Apparently Tibby told Douglas about me."

"You know, my feelings are hurt. I thought this thief business was going to be our secret, and now half of London knows."

"Very amusing. And I'm not giving you any of the duke's cigars."

"That was part of our agreement, Sullivan."

"He shot at me. Get your own cigars."

With a snort, Bram pushed back to his feet. "Have it your way, then. I'm off to be charming at the Fordham soiree. The duke's supposed to be there — did you dispose of that damned fertility idol?"

"I couldn't carry it, but it's now cockless. And that bit, you can have."

"God, no. For once, though, I'm looking forward to conversation with Levonzy. I shall be very sympathetic."

Sullivan watched Bram walk to the door. Frowning, he debated whether to say anything else. *Damnation.* "Bram?"

Lord Bram paused with the door half open. "Hm?"

"Keep an eye on Lady Isabel, will you? I put her up on a horse today, and she was so pleased that she . . . hugged me. Some of her friends saw us."

The door closed again. "You're the devil of a puzzle, Sully," Bram said after a moment. "You'll talk about thieving and being shot at, but you leave out the bit where the girl —"

"It was completely innocent," he interrupted, craning his head to look back in the direction of the door.

"Unlike the kiss."

"Kisses."

"Bloody hell." Bram returned to the chair and sat again. "I'm not one to advise on matters of the heart or the bedchamber, but . . . is it your intention to ruin this girl?"

"No! Of course not. Why would you even ask that?"

"You haven't been overly fond of my breed, ever. And less so since I dragged you back from the Peninsula."

"Which you shouldn't have done."

"Yes, I should have, since you joined only because I was forced to it."

"That's a rumor you began," Sullivan said, stifling a grin.

"Sometimes rumors are true. Which is why I have to wonder whether this business with Isabel Chalsey is some twisted kind of revenge against Tilden."

"Tibby never did anything to me but witness one of my ill deeds. And I'm not mad enough to fool myself into thinking . . . anything. . . ." He trailed off.

"Be careful, Sully. I can only save your life so many times before it becomes tiresome."

"I'll keep that in mind. Watch her tonight, will you, Bram?"

"I watch everything."

As Bram left, Sullivan sat back to sip his brandy again. Whatever his position in the world, he was accustomed to being responsible for his own destiny and actions — and no one else's. Now, though, he abruptly had someone else whose well-being concerned him. And all he could do was hope that Isabel's friends were truly that, and wait until morning.

And think of her for every moment between now and then.

"How is your head?" Lady Darshear asked, putting her palm against Isabel's cheek.

"I'm fine, Mama," Isabel replied, elbowing Phillip to gain a bit more room on the coach seat.

"If you say so."

In truth, Isabel wasn't certain how she felt. Feigning an aching head had been silly, but she couldn't rid herself of the feeling that something was wrong. Her outing with her friends had been perfectly enjoyable but for a few whispers and giggles where she'd been left out of the amusement. She couldn't remember being excluded even from the most inane conversation before, but it was also entirely possible that she was looking for something that wasn't there. For something to be wrong when it wasn't.

Barbara had congratulated her for riding Molly, but only Barbara knew how difficult it had been for her to do so. Eloise Rampling and Oliver had said nothing, and no one had commented about her embracing Sullivan. Perhaps they understood that it had been perfectly innocent, as had her parents. Or even better, perhaps they hadn't seen it at all.

Because it hadn't been completely innocent. She wouldn't have embraced Phipps or Delvin for helping her. Or Oliver. One of her family, yes, but not with the same breathless . . . joy she felt in the presence of Sullivan Waring.

"Do you remember the Fordham ball last year?" her mother asked. "Your dance card was nearly obliterated, it filled so quickly."

Isabel chuckled. "And Phillip was nearly blinded, so many cards were thrown at him."

"I can't help being irresistible," her brother drawled, "though I'm not so pretty as Tibby."

"Thank goodness for that. I would be terribly jealous." In truth she did feel pretty tonight. She'd worn her newest gown, a deep burgundy with lace at the neck and sleeves, ribbons of the same color twined through her blonde hair. If not for that nagging sense of trouble in the back of her mind, tonight would have been nearly perfect.

It still could be perfect, she told herself. The trouble could all just be in her head, because she knew the truth of why she'd embraced Sullivan. And that was because she hadn't been able not to.

It had begun as a game, but it wasn't anything near that any longer. It was wrong, and forbidden — and all the more tantalizing because of it. Like Juliet and Romeo, except that this Romeo wasn't from a hated rival family. He would have been acceptable, except for the niggling fact that his father had been married to someone other than his mother. And his father wouldn't claim him. From what she'd overheard this morning, Lord Dunston would never acknowledge Sullivan as his own son.

"Isabel?"

She shook herself. From her mother's tone, it wasn't the first time she'd spoken. For heaven's sake, she was about to attend the grandest ball so far this Season. She could dwell on her unfortunate obsession with Sullivan Waring later. "Yes?"

"What in the world has you so distracted?" the marchioness asked.

"I rode a horse today," she improvised. "I'd like to brag about myself, but everyone would just think me odd."

"*We* don't," Phillip supplied, giving her a very brotherly smile. "No odder than usual, anyway."

"Oh, thank you very much."

"Phillip," their mother chastised. "We're

proud of you, Tibby."

"Very proud," her father echoed. "In fact, I was thinking we might purchase that chestnut mare for you. Or I'm certain Mr. Waring wouldn't mind a trade, her for Zephyr. And then when you're more comfortable later on, we'll get you a younger, more spirited animal."

"No!"

"I beg your pardon?"

Realizing she'd spoken far too stridently, Isabel sat forward to take her father's hand. "If I give up Zephyr, it's the same as saying that I can't accomplish this. And I truly want to be able to ride her."

"Very well. So long as you're willing to continue to put in the work that is required."

"I am."

Thank goodness he'd given in. Because giving up Zephyr would mean giving up Sullivan. He might be bad for her, but she absolutely wasn't prepared to let him go. Not yet. Not even if it was selfish, and not even if it meant a great deal more trouble.

As the coach rocked to a halt, a yellow-liveried footman hurried up to pull open the door and assist their party to the ground. Once again Isabel banished Sullivan Waring from her thoughts. She could dwell on him later, in her dreams.

Phillip offered his arm, and with a smile she wrapped her fingers around his dark sleeve. Tonight there would be three waltzes, a quantity almost unheard of at any one event. Did Sullivan dance? Did he know the waltz? He'd been raised as a gentleman, he'd said, but the waltz was just becoming more popular than scandalous in London. Of course, he'd spent time in Europe where it had begun, so perhaps he did know it.

On the other hand, what did it signify? They would never dance together, because he would never be invited to any soiree, much less the Fordham ball. *Pay attention, ninny,* she reminded herself, stepping forward with her parents and older brother.

The butler announced her family, and they strolled together into the largest of the conjoined ballrooms at Fordham House. "What a sad crush," her mother exclaimed happily, and Isabel nodded in agreement.

She caught sight of Eloise Rampling halfway across the room and waved, but her friend turned and scampered off in the opposite direction. Considering that she could barely see her own hand in the crowd, she didn't know how anyone was supposed to find a particular person and hold a conversation. Still, that seed of uneasiness in her chest stirred a little.

"Relent a bit, will you?" Phillip complained. "Before you break my arm off, preferably."

She hurriedly loosened her grip. "Apologies."

He chuckled. "No worries." Unexpectedly he put his hand over hers. "Are you certain something's not bothering you?" he asked more quietly. "I wish I'd been there to see you ride. I hope you're not ang—"

"I didn't expect a parade or a royal decree, Phillip," she broke in, putting the smile back on her own face. "Nothing's troubling me. Truly."

"Very well." He looked past her shoulder. "There's Barbara, then. Must I stand by you? She makes me nervous."

"Only because she wants to marry you."

"Yes, that's it precisely."

She released his arm. "Go, then, you coward."

"Thank you." With a jaunty grin, her brother strode into the crowd.

"Was that Lord Chalsey?" Barbara asked, joining her in the crush.

"Yes. He saw an old friend from university and ran off." Isabel took in her friend's blue and yellow silk gown. "That's the material you chose at Mrs. Wrangley's, isn't it? Oh, it's lovely."

Barbara curtsied. "Thank you." With a quick glance around, she took Isabel's hand and tugged her toward one of the dozen doorways. "Come with me," she said in a lower voice. "I need to talk to you."

Isabel frowned, then swiftly smoothed away the expression. "What's going on?" she asked, allowing herself to be pulled along. "You haven't found someone to replace Phillip, have you?"

They finally found a quiet alcove, and Barbara sank against the far wall. "It's Eloise," she whispered.

"What's happened? Is she well?"

"She's been talking. To everyone. About you lusting after a stableboy."

Isabel's heart rattled and froze. "Oh, no."

"Yes. I told her to stop it, but she —"

"You were whispering with her all afternoon, Barbara," she interrupted, scowling. "You might have said something to me before now."

"I was attempting to make a jest of the whole thing. I thought she must have understood that you would never think of such a thing."

But she was thinking of such a thing. Isabel blinked. "You still should have told me."

"I know, I know. But I'm telling you now. You need to say something."

"What would I say?"

"That you certainly have no designs on a stableboy, or that Oliver's stolen your heart and you felt . . . pity for Mr. Waring."

"He's not a stableboy." Nor had Oliver stolen her heart. The Sullivan family, legitimate or otherwise, had only one thief who interested her.

"Yes, but —"

"He's not," Isabel insisted. "I know that's probably what Oliver wants everyone to think, but Sullivan Waring is a very well respected horse breeder. And he helped me ride a horse. Why shouldn't I have thanked him?"

"I don't think you should be worrying about the definition of Mr. Waring's employment," Barbara returned, her own frown deepening. "He's a by-blow with no confirmed parentage, and Eloise is whispering to everyone that you've . . . been with him."

Isabel blanched. "That's nonsense!" For a long moment she stared at Barbara while she tried to pull her scattered, half-panicked thoughts together. "No one will believe her," she finally said. "I have a great many friends here tonight. They'll know that I wouldn't do such a thing."

"Tibby . . ."

Barbara's look reflected everything that

Isabel was already thinking. Rumors. All she could do to defend herself was deny them, and that only brought them more credence. Ignoring them was equally useless. But at least that way had a little dignity to it. And she did have friends. She knew she did. Barbara was a friend, and she didn't believe the rumors. There had to be others. She'd grown up with these people. And for heaven's sake, as long as her virtue remained intact, who the devil had a right to care if she had become friends with a horse breeder?

"Let's go back inside," she decided.

"But —"

"It's just Eloise, spreading a nasty rumor. I have as much chance of being believed as she does. And I have truth on my side." And hopefully enough resolve to refrain from doing physical injury to her former friend.

"Very well," Barbara said with clear reluctance. "Unless you think you might prefer just to return home and wait for something else to distract everyone's attention."

That was probably a very wise idea. But the thought of running was supremely distasteful. All right, so she'd kissed him, and so she wanted to kiss him several more times — that was not why the rumors were flying. What Eloise had seen had been innocent. Relatively.

Before they left the alcove, she hugged her friend. "Thank you for telling me."

"Yes, well, I only hope I'm wrong about how busy Eloise has been."

As soon as they reentered the main room, Isabel knew that Barbara hadn't been wrong. Eloise had been very busy, indeed. Everyone seemed to be looking at her, and not in the usual friendly, smiling way they generally did. *Oh, dear.* She needed to inform her parents and Phillip before someone else did.

She found them by the dessert table, her father talking with her brother, and her mother looking a bit . . . bewildered. "Mama," she said, taking the marchioness's hand.

"Tibby, there you are. So who's filled your dance card tonight?"

"No one. That's —"

"Oh, please. Don't jest ab—"

"Mama, listen to me." Isabel motioned her family closer, and told them what Barbara had told her. By the time she finished her brief dissertation, her mother's face had paled, while Phillip and her father both looked ready to throttle someone.

"This is ridiculous," Phillip snarled.

"So far I haven't heard anything," the

marchioness said a little shakily. "Perhaps you exaggerate, Barbara."

To her credit, Barbara still stood close by them, though her pleasant smile looked more and more strained. "I think you would be the last people to hear. That's the way rumors work, isn't it?"

"Yes, it is," Phillip said grimly. Then his expression eased, and he held out his hand. "Lady Barbara, if you're not spoken for, may I have the next dance?"

This time Barbara blushed. "Of course you may."

Phillip glanced at Isabel. "And I want the dance after that with you. Save it for me."

She smiled, grateful. "I don't think that'll be a problem, but it's yours."

While Phillip and Barbara headed for the crowded dance floor, Isabel marked her dance card, putting Phillip's name beside the country dance which would take place next. Otherwise, the card was empty. Empty. At the Fordham ball. A low shiver ran through her.

"This is ridiculous," Lord Darshear hissed. "Where is Eloise's family? I'm going to have a word with her father."

"Lord Rampling never attends these events," Isabel contributed. Of course she knew that; until today she and Eloise had been friends. Good friends. Or so she'd thought.

"What about her mother? Where's Lady Rampling?" her mother put in, her own expression going grimmer as every moment passed without a single gentleman approaching them. "I have a few things I'd like to say to Martha."

Isabel shook her head. "This is just silliness. Don't make it any worse than it is, Mama. I'll go find Eloise and tell her to stop it."

It took several minutes to convince her parents to stay where they were and not begin an all-out attack on every gossip in the house, but finally she slipped away and went looking for Eloise Rampling. She found her friend surrounded by other young people, and squared her shoulders.

"Eloise?"

The petite brunette jumped. "Oh, Tibby. I thought you might have decided not to attend tonight, so you could spend the time with your stableboy."

A low snicker of laughter sounded around them. It took every ounce of control Isabel possessed to keep from bloodying her friend's pert upturned nose. "I'm sorry, Eloise," she said slowly, racing to keep her mind ahead of the pace of her words, "but are you talking about when I tripped in the stable yard today and Mr. Sullivan Waring kept me from falling on my face in the mud? I suppose that might sound romantic, but actually I was just grateful not to have ruined my gown."

That garnered a few more chuckles, less nasty this time. Was this how it was for Sullivan, when he had dealings with her kind? If so, she understood now why he didn't like the aristocracy. She wasn't fond of them herself at the moment, and she was one of them.

"I heard a rumor," a low voice drawled behind her, and she stiffened. Keeping her expression light and easy, she turned around. And blinked.

"Lord Bramwell?"

The tall, black-haired, black-clothed duke's son sketched a lazy, elegant bow. "Someone told me that Lady Isabel Chalsey is the finest, most elegant dancer in attendance tonight. Would you care to oblige my curiosity?" He held out his hand to her.

"Now?"

He glanced over his shoulder at the exuberant crowd of dancers. "I have to test your mettle before I commit to requesting a waltz."

The notorious Lord Bramwell Lowry

Johns seemed to be performing a rescue. Dipping in a curtsy and doing everything she could to keep the gratitude and relief from showing on her face, she clasped his fingers. "You are very wise, my lord," she said aloud as they walked over to join the other dancers.

"So I keep telling everyone."

"And you have quite excellent instincts," she observed, timing her comments to the moments when the dance brought them together.

"Yes, well, an angry little birdie mentioned that you might be in need of an ally tonight."

She turned and nearly missed a step. Sullivan had arranged this? She wished she dared ask that question aloud, but being overheard speaking about him certainly wouldn't improve matters for her, or for him. But he'd thought of her, and he'd sent help. Unlikely help, but help indeed.

"It's still very nice of you," she said as they joined hands and circled again.

Lord Bramwell gave her a dark smile that unsettled her a little. "I'm not the least bit nice. I enjoy having people owe me favors. Now you owe me one."

"I —"

"And I'm about to make it two favors. Stay away from the angry bird, Isabel. He's on a path with no safe haven in sight. And you don't want to be there when pheasant season begins."

A shiver ran through her again. "Have you told him that?"

"He knew when he began this that it wouldn't end well."

"What if . . ." She hesitated. Why in the world should she trust this man? Even as she asked the question of herself, though, she knew the answer. She trusted him because Sullivan trusted him. "What if I can convince him to leave this path?"

Eyes black as pitch assessed her. "Someone is going to lose," he said finally, joining in the applause as the dance ended. Then he placed her hand over his arm while they looked for her parents. "Stand close to him, and it will very likely be you."

"Where will you stand?"

He shrugged. "I'm a shifty, self-serving sort of fellow. I suppose it depends where the greatest benefit to me lies."

As he smiled and handed her off, Isabel didn't know whether she believed him about that or not. He did have a very changeable reputation. But he'd made an appearance, and he'd helped her tonight. As for —

"Isabel, there you are," Oliver said, nodding at her parents as he reached her side.

"I hope I haven't arrived too late to secure a place on your dance card."

Hm. Perhaps now that Lord Bramwell had smiled on her, everything wasn't as lost as she'd begun to fear. "You may have your pick, Oliver."

"Then I choose the first waltz."

"It's yours."

Phillip returned to claim her for the next dance, and she did finally end with an adequate complement of partners. It hadn't been easy, though, and it wasn't something she looked forward to encountering ever again.

And charming as she tried to be, Lord Bramwell's words kept running through her mind. Because he'd been very correct about Sullivan. Mr. Waring was headed toward a very bad carriage wreck. And she'd already lived through one of those. She wasn't certain she could face another.

CHAPTER 15

Sullivan stifled a yawn. He generally enjoyed the early mornings, and particularly those when he attended Tattersall's horse market, but this morning he would rather have arrived early at Chalsey House. Bram hadn't bothered to return after the ball to report on Isabel's reception there, and he'd tossed and turned all night imagining her ruination.

A light fog blended ground with sky, the stables and auction pens gray and gloomy despite the flurry of men and horses around them. He listened for anything interesting, but most of the men about the paddocks at this hour were stableboys and grooms, and even if there was any good *ton* gossip to be had, they probably wouldn't have it. Not yet, anyway.

One of his sale animals came up behind him in the holding pen to nuzzle his shoulder. "You want an apple already?" he asked, digging one out of his pocket as he turned around. "Here you go, Ariadne."

The pretty chestnut mare nickered, taking the fruit from his hand and munching down on it. If people were as easy to decipher as horses, he could have been king by now, he reflected with a short grin, patting Ariadne on the neck.

The shovel handle caught him in the back of the knees, sending him to the ground almost before he realized he'd been struck. Instinctively Sullivan rolled sideways, grabbing the sturdy railing of the pen to help him to his feet again. Four men advanced on him, none of them familiar, and all of them armed with shovels.

"Good morning, gentlemen," he said darkly, crouching, the old battle lust stirring his blood. "Apparently we have a disagreement. Care to tell me what it is?"

"You need to learn to keep to your own kind, boy," the largest of them growled, swinging the shovel at him.

Sullivan blocked it with his forearm, closing in to deliver a hard jab to his attacker's throat. With a gurgle the fellow dropped. Grabbing the shovel out of the man's hand, Sullivan swept the second cove's legs out from under him. A shovel slammed across his back, stunning him. He swung again as he stumbled forward, connecting with someone's arm. A handle cracked across the side of his head, and he went down into the dirt.

Damnation. Where the devil were his own lads? Rolling over onto his back, he blocked another blow and slammed the head of the shovel into someone's gut. As he scrambled to his feet, he caught sight of a figure standing at the corner of the stable building. With a grim smile Oliver Sullivan ducked out of sight.

The attack abruptly made sense — though the knowledge didn't make it any less painful. He struck out again, whipping sideways to catch one of them with his elbow. They might be hired ruffians, but he'd been a soldier for four of the past five years. The gouge in his thigh ached, but he ignored it.

They'd obviously come to hurt him, but had they come to kill him? He didn't think so, or that first blow would have been to the back of his head rather than to his legs. But he didn't have any promise of money keeping *him* from using lethal force. And ever since he'd returned home he'd been spoiling for a good fight.

A hard fist met his shoulder, and he staggered back a step, throwing another punch in response. This would have been so much more satisfying if Oliver had stayed to fight his own battle. But with his half-brother gone and himself outnumbered four to one —

"Is whatever he's paying you worth a cracked skull?" he panted.

Two of them grabbed him, shoving him back against the hard wooden railings of the pen. "Depends on whose skull's being cracked," the first one rasped, then reared back his fist and punched. Everything went blurry, until another fist connected with his chin. Then the gray morning went black.

He opened his eyes to someone shaking his shoulder. Striking out, his fist connected. The sound of a surprised yelp echoed around the yard.

"Mr. Waring! For God's sake!"

Sullivan blinked hard. "Damnation, Halliwell, help me up."

"We chased those brigands away," his groom said, as he lifted one shoulder and Samuel pulled him up by the other. "For a moment we thought they'd murdered you."

"No, they just wanted to give me a message." Gingerly he shook dirt and straw out of his clothes and touched one hand to his bruised jaw. His skull and ribs hurt, as well, but none of the fellows who'd attacked him would be dancing tonight, either. If he had anyone to tell about the incident, they'd be fairly easy to identify.

"Lord Massey's back at our wagon, asking after Spartan," Samuel informed him, retrieving the gloves Sullivan had dropped and returning them.

So a little beating and then back to business. Considering his mood toward Massey's kind at the moment, the viscount was not going to like how much Spartan was going to cost him. And as for Oliver . . .

Sullivan clenched his fists. Obviously this was because of Isabel. Walking over to a water barrel, he dunked his head. The cold water shocked away his grogginess, and he stepped back and shook out his hair.

Oliver considered him a threat? A rival? That was interesting, since Isabel and her parents would be foolish to let her dally with a horse breeder, even one of unacknowledged aristocratic lineage, when a viscount was panting after her. Oliver seemed to be worried about something, though. And it wasn't a business rivalry, for damned certain.

For the moment he pushed back his anger. Riding Tilden down and beating him might give him some satisfaction, but it would also end with him in shackles. It was too soon for that, since he still had three paintings left to reclaim, three more opportunities to dig at Dunston's hypocrisy.

Even with that in mind, he couldn't help thinking about Isabel. He knew she liked him; from the moment she'd begun ordering him about he'd known that. But did she like him enough to threaten Oliver's pursuit of her? Apparently so.

"Mr. Waring?"

He blinked. "Yes. I'll go see to Massey. Halliwell, you have the papers for the other three animals?"

"I do, sir."

"Good. After I sell Spartan I'll need to go see to Zephyr's morning training. Take Hector out when you return and run him. He's to go off to Lord Esquille's tomorrow, and I don't want him trampling Esquille's mares when he's supposed to feel romantic."

"Yes, sir. Do you want an escort?"

"What?" He noted Halliwell's look, and touched the bruise on his chin. "No. They did what they came to do. They won't be back." At least not until he did something else about which Oliver could disapprove.

"I have to say, Phillip, I wasn't terribly enthusiastic to have Lord Bramwell Johns here as one of your dinner guests last month, but perhaps I've underestimated his character." Lady Darshear deftly changed the thread color of her embroidery and continued sewing. "If he hadn't danced with Tibby last night, she might have had a difficult evening. We all might have."

"It's all frip and folly anyway," Douglas put in, setting aside the book on horse breeding he'd found after Isabel had set it aside. "How can people be angry that we hired Sullivan Waring? Everyone wants to hire Waring."

Isabel gave an indignant snort — or at least she hoped it sounded more indignant than panicked. "They're not angry. They think they've found some good gossip, that I'm mooning over Waring or something, simply because I hugged him after he helped me ride a horse."

"You should have been more careful, Tibby," Phillip commented. "Especially with Oliver Sullivan hanging about."

"You were happy as a kitten with twine when I hired Mr. Waring," Isabel shot back, "and *you* were the one who knew of his connection to Oliver."

"There is no connection, officially."

"Don't tangle the circumstances any more than they already are, Phillip. Sullivan *is* Dunston's son, whatever anyone's willing to say about it publicly." Seeing the look her parents sent one another, Isabel swallowed. "So the entire thing's just ridiculous. And I'm certain it won't be more than a day before someone else does something more scandalous than thank someone for their help, and everyone will forget my . . . whatever it is we're calling it. Act of gratitude, I suppose."

"You do have a point," her father noted. "But please be cautious. There's no sense in giving even a rumor teeth."

"People are still stupid."

"As a whole, I tend to agree," the marquis returned. "And for your own sake, my sweet one, pray keep that in mind."

"Oh, I will."

She would definitely keep it in mind. Whether it changed her actions, though, was another matter entirely. Last evening had been a rather eye-opening experience.

The butler came into the morning room and sketched a bow. "My lord, Mr. Waring is here. You asked to be informed."

The marquis winced, then pushed to his feet. "So I did. Excuse me a moment, everyone."

Her heart skipping a beat, Isabel practically leapt to her feet, as well. "What do you want with Mr. Waring?"

His wince deepened into a pained expression. "I want a word with him, Tibby. None of your concern."

"I paid him to accomplish a task for me," she pressed, following him as he exited the room. "I expect him to finish it."

"At the expense of your reputation?"

"I won't embrace him again," she said, knowing full well that she was lying. Nothing else seemed to matter where Sullivan Waring was concerned; nothing but being able to be in his presence. "For heaven's sake."

"I know you like to have your way, Isabel," her father countered, continuing down the hallway, "but I suggest you choose your excitement more wisely. We'll find someone else to finish Zephyr's training."

"You said Sullivan Waring was the best."

"The best is not worth another night like the last one. You were devastated."

"I was not devastated. I was angry. I'm *still* angry. I thought better of Eloise. And everyone else who whispered about me. Ridiculous. All of them."

"You say that now, but I doubt you'll feel the same if no one comes to your rescue next time."

She wasn't so certain about that. There were worse things she could imagine, and this was one of them. Her fingers shaking, something like panic tightening her chest, Isabel reached out to put a hand on her father's shoulder. "I am nearly twenty years old, Papa," she said, her voice mostly steady, "and I am perfectly capable of working with Mr. Waring."

"Isa—"

"Leave it be, Papa," she insisted. "I'll take care of it."

For a long moment he looked at her, the deep brown eyes beneath his straight brows serious. "Then do so, Tibby. Because of who he is, people notice him. And because of who he isn't, you need to watch your step in his presence. Even more carefully now. Do you understand?"

"Yes, I do. Now, if you'll excuse me, I have another riding lesson this morning."

Her father obviously thought that was a very bad idea, and the logical part of her agreed. The other part, the one that had apparently taken control of her actions over the past several weeks, was hard-pressed not to run out to the stable yard. When had this happened? And why couldn't she seem to listen to sense, even from herself?

Assuming a civilized walk and smoothing her skirts, she left the house. The stable yard was filled with its usual quotient of horses and grooms, but at first glance she didn't see Sullivan. Not at second glance, either.

"Phipps," she said, spying the head groom, "I thought Mr. Waring had arrived."

"He's in the stable, my lady." A muscle in his cheek jumped. "You might want to give him a bit of distance this morning."

"Why is that?"

"I — I couldn't say, my lady."

"Then I shall go see for myself." Drawing her abrupt sense of uneasiness back in around her, Isabel trudged over the soft ground and into the building. She paused in the doorway, then saw his head and shoulders inside Zephyr's stall. "I see you managed to be prompt this morning, Mr. Waring," she said, continuing forward and unable to help the grin that touched her mouth.

Sullivan kept his back turned as he fastened a bridle over Zephyr's harness, and then a lead line to that. "I try to please, Lady Isabel. How was your party last evening?"

She frowned. "Did Lord Bramwell say something to you?"

"No."

"Well, I know you asked him to dance with me."

He shifted, fastening a saddle blanket

across Zephyr's back. "I asked him to keep an eye on you. The dancing was his idea." He paused. "Bram's a notorious womanizer, you know."

"Yes, he's told me that himself." Isabel put her hands on the board topping the near wall of the tiny enclosure. "Since you might hear it elsewhere, I'll tell you that there were a few uncomfortable moments last evening, but they passed quickly."

"I'm glad, then."

She slapped her hand on the wood. "Sullivan Waring, look at me when I'm speaking to you."

His broad shoulders lifted and fell, and then he turned around. "As you wish."

Isabel gasped. "What happened?"

One of his sleeves was torn at the elbow, and he'd lost a button off his waistcoat. The damage to his clothes was secondary, though, to what she saw on his face.

Sullivan had a deep red scratch across his throat, and a black and blue bruise crossing part of his mouth and the left side of his chin. His left eye was circled by a painful-looking black bruise, and his brown and golden hair looked as though he'd combed it by dragging his fingers through it.

"What happened?" she repeated, reaching over the stall to touch his chin. His skin felt warm before he ducked backward, away from her fingers.

"I had a disagreement."

"With what, a bear?"

He grinned briefly, wincing as the movement pulled the bruise over his mouth. "Several of them." Taking the lead line in one hand, he unlatched the stall door with the other. "Do you want to ride Molly today?"

"Not until you tell me who did this to you."

"I'll assume that's a no, then. Come along, Zephyr."

Taking a deep breath, Isabel folded her arms across her chest and refused to move out of the way. "Answer me."

Ice-green eyes met hers, then moved away. "I don't live among tea-drinking dandies, Tibby," he finally said. "Don't trouble yourself about it."

"It does trouble me, Sullivan. Tell me."

He stopped directly in front of her, Zephyr behind him. "I was here at the appointed time, and I'm able to train your mare as per our agreement. Why should anything else concern you?"

"Because it does."

"It shouldn't."

"And you 'shouldn't' be arguing with me,

and we 'shouldn't' have kissed," she re-torted. "We're friends, Sullivan, and I want to know —"

" 'Friends'?" he interrupted. He grabbed the front of her dress in his fist and yanked her up against him. "Are we friends, Lady Isabel?"

Her heart hammered so hard he could probably hear it. "Y . . . yes, we're friends. You —"

"Are you shunned when you embrace your other friends?" he broke in again, his voice deepening to a low, sensuous growl. "We talk in secret. We kiss in secret. Any suspicion of even friendship between us gets you slighted and me pummeled."

Desperately Isabel tried to follow the conversation rather than the heady rush of her blood beneath her skin. "Someone beat you because I hugged you? That's —"

"I'm not worth the trouble as a friend, Tibby," he murmured, the sound of her nickname lingering intimately in the air between them. "You have friends. Friends who don't cause you trouble. So do I. I'm not here for friendship."

If her heart beat any faster she was going to faint. "No, you're here because I'm blackmailing you."

He shook his head, pulling her a breath

closer. "I'm here because I want you. Your touch. Your body. *That* is what I would take a beating for."

Oh, goodness. "Sullivan, I want —"

"Before you finish that, consider what rumors of an innocent embrace did to you. And if you're going to say you want to be my friend . . ." His voice shook as he spoke those words. "If you want us to be friends, friends don't do this."

He brought his mouth down over hers. Hard and ruthless, stealing her breath and the strength from her bones. Oh, she wanted to sink into him, to climb inside him and never emerge until she'd figured him out. Her seeking tongue tasted salt; his blood, probably from the blow to his chin.

She moaned, grabbing his shoulders, the back of his neck, into his wild hair with her hands. The taste of him excited her beyond words. It was the most intimate thing she'd ever felt. And he wanted more. More, when just this could destroy her.

With the fist still wound into the front of her dress, he abruptly pushed her away. "Consider all of that before you answer me," he said brusquely, releasing her to wipe the back of his hand across his mouth. "Consider all of the ruin I could bring to your reputation and your future, all of the peril I could bring to your heart, because you and I both know that this leads to nowhere but ruin."

Brushing her back another step, he led Zephyr forward. "And when you've considered," he went on in the same heated, barely controlled tone, "if it's damnation you want, then I'll see you inside this stable at midnight tonight. If you have any sense at all, I'll see you in the morning when I come to tend your mare."

"But —"

"But right now if I set eyes on you again, I'm liable to wreck both of us. So go inside your house, Isabel, where you'll be safe."

She wanted to argue, to protest that he wasn't allowed to order her about. *She* was the one who dictated to *him.* Isabel watched him leave the stable, caught her breath, and waited until the heat she felt in her cheeks faded.

He was right; she needed to consider what she wanted very carefully. And so she gathered her skirts and ran back into the house. He'd been wrong about one thing, already. Knowing he was just outside didn't leave her feeling safe at all.

CHAPTER 16

Isabel flipped open the cover of the pocket watch she'd borrowed from Douglas. That was to say, if and when he missed it she would claim that she'd borrowed it.

Ten minutes until midnight. Sullivan had picked a good evening for his ultimatum: Parliament had an early morning session tomorrow, so no late-night events had been scheduled. By now the house was quiet, and as far as she knew, everyone had gone to bed.

She'd put on her night rail, but that had been because Penny was there to help her dress for bed. The maid would have been suspicious if she'd announced her intention to sleep in her gown. She'd blown out the candle on the bed-stand, again just as a precaution against any of the footmen on their way to their quarters seeing that she remained awake.

At the same time, she hadn't crawled

beneath the covers of her very comfortable bed. In fact, she still sat at the dressing table, where she could eye Douglas's watch every two minutes as midnight crept closer. And one thing had become clear: Sullivan Waring knew her better than she expected.

From the moment she'd begun ordering him about, he'd probably realized that she had more than revenge or blackmail on her mind. He'd kissed her first, but since then she'd looked for every opportunity to kiss him or to be kissed by him again. And yes, the only conclusion to this would be her ruination. At the same time, this seemed the most likely and logical step in her . . . growing up, in the opening of her eyes that had happened to her since they'd met.

She checked the pocket watch again. Six minutes. If he'd been reconciled to his father and the Sullivan family, then a connection between them might have at least been imaginable. As it was, with him climbing through noblemen's windows and getting shot at in order to recover a handful of paintings he couldn't even show anyone, he was very likely going to end up dead. And if anyone saw them together, she would wish herself dead.

Clearly she wasn't going to marry him. He wanted to . . . to fornicate with her. And she wanted his hands on her, his mouth on her, in ways she could only imagine. Would it be worth the risk? The loss of her virginity? She supposed that would depend on who she married afterward. Oliver was definitely interested in her, but the more she saw how he treated Sullivan, the less she wanted to spend any time with him. She'd begun to think she only did so to keep him from suspecting just how much she liked Sullivan. Obviously once she gave her purity to Sullivan, Oliver would want nothing more to do with her. And she honestly didn't care. If she even wanted to marry, she supposed there would be men who would overlook her lack of chastity in exchange for a generous dowry.

But it was more than her purity that would be lost, and she needed to consider that, too. Until last night, she'd been one of Society's favorites — their darling, always mobbed at soirees, never without friends or dance partners. Until last night, she hadn't realized how tenuous a thing that popularity was. It brought up more questions for her. Did her popularity make her who she was? What would happen to her if she lost it? And was she willing to risk that?

Four minutes. "Damnation," she muttered, clicking the watch closed again. All she had to do was stay where she was, and she would be safe. Not safe from wanting Sullivan, from being interested in him, but safe from his kisses and from being ruined by him, and from having to answer those questions.

She dropped the watch into a drawer and stood to pull on her thin dressing robe. She'd spent the past two years dancing through ballrooms and flirting, because that was what young ladies of good name did. She didn't believe in love at first sight or fate or any silly thing of the kind. But once Sullivan Waring had entered her thoughts, he'd never shown the least inclination to leave them again. And she didn't think he ever would. Not until she went to where she wanted and needed to go.

Taking a breath, she slowly opened her bedchamber door and slipped cautiously into the hallway. She could still change her mind. She could still stop in the kitchen to get herself an apple and then go back upstairs to bed. That had been her plan the night she'd stumbled across Sullivan robbing the house.

She hesitated at the door to the kitchen. Sullivan Waring was a wrecked, angry lawbreaker who worked with his hands to make his living. And she was being pursued by a wealthy viscount who would one day be a marquis, and who actually bore a very close physical resemblance to Mr. Waring. Hm. So if she could pass by the temptation of Sullivan, she could still have someone she didn't want, but who looked just like him.

Temptation. Yes, she wanted an apple, but not one from the kitchen. Tonight she felt hungry for the very one the serpent had given to Eve. And she would probably lose her paradise, too, as a result. Because for all his similar physical attributes, Oliver did not possess the one quality that drew her to Sullivan: that sense of being alive, which he fought for and earned every moment of his life and the time they spent together.

Practically before she even realized it, she was out of the house and into the murky darkness of the stable yard. With a silent curse she kicked out of her shoes and laid them behind a stone bench out of easy sight. No sense ruining them — or giving anyone a clue that she'd been elsewhere than in her own bed during the night.

The door to the stable already stood open an inch or so. None of the stableboys would have left it that way if they wanted to keep their employment at Chalsey House. Biting her lower lip and making her hands as steady as she could when her heart beat faster than a drummer's tattoo, she pulled it open another few inches and slipped inside.

Without the pale cast of moonlight, the inside of the stable building was as black as pitch. She could hear the rustling and breathing of two dozen horses, but other than that, nothing.

"Sullivan?" she whispered almost soundlessly. The grooms and stableboys slept in a separate room at the back of the stable, and she had no intention of waking them even if Lucifer himself appeared before her. "Sullivan?"

A hand slid over her shoulder and across her mouth. "You're very prompt," Sullivan's low voice murmured against her left ear.

Her entire body shivered. Excitement, lust, trepidation — she didn't know. As he took her shoulders and turned her to face him, she didn't care. She'd never felt as alive as she did at that moment.

Lifting onto her toes, she tangled her fingers in Sullivan's hair and dragged his face down to meet hers in a deep, open-mouthed kiss. He wrapped around her like molten fire, pressing her back against the wall as he pulled her hard against him, his mouth as eager as hers.

"Sulli—"

"Don't talk," he murmured back, slipping his fingers beneath her robe to pull it from her shoulders and toss it over the railing of the nearest stall. "You'll change your mind."

"No, I w—"

He kissed her again, making her moan. As his palms trailed down her bare shoulders and along the arms she had tightly locked around him, she could feel the calluses on the pads of his fingers. He'd said he was no soft-handed dandy, but she hadn't expected the touch of his skin against hers to be so intoxicating.

As those same rough-edged fingers slipped beneath the narrow shoulders of her night rail, she felt close to losing herself in him. "Don't tell me what to do," she managed, breathing in the leather-and-soap scent of him. "And don't interrupt me."

He backed away an inch or two. As her eyes adjusted to the gloom she could make out his gaze, aggravated and amused at the same time. "May I suggest that you keep your voice down, then?"

"I am," she retorted. It was difficult to be quiet and commanding at the same time. Especially when he reached for her night rail again and slowly pulled the left shoulder down to her elbow, then closed on her for another slow, plundering kiss.

"If it were anyone else . . ." he muttered, his fingers trailing along her bared shoulder.

"What do you mean by that?"

She felt his smile against her mouth. "Nothing. Give me your orders, Lady Isabel."

Moaning again, she bared her throat to his kisses. And she realized what he meant. No one else ordered him about. He didn't tolerate it. Except from her. "Take off your shirt," she whispered shakily.

He kissed her again, tipping her head back with the force of his embrace. "I want you," he growled, removing his hands from her and yanking his own shirt free of his trousers. He pulled it over his head and cast it beside her robe. Sullivan tried to close on her again, but she held him back with her hands against his bare chest.

Soft skin met the pads of her fingers, the hard muscles beneath flexing under her touch. Physically she was no match for him, but he nevertheless stopped his advance.

"Changed your mind?" he breathed, his eyes narrowing.

"Put a blanket down," she countered. "I don't want to get dirty."

"You will be dirty," he returned, stepping over for a handful of saddle blankets and spreading them over the floor of an empty stall. "The kind that won't wash away."

"I thought you were supposed to be seducing me." Uncertain of exactly what her part in this was supposed to be, she followed him into the straw-and-blanket-covered box.

"You're barefoot," he announced, his gaze sweeping over her and lingering at her bare ankles and feet.

"I left my shoes behind a bench," she returned. "I didn't want anyone to know I'd —"

"Been doing anything naughty?" he finished. "With someone completely unacceptable?"

"I know who and what you are, Sullivan," she snapped, her voice rising a little before she managed to quiet herself again. "So are you trying to drive me away, or are you frightened of me and you're just wasting my time in hopes that I'll leave?"

"Bold words for a good, virginal chit," he murmured, looking at her with so predatory a gleam in his eyes it made her swallow. He hooked a finger into the neck of her night rail and tugged her closer. With his other hand he pulled the clip from her hair, and the long, honey-colored waves fell past her shoulders. "If you hadn't come down here, I probably would have climbed into your window to get to you. What do you think of that?"

She shivered as his fingers tangled and tugged into her long hair, as she ran her palms up his warm, well-muscled chest, as the meaning of his words sank into her. He'd said that he'd given her a choice about this, but now she wasn't so certain. And the idea that he would have pursued her back into her own house aroused her.

"I think you should stop talking so much," she stated. "Unless that's all you have to offer."

"By God, you have a mouth on you." A brief smile touched his face again. "And now you'll have mine on you." Sullivan took two handfuls of the material above her breasts and ripped. The entire front of the flimsy cotton gown tore open from top to bottom. She gasped.

Before she could recover her heated, scattered wits, he slid his hands around her bare waist, pulling her against him again. Then he kissed her once more, his tongue boldly exploring her mouth. Good heavens, he was strong, and sure of himself. One large hand trailed up her stomach to cup her left breast. Her nipple hardened, pebbling against his palm.

Pure sensation flooded her, stealing her

breath. Only a useless scrap of clothing hung from her shoulders and down her back, as his capable mouth traveled down her chin and throat, down to . . . oh, heavens.

Sullivan took her breast into his mouth, sucking and licking her tight nipple. "God," she whimpered, clutching her fingers into his hair.

Her legs felt boneless. He seemed to realize that, because he lowered her onto the rough blankets, his mouth still fastened to her breast. She felt the tug of his lips all the way down her spine and to the private spot between her legs. She heated and dampened, groaning and lifting her hips helplessly in response.

"Sullivan," she whispered shakily.

"You ordered me to stop talking." He moved his attention to her other breast, crouching on all fours over her like a tawny-haired lion feasting on his very willing prey. "If I were to say something," he continued in a low, sensual tone that rumbled through her where they touched, "it would be that you are breathtaking."

Breathing hard, Isabel put her hands on his shoulders, kneading her fingers into the hard, taut muscles there. She closed her eyes; everywhere they touched felt heated, silk-soft flames that sank deeply into her, straight through her veins to her fast-beating heart.

When his palm coursed slowly down her belly to her abdomen, her eyes flew open again. Fingers trailed through her light curls and then touched her . . . there. She gasped.

"I excite you," he murmured, lifting his head to look her in the eye. "You want me." Still watching her, he moved his fingers deeper, parting her. Then he slipped inside.

She bucked. Something that sounded like his name blurted out from her lips, and he covered her mouth with his free hand.

"Shh," he cautioned, glancing briefly over his shoulder before he returned to his exploration.

This was too much. "Sull . . . Sullivan," she managed, gasping his name as quietly as she could.

"You're the one giving the orders, my lady. What shall I do to you next?"

Oh, God, she had no idea. *More,* her body told her. She craved it. *More.* "I —"

"Shall I remove my trousers, perhaps?"

His voice wasn't entirely steady, either. That realization actually calmed her a little, though not nearly enough for her mind to be of any use. She could barely form words, and he still had clothes on. "Yes. Remove them. Now. And your boots." There. She still had some control — of herself, if not of him.

He swiveled to sit beside her. It seemed very important to continue touching him, so she sat up and shrugged out of the ruined remains of her night rail. Running her hands down his back and shoulders, kissing the nape of his neck, she tasted the salt of his skin. Intoxicating. As his muscles shuddered beneath her touch, she realized that she did have some control over him. Her touch affected him, perhaps as much as his did her. She wet her swollen lips.

"I've changed my mind."

He froze. "Beg pardon?"

"Not about that," she said, further reassured by his reaction. "I mean, I think *I* should remove your trousers."

"Oh. Please proceed, then."

She pulled him onto his back. Wherever this wanton, brazen miss had come from, she was glad of it. After all, he'd said that he wanted her, but she wanted him, as well. And she might as well be an active participant in her own ruination.

His dark trousers tented at the crotch. For a second the brazen miss nearly turned tail and ran, but Sullivan pulled her down across his chest and kissed her again. His skilled fingers flicked across her sensitive nipples, and she writhed against him.

"Touch me," he breathed, taking her hand and placing it over the bulge in his trousers. "I want you to touch me."

Even through the material he felt warm and hard. Tentatively she squeezed, and he dropped his head back, moaning. Isabel shifted so she could reach him, and with shaking fingers she unbuttoned his trousers. It was impossible to concentrate with his hands roaming her bare skin, but she managed to open the last button. "Lift up," she ordered.

"As you wish."

Sullivan complied, and she tugged his trousers down his hips. He came free, erect and magnificent. "My," she breathed. "That —"

"Is about to be inside you," he finished, shrugging his trousers the rest of the way off and kicking them aside.

And she'd thought she hadn't been able to breathe before. He rolled them so that she lay on her back again, looking up into ice-green eyes made darker by the gloom of the stable. With his knees he nudged hers apart, sinking down between them so that she could feel his hard erection pressing against the inside of her thighs.

Ruined. She was going to be ruined. And she wanted him to hurry up with it. He kissed her again, nibbling at her lips and her throat, driving her half mad with desire. She felt drawn tighter than a bowstring.

"Sullivan, hurry," she panted.

"Hurry with what?" he whispered. "Tell me what you want, poppet."

Good Lord. "I want you inside me," she said, using the same phrase that he had.

"As you wish." He angled his hips forward, sliding between her folds and pressing inside her.

She could feel every inch of him as he entered her. Time stopped. Nothing existed but him and her heartbeat. For a second a sharp pain made her gasp, and he covered the sound with his mouth over hers.

"I'm sorry," he said unsteadily, stilling over her. "You may have to pretend feeling that again for your husband."

At the moment she did not want to be reminded that the two of them had absolutely no future together, but as he slowly began to move again, she didn't care. Not about anything but the sensation of his body inside hers. Isabel grabbed on to his shoulders, lifting her legs to lock her heels around his hips.

Again and again he entered and retreated,

driving her into the rough horse blankets. Her body felt both a part of her and separate, all of her moving swiftly toward the edge of a very high cliff. And then abruptly she went over the edge.

"Oh, my," she squealed, muffling the sound against his shoulder. She stiffened and convulsed, shuddering.

Sullivan's own movements quickened, and then he pulled away from her, shaking. She didn't know everything, but she had a sense that lovemaking was not supposed to end that way.

"Sullivan?"

"Apologies," he grunted. "We can't have you getting with child."

She hadn't even considered that. Paling, she stroked his arm as he grabbed a cloth to clean himself. "Thank you."

"You're still ruined, my dear," he returned, softening the words by leaning down to kiss her again, very gently.

"Half the people I know considered me ruined yesterday," she said, breathing hard and still feeling weightless. "Facts be damned."

With his brief smile, Sullivan lay back, tucking her against his shoulder. "I'm glad you see it my way," he said quietly, twining his fingers through her hair.

"Your way?"

"The stupidity and backbiting arrogance of the *haute ton*."

"Oh." She wished that her brain would begin working again, because she wasn't entirely certain what he was talking about, or that she would agree with it if she was. "Not everyone's like that, you know," she ventured anyway.

"I admit the exceptions. You, Bram, Lord Quence and his family, one or two others." He lowered his fingers from her hair to draw lazy circles around her breasts.

Low heat began in her again. "Is that why you kept wanting me to order you to ruin me?" she asked, half wishing she could just keep her silence. "So that I could be one of your exceptions?"

She felt the rise and fall of his chest as he drew a breath. "You are an exception," he said after a moment. "We shouldn't stay; someone might come around to check on the horses."

"So you're finished with me now?" Isabel sat up. "You did what you needed to do, and now off you go?"

"What would you have me do, Tibby, ask your father for permission to marry you?" He scowled. "And I'm not finished with you." Putting a hand on her shoulder, he drew her in close again for another heart-stopping kiss. "This is complicated. I find myself . . . obsessed with you. Keeping my hands off you . . . I couldn't do it. I can't."

That sounded delicious. "Obsessed. I can sympathize with that feeling," she said. Unable to resist touching him, she drew a finger along his left shoulder. A hard knot in his skin stopped her. "Is this where you were wounded?"

"Yes."

She let her hand glide down to rest on his left thigh. "And this is from the splinter you got the other night?"

He chuckled quietly in the near-darkness. "Keep touching me there and we'll never leave here," he whispered. "And yes. A large splinter."

"More like a fence post," she returned, gingerly running a finger along the bandage he'd wrapped there.

"Are you talking about the wound, or my physical attributes?"

"Very amusing. And you're changing the subject."

"What subject? That I want to have you again?"

Oh, my. "That you're disparaging everyone I know. I'm not certain how I feel about that."

Sullivan climbed to his feet, naked and stunning as any Greek statue she'd ever seen. He pulled her robe off the wall and handed it to her. "You should dispose of your night rail," he said.

"I suppose I would have a difficult time explaining the fact that it's been torn in half," she agreed, becoming annoyed that he continued to avoid discussing the way he'd pulled her into his little world of hatred.

He sat again, pulling on his trousers and his boots. "And I shall see you in the morning."

"Why are you suddenly in such a hurry?"

"I'm not. You know we can't stay here."

"But . . ." *But I don't want you to leave.*

"Whatever you seem to think, I don't want you ruined."

She eyed him as he donned his shirt and tucked the tail into his trousers. As he pulled his dark waistcoat and jacket on, the answer occurred to her. He had another appointment this evening. "You're going to burgle someone else. That's why you're in such a hurry."

He helped her to her feet, curling her hair around his fingers again. "Not tonight. Tomorrow," he returned, tugging the front of her robe closed and knotting the tie for her. "Be careful, Tibby. Neither of us will be able to explain this. I'm in a hurry because if I don't leave now, if I lie here with you in the dark, I won't want to leave at all. Good night, poppet."

With a last soft kiss he was gone. Isabel stood where she was for a moment, listening to the sounds of the stable again. So that was that. He'd wanted her, he'd taken her, and now he'd decided it was perfectly acceptable both to just go off to his other amusements and to inform her in advance — *again* — that he had another burglary in mind. And she hadn't even told him not to do it, this time. Perhaps he had a reason for thinking she'd turned against her own kind, after all, and perhaps he was correct.

Putting aside the thought that he meant to risk his life by stealing a painting from someone who'd be happy to put a ball through him, now she seemed to have become an accomplice. If she said nothing, she *was* an accomplice. And if she spoke, she would be responsible for Sullivan being jailed or hanged or transported.

But even with all those doubts, foremost in her mind was the question of when she could be with him again. Oh, she'd made a terrible mistake. And what had been complicated before was now so tangled she doubted she'd ever be able to find her way through it to the other side.

CHAPTER 17

Sullivan made his way behind the Chalsey House stable. Once he was out of view, he stopped and leaned back against the wall.

For a moment he tried to form a plan of action, decide what he needed to do next, but nothing came to him. Nothing but images of Isabel spread beneath him, of the heated enjoyment on her face as he'd moved inside her, and of the abrupt disappointment there when he'd mentioned recovering another painting.

What the devil had he expected? That bedding her would make her other than what she was? "Idiot," he muttered, sinking farther into the shadows as she emerged from the stable, barefoot and her ruined gown in her hands, the robe held tightly around her lithe, otherwise nude form.

She sat on the bench just outside the door, using the gown to clean off her feet. Once she'd pulled on her slippers she took a last look around the stable yard and then ducked back into the house. That was as far as he could watch over her; once inside she was on her own.

It had never aggravated him before that he wasn't welcome inside most of the elegant houses of London; he'd simply grown up that way. It aggravated him now. Because yes, in the back of his mind the thought of having Isabel, the belle of every ball, the perfect daughter of a perfect family, had appealed to the dark parts of his soul. But in knowing her, in talking with her and holding her, he'd never met a more witty, forthright person. And he'd told her the truth. He had become obsessed.

And if he stayed about any longer tonight he would end being caught staring up at her window with a damned moon-eyed smile on his face. With a quiet curse he slipped off the Chalsey property and retrieved Achilles from the public stable where he'd stashed the stallion.

He knew bloody well what he was, and what he'd managed to do with his life despite it. Even becoming a thief hadn't bothered him — those people had acquired something that belonged to him. Now, however, for the first time in a very long time, he felt . . . wanting.

So what was he supposed to do about it? Go talk to Bram? He wasn't in the mood for jaded observations or sticky questions from the too-observant cynic. It would have been good to talk with Phin, but Phineas Bromley was somewhere in Spain. Any bit of clever strategy and logic was there with him.

As he looked up, he realized he'd turned up Bruton Street. He pulled Achilles to a stop. Directly on his left, its orderly windows overlooking the street above a precisely planted rose garden, stood Sullivan House. He'd probably find a few of his mother's paintings inside there, but he would not step foot through that front door — or any of the two dozen windows. Not for anything.

This, in fact, was probably the closest he'd been to the house in years, if ever. When he'd confronted Dunston about the missing paintings, he'd been in Warwickshire, at Dunston Abbey. And that encounter had occurred outside.

He swung out of the saddle and led Achilles to the foot of the drive. Just short of the drive, rather. For a long moment he looked up at the dark windows. Inside would be the Marquis of Dunston and his mousy wife Margaret Sullivan, the marchioness. Oliver had his own residence, but Dunston had two other brats aside from his eldest — another boy, Walter, and a young daughter named Susan.

Slowly Sullivan squatted down and picked up a loose rock from the drive. He straightened, hefting it in his hand. It was petty, and foolish, and probably beneath him, but he threw it anyway. Hard.

With a sharp crack and brittle ring, glass shattered. Mounting Achilles again, he reined in and watched as one by one lights flickered on in the windows. It didn't improve his mood any. With a grim shake of his head, he sent Achilles trotting off into the darkness again.

"What the devil happened to you?" Bram Johns asked.

Sullivan looked up from saddling Achilles. "Beg pardon?"

Bram motioned at his face. "You've gone black and blue. Not a new fashion, I hope. Looks ghastly."

He'd nearly forgotten the beating. Had that only been yesterday? "Apparently I overstep where I shouldn't," he said dryly. "What do you want?"

"Can't a friend simply stop by when the occasion presents itself?"

"For you to be awake and about before

ten o'clock in the morning, Bram, is an occasion in itself." It took a great deal of effort not to jump on Achilles and charge off to Chalsey House. He wanted to see Isabel again, and with an urgency that surprised and worried him.

"Very well, you've caught me out. Yes, I have a reason for being here."

Sullivan counted to five. "Which would be?" he prompted.

Lord Bramwell glanced at the busy stable around them. "Do you really wish me to speak of your affection for sheep here, in front of every —"

"Oh, stop it," Sullivan grumbled, noting the chuckles coming from his employees. "Outside, then."

Bram led the way outside. When they were out of everyone's earshot, he stopped. "I have a favor to ask of you. Two, actually."

Sullivan eyed him. "What are they?"

"Firstly, I'm having dinner tonight with Quence. Have luncheon with him."

Sullivan frowned, dread tightening his chest. "Why? Did something happen to Phin?"

"No. But Phin's older brother is not doing as well as we might have hoped. For some reason he likes you, so you should visit him. God knows Phin would never ask, even if he knew, so I am. Asking, that is."

Another piece of the puzzle that was Bramwell Lowry Johns. He broke female hearts with regularity, but the condition of the crippled brother of a friend was a cause for action. And there *he* was, Sullivan reflected, throwing rocks through windows. "I'll send over a note inviting myself to a late luncheon with him and Beth," he agreed, frowning. "How well is not well?"

"A cough and a low fever, according to Beth. It could be nothing, but then it could be something."

Sullivan nodded. "What's the second favor, then?"

"Don't visit Fairchild's home tonight."

That surprised him. "You're the one who told me the painting was there," he shot back.

"Yes, but the last time you house broke, the duke nearly put a hole through you, and Fairchild's got an even fouler temper and a sharper aim than Levonzy."

"You're worried about me?"

"It's entirely selfish, I assure you. You're one of the few people who has a worse father than I do. It helps me maintain a certain perspective."

"I see. Well, as luck would have it, I believe I've already been shot and shot at enough times that I'm well nigh invulnerable now. So go do whatever it is you do in the mornings, and I'll see to my own affairs."

"That's a bit harsh," Bram returned.

"Well, I'm in a hurry. I don't wish to be late."

"To your horse training appointment? I think you're safe there, Sully. If Lady Tibby was going to hand you over to the authorities, she would have done it by now."

Tibby. Mentally shaking himself free from the abrupt image of Isabel with her long blonde hair framing her face, her heated gaze steady on his as he entered her, he shrugged. "I'd prefer not to take that chance."

Bram folded his arms. "So you're going to visit Fairchild tonight?"

"Yes."

"You're taking this too far, Sullivan."

"With you as the voice of reason, I'll take my chances."

"If I had a heart, it would be wounded. What do you truly want from this? You'll never be able to show them off."

"I want justice. The rest doesn't signify." After last night he couldn't even express in words what it was he wanted any longer, but he did know one thing. These people — Dunston, especially — had taken enough from him. And if it took getting caught to finally expose the marquis for the hypocrite he was, Sullivan was willing to risk it. Or he had been, until yesterday. Until last night.

He arrived in the stable yard of Chalsey House just as the area church bells rang the ten o'clock hour. By now the stableboys knew to expect him, and Molly had already been saddled on the chance that Isabel would wish to ride her. The stable hands had left Zephyr to him; it wasn't that he didn't trust them to know their jobs, but rather that this horse would bear responsibility not only for Isabel's safety, but for her continued peace of mind.

Today he put a bridle on her again in addition to her harness, and then cinched the saddle around her middle. He led her out of her stall and, talking to her softly, placed two bags of sand over the saddle. Zephyr fidgeted a little and flicked her ears, but other than that made no sign of being distressed. "Good girl," he murmured, giving her an apple out of the barrel.

A soft breeze brushed across him through the open stable doors, a faint scent of citrus above the smell of horses and hay and leather. The hairs on his arms lifted. Isabel.

He closed his eyes for a moment as he inhaled, then pulled himself back in to the present and turned around. "Good morning," he said.

She stood in the doorway, her hunter-green riding gown snug on her slender figure, and a matching hat perched jauntily on her head. Warm desire hit him again, softly at first, and then stronger and deeper like ocean waves during a storm. God, he wanted her again.

"Good morning," she returned, color creeping up her cheeks.

"I came on time," he went on after a moment, knowing that he'd begun to babble.

"Yes, I see that you did." Her gaze swept the length of him, and his cock stirred in response. "I'd like to try riding again today."

That only reminded him that he'd ridden *her* last night. "Good. Let me work Zephyr a bit, and then I thought we might take a ride through Hyde Park."

"Out of the stable yard?" Her color fled again.

"At a walk. And I'll be right there."

"I don't know about this."

"I leave it up to you." Her older brother walked up behind her. "My lady," Sullivan finished, not certain whether he was more annoyed or grateful that they couldn't stand there just looking at one another all morning.

"What?" Lord Chalsey said, pausing to kiss his sister on the cheek. "You're going riding this morning? That's splendid, Tibby."

"I'm not certain whether I am or not."

"I'd love to go with you, but a group of us who graduated from Oxford are going up to see one of our professors. He's retiring before the next term begins."

"You mean he's retiring and you want to show off Ulysses," Isabel put in, her gaze still on Sullivan.

"Yes, yes, I can't help if I have the most splendid hunter in London. Well, actually, I can help it." With a chuckle, he offered his hand to Sullivan. "Thanks to you, Mr. Waring."

If Chalsey had any idea what he'd done last night, they would be exchanging blows rather than quips, but since he had no wish to beat or embarrass Tibby's brother, Sullivan forced a return smile and shook hands.

As the earl moved past them, Phipps in tow, Sullivan shook himself. "If you'll excuse me," he said to Isabel, motioning for her to step aside so he could leave the stable with the mare.

"Certainly, Mr. Waring."

Their hands brushed as he walked by, and he briefly squeezed her fingers, releasing her

309

before anyone could notice. Good God, this was a hundred times worse than before, when he'd wanted her without seriously thinking it could ever happen. Now her scent, her touch, her taste — they filled him so full he could barely think straight.

"Come with me," he said, just barely resisting the temptation to brush a stray strand of honey-colored hair from her face.

Nodding tightly, she followed him to the center of the yard. He let out the lead line, allowing Zephyr to trot about in a wide circle for a few moments while he watched her move with the bags of sand on her back. She had a smooth gait, thank God, because the last thing Isabel needed was a tooth-rattling every time she rode her prize mare.

"She looks very fine," Isabel said from beside him.

"So do you," he murmured back.

"Stop it."

Yes, he probably should. "Whoa, Zephyr," he said aloud, the longe whip still on the ground in front of them. The mare pranced to a halt. Taking a breath, Sullivan held the line out to Isabel. "Take her through her paces."

"But I don't know how," she protested.

"You do, but I'll be right here. Zephyr should become comfortable with your voice and your touch."

Again she gazed at him, clearly reading more into his words than what he said aloud. For a moment he thought she would refuse, put her hands behind her back, and move away as she'd done before. Instead, and after a lengthy hesitation, she held her hands out for the line.

Zephyr's ears flicked again, and she stomped one foot against the soft ground. "What do I do?" Isabel asked.

"Flip the line once, and tell her to walk on. Keep the line loose and a little ahead of her. When you want her to stop, say, 'Whoa.' Or 'Trot' if you wish her to trot. Be confident."

"That's easy for you to say," she muttered. "Don't go anywhere."

"I won't."

She took a deep breath. "Walk on, Zephyr."

Lady Darshear sat back in her chair by the sitting room window and looked at her husband. "I think we may have a problem."

Harry Chalsey, the Marquis of Darshear, took a last look at the clock on the mantel. He'd missed most of the early session of Parliament, and he wasn't certain he was happy to have stayed home this morning.

"He's helping her with something we've tried and failed at for years."

"That's not brotherly affection in his eyes."

No, it wasn't. Nor was it sisterly affection in hers. "Sending him away now might confirm those blasted rumors."

"Or it could signal that we're attempting to maintain a proper household. Harry, we have to do something. He's . . . common."

"He's not common. And he has a damned fine reputation."

"As a horse breeder! You can't want him for a son-in-law. Or worse. His own family won't recognize him. And what if he has nothing honorable in mind at all? You've seen what just rumors can do. Heaven help us if it becomes fact. Heaven help Tibby."

"Perhaps we're reading between lines that aren't there," he said after a moment, not certain he believed what he was saying, himself. "There's nothing wrong with a friendship. And as soon as the next scandal erupts, the few rumors there are about this will vanish."

"You are too lenient, Harry. Indulging Tibby in her high spirits is one thing. Allowing this to continue is not doing her — or us — any favors. Especially when she's being courted by Oliver Sullivan."

"I know that, Helen," he said more sharply. "But stepping in when no intervention is required could set her against us. And then who will she turn to?"

The marchioness frowned. "Very well. But we are all going to keep a very close eye on this. You may admire him, but that doesn't make him acceptable."

"I know. Once Tibby's able to ride, he'll be gone. And she'll be able to indulge in something new, and life will go on as it should."

"I hope you're correct. But I will not just ignore things until then."

"Nor will I."

Isabel rushed into the house to scribble out a note to Barbara Stanley, canceling their luncheon. A few weeks ago the thought that she would favor riding a horse over luncheon and shopping with Barbara would have both amused and frightened her.

But her cancellation today actually had nothing to do with horses at all. It was the fact that she would be spending a part of the day with Sullivan. There would probably be more rumors, but after last night, she couldn't bring herself to care. Not now. After all, people would carry those blasted tales whether she behaved or not.

"Ready?" he asked, guiding Molly up to the mounting block as Isabel rejoined him in the stable yard.

Of course, riding was actually involved. Squaring her shoulders, she stepped onto the block and held out her hand. "Ready," she said, grateful that she sounded steadier than she felt.

Sullivan placed her hand on his shoulder, and cupped his own hands for her to step into. Muscles flexed beneath her fingers as he boosted her up into the sidesaddle. For a moment, as she settled herself and looked down at his upturned face, at that stray hair across one green eye, she wanted to lean down and kiss him. And she didn't care who might see it.

Abruptly he cleared his throat and looked away. "You remember how to hold the reins, yes?"

She took a breath. "Yes."

He showed her a short line, which he buckled to Molly's bridle. "I'll be holding this from beside you, so you're not going anywhere you don't want to be."

Isabel nodded, gathering the reins in her hands as he'd shown her. Beside her Sullivan climbed into the saddle of the massive black Achilles, while beyond him Delvin the groom mounted another of the family's horses. *Drat.* She supposed she had to have a chaperon, though, even when the ride wasn't a social occasion.

"Stay well back, Delvin," Sullivan said on the tail of her thoughts. "Molly's as calm as they come, but I don't want anybody galloping up on us unawares."

Delvin touched his forelock. "Aye, Mr. Waring."

With an encouraging smile, Sullivan nudged Achilles in the ribs. "Let's go," he said. "Tell Molly to walk."

Trying to keep her hands from shaking, Isabel flicked the reins. "Walk on, girl," she instructed, making her voice as friendly as she could.

They started off, and she didn't fall out of the saddle. "Good girl, Molly," she whispered, patting the mare on the neck.

On his own, Sullivan probably would have been trotting or cantering or standing in the saddle as he rode up the street toward Hyde Park, but she couldn't believe she was on horseback in the first place. Walking at a very sedate pace was adventure enough. For a moment Mary's screams echoed in her mind, and her hands tightened on the reins. That couldn't happen today. Today the horse would do as *she* said. She wouldn't let it be otherwise. Sullivan wouldn't allow it to be otherwise.

A milk cart rattled by, and she tensed again. "Watch Molly's ears if you're not certain how she'll react," Sullivan's low drawl came from three feet away. "See? She heard my voice, then went back to listening for your commands."

"Yes."

"If you catch her listening to something else more than to you, remind her that you're there."

Isabel nodded. "I'm being silly, I know."

"No, you're not. You're being very brave."

"Oh, please."

The expression on his lean, handsome face remained serious. "I'm not teasing. You have a very good reason for your fear. All I can do is point out the ways you can prevent another accident from happening. You're the one who's decided to make the effort of learning."

She smiled. She couldn't help it. "Thank you, Sullivan."

Smiling back softly, he inclined his head. "You're welcome, Isabel."

As they stepped onto the Hyde Park trail, she couldn't help glancing about to see who else might be visiting. Carriages seemed to be everywhere, and without any difficulty she spotted at least a dozen riders she knew by sight, if not by name. And they would all see her riding with Sullivan Waring.

So there would be more rumors. Except that this time they would all be true. And if Sullivan was caught breaking into another house tonight . . . Oh, she didn't want to ruin this moment. In fact, she wanted a thousand more like it. But she couldn't. "May I ask you a favor?" she began, knowing she was heading straight for disaster.

"What is it?"

"Don't break into anyone's home tonight."

His jaw clenched. "Isabel —"

"You see all those people looking at us?" she broke in. "I don't mind that they know we're . . . friends. I don't even think I care what rumors they might conjure. But do you know what will happen to you — to me, now — if you're discovered? Or if you're hurt?" Her voice caught.

" 'Friends,' " he repeated darkly. "Back to that again, are we?"

Oh, dear. "Are you going to leave me here if I say yes?"

Lips tightening, he shook his head. "I won't leave you stranded, regardless."

"Then yes, I think we are becoming friends. And as a friend, I'm asking you to please stop risking your freedom and your life to —"

"And *your* reputation."

"Yes, mine, too."

"Selfish."

Men and their vendettas. "*You're* selfish," she retorted, warming to the argument. "And you can't even see it, can you? I had no idea that that painting Oliver gave us actually belonged to someone else. Who are you trying to hurt?"

"No one," he said stiffly. "I want what's mine. If I attempted to get it legally, you know I would lose."

She eyed him. "You're trying to hurt Lord Dunston. Your father."

"Do not call him th—"

"And then there's me," she pressed, unwilling to begin a fight over how much his father influenced Sullivan's life, whether he would acknowledge that or not. "Last night has consequences for me, whether you . . . took precautions or not."

"You came to me. Don't blame me for the loss of your virginity, Isabel."

Her cheeks warmed. "I don't mean that. For heaven's sake. You are in my life, Sullivan, and I like having you there. Generally."

"Ah. I'll do as I please, then. As will you, I expect."

"What's that supposed to mean?"

He jerked on the reins, and Achilles whinnied and stopped. Belatedly she halted Molly, as well, before she reached the end of the short lead line. "I don't understand why you're trying to protect Lord Fairchild," he half growled. "He has something that belongs to me. And he'd be happy as anyone else to spread nasty rumors about you."

Fairchild? That was his next burglary? "I'm not trying to defend him. I'm saying he may not be aware that he's done anything wrong. And I'm asking you not to endanger yourself. Besides, you can't rob him tonight. He and Lady Fairchild are holding a masquerade ball."

"I'm aware of that. You're attending, I presume?"

"Sullivan, don't do this."

He looked at her for a long moment. "Would you listen to *my* guidance in *your* life? Would you bid Tilden good day and good riddance if I asked you to?"

Oh, goodness. He was jealous. A thrill ran down her spine. "I —"

"We obviously come from two different places, and have two different lives, Isabel. I want another night with you. More than one. But we don't belong together. In daylight you're my employer. And don't

319

think I haven't noticed you looking about to see whether any of your acquaintances have seen us together." He drew a breath. "I should stay away from you. You make me forget things I should always remember."

"Sullivan, I don't care about rumors," she said, pain stabbing into her heart as she realized that if she couldn't bring him to his senses she might very well never see him again after today. "I called us friends, and we are."

"I don't want to be your friend." He looked away. "Not just your friend. It's not enough."

"But you —"

"You'll be riding Zephyr by the end of the week. After that, you won't have need of my 'friendship' any longer. That will be safer — better — for both of us."

He clucked at Achilles, and the horses started off again. And abruptly the most significant event of the day was not that she was riding a horse, but that within a week's time she would see the last of Sullivan Waring. He was right: Friendship might be part of it, but it wasn't enough. And she had no idea how it could ever be more. Whether she wanted it to be was an even more complicated question.

CHAPTER 18

The idea of dressing as a butterfly had seemed a brilliant one. In practice, however, Isabel was beginning to realize that the costume had certain flaws. For one thing, the opalescent wings had nearly knocked the glass of Madeira out of her mother's hand, and now she was faced with Eloise Rampling, who'd dressed as a yellow butterfly.

Personally she preferred the deep blues and purples she'd chosen, and the swirls of makeup in the same color that glittered on her cheeks. Tonight she felt free and exotic, and even with the curious, sly looks she'd been receiving, enough gentlemen seemed taken by her that her dance card was nearly full.

She'd saved an early waltz at Oliver's request, and she smiled when she saw him in his tiger's half-mask making his way over through the crowd. "Good evening," she said. "You look very striking."

He'd worn black with an orange waistcoat, sleek black leather gloves adding to his rather predatory appearance. It was quite . . . enticing, actually, and for a moment she felt guilty that she found Sullivan's half-brother attractive.

He inclined his head and held out his hand for her dance card. "Tilden's carriage suffered a broken wheel," Sullivan's low voice came, "and he won't be attending until much later."

She blanched. Thankful that the streaks of color across her face would cover her loss of composure, she gripped Sullivan's black-clothed arm. "What are you doing?" she whispered fiercely.

"Claiming a waltz," he said, writing *Tiger* beside the dance and then handing the card back to her. "I see you've saved one for me."

"But —"

He took her hand, squeezing her fingers lightly as he bowed over it. "I wanted to see you somewhere other than the stable. Tell me to leave, and I'll make myself scarce."

"How did you know Oliver would be dressed as a tiger?"

Sullivan gave a short smile. "I have my sources."

"Have you . . . retrieved anything yet?"

"Not yet. Later."

He meant to dance with her and then go steal a painting. Being caught out at either activity could be deadly, and so she would never admit to him that she felt just the slightest bit excited by it all. "Are you trying to be discovered?" she asked instead.

"Not tonight."

"Oliver," her brother said, coming forward to shake his hand. "I should have opted for a more dangerous beast, I think."

"Nonsense, Phillip," Isabel put in, so Sullivan wouldn't have to do more than smile beneath the half-mask, "a stag is very majestic."

"The antlers are blasted heavy. I'll grant you that."

The music for the waltz began, and Sullivan held out his gloved hand to her. "Excuse us, Phillip," Isabel said, and clasped the waiting fingers.

They walked over to the large, crowded dance floor, and Sullivan slid an arm around her waist. She was just about to ask him whether he actually knew how to waltz when he swung her gracefully into the dance.

Oh, yes, he could waltz. He moved like a natural athlete, with the same easy grace he showed in the stable yard. From behind the orange and black half-mask, pale green eyes glittered at her.

"You are insane," she whispered. "Completely mad."

"As you know, I'm fairly comfortable with wearing a mask."

"You're surrounded by dozens of the people you've stolen from. What if I decide to turn you in?"

"That won't happen, poppet," he returned.

"And how do you know that?"

"Because you're a bit mad, yourself. You are dancing with a horse breeder." He gave his brief smile. "Should I dance with anyone else this evening?"

"I think that could be exceedingly dangerous." Besides, she didn't want him dancing with any other ladies. He'd come to dance with her.

"You had no trouble finding partners for this evening?" Sullivan asked. "Your dance card looked full."

"Nearly so. But my dance card is my concern. Not yours."

"I could dispute that, but this waltz is too brief, as it is."

He drew her subtly closer. All she would have to do was lean up just a little, and she could kiss him. Everyone would think it was

Oliver, so Sullivan would be safe, but she would still be ruined. She sighed.

"Penny for your thoughts, Tibby," Sullivan murmured.

"I was just thinking that I'd like to kiss you right now."

Sullivan lost a step, and they nearly stumbled. "Lucifer, Tibby."

She grinned. It felt powerful, to know that she could unsettle this man. Heaven knew he unsettled her, but in a way she was very much coming to enjoy. "What if my dance card had been empty?"

"I would have danced with you."

"And what if it had been full?"

"I would have clubbed someone over the head and danced with you."

He smiled as he spoke, but considering some of his previous actions, he might very well be serious. As they swayed and turned to the music, she let herself sink into his embrace, following his sure steps and guided by his strong arms. Dancing with him was magnificent. For a moment she allowed herself to pretend that he wasn't there in secret, that he'd been invited. She would love to dance every dance with him. And if he'd asked to call on her, she would have said yes in an instant.

When she finally glanced away from him,

a great many of the other guests were watching. It might have been because they made a striking couple, or it could have been the ridiculous smile she wore because she couldn't help herself. Either way, two things were very clear: She liked Sullivan Waring very much, and he needed to make an exit before Oliver arrived.

As the dance ended, far too soon, he joined in the applause and then took her hand in his. "I need to go," he murmured, running his gloved thumb along her palm. "If anyone aside from Tilden realizes something is amiss, claim ignorance. As far as you know, I'm him."

She nodded, and with another smile he vanished into the crowd. He needn't be so concerned about her reputation; aside from that very first kiss, she'd gotten herself into this. And tonight she could have declined to dance with him. She'd wanted to dance with him.

"I say, Lady Butterfly," a stout boar's head said, approaching, "I believe this quadrille is mine."

Isabel held out her hand. "Of course, Mr. Henning. Or Master Boar, rather."

Francis Henning snorted. "It was only after I arrived here that I realized everyone calling me a boar wasn't trying to insult me.

You know, a boar, or a bore."

She forced a laugh, hoping she sounded as though she appreciated the rather . . . silly attempt at humor. At least he wanted to dance. "Then, to avoid trouble, I'll call you Mr. Henning."

As the dance began, she glanced about for Sullivan again, but he was gone. He'd begun their acquaintance as a mystery. Unlike any other mystery that had caught her attention, however, the more she discovered about him, the more interesting he became. And the fact that he'd come by tonight to steal a painting seemed secondary. Because he'd also come to dance with her.

Sullivan placed his latest acquisition — re-acquisition, rather — on the wall in the small, concealed back room of his cottage. Twelve recovered paintings. Two to go. And then he supposed he could stop, though it seemed a shame to do so when every burglary served as another jab to Dunston's well-fed gut.

He lifted the lantern, the only light in the room. He'd told Tibby not to trouble herself over him, and as far as he knew no one in Fairchild House had had the slightest clue that he'd visited them tonight — and right in the middle of a bloody soiree. They would discover the theft in the morning, and whether they blamed it on one of their invited guests or not, shortly thereafter Dunston would hear about it, as well. And he would know who the real culprit happened to be. Good. Threats and beatings, and still he did exactly as he pleased.

Before he left the room he emptied his pockets of the silver card salver, the engraved pocket watch, and the pair of ivory-handled dueling pistols he'd liberated along with the Francesca Waring Perris painting. The trinkets joined the dozens of others he'd acquired, because while he wanted Dunston to know who was behind the thefts, Sullivan preferred that Bow Street did not.

Slinging his coat over his shoulder, he closed and locked the door behind him. His housekeeper made a fair roast, but he didn't want Mrs. Howard connecting him with several thousands of quid worth of stolen property.

His bedchamber lay upstairs, but it was barely one o'clock in the morning and he didn't feel ready for sleep. Instead a restless energy coursed through him, as it often did when he managed to commit a burglary and vanish back into the night unscathed. This time it was worse; he'd danced with Isabel.

In front of everyone.

In the past he might have sought out one of Society's female outcasts to keep him company for the remainder of the night. Street whores were too pitiful and desperate to tempt him. But the chits who'd known better, who'd reached too high and fallen, or made the wrong choice in male companionship, those who knew what they were getting into — them he could appreciate.

Tonight, however, he didn't want some random woman; he wanted Isabel. And at the same time he worried that he would be responsible for making her into one of the fashionable fallen. Tonight had been risky enough. Did he dare make it worse? "Damnation," he muttered, heading into the front room to rummage about for a bottle of claret and settling for whiskey.

After he downed half a glass, though, he set it aside again and stood. Then he grabbed his dark thievery coat and left the house. At the least he could reassure himself that Tibby had returned home safely, and that she didn't have to worry about being ruined in the morning papers. Yes, that was all he wanted. To talk with her again.

Deciding that Achilles had done enough today, he saddled his bay gelding, Paris, and rode into Mayfair. He left the beast at the local public stable, having to awaken the annoyed groom to do it, and went the last half mile on foot. All the way to Chalsey House he debated again whether he should even be there, much less go in to see Isabel.

The lights, however, still flickered inside. Apparently the masquerade ball hadn't provided enough excitement for the evening. Or it had been so momentous that the Chalseys were still discussing it. And they weren't alone. As he moved closer, using the shadows of the elm trees lining the street for cover, he caught sight of a pair of carriages stopped on the shallow drive. The Stanley coat of arms would be her friend Barbara and her parents. The other one brought a scowl to his face. Tilden. The late-arriving tiger remained in the hunt, apparently.

The front door opened, letting light flood onto the drive, and he swiftly ducked into the shadows. Lady Barbara, her younger sister, and her parents, together with the members of the Chalsey household, stepped outside to say their good nights. Sullivan drew a slow breath as he caught sight of Isabel. She still wore her gown of deep blue and violet. Even with her wings detached she looked ethereal, like a figure of mist and twilight, her blonde hair hanging loose in the back and woven with ribbons the same color as her dress. A precious gem among stones. In a better, more perfect world, *his* gem.

Lord Tilden had remained inside; apparently he hadn't finished with his visit yet. As the family returned to the house, Sullivan closed his eyes. He should leave. He should return home and go to bed, or find some pretty blonde harlot who wouldn't care which name he called her.

Oliver would continue courting Isabel, wed her, and she'd deliver some plausible excuse for the loss of her virginity. As long as Sullivan Waring's name wasn't mentioned as the deflowerer, Tilden probably wouldn't care. They would have lovely children, young lords and ladies, and he would never set eyes on any of them unless someone came to purchase a prize horse. He'd certainly never be invited to the wedding — not that he would attend. Not that he would ever want to see her given away to someone else.

"Devil take it," he murmured, and started back toward the north side of the house. He couldn't have her forever, but he had her now, and would take whatever she was willing to give. That was what he'd been reduced to: scavenging and begging for scraps.

The vine-covered trellis climbing the wall

passed by young Douglas's window rather than his sister's, but just above that the roof flattened out. Some of his burglary skills had uses he hadn't imagined before this.

Once up on the roof he moved quietly back until he was crouched five feet above the third window. When he'd first broken in there, Bram had given him a sketch of the entire house. One could never be too cautious, and he didn't like being left with only one way in or out. Being caught might cause more humiliation for the Marquis of Dunston, but that couldn't happen until he'd exhausted every other means of revenge.

Gripping the overhang with his fingers, he hung over the side of the house. Pushing gently against the window with one toe, he felt it give. That made things easier. He wedged the toe of his boot into the opening he'd made, and swung the glass wide open. After that it was a simple matter to let go with one hand until he grabbed the top of the casement and then eased himself into the room. Getting out would be another problem entirely, but at the moment he didn't care.

The second after he stepped inside her bedchamber the door handle rattled, and he ducked behind the large mahogany wardrobe. Isabel's maid entered the room. "Who left you open?" she said to the window, closing and latching it before she set out Tibby's night rail, made down the bed, and stoked the fire in the small fireplace.

Sullivan remained motionless in the corner, glad he'd worn dark colors. The maid left the bedchamber door open as she exited, and after a silent count to ten, he edged away from the wall and toward the hallway.

He could hear them somewhere downstairs, talking and laughing. Tilden's smooth voice made him clench his jaw, but this was not the time or the place for a brawl, however much he owed Oliver a black eye and a good nose-bloodying. He might win the fight, but he would lose any chance of ever seeing Isabel again. It was more important that everyone seemed to be in good humor; they hadn't discovered his ruse, then.

Finally he heard the good nights, and the front door opening and closing. His heart began to beat faster — not with apprehension, but with anticipation. He might be a nonentity to the rest of good Society, but he hadn't become one to Isabel. Not yet, anyway.

Returning to his shelter behind the wardrobe, he waited as footsteps and voices began trailing up the stairs. It seemed like hours before Isabel and her maid entered her room, closing the door behind them. Soft citrus spun into the air, and he went hard.

"Shall I lay out your morning dress, my lady?" the maid asked, as she helped Isabel unbutton the back of her stunning gown.

Sullivan saw her glance toward the wardrobe, and he deliberately moved, putting a finger over his lips. Isabel gasped.

"What is it, my lady?"

"Oh, it's nothing," Isabel said hurriedly. "A yawn. Penny, you may go. I'll see to the rest myself."

"But your gown —"

"I'll manage. Thank you. I'm just frightfully tired."

The maid dipped a curtsy. "Very well, my lady. Shall I wake you at nine o'clock again?"

"Yes. That will be fine. Good night."

"Good night, Lady Isabel."

As soon as the door closed, she stalked up to Sullivan. "What the devil are you doing in my bedchamber?" she hissed.

"That wasn't the reception I was hoping for," he said dryly, unable to resist reaching out to stroke her bare throat with his fingers.

"Does this mean you decided against robbing Fairchild House after all?"

"No. The painting's safe in my house."

"Sulli—"

"I just wanted to make certain that nothing happened to you after I left. That no one had any idea I was there." Running his fingers down her arm, he took her hand. "Are you well?"

"Yes. Oliver knows something, but he didn't accuse anyone of anything. Apparently several ladies saw his skill in dancing with me, and were interested in claiming the last waltz of the evening."

He drew her hand up to his lips, kissing her knuckles. He felt her fingers tremble beneath his, and smiled a little. "Good."

"He'll know tomorrow that you burgled Fairchild's house. And he'll know for certain that it was you I waltzed with."

Sullivan felt his smile fade. "If he asks directly, you have to tell him that you thought he was the tiger, being mysterious. I doubt he'll press the issue. He can't, without admitting I bested him."

" 'Bested him,' " she repeated. "Please tell me that I'm not some sort of prize in a tug-of-war."

"You're not." Yes, it had crossed his mind, but not any longer.

"Humph." Isabel pulled her hand free and

turned her back on him. "Undo my dress."

"As you wish," he murmured, shifting her long blonde hair over her shoulder so he could reach the row of buttons running down her back. As he opened each one, he kissed the skin he'd bared. "Does this mean I'm to stay?" he asked between kisses.

"I haven't decided yet," she returned, her voice breathy and not quite controlled. "You did dance rather well tonight."

"Thank you. So did you. It made me wish that wings were fashionable riding attire."

He wanted to ask her what interesting things Oliver had said to her when he finally appeared, but that would be a sure way to get him thrown out the window, and it was a good twenty feet to the very prickly-looking rosebushes below. Aside from that, he wasn't entirely certain that he *did* want to know whether she found Lord Tilden's attentions flattering, or whether she would accept when he offered for her. Because he would offer for her; Sullivan was certain of that.

"Perhaps this will help to persuade you," he said aloud, slipping the dress forward over her shoulders, letting his hands drift down to graze her breasts. He lingered there, circling his fingertips closer and closer until he pinched her nipples lightly between thumb and forefinger.

She gasped, sagging back against his chest as he continued his ministrations. It fascinated him, that she could be so sought-after as a wife and yet he was the first one inside her bed, inside her body. She fascinated him, probably too much. A sane man, even a heathen such as he, would have thought twice — or thrice — about bedding a young lady in her father's own house.

He'd had only one thought, and it had been a constant one almost since he'd first kissed her. And even last night in the stable hadn't been enough. Not nearly. In fact, that had only made his yearning for her worse.

Pushing the gown down past her waist, he lowered his hand to her stomach, and then farther, slipping his fingers through her curls and pressing up against her. God, she was damp for him. Forcibly turning her to face him, he bent his head down to kiss her.

She opened her mouth to him, her tongue flitting between his teeth and making him groan. Isabel slipped her hands beneath his jacket, pushing the heavy thing off his shoulders. He shrugged his arms out of it and dropped it to the floor. "Poppet," he murmured against her mouth, sliding his arms around the swell of her hips and pulling her up against him.

In his arms she seemed so fragile, but she had more courage than some soldiers he'd known. In order to keep him under her control she'd chosen what had probably been for her the most terrifying course she could imagine. And today she'd ridden a horse in Hyde Park.

Isabel pulled his shirt free, her warm fingers gliding up his chest, bare skin against bare skin. His cock strained at his trousers, the ache painful and welcome at the same time. He yanked his shirt off over his head so he could resume kissing her.

"I wasn't worried about me, you know," Isabel muttered, going to work on his trousers. "I just didn't want you to get in any more trouble."

"Me get into trouble?" he repeated, lifting her in his arms to carry her to the bed. "You *are* trouble, Isabel."

Sullivan sat on the edge of her bed so he could remove his boots. Both they and he seemed incongruous in a bedchamber filled with lace pillows and bed hangings, and yellow and pink flowers and clippings of French gowns from the latest fashion plates.

"What are you looking at?" she asked, sitting up behind him. Her hands exploring the muscles of his back and shoulders made him shudder.

"Your perfect life," he admitted quietly, mindful that her younger brother had the room next to hers. "I truly don't belong here."

"But you are here," she returned, pulling at him until he gave in and lay back. "And if I'd asked you to go when I saw you lurking in the corner, you would have."

"I wasn't lurking." He looked up at her. "And are you so certain I would have left?"

"From the moment you broke into this house," she answered, leaning down over him and kissing his chest with a feather-light touch that stole the air from his lungs, "you've left me half mad with annoyance and frustration, but you've also been the most . . . intuitive and honest man I've ever met."

The compliment made him smile. "You neglected to mention lust. I think that's persuaded you more than anything else."

"It has not."

"Are you certain?" He lifted his head, taking one of her breasts in his mouth.

She moaned, the splayed fingers of her hands digging into his chest. God, he wanted her. But it wasn't just that. He liked conversing with her. And dancing with her. A few of her peers might be polite to him, but if they conversed at all, it was about horses. With her, he could chat — and argue — about anything. He liked arguing with her.

Sullivan finished removing his trousers and went back to kissing her. Whatever his body craved, simply putting her on her back and rutting wouldn't do. He might not be a gentleman, but he wasn't an animal, either.

"Sullivan," she murmured shakily, jumping as he trailed his hand up the inside of her thighs, "may I touch you?"

She *was* touching him. For a moment he frowned, before he realized where her gaze was. "Please do."

He steeled himself, leaning back on his elbows, as her hesitant fingers stroked his cock, then wrapped around it. It would have been easy to let go right then, but he gritted his jaw and fought against it as she explored him.

"This feels good, doesn't it?" she whispered, her voice growing huskier. She stroked along his length again.

"Yes, it does," he grated, trying to keep his eyes from rolling back into his head. He reached down to take her hands, pulling her away from him. "Time for another riding lesson, Isabel."

"Wha— *Oh,*" she returned, her eyes widening. "Show me."

Guiding her right leg over his hips until she straddled him, Sullivan sat up to kiss her again. Then he put his hands on her slim hips and pulled her down, watching as his member slid slowly up inside her. Her warm, tight heat engulfed him, and he moaned again. "Isabel."

He showed her, up and down, up and down, while he lifted his hips to meet her. She learned quickly, and he gave in to the pleasure of it all, thrusting up into her, teasing at her breasts until she gasped and climaxed. Sullivan wrapped his arms around her back, twisting them until he was on top and she lay on her back looking up at him. Harder and faster, deeper he pushed and retreated, until he felt himself crossing the edge.

At the last moment he left her, holding her tightly against him as he came. They lay tangled together for a long moment until he could breathe again. Then he rose and went to find one of her pretty monogrammed kerchiefs so they could clean themselves.

As he lay down again beside her, she slipped her head onto his shoulder and he curled an arm around her. "Sullivan," she whispered, her breathing still hard and her pulse fast under his fingers, "you feel very good."

He chuckled quietly. "So do you, poppet."

Too good, in fact. For Lucifer's sake, he nearly hadn't left her. He would have risked ruining the remainder of her life simply because he could barely stand the thought of not . . . finishing with her. Him. The child of exactly such a mistake.

"Oliver escorted us home tonight," she said after a moment, her fingers absently roaming his chest. "He finds every way he can to ask whether you've been here or not without actually mentioning you. It was almost ridiculous tonight, the way he couldn't ask why I told him I'd already waltzed with a tiger."

"That's because according to the Sullivan family, I don't exist," he returned. "It makes it difficult for him to not tolerate me publicly."

"He's been very nice to *me*. I know you detest him, and I don't like the way he talks to you and about you, but when you consider it, neither of you are to blame for anything."

Except for hiring thugs to beat him, but that was a private matter to be settled just between Oliver and him. "Perhaps not for the beginning of it," he said aloud, "but for our actions since we became old enough to know better, yes, we can be blamed."

"You have reasons for your anger. Both of you. I understand that. But you needn't make things so difficult for yourselves, or for one another."

"How else would you have us — me — behave?"

"With more tolerance."

"Tolerance doesn't erase sins, Isabel."

She might have thought he referred to the burglaries, but he could be blamed for much worse than that. He'd made a possibly fatal misstep; he'd begun to fall very hard for the daughter of a nobleman.

CHAPTER 19

Isabel gazed out her window into the dim predawn darkness. "How in the world did you get in here?" she asked. "Someone surely would have seen you coming through the front doors last night."

Sullivan came up behind her, his warm hand sliding down beneath her robe to cup one breast. Sighing unsteadily, she leaned back against his chest. Four hours. She'd never felt as decadent, or as sated, in her life. And his touch still made her tremble.

"I swung down from the roof," he said matter-of-factly, leaning down to brush his lips against the nape of her neck.

Oh, goodness. "You won't be able to leave that way."

"Thinking about how to get rid of me already?"

Thankfully he didn't sound annoyed. "It's nearly daylight," she returned. "I think we both know what'll happen if you're seen here with me."

"Yes. A convent or life in the country for you, and transportation or a hanging for me, most likely."

"Not for this," she protested, reaching around to knock him on the hip. "You would only lose your livelihood because no one would ever purchase a horse from you again."

"Perhaps I should just jump out the window and be done with it, then."

Through the trees down below she made out a milk cart rattling down the street. Some of the servants were likely already awake, then. "I'll check the hallway; you follow me."

"No. I'll manage. Get back in bed, poppet." Turning her to face him, he kissed her softly on the lips.

"Sulli—"

"I'll see you in" — he pulled out a battered pocket watch — "five hours."

He released her, starting for the door. Isabel felt abruptly cold, inside and out. She followed him, grabbing his wrist, and he stopped.

"What is it?"

"May I ask you a question?"

Sullivan nodded, his elegant brow lowering.

"If . . . if circumstances were different, would you still . . ." She trailed off, not certain how to ask the question, and even less sure she wanted to hear the answer. She seemed to be careening straight toward disaster, though, and the more she knew about the path ahead, the better. Hopefully. "Would you still like me?" she finished.

He looked at her for a long moment, his eyes showing green and serious as the sun neared the eastern horizon. "If circumstances were different," he said slowly, pulling her up against him again, "I would knock at your front door in the middle of the day and ask your father for permission to court you."

For a second it looked as though he'd intended to say something different, and her heart stammered. Did he care that much for her? Was he thinking the same things she'd begun to daydream about? His presence had drawn her from the very beginning. Now, though, he didn't need to be anywhere in sight for her to be consumed with thoughts of him.

"This is not going to end well, is it?" she whispered.

He drew a finger along her cheek. "No," he murmured back. "Not as far as I'm concerned." Sullivan kissed her. "And if you knew what was good for you, you would dismiss me from your service and hire someone else today."

As he released her and quietly pulled open her bedchamber door, Isabel knew that he was absolutely right. But the moment he vanished from sight, closing the door behind him, she wanted him back there again.

They were both being stupid, and reckless, and she'd never felt more conflicted. He should not have been there, they should not have been together, and at the same time she was quite certain that she would do it all over again in a fast heartbeat.

But what happened next? What did she want to happen tomorrow, or the next day, or in a year?

A tear plopped onto her arm. Slowly she brushed it away. The only thing she could hope for was that no one else discovered her secret, and that the gossips would find some other hapless target. She wouldn't be participating in that fun, however. Lately she'd developed an aversion to speaking ill of other people.

Isabel donned her night rail and crawled back beneath the disheveled covers. Her sheets, though, smelled like him, stirring desire even after a night of indulgement. She tossed and turned restlessly for a quarter of an hour, then rose to go sit by the window and attempt to read.

She jerked upright as a knock sounded at her door. "Come in," she called, blinking. Good heavens, it was light outside. How long had she dozed in her reading chair?

Douglas hurried into the room, shutting the door behind him. "Did you hear? Oh, of course not. But what are you doing out of bed?"

"I'm reading," she lied, setting the neglected book aside and standing. "What time is it?"

"Half eight. I wanted to wake you half an hour ago, but I thought you might kick me if I did."

"Very wise of you. What did I not hear?"

"Alders got it from the venison man that Lord Fairchild was burgled last night. And listen to this — apparently it happened *during* the masquerade. Mayfair's screaming about the Marauder. Waring's going to get himself caught, if he keeps taking chances like that. Did you know he would be there?"

"What makes you think it was Sullivan?" she asked, wondering why she bothered with the deception and already knowing the answer to that question. She wanted it to be someone else.

"Zooks, Tibby, give me some credit. A

painting was taken. According to Alders's source, anyway."

" 'Alders's source'?" she repeated. "He's a butler."

"With a good ear for news. You know it was Waring, Tibby. I like him. You know I do. But he's got to stop stealing from people we're acquainted with. If it ever gets out that we knew what he was up to, no one will ever speak to us again. Or we might even be arrested."

"Well, he'll be here at ten o'clock. I'll mention that to him."

"Oh, that reminds me. Oliver sent over a note. He's coming by in an hour, and inquires whether you'd like to go for a morning drive in Hyde Park."

She frowned. "He might have mentioned that last night." Wonderful. Another complication. If Lord Tilden ever — *ever* — found out with whom she'd been sharing her bed, there would be bloodshed. She was certain of it. And oddly enough, preventing that was the only reason now that she continued to see him.

Douglas grinned. "Perhaps he dreamed of you and felt inspired."

Isabel knocked him in the side of the head. "You're an evil boy, and one day I hope you meet a young lady who drives you mad."

"I already have you."

"Go away, and send Penny up so I may dress, will you?"

He sketched a bow. "As you wish."

That reminded her again of Sullivan. "Stop it. I am not imperious."

"But the entire male population of the *ton* worships you, *ma petite*," her brother cooed, taking her hand and bowing over it. "We would all die horribly for you."

She shook him off, grinning reluctantly. "If you'd seen me at the Fordham soiree, you wouldn't be saying that."

"Phillip told me. Eloise Rampling is a damned backbiting bagpipe."

"Douglas," she chastised.

"Well, don't let her little lies bother you. Fairchild's went well, didn't it?"

"I had a dozen dance partners." And she'd scarcely noticed any of them, or the dances, when she stood to one side. The man she'd most wanted to dance with had been there. Nothing else mattered.

"Go driving with Tilden, then. That'll show everyone."

It might help to repair her reputation, at that. Knowing how little the two half-brothers liked one another, though, it also made her feel like a traitor. Discovering a mystery and participating in a deception were two very different things. Isabel rubbed her temple.

She shooed Douglas out of the room and sat to brush out her hair. By the time Oliver arrived, she and Penny had managed to turn her out presentably, and she'd headed downstairs to devour her breakfast. Being with Sullivan certainly left her famished. "Good morning," she said, dipping a shallow curtsy as the viscount strolled into the morning room.

"And here I am yet again," Oliver said, bowing his head in return. "Your household must be tired of seeing me so often."

"Nonsense. Thank you for inviting me to go with you."

"My pleasure." He held out his arm. "Shall we?"

With Penny and Oliver's liveried groom sitting on the narrow bench behind the seat, Oliver drove the phaeton to Hyde Park. At midmorning it was crowded, and she braced herself, ready to be as charming as possible to everyone they met.

It took less than five minutes for her to realize that they weren't going to meet much of anyone. Carriages mysteriously turned down other paths, horsemen suddenly saw something of interest in the opposite direction, walkers had flowers to examine on the far side of the beds.

So no one had forgotten the rumors Eloise Rampling had worked so diligently to spread. Evidently she wasn't as enticing without her butterfly wings. She'd truly thought Eloise had been her friend. Some of the people who avoided her today had been her friends, as well, though apparently the word didn't mean the same thing to them that it did to her.

When she looked over at Oliver, his lean face bore a grim, angry expression. As he caught her gaze, he put on a strained smile. "Everyone seems a bit preoccupied today," he offered.

"Yes, I suppose so."

He'd heard the rumors; he knew precisely why no one slowed to speak with them. With Oliver present the worst anyone could do was pretend not to see them; if she'd been alone, she would likely have been given the cut direct. And as they turned back to Chalsey House she hoped that for once Sullivan would have come and gone already.

Oliver's restraint actually surprised her a little, considering his previous venomous reaction to his half-brother. And it probably meant something that he was still willing to socialize with her even with the rumors of her infatuation with a horse breeder flying about. Isabel stifled a scowl. Perhaps she should like Oliver more than she did.

As they pulled into the stable yard a groom came out to hold the team, and Oliver hopped to the ground. "I apologize," she said quietly, as he came around to help her down from her seat.

"You've nothing to apologize for," he returned. "You've done nothing but show charity. It's not your fault your good deeds have been abused by others with less pure intentions than your own."

"I prefer to think that an innocent conversation was misinterpreted for no reason other than malice," she offered, trying not to hesitate as she said the word "innocent." It didn't seem as though she'd ever had anything innocent in mind where Sullivan Waring was concerned.

Lord Tilden smiled at her. "You are good to say so. But don't be so charitable that you allow harm to come to you, or to your reputation." His gaze moved beyond her, and his eyes narrowed. Before she could open her mouth to respond, he'd pushed past her.

She whipped around to see Sullivan emerging from the stable, Zephyr's reins in his hand. *Oh no, oh no.*

"You have some damned nerve, coming here yet again after the trouble you've caused," Oliver snapped, closing on his half-brother.

Sullivan sent a glance his way, then continued with what he was doing. Her heart pounded, as much from seeing him in daylight as from what was likely to happen next. "Oliver!" she called.

Lord Tilden slowed. "Go inside, Isabel."

"Only if you'll sit to have some tea with me," she returned, her gaze on Sullivan. The muscles in his jaw clenched, but otherwise he gave no sign he could hear either of them.

"I'll join you in a moment. If you're too kind to do what's right, I'll do it for you."

Gathering her skirts, Isabel rushed across the yard, putting herself between the two tall men. "You will not do anything," she snapped, backing toward Sullivan as she faced down the advancing viscount.

"Move aside, Isabel," Oliver ordered.

"There's no need to put yourself between us, my lady," Sullivan said. "Lord Tilden wouldn't dare begin a fight with me face-to-face. It wouldn't look at all proper. He likes to hire fists to keep his own from getting bloodied."

"I have no idea what you're babbling

about," the viscount retorted.

"Don't flatter yourself. You're not that clever, Tilden."

Isabel glanced behind her at Sullivan. "Your face. That was Oliver's doing?"

"Not according to him. But then he's never done anything improper, according to him."

"Move aside, Isabel. This doesn't concern you."

A hand gently settled on her shoulder. "It's fine, Tibby," Sullivan murmured. "Go inside."

"My God."

At the sound of the exclamation, she looked back at Oliver. His angry gaze had moved from Sullivan to her. More specifically, to her shoulder, where Sullivan still touched her. In the same moment, the blood left her own face. *He knew.*

"You're finished, Waring," Lord Tilden spat. He glared at her for another moment. "Poplolly." Without another word he turned on his heel, stalked back to his phaeton, and climbed into the seat.

"Oh, no," Isabel breathed, her heart beating so fast she began to feel dizzy.

"I would have let him leave," Sullivan grated, "except for what he just called you." He dropped the lead line and strode toward the drive.

"You think I care about that?" she retorted. "He said you were finished."

Sullivan stopped. "That bit doesn't worry me."

"I don't know why not. And please see to Zephyr. I don't want her running off because someone called me a foul name."

His jaw working, Sullivan returned to the mare and caught her reins. "That's the only part I'm concerned with." He tugged on Zephyr's reins and walked the mare forward again.

Isabel followed him. "I don't think you should take his threat so lightly," she went on, nearly treading on his boot heels.

"He's not going to do anything. He can't."

"Forgive me for not simply taking your word for it. If he accuses you publicly of wrongdoing, and me of being with you, name-calling will be the least of my worries."

"He's his father's darling. If he wants to keep his inheritance, he'll have to do exactly as Dunston says. And Dunston doesn't want a public scandal anywhere close to him. You and your reputation are therefore perfectly safe, my sweet one."

"I wasn't referring to . . . us," she said, gesturing between them and then self-consciously glancing about the yard. For heaven's sake, if Oliver didn't ruin them, she would take care of it herself. "I meant the robberies. You robbed my house. I hired you the very next day. And everyone knows I got at least a glimpse of the burglar."

He sent her a slow smile that made her mouth dry. "You've done more than get a glimpse."

"Pay attention to what I'm saying. For heaven's sake." If Oliver went against Dunston's wishes, it wouldn't be her reputation that would hang by the neck on Tyburn Hill. "This might all be a game to you, but I am worried."

"About your ability to find a proper and worthy husband. I know that." His grip on the reins tightened, then loosened again. Broad shoulders lifted and fell with his deep breath. "Then I suppose our fun is over."

Isabel blinked. "What?"

"You're worried about your future. We both know I'm not going to be a part of it. So stand back and let me work Zephyr. Let Oliver have his tantrum and then tell him you were just . . . infatuated with me because you'd never conversed with a horse breeder before. Oliver is the one you want, isn't he?"

For a brief second he sounded like a boy

whose best toy was being taken away and given to someone else. Then he lowered his head, brushed the lock of brown and gold hair from his eyes, and led Zephyr across the yard.

Isabel's hands were clenched so hard the nails were near to drawing blood. She relaxed her fingers, flexing them. The pain, though, wasn't in her hands. It was in her heart. No, Oliver Sullivan wasn't the man she wanted in her life. And Sullivan Waring *couldn't* be.

That wasn't quite true, though. She could have Sullivan, if she didn't ever wish to go to a party in a fine house again, if she never wanted to dance with the sons of dukes and viscounts, if she wanted all of her friends — and probably her own family — to turn their backs on her literally and figuratively.

Strangers, she could bear. But her parents? Phillip? Douglas? And how long would Barbara continue to defend her against the truth?

Oh, it was ridiculous. Even if she understood the hypocrisy of it all, how could she even be thinking about destroying her life for him? What had he done for her, anyway? Yes, he kissed very well, and the . . . other things were exceptional. But her own friends were carrying tales about her now, and the man who'd been pursuing her for weeks had just called her a whore and stalked off.

Yes, Sullivan did seem to understand her, and he was kind and patient, and she could say whatever she wished to him without fear of her words coming back to haunt her. She felt . . . important when she stood in his company, not just some pretty chit of good fortune to complement a matching set of silver candlesticks and a butler.

"Tibby?"

She turned around at the sound of her mother's voice. The marchioness stood a few feet behind her, her generally amused expression surprisingly serious. "What is it, Mama?"

"Come inside, why don't you?"

Isabel looked back at Sullivan. "But Zephyr —"

"We need to chat, my dear. And you need to stop staring at Mr. Waring like that."

Oh, dear. Clearing her throat, Isabel put a surprised look on her face. "I wasn't staring at anyone," she lied, smoothing at her dress before she retreated from the yard. "But yes, we haven't had a good coze in a long while, and I would welcome a nice cup of tea." *But only because it was too early in the day for whiskey.*

Sullivan pretended not to watch as Lady Darshear came outside to claim Isabel. He pretended not to notice the mutterings going on among the stable staff. And he pretended that he was content with having told Tibby they needed to stop seeking one another out.

Of course it was the right thing for her; the only better thing would be if he'd never touched her in the first place. But he had touched her, and he wanted to do so again. And he wanted to break in half Oliver or any other man who presumed to touch or speak ill of his Isabel.

Clenching his jaw, he leaned in against Zephyr to tighten the cinch of the side-saddle. *Concentrate,* he ordered himself. If he wouldn't allow himself to touch Tibby again, then he needed to leave her employment as soon as possible. Because whatever difficulties and dangers he'd faced during war, he wasn't certain he could manage to continue gazing at her while knowing he could never touch her again.

He straightened. "You, Delvin," he called, looking over at the stableboy, "what do you weigh, nine stone?"

"After a meal, yes, Mr. Waring."

A bit heavy, but it was much closer to Isabel's weight than he was. "Come here. Have you ever ridden sidesaddle?"

The boy blushed as the rest of the yard staff laughed. "No, sir."

"Well, you're going to do it today. Are you nervous?"

Frowning, the boy met him at the mounting block. "Yes, sir."

"Good. So will Lady Isabel be."

He'd lain across Zephyr's back, attached sacks of sand and flour with flapping ribbons on the ends, everything he could think of to accustom her to being ridden. Now they needed to make an attempt with an actual rider, and there was absolutely nothing that would make him risk Tibby and her fragile new confidence by having her be the first.

Phipps approached to help, and while Sullivan talked soothingly to Zephyr, Delvin managed to arrange himself somewhat gracefully in the sidesaddle. The mare backed a few steps, but Sullivan kept pace with her, letting her walk out her nervousness and reassuring her. Finally her ears flicked forward again, and he breathed a sigh of relief.

"Good girl," he said, stroking her neck.

"Delvin, take the reins, but don't try to guide her with them. I'll do that to begin with."

"Yes, sir."

They wound back and forth across the yard, Sullivan gradually letting Delvin begin to guide the mare as she became more accustomed to both someone on her back and having that person direct her movements. Even to his own critical gaze Zephyr was coming along beautifully.

Finally he unclipped the lead line and stood back. In one way he felt like a proud papa watching his offspring take their first steps. On the other hand, if the afternoon's lesson went half as well, Isabel could ride Zephyr tomorrow. And then or the next day, he would be finished. They would be finished. And he would go home, go back to his work, and probably never see her again.

As much as just the thought of that bothered him, he knew that leaving her be was the best, wisest thing to do. If there was an alternative, he had no idea what it might be — though he'd be willing to pay a great deal of money to find one.

CHAPTER 20

"If you're going to say something awful to me, I wish you would just get on with it." Isabel clenched her teacup, gazing into the reddish brown liquid so she wouldn't have to look at her mother's serious, thoughtful expression.

"What makes you think I have something awful to say?"

"Because you said we needed to talk and now you haven't spoken a word for nearly twenty minutes."

"Very well. We'll talk." The marchioness drew an audible breath. "At least look at me," she continued. "You're huddled in the chair like a frightened kitten."

"I am not." She was only bracing herself. Isabel straightened, finally meeting her mother's gaze. The somber look she received didn't leave her feeling any more encouraged. With a breath of her own she decided that perhaps she could improve the situation before anything unpleasant could happen. "Did you see that Zephyr's wearing a saddle now? Can you imagine that I might be riding her within a few days?"

"No, I can't. That is truly remarkable." Her mother smiled. "For you, more than for Zephyr. I can't tell you how proud I am of your courage."

There were other things of which she would be much less proud. "Thank you. Sullivan's a grand teacher."

" 'Sullivan,' " Lady Darshear repeated. "You're on a first-name basis with Mr. Waring?"

"We've become friends," Isabel hedged. If her mother had any idea how very close she and Sullivan were, she would end this conversation locked in her room.

"How does he address you?"

Now she needed to decide: Could she evade, or was she willing to outright lie? Telling the truth was absolutely out of the question. "What are you implying?" she settled for.

"I've heard the rumors, Isabel. Don't dissemble."

"So you believe Eloise? For heaven's sake, Mama. She saw me thanking Sullivan for helping me ride a horse for the first time ever. I smiled at him. I may even have hugged him. I don't recall." At least that bit was fairly close to the truth.

"You need to be more cautious about your friendships, Tibby. You're being courted by the man's half-brother. How do you think Lord Tilden felt upon hearing those rumors? And yet he had the grace to ask you out driving this morning."

"How is it grace to continue verbally attacking a man whose birth was no fault of his own and who's only attempting to do a job for which I hired him?" she retorted. "Or to hire men to beat him?" Or to call her horrid names, but she left that part out.

Her mother's frown deepened. " 'To beat him'?" she repeated.

"Yes."

"I understand that you feel . . . compassion for Mr. Waring's unfortunate position. But you made Lord Tilden's acquaintance first. You must take him into account. And your own future. If you'd never met Mr. Waring or allowed his presence to disrupt your life, Oliver would likely have offered for you by now. Do you realize that?"

It had occurred to her, but not in the way her mother meant. And it angered rather than alarmed her. She most likely would have turned him down, just as she had the other four gentlemen who'd proposed previously. But while she'd worried over wounding his feelings, she obviously needn't have concerned herself. If he'd truly cared for her, he wouldn't have called her that name. "If my friendship with someone is enough to put Oliver off," she said aloud, "then I don't want him to offer for me."

"When that 'someone' is his *illegitimate* half-brother, you can't expect him to react otherwise."

"And once again, the state of his birth is *not* Sullivan's fault."

"And once again, I am not discussing Mr. Waring. I am talking of your future, Tibby. Don't be childish."

Isabel didn't think she *was* being childish, but arguing with her mother wouldn't prove that point. "Sullivan will be finished here in just a few days," she said. That fact troubled her much more than hearing she might have missed out on a proposal of marriage from his half-brother.

"I'm sorry that you can't continue your friendship with Mr. Waring," her mother said after a moment. "He does seem to have some very good qualities. But you need to pursue an acquaintance that won't leave you ridiculed and alone, my dear. There is nothing good that can come of you knowing that man, no matter how much you might wish otherwise."

Abruptly Isabel felt like crying. "I am very aware of that," she said quietly, and set aside her tea. "If you'll excuse me, I would like to attempt riding Molly again so I won't be a complete nodcock when Zephyr is ready for me."

"Come here." Lady Darshear held out one hand.

Isabel walked over and clasped her mother's fingers. Their hands were the same size now; she supposed it had been that way for some time, but it had never occurred to her before. She wasn't a child any longer, and not simply because she had been intimate with Sullivan Waring. Recently she'd learned several lessons about friendship and rumor, and she didn't think she could go back to being the girl she'd been before even if she'd wanted to.

"We are very proud of you for learning to ride, Tibby. And I'm proud that you haven't cut someone based on the opinions of others. But your life is here, and so you must follow these rules. Do you understand?"

"I understand."

The marchioness squeezed her fingers and then released her. "Good. Come shopping with me. And wear a bonnet today; we don't want your nose turning red with the Fontaine ball tonight."

"Yes, Mama."

She spent the entire morning and part of the afternoon on Bond Street looking at hats and brooches and gowns with her mother, so restless in her own skin she could barely stand still. The other shoppers they encountered were polite, though they seemed to spend much more time speaking with her mother than with her. So she wasn't being cut as she'd expected to be, but what, taught a lesson? Don't associate with inappropriate persons? At least Sullivan Waring made his own way in life, rather than relying on a name or a title handed down without merit or consideration just because of someone's birth parents.

"You see, my sweet?" the marchioness said as they climbed back into the barouche amid the stacks of boxes and packages they'd accumulated. "You haven't done any permanent damage. Just . . . be more cautious from now on. And if you wish, your father can ask Mr. Waring to terminate his services with us. Then you can avoid any further encounters with him."

"I still want Mr. Waring to train Zephyr for me," she returned, just barely keeping her voice steady. "I trust him above anyone else in this."

Her mother didn't like that; Isabel could see it in her eyes. But the marchioness didn't say anything more, so she kept away from the subject, as well. Inside, though, her blood hummed through her veins. She couldn't explain it, except that the more she saw how easily people she'd counted as friends could turn their backs on her because of a rumor, the less she wanted anything to do with them. And the more she wanted to see Sullivan again, so he would know that she wasn't one of those hypocritical aristocrats he disliked so much.

Once they returned to Chalsey House, Isabel threw off her bonnet and hurried through the foyer to the back of the house. Prompt as Sullivan was, she would barely have another twenty minutes before he'd finished Zephyr's afternoon lesson. Everything was a mess, and nothing could be the way she wanted it, and only if she was very lucky could she hope to avoid ruin. And at the moment she wanted to kiss Sullivan Waring so badly it physically hurt.

He stood in the middle of the yard, watching Zephyr walk a wide circle around him, the youngest stableboy on the mare's back. And even with renowned pieces of horse-flesh about, Sullivan was the most magnificent specimen in sight. Anywhere, she was beginning to believe.

"What do you think?" he asked as she approached, no sign of his earlier frustration in his voice. "She's ready for you, if you're ready for her."

She couldn't think at all. "May I have a word with you?" she demanded, her voice tight.

Sullivan's brow lowered. "Certainly, my lady. Delvin, keep her at a walk. And don't circle in one direction only."

The stableboy tugged on his forelock. "No worries, Mr. Waring."

He followed her into the stable. "Please leave us," she said to the building in general, and immediately the remaining grooms shuffled past them out into the yard.

Sullivan's frown deepened. "If you're going to tell me to leave, you might as well do it in front of —"

She grabbed his hair, yanking his face down to hers. She kissed him ferociously, tasting him, wrapping herself into him, wishing she could crawl inside him. After a surprised second during which her heart stopped, he began kissing her back, drawing her up against his hard chest.

Time floated away. Kissing Sullivan, having him kiss her — this was what she wanted. His arms around her, his scent on her skin.

He moaned against her mouth. "Tibby."

"Shh." She kissed him again, his mouth, his throat, his chin, everywhere she could reach.

"Tibby, stop." Taking her shoulders, he pushed her backward. Not far, but far enough to break her hold on him. "Stop. Someone will see."

"What do you care?"

"You are a good person," he said, ignoring her batting hands. "I do not want to see you ruined because of my sins."

"*Your* sins? We've both sinned."

"Every time I touch you, letting you go gets . . ." He drew a harsh breath in through his nose. "I am not . . . good," he said slowly, obviously searching for words. "I steal. I've killed for my country. I . . . hate your kind. You're an exception, but that doesn't change anything. I'm no good for you, and I honestly can't think of any way that making off with you would benefit me."

"But you've thought about it. About making off with me."

"I've thought about riding a colicky horse through Dunston's townhouse, too, but I've never done that." Brief humor touched his face before he sobered again. "No more of this, Isabel."

"Don't tell me what to do," she snapped. Giving up trying to embrace him, she pushed back and stalked a few feet away. "My mother said that if I hadn't hired you, Oliver probably would have offered for me already."

His expression grew even darker. "No doubt."

"So he judges that my . . . error in calling you a friend is enough to prevent him from asking for my hand? That certainly isn't love he's fighting against. It's his own pride. And yours."

"Does he love you?" Sullivan asked quietly.

She shook her head. "He likes me. Liked me. At the beginning of the Season he danced with two dozen other ladies. Apparently he found me the least objectionable. Until now, at least."

"Yes, he's a sterling character." He folded his arms across his chest. "He used to spit at me when we crossed one another's path as children."

"You steal from people," she retorted. "Whose character is more sterling?"

"Do you really want to compare me with that —"

"Oh, stop it. This isn't your fault, and it

isn't his. Or it wasn't to begin with. Since then I don't think either of you have acted appropriately, and neither have I — so don't try to throw that back at me."

Sullivan looked at her for a heartbeat. "Do you — did you — love him? Oliver bloody Sullivan?"

"I love you," she shot back, then clapped both hands over her mouth.

His lean face went white. Ice-green eyes fixed on her face, he backed away until he came up against the stable wall.

"Sullivan?" she managed, her voice squeaking.

He turned and left the stable.

Isabel sat down hard on an upturned barrel. She'd done it now. Of course they could never have any kind of future together, but she'd managed to ruin today, as well. And any other todays they could talk themselves into. "Idiot," she muttered, sinking her face into her hands.

Someone by the door cleared his throat. She started to her feet, Sullivan's name on her lips. Thankfully she didn't utter it aloud. Delvin the stableboy stood in the doorway. "What is it?" she snapped, her temple beginning to throb.

He bowed, tugging on his lanky brown forelock of hair at the same time. "Begging your pardon, my lady, but Mr. Waring says if you wish to ride your Zephyr today, you'd best come out of the stable."

He had, had he? "Oh, yes. Thank you," she said aloud.

Riding a horse no one had ridden until two days ago. Very well, now she was nervous again. And hopeful. Or at the least, less dejected. In fact, if one or two more emotions filled her skull and her chest, she was very likely going to suffer an apoplexy and drop dead.

Shaking herself, she left the stable. Sullivan had his back to her as he spoke to Phipps. "I'll be a minute, Mr. Waring," she called, hurrying for the house. "I need to change."

He ignored her. She nearly let that go — until she considered that she'd done nothing wrong, and he'd been the rude one. Twice now.

"Mr. Waring," she repeated crisply, coming to a stop. "Pray look at me when I'm speaking to you."

He turned on his heel to face her, his movements as spare and precise as the soldier he'd once been. His expression was unreadable. "Yes, my lady."

"I'll be back in a moment. You are not to leave."

Sullivan inclined his head. "As you wish."

He watched her into the house, her skirt gathered in her hands as she ran. *God, God, God.* She *loved* him. What the devil was he supposed to do with that? Sweep her onto the back of his horse and carry her off to his castle? The worst of it was that he wanted to. He wanted to take her into his arms in front of everyone and have . . . nothing happen. No one to frown, no one to be ruined. But whatever she said to him, that could never happen.

"Mr. Waring?"

Sullivan started, looking back at Phipps. "Apologies," he said shortly. "Yes. Please bring Paris out for me."

Concentrate, damn it all. He'd ridden the bay gelding today on purpose; Zephyr was a mare, and as much confidence as he had in her, neither did he want to be riding a big stallion like Achilles when Isabel took her seat for the first time.

Phipps hurried off, and Sullivan busied himself with checking and rechecking the cinches on Zephyr's saddle, making certain the reins were straight and that he had apple slices in his pockets. The mare shifted, obviously picking up on his nervousness, and he took a breath to steady himself.

It didn't change anything. What she'd said

didn't change anything. She would still carry on with her life of parties and rides in the park, and he would raise horses and reclaim the remainder of his mother's paintings and otherwise avoid having anything to do with Dunston. He closed his eyes for a moment. Until now he might have hated his relations, but he'd never hated his life before. Until now.

"I'm ready."

Sullivan opened his eyes again and turned around. She'd donned her hunter-green riding dress, snug in all the right places, deliciously curved at her breasts and hips. For a second he took her in, not certain whether or not he was imagining the scent of citrus in the air around her.

"Well?"

He cleared his throat. "Apologies. Do you want to attempt this today?"

She sent a nervous glance at Zephyr. "It seems like my best chance," she said after a moment. "I'd hate to go to all this effort and then miss my moment."

"That's rather blunt, don't you think?" he murmured, leading Zephyr to the mounting block.

"I have no idea what you mean, Mr. Waring. What should I expect?"

"Zephyr's more energetic and less experienced than Molly, so she'll probably be shifting her weight more. Just shift your weight with her, keep yourself centered above the saddle. I'll be on Paris, with a lead line in case she gets away from you."

The worried look on her face deepened. "Is she likely to get away from me?"

"No. She's a good girl. Just remind her of that. Talk to her, as you did Molly. She knows your voice, and she likes you."

Isabel lifted an eyebrow, though she kept her gaze on the mare. "Isn't that interesting?" she said, walking carefully forward to pat Zephyr on the neck. "She likes me, and she lets me know it."

Apparently Isabel had had enough time to realize that he was a complete and utter nodcock. It hadn't taken very long. "You two should have a long and happy partnership," he offered. "You're well suited to one another."

"And yet you had originally decided she should be a brood mare."

And she was angry. His jaw clenched. "I make mistakes."

"Yes, I've become aware of that. Now shall I ride, or have you changed your mind?"

Damnation. He took her arm to help her onto the mounting block, gripping her harder than he needed to. "Stop it," he whispered.

"Stop what? She's my animal; I may converse about her if I wish to. You certainly can't prevent me from doing so."

Taking a step closer, he yanked her back, pulling her against his chest. "What good would it do," he hissed, "for me to tell you how I feel?"

"Let me go."

"Not yet." He shifted, making certain anyone watching from the house would see only his back. "You're the cruel one, Isabel. You shouldn't have said it."

She wrenched her arm free. "I didn't mean to," she retorted. "You keep setting me off balance."

Well, this was becoming more interesting. "You 'didn't mean to'?" he repeated. "Telling me your deepest feelings was an accident?"

"Yes. Should I apologize for not dissembling?"

Sullivan leaned in, inhaling the scent of her hair. "No. I will apologize for not being what you deserve." Phipps trotted up, Paris and the groom's mount in tow. "Now let's get you on this horse, shall we?"

"I'm not finished arguing with you."

"We can fight on the way to the park, then. Not standing here."

He felt her sigh. The urge to close his arms around her was so strong that he'd shifted before he could stop himself. Hoping Phipps hadn't noticed, he moved his grip to her waist and lifted. With a small gasp that sent arousal shooting through him, she slid onto the sidesaddle.

Keeping one hand on her and one on the reins in case either lady or mare panicked, he held his breath. Zephyr was no matronly fifteen-year-old companion mare, and she would know she bore a new and nervous rider.

Isabel's face was white. She wasn't angry with him at the moment, but given the circumstances he would almost prefer that she was. "You look very fetching up there," he whispered.

Color touched her cheeks, and she broke her stare at Zephyr's ears to glance down at him. "Don't compliment me if it's just words," she ordered.

Shifting his grip to the lead line, he moved around and swung up onto Paris. "I've meant everything I've ever said to you," he returned. And some things he would never say aloud.

CHAPTER 21

Isabel's entire family happened either by accident or by incredible coincidence to be home for the momentous occasion. She put aside the fact that this meant they were watching her, and instead waved two fingers — the most she dared — at them where they stood gathered on the front portico to watch her ride Zephyr down the front drive and out into the street.

"Brava, Tibby!" her father called, real pride in his voice.

"We'll return shortly," she ventured, concentrating to give just the correct amount of pull to the reins. With a twitch of her ears Zephyr angled smoothly to the right.

Tall and straight in the saddle just two feet to her left, Sullivan smiled. "Well done," he murmured.

"Thank you." She risked loosening the reins with her left hand to pat Zephyr on the neck. "Good girl."

Riding Zephyr felt immensely different than riding Molly. The gray moved like a coiled cat, ready to spring into a trot or a gallop at any moment. But she didn't; she stayed at the placid walk Isabel had called for. "It feels as though she would do anything I asked," she said aloud.

"She would. It will take time for the two of you to learn from one another, though," Sullivan cautioned in the warm, relaxed voice he always used around horses. "If she does something you don't expect, keep in mind that it's not on purpose. Just be patient and reassuring, and bring her back to where you're both comfortable. A walk first, then a trot."

"And don't fall off," she added with a nervous chuckle.

"Falling off happens," he returned matter-of-factly. "Don't be frightened of it. Just be ready. You'll probably tend to go over backwards. Grab the pommel to try to keep your balance. If you can't, then try to curl up. Don't land flat on your back if you can avoid it, because that'll knock the wind out of you."

"I am not reassured."

He shrugged. "If it happens, it happens. But it won't today."

She risked a glance at his smiling, handsome face. The face she wanted always looking back at her. "How am I ever to relax when every moment I must be ready for disaster?"

"It'll get easier. Like learning to walk. You've mastered that and don't give it much thought, do you?"

"I've been walking since the age of one. Eighteen years of practice."

Sullivan chuckled. "Yes, but it took a year or two for you to get very good at it. And you're not a newborn now."

"I feel awkward as one."

"You look very competent. And exquisitely lovely."

"I told you to stop that." She scowled at him. "I gave you a very nice compliment. The nicest one I can possible give, I think. If you can't or won't return it, then stop saying anything else."

"It does pale in comparison, doesn't it?" he noted after a moment. "But it hurts less."

"For you."

Sullivan looked away. "Very well," he said finally, looking back at her. His ice-green eyes held secrets she couldn't put a name to — but she knew they belonged to her. All of them. "I love you," he went on in the low, intimate voice that made her tremble. "I want to see you, to talk to you, to hold you, every moment of every day. You make me want to be things that I can't possibly be."

His voice broke, but she kept her silence. She had no idea what she could ever say. A tear touched her cheek, and she hurriedly brushed it away before anyone at the entrance to Hyde Park where they rode could see it.

He cleared his throat. "You make me wish to be someone else. A man who could do those things in the light of day without fear of ruining you and destroying me. I've never wished that before, Isabel." His gaze held hers. "Do you feel less pain now?"

She shook her head, another tear following the first down her cheek and then into oblivion on the back of her glove. "No."

"Neither do I."

"Sullivan Waring!"

The deep, strident voice made her jump. Zephyr sidestepped, tossing her head, her ears flattening. *Oh, God.* Isabel pulled up on the reins. The mare backed, snorting.

"Whoa, girl," Sullivan said easily, not moving otherwise except for a subtle shift of his booted foot that kept Paris even with them. "Tibby, talk to her. Watch her ears."

"Whoa, girl," she repeated, not daring to let go of the pommel or the reins to pat the mare. "Good girl. That's it. I'm sorry I startled you."

Zephyr's ears lifted, twisting to listen to the stream of soft words she continued to babble. The mare stopped fidgeting and lowered her head to nibble at the grass beneath her feet.

"Well done, my lady," Sullivan murmured.

When she finally looked away from Zephyr's ears, she realized that Sullivan had his hands in the air, his own gaze on the nearest of the half dozen mounted men encircling them. The men with pistols aimed at his chest.

"What is the meaning of this?" she asked, using every ounce of will she possessed to sound offended and not terrified that someone was about to shoot Sullivan.

The closest of the men, dressed as all of them were in a blue greatcoat with a scarlet waistcoat beneath, sent her a glance. "This is official Bow Street business, miss. Stay cl— "

"Lady Isabel Chalsey," Sullivan interrupted. "You will speak to her with the respect she is due."

The man's jaw twitched, and he inclined his head. "Apologies, my lady. We're here under orders. Please stand clear." He returned his attention to Sullivan. "Mr. Sullivan Waring, by order of the chief magistrate, you are under arrest for theft."

"This is ridiculous!" Isabel stated. Talking was difficult with her heart in her throat, but these men looked ready to shoot. How had they found him? How could they simply ride up and arrest him right when he'd said that he loved her? She took a breath to steady herself. "Mr. Waring has been training my horse. I have no idea what —"

"Apologies, my lady, but we have good information that Waring is behind the Mayfair thefts over the past few weeks. He's to come with us immediately."

"No," Sullivan stated.

The pistols lifted again. One of the men dismounted, a pair of iron manacles in his hand. "Dismount before we force you to it," the ranking Runner said.

"Lady Isabel is my responsibility," Sullivan said in the same even voice he'd been using. "I will not abandon her here."

"You've got a groom there," one of the others said, gesturing at Phipps.

Isabel had forgotten the head groom was even present. He sat on his horse a short way behind them, his face gray. She imagined hers looked much the same. They'd found Sullivan, and they knew — they *knew* — what he'd done. That he was the Mayfair

Marauder. Who had told them? "Who provided you with this ridiculous information?" she asked aloud.

"We're not at liberty to say."

"I'll say." Oliver Sullivan, Lord Tilden, rode up behind the mounted Runners. "I've been forced to do my civic duty, Isabel. My apologies on the timing of it. I'll see you home."

"You will do no such thing!" she retorted, returning her gaze to the lead officer. "Mr. Waring is in my employ. I require him to return me to my home. You may follow us there if you wish." It wasn't much, but it might give them a little time to think of something.

"Mr. Waring is to come with us immediately," the leader repeated.

"I don't understand. Lord Tilden has no proof to support his accusations. In fact, the only reason he —"

"Phipps," Sullivan interrupted. "Take the lead line. And don't you move more than three feet from Lady Isabel all the way home or I will hear about it and hunt you down. Is that clear?"

"Yes, Mr. Waring."

"Sulliv—"

"Everyone is watching, Tibby," he said in a low voice, slowly dismounting as the pistols followed his every move. "Supporting me will only hurt you. Stay quiet, keep your chin up, and go home."

She clamped her mouth shut. Finally she looked beyond their small circle to see what looked like half of Hyde Park's visitors gathered around them, everyone muttering and sending as many looks at her as they did at Sullivan. She hadn't even noticed them, and now that she had, she didn't care. "Proof, sir. What is your proof?"

"Don't you worry about that, my lady. On Lord Tilden's statement we have men going to Mr. Waring's home to look for the stolen items. You were burgled yourself, weren't you?"

Oliver moved in. "There's no need for that, Mr. Seifley. Let's get you home, Isabel."

"Stay away from me. As if I would want anything to do with you after what you said to me."

Sullivan grasped her foot, making her jump and putting the Runners on edge all over again. "For God's sake, go home, Tibby. Please," he murmured, pretending to adjust the reins for her. "I never wanted this to hurt you. Stay away from me. Better yet, kick me first, and then go."

"I will not," she murmured back. Then

she straightened. "Very well, gentlemen. Phipps, take me home at once."

The groom crept in to take the lead line from Sullivan, then turned Zephyr away from the group. Isabel kept watch over her shoulder, making certain no one shot Sullivan. When the manacles closed around his wrists he sent her a last look and then turned his back.

Isabel felt sick to her stomach. She swallowed hard, fighting the urge to retch in the middle of the park. How could they simply ride up and arrest him? Once they had their proof, the only thing left would be to learn what his punishment was to be. Oh, God, what if they decided to hang him? *No, no, no.*

"My lady," Phipps said from beside her, "we need to return to Chalsey House."

She blinked. The Runners were on their way to Sullivan's cottage. They didn't yet have any proof other than Oliver's accusations. "No," she said aloud.

"No? But —"

"*I* will go home," she stated much more confidently than she felt. "You will go to Lord Bramwell Johns's home and tell him exactly what just transpired. Do you know how to find his residence?"

"Yes, my lady. But Mr. Waring said I

should see you home. He said that expressly."

"Phipps, you are in *my* family's employ. Not his. Now go!"

With obvious reluctance he detached the lead line from Zephyr's bridle and swung back up on his own horse. "Please be cautious, my lady. You will be alone on the streets."

She was more worried that she'd be riding without assistance. "I am not going to ask you again, Phipps."

He gave a curt nod, kicked his mount in the ribs, and galloped away. Isabel took a deep breath. She was not ready for this. Worse, though, would be to simply go home without trying to do something to aid Sullivan.

"Walk on, Zephyr," she said, and flicked the reins as Sullivan had shown her. The mare started off as easily as if they were still in the stable yard with ready assistance right beside her.

A large chestnut gelding trotted up beside her and slowed to match Zephyr's pace. "Isabel, don't be stubborn," Oliver said. "Let me see you home."

"No, thank you," she returned sharply, ready to try a trot except that she didn't want him to see her awkwardness with it.

He would find a way to blame her uneasiness on Sullivan, and he'd done enough of that.

"Mr. Waring is a thief," he continued. "It was my duty to see him arrested."

"Ballocks," she snapped, finally turning her head to glare at him. "You had him arrested for no other reason than the fact that you are a small-minded, jealous, pitiable man."

His elegant brow lowered. " 'Jealous'?" he repeated. "I most certainly have never been jealous of a . . . a horse breeder. He works for a living, for Lucifer's sake."

"That is precisely the point I will make to anyone who will listen," Isabel retorted, wishing she knew how to hold on during a gallop. She wanted to fly home, to get help. "I will tell everyone that you, born with every privilege imaginable, stooped to making accusations against your half-brother simply because you couldn't stand the thought of him being happy."

"And you are the reason for this happiness you think he's found, I presume?" His tone lowered, and she stifled a shiver. "That should create some interesting gossip."

"Oh, don't you trouble yourself, my lord. By the time I begin telling everyone about your small, black soul, I'll have a much bet-

ter tale to hand. About where those paintings came from in the first place, perhaps."

"You wouldn't dare."

"Wait and see." Tired of both the conversation and the snail's pace, she flicked the
reins again. "Trot, Zephyr. And you, my
lord, will leave me alone. If I ever set eyes
on you again, it will be too soon."

As Zephyr sped her pace, Isabel had to
grasp the pommel. She balanced herself
again, and let go. If Sullivan received credit
for nothing else, he was a very fine riding
instructor. And he'd trained a fine horse.

And she needed to save him.

It seemed as though it took her forever to
reach Chalsey House. As she rode up the
drive and past the house to the stable yard,
she didn't even take the time for a moment
of self-congratulation. It could wait.
"Delvin! You, Smith! Harness our fastest
pair to the coach at once!"

Apparently they were surprised enough
both by her appearance and by her shout-
ing that they ran to do as they were bid.
That, though, left her alone to climb down
from the horse. She'd never had to do that
on her own; Sullivan had always lifted her
down.

"Tibby?" Douglas strode into the stable
yard from the house. "What the devil are

you doing? And where's Waring?"

"Oh, thank goodness. Douglas, help me down!" she commanded.

He lifted his arms, and she half fell onto him as she dismounted.

"Good God, Tibby, you've broken my arm."

"I have not. And I need your help."

"With what?"

"Sullivan's been arrested. Bow Street's sending men to look for the stolen property he's accused of taking. I sent Phipps to go tell Lord Bramwell Johns, but who knows whether he's home or not. So you and I must go and remove all of the stolen paintings before anyone else can use them against him."

Her younger brother blinked. "Are you mad?" he finally squeaked. "Do you have any idea what could happen to us if we're caught helping a known thief?"

"I don't care. Now say you'll assist me, or I'll find someone who will."

"Damnation," he muttered, glancing back toward the house. "They are going to ship me off somewhere for this, you know. And you, too. And don't say you don't care, because I know y—"

"I love Sullivan," she interrupted, frustrated tears welling in her eyes again. "And

I'll help him, with or without you."

"By God," her brother stammered, staring at her. "By God."

"I know, I know. It's impossible. But at the moment there's something I can do to help him, and so I will. Will you assist me?"

Still slack-jawed, he nodded. "I'll help. But if Mother and Father sell me to the Americas as an indentured servant, I'm going to be very annoyed with you."

"They'll sell me, as well, so you can be as annoyed with me as you wish."

Together they hurried over to the coach. She'd selected it because it had the most room inside for hiding stolen items. As Douglas waved aside Eugene the driver, though, and climbed up to the high perch himself, she had to wonder if she'd thought even this much through.

"Why are you —"

"Get in, Tibby. I won't have any of the servants arrested for assisting us in assisting him."

He had a very good point. She clambered into the coach and closed the door. "Go!" she yelled. If she couldn't save Sullivan Waring, at least they would both go down fighting.

He could have gotten away. The Bow Street

Runners wouldn't have expected a captive wearing shackles to run, and he would pit Paris against any of the broken-down nags they rode in a quick second. A few weeks ago, he might have attempted it — lost what reputation he had, lost his cottage and his stable — to stay out of gaol.

After all, an attempted arrest would have done as much damage to Dunston and his illusion of perfection as having his bastard son hanged. Nearly as much, anyway. It didn't look at all well for a son — even an illegitimate, unacknowledged son — to be arrested for burglary and theft.

Sullivan glanced at the curious crowd still surrounding him, then looked over his shoulder at Tibby just beyond, ably mounted on Zephyr and arguing over something with Phipps. She would now face hell because of him. And the larger the disturbance he made, the worse it would be for her.

So he allowed the men to shove him back on Paris, sat as they pulled the reins over the gelding's head, and kept his silence amid the growing jeers and catcalls as they led him away toward the Old Bailey. He supposed that that was what he'd expected to come of all this in the first place.

Bram hadn't needed to tell him that

sooner or later his deeds would catch up to him, because he'd known it already. The difference now, though, was that striking back at his so-called sire wasn't his foremost concern. That honor went to the young lady currently leaving Hyde Park and scurrying home posthaste.

He hoped she had enough wit to appear as shocked as anyone else by his actions. She needed to think about self-preservation; not about him. And only to himself would he admit that he wished it could be otherwise. From the look of things, he would have a great deal of time to make that wish.

CHAPTER 22

"How do you know if this is even one of the stolen paintings?" Douglas asked, hefting a small landscape under one arm and an Egyptian urn in the other hand.

"Just put everything in the coach," Isabel said, taking another painting off the wall. "We can sort them out later."

"But someone's going to get suspicious when they arrive here and all the walls are bare."

"They're going to be more suspicious if we're here removing everything from the cottage when they arrive."

"Not everything," her brother returned. "I haven't seen anything of ours yet."

She hadn't, either. Her one and only visit to Sullivan's home had been limited to the hallway and front room, and she had no idea where he kept the paintings he'd reclaimed — or even if he kept them here at all. All she knew was that they didn't have time to be wrong. "Just take all the paintings you see. Most of them are Francesca Perris. Some of them are bound to be the missing ones."

"This is interesting."

Isabel yelped at the low drawl, straightening so fast she nearly dropped the painting she'd just liberated. As she turned toward the door, her heart began beating again. "Lord Bramwell."

"You're breaking the law, you know," he said, nodding at Douglas as her brother reappeared from behind a chair.

"Bow Street will be here at any moment," she pointed out, putting a pair of candlesticks into the sack she'd found.

"Then you'd best go and leave this to me," Levonzy's son returned.

"Leave it to you? *I* am helping Sullivan. You're standing there talking."

Brief amusement crossed his lean face. "It's one of the things at which I excel. I also happen to know where Sullivan keeps what he's taken, and I've brought help. So I suggest you cease robbing the poor fellow of his legitimate possessions and come with me."

Pushing away from the doorframe, he turned down the hallway. With a glance at her, Douglas put down the armload of items

397

he'd gathered and followed Lord Bramwell. Isabel looked about at the bare walls of the front sitting room. They already had a dozen paintings stashed in the coach, and whoever they actually belonged to, there wasn't time to return them to their place. She hurried after the men.

She hadn't even seen the door set into the back of the kitchen pantry. It was paneled in the same oak as the rest of the kitchen, and when closed it simply blended into the back wall.

"Excuse me, my lady." A stocky man dressed in Johns family livery squeezed past her out of the hidden room. Under his arms were two paintings.

"Thank you, Lord Bramwell," she breathed, eyeing the half dozen men busily removing everything from the small, windowless room and carrying it to two wagons stopped behind their coach.

"I'm not doing it for you, Lady Isabel. And call me Bram."

"Yes, he's your friend." One of the few Lord Bramwell seemed to have, as she recalled.

"He is."

"Do you trust these men?" she asked, avoiding the use of his nickname. Sullivan might be a self-confessed thief, but Bramwell Johns was the one who . . . frightened her a little.

"I pay them enough to make them trust-worthy," he returned. "Now you and your brother need to leave. Tilden's information might have caught Bow Street flat-footed, but for an arrest like this they know they'll need to move swiftly — or risk irritating all the people who've purchased mounts from Sully."

He hadn't mentioned Sullivan's father, and that had likely been intentional. "But —"

"They'll be here soon, my lady — and you can't be."

"I'm the reason he's in this mess."

Lord Bramwell shook his head. "Sullivan and Lord Tilden have two things in common — their father, and you. This would still have happened without you. Perhaps not the arrest, but the scandal, yes. The only difference is that with you about, he won't want to attempt fleeing." Johns stepped back to allow her to leave the kitchen. "I told him he was a bloody fool, risking his life for a chit. You are apparently something unusual."

Her heart skittered. Had Sullivan told him that? Did Lord Bramwell suspect how dear a horse breeder had become to this "chit," as he called her? "Thank you for telling me."

"You're welcome. Now go home, before you make this even more complicated."

"I —"

Lord Bram took her by the elbow and practically dragged her outside. He probably would have flung her headfirst into her own coach if she hadn't grabbed the doorframe.

"Will they release him if they find no proof?" she asked, as Douglas climbed back up to the driver's perch.

His lips thinned. "Probably not. He's been accused by a future marquis, who is apparently willing to see some damage done to his own reputation. It'll be a matter of proving him innocent rather than finding him not guilty."

"Then what are we to do?" she demanded, her voice getting more shrill as the scope of the disaster began to truly sink into her heart. "He . . ." She forced herself to calm down and lowered her voice. "He isn't innocent."

Black eyes regarded her for a moment. "I have a thought or two on the subject," he finally said. "But if you don't return home and *be* innocent, his betters will see him hanged on principle alone. They don't like having a wolf in with their pretty sheep, my dear."

She climbed into the coach. "I am not a sheep, Lord Bramwell."

"No, I do believe there's a bit of wolf in you," he said with thinly veiled amusement, and closed the coach door. "Go!"

Douglas whistled at the team, and they rumbled down the rutted drive. Bram watched for a moment to make certain the stubborn chit didn't change her mind and attempt a second attack on the house, then went back inside.

"Hurry it up, Grimes," he ordered the most senior of his footmen. "And be careful with those paintings."

"Yes, my lord."

Much as he hated to admit it, Lady Tibby had a point: In the eyes of the court, a lack of evidence would not equate with innocence. Not when a lord had accused a so-called commoner. He returned to Sullivan's hidden den and opened the trunk set against the back wall.

Filled with blankets and an old quilt, it could stay — except for the one item tucked into the corner. Bram lifted the black half-mask, apparently a replacement for the one Isabel had pocketed the night Sullivan had robbed her home. He sighed. Apparently he

401

would have to squeeze in an unforeseen engagement between dinner and dancing at the Fontaine ball and dessert with Hannah Price, the latest diamond to grace London's stages — and his bedchamber.

"We should not be going out tonight," Phillip said, sinking into the corner of the coach.

"I agree," Isabel added from beside him, wondering what her parents would think if they knew that just a few hours earlier this very coach had been filled with paintings and knickknacks from Sullivan Waring's home, items which now rested securely in the tack room of the stable beneath a pile of straw and blankets.

"It's certainly not our fault that we hired Mr. Waring," her father put in, though his expression looked as dour as Phillip's. "We had no idea that he was the Mayfair Marauder."

"That's not the problem, Harry," Lady Darshear countered. "The rumors of Tibby's affection for Mr. Waring will be on everyone's tongues again tonight. And I thought we'd made it through that fiasco."

"I'm not going to apologize for anything," Isabel stated. "And I think the problem is that Sullivan's in gaol, not that people are talking about me."

"You may think differently when we arrive at the soiree."

"Yes, Mama. I'm certain it will be unpleasant." She drew a breath. "That is why I would prefer to go see Sullivan at the Old Bailey instead of attending the Fon—"

"What?" her mother gasped. "What?"

"Everyone's already condemned him," she pressed on, ignoring the fact that he had actually committed the crimes. He'd been driven to it, for heaven's sake, and he'd taken only what was his, with just enough other items that no one would suspect him. "This is all just because Oliver decided he didn't like me riding with Sullivan. It's my fault." Lord Bram might have disputed that, but she knew that she was correct. And that made this worse than it already was. She'd told Sullivan that she loved him, and then everything had fallen apart.

"It is not your fault. And how do you know that Mr. Waring didn't have anything to do with the thefts?" Her mother continued to look grim and disappointed, as she had since Douglas had driven the coach back up the drive.

"You know what I heard?" Phillip contributed. "All of the missing paintings were done by his mother."

The marquis sat forward. "You mean *he*

was the one who broke into our home and threatened Tibby? That —"

"No one threatened me," she broke in, her throat constricting and panic seeping into her chest. "I scared that man away. Remember?"

"Francesca W. Perris," he went on. "The *W* could very well stand for Waring."

"Oh, good heavens." Her mother fanned at her face. "What have we become involved with? Tibby, please tell me if you know anything more."

A tear ran down Isabel's face. She felt it fall, felt a second one follow it. Her feelings for Sullivan had been difficult enough to reconcile when no one suspected anything about his late-night activities. To whom was she supposed to be loyal? And who was she supposed to betray?

"Isabel?" her mother said again, more quietly. "You do know something. Please, please tell us."

A sob broke from her throat, and she flung herself across the coach into her mother's startled arms. It was too much. How was she supposed to know what to do? Oh, she was so stupid. So stupid.

"Tibby?" Her father awkwardly patted her shoulder. "We know you liked him. He taught you to ride, after all, and that —"

"His mother died while he was away at war," she said, her voice muffled against her mother's shoulder. "When he returned home, Dunston and Oliver had stolen all of the paintings his mother had left for him. His entire heritage, and they took it because her house was on their land, and because they could. Who would find in favor of a horse breeder against a marquis? He just wanted them back."

"Good God," the marquis murmured.

"He told you this?" Phillip asked, his voice as shocked as her parents'.

"He would have stopped after he got the last painting. There were only two more. But Oliver knew, because Lord Dunston knew. They didn't want to raise a stink — or Dunston didn't, but then Oliver saw that Sullivan and I were . . . friends, and so he went to Bow Street, and now they're going to hang Sullivan. I know they are."

She couldn't stop babbling. Apparently she could say anything about Sullivan and his situation except what truly mattered. As long as she kept talking and kept her face buried in her mother's shoulder at least she wouldn't have to see the shock and dismay undoubtedly showing on the faces of her parents and her brother. Oh, and she'd even managed to tangle Douglas into this mess.

405

"Tibby, you must stop crying," the marchioness said urgently.

"I can't," she wailed.

"Harry, stop the coach," her mother commanded.

He rapped on the ceiling and the carriage rolled to a halt. "Helen, what —"

"You and Phillip must get out for a moment," she went on. "Immediately."

Sniffing, Isabel straightened. She'd seen that look on her mother's face only a few times in her entire life. The last time had been when Douglas had brought a live goose into the dining room at Burling and it had both driven away the half dozen invited guests and committed an act of cannibalism before they recaptured it. No wonder the men fled outside and closed the door behind them.

Her mother looked out the window and made a shooing gesture, no doubt to send them farther away. Then she faced Isabel again. "Are you with child?" she asked bluntly, her face white around the edges.

"N-no!"

"Thank God for that. Why the tears, then?"

"Because . . ." Isabel closed her eyes for a moment. Obviously she was in this well over her head. The difficulty was whether telling anyone else would help, or make things even worse. Her mother, both her parents, had never been anything but sympathetic and understanding up to this point, though. She was the one who'd gone completely mad. "I love him," she said aloud.

The marchioness didn't look surprised. "Last year you loved John Hilgrandt. And Clark Winstead."

"This is nothing like that. For heaven's sake, Mama, you know I never meant that seriously. John was simply amusing, and Clark danced well."

"What about Oliver?"

"I despise him."

"Did this happen before or after he had Mr. Waring arrested?"

"Before. Or at least I'd finished with him well before that. The only reason I didn't tell him so was that I thought he might blame Sullivan. Oliver likes everything that he's supposed to, and nothing that he's not."

Her mother sat back, her hands folded in her lap. "And what, precisely, is wrong with that?"

"Nothing, I suppose." Isabel shrugged as she wiped at her cheeks. Her eyes felt puffy. "It's just . . . ordinary. I realized several weeks ago that I didn't know anything about his interests because I'd never cared to ask.

And he doesn't know anything about mine."

"But Mr. Waring does?"

"He did manage to get me up on a horse. And he's very smart. And well educated. I think his mother kept hoping that Dunston would acknowledge him, so she raised him to be a gentleman."

"But Lord Dunston hasn't acknowledged him, and he's not a gentleman."

"I know." Her voice broke. "I know it's impossible. I may be acting like a fool, but all of my faculties haven't deserted me. I've traveled a hundred miles in my mind, just to find a way that everything could be the way I want it to be."

The marchioness gazed at her for a long moment. "And where have you ended up after all of your travels, my dear?"

"Right back here. I don't know what will happen, Mama, but if there is anything — *anything* — I can do to keep Sullivan Waring from being imprisoned or killed, then I will do it. Because even if I had to live on the streets and beg for food, it would be better than feeling the way I feel when I think about what is probably going to happen to him."

"I wish I could be certain this isn't one of your dramatic flourishes, Isabel. Because you may talk about living on the streets, but

I think you have no idea what your decision to support Mr. Waring would truly do to you."

Her mother had a point. She'd always been headstrong and given to "dramatic flourishes," as her family called them. Her interest in Sullivan had begun as one. She knew how she felt, but of course they would have little reason to believe her. Isabel squared her shoulders. "Then I think we should go to the Fontaine ball, and I will show you that I am very serious about him, and that I understand the consequences. Afterward, though, I will go to see him."

"We'll see about that." The marchioness opened the coach door. "Harry, Phillip, you may return. We're going to have a very interesting evening."

CHAPTER 23

"What did you do with them?"

Sullivan remained where he was, leaning against the back wall of his small, stone-lined cell in the cellar of the Old Bailey, and kept his expression still. "You're going to have to be more specific," he said.

The magistrate adjusted his white wig, glaring from him to the pair of Runners standing beside him and back again. "I do not interrogate prisoners," he stated. "I'm only here because of the alleged circumstances of your birth, and the status of the victims of your crimes. So I suggest you cooperate before I have you moved to less pleasant surroundings."

"I may have sold a horse or two for a larger profit than warranted," Sullivan returned, still not moving, "but other than that and the rabid ravings of Lord Tilden which I witnessed, I have no idea why I'm here."

The magistrate, who hadn't bothered to introduce himself, pulled several folded papers out of a satchel and waved them in the air. Whether the gesture was supposed to frighten him or the man's subordinates, Sullivan had no idea. Everyone seemed very red-faced, which boded better for him than he would have expected.

"I have a half dozen letters from supporters of yours," the magistrate went on, putting the papers away without letting anyone else get a look at them. "Well-placed supporters. Apparently you expected that your acquaintance with various noblemen would keep you away from the hangman. You, sir, are incorrect."

"Perhaps it's just that several nobleman are aghast that you would arrest someone for no good reason, and they're informing you of that fact. That's merely supposition on my part, of course."

People frequently didn't know how to address him. Of course he was Mr. Waring, but Dunston had done a poor job quashing the rumors of his noble birth. Or, more likely, his mother had done a fine job making certain all of her well-placed clients knew whose son he was. So legally he wasn't nobility, but socially he wasn't common, either. A bit of a bother for everyone concerned.

He'd never particularly enjoyed being an oddity, but tonight it was proving to be interesting. And he'd ended up by himself in one of the more accessible cells at the Old Bailey rather than being thrown headfirst into some rathole in Newgate Prison. That could also mean that they meant to try him quickly, but since he expected the same outcome whether it occurred in a sennight or a year, he'd rather have room to lie down in the interim.

"Well, if it's merely the nobles rattling their holy sabers, then I suppose we have nothing to worry about. They'll find a new cause by morning. And you can rot in there until you tell us where you've hidden those things you stole from your betters."

Hm. A few weeks ago he would have confessed merely for the embarrassment it would bring to the Marquis of Dunston and his family. It was still tempting; obviously he wasn't being treated as a common thief, so it wouldn't take much to raise an impressive ruckus. On the other hand, a few weeks ago he hadn't been in love — he'd never expected to be in love. And he was finding that he couldn't love Isabel and be reckless at the same time.

He'd already made things worse for her than she could ever have managed on her own. A confession of thievery on his part would absolutely ruin her. And so he merely lifted an eyebrow. "I still think it would help if you could manage to tell me what I'm accused of stealing. Perhaps I made off with a horseshoe or some toasted bread by mistake."

One of the Runners snorted. The magistrate slapped the fellow on the back of the head. "This is a serious matter, Danning. A viscount has accused this man of being the Mayfair Marauder. We will find the evidence, whether he cooperates or not."

Danning rubbed his skull. "But I went to his house myself, sir. Looks as though a bull trampled through it, but none of us found any of the stolen items from the list."

"Then go back and look again. If there was one concealed room, there may be more."

The runner nodded. "Yes, sir. Come along, Howard."

Sullivan watched the conversation in growing confusion. They'd found the hidden room, but nothing inside it. And a bull had trampled through his home, apparently. "Excuse me," he drawled, unable to resist, "but it sounds as though I may have been robbed."

"If it was one of your partners, we'll find them, too. And we'll see whether you still make jests when you're standing before the bar — or when you've a rope around your neck, *Mr.* Waring. Good evening."

The three men left, and Sullivan bent his legs to sink down onto the cold stone floor. It didn't make sense. They'd found the room. Had it been Bram? His friend was the only other one who knew about his dealings, aside from Isabel and her brother. But Bram wouldn't have trampled the rest of his house.

Ice shot down his spine. *Tibby.* She'd gone to his cottage and taken away whatever she thought might have been stolen. She'd been in there with Bow Street on the way. If they'd caught her inside . . .

This had to stop. He admired her courage, and her loyalty to him absolutely left him stunned and humbled. But he was, as Bram would say, a losing proposition. She needed to stay far, far away from him. Better yet, she needed to join the undoubtedly growing group of gossips who'd already condemned him.

He would lose her, of course, but then he'd never really had her. Sullivan closed his eyes. Would she come to his hanging? It would give him strength, to see her there. *Good God.* The amount of his strength would hardly matter shortly thereafter, and he didn't want her to see that. Ever.

There was no question, after all, that he would be found guilty. He'd committed the crimes of which he was about to be accused. His only shield had been that he'd reckoned Dunston and his spawn would never turn him in. Clearly he hadn't added Isabel Chalsey into his calculations, or the fact that Tilden would be courting her. Jealousy apparently overwhelmed honor.

He gave a small smile. So he'd finally managed to make his privileged half-brother jealous. That was something, he supposed, even if it would end up costing him his life.

The door at the end of the corridor rattled and opened. He ignored it; they'd attempted their so-called interrogation on him for the night. Some other poor bloke could have his chance now.

When the dozen or so other prisoners in the cells around him began whistling, though, he opened his eyes. Whatever was going on didn't seem to be usual. One of the prison's guards tromped up and stopped in front of his cell.

"You've a visitor. On your feet."

It was probably Dunston come to gloat.

"I'm quite comfortable here, thank you," he returned, leaning his head back and closing his eyes again.

"Sullivan," a female voice whispered, and the scent of citrus touched him above the stink of his surroundings.

He shot to his feet.

The figure on the far side of the metal bars wore a heavy dark cloak with a hood, but was still clearly female. And with everything he'd decided about the benefits of her staying away from him still in the back of his mind, he strode to the front of the cell, helpless as a moth to lamplight.

"What the devil are you doing here?" he whispered back harshly, his voice unsteady.

"I wanted to see you." Isabel started to push the hood back on her shoulders.

Swiftly he reached through the bars and tugged it up again, concealing her face from the rest of the hallway's occupants. "You can't be here," he said, using the same low tone she'd begun.

"Obviously I can."

"This is dangerous, Isabel. How in the world did you even get here?" He blanched. "You didn't ride, did you? If Zephyr became startled, you might —"

"Shh." She pressed her gloved fingers against his lips. "I didn't ride." Withdrawing her hand before he could grab it, she gestured a short way down the corridor at another cloaked figure, taller and thicker than she, who approached in their direction.

"Who?"

"My father."

"Your —" He broke off, stunned. "My lord."

"Mr. Waring."

"My lord, you must get her out of here. Please. If anyone sees that she's come here to visit me, nothing you do will preserve her reputation."

"Oh, I'm aware of that. And believe me, we tried everything short of locking her in her bedchamber to convince her." The marquis retreated a short way down the corridor again, evidently he was willing to give them some privacy.

That left it to Sullivan, then, to make her see reason. "Don't be so stubborn, Isabel. Don't you realize what would become of you? You love to dance. You'd never be asked onto a dance floor ag—"

"I attended the Fontaine ball this evening," she interrupted, reaching through the bars again to grab his shirtfront. "I didn't dance at all, except when Lord Bramwell asked me to waltz. Oh, and Phillip partnered me for a country dance. And Papa."

He watched her expression, what he could see of it beneath the cloak in the dim light. "I'm so sorry," he murmured. "I should have realized what Tilden meant to do. He made the threat clear enough. I could have been far away from you when they came to arrest me."

"I don't want you to be far away from me." Her hands shook. "And I don't care about dancing. Those stupid people. All they care about is that they're on the right side of any gossip."

"But I did what they accuse me of." Whispering, Sullivan curled his fingers around the bars between them to keep from touching her. "You went to my cottage, didn't you? They said it was in shambles."

"I didn't know where you kept everything. I'm afraid I have some of your own things, hidden away."

"Keep them," he said shortly. Better her than Dunston. "You don't have any of the . . . other things?"

Isabel shook her head. "Your . . . friend took them away." She glanced down the corridor. Whatever her father had said to the guard, it had kept him well out of earshot, but Sullivan appreciated her discretion, anyway. Hanging was one thing he preferred to do alone.

"Good," he said aloud. "Then go home. Be affronted that I tricked you. Do whatever you need to, Tibby. I have nothing to lose."

"Don't be such a martyr," she snapped.

His lips curved. "Don't order me about. I don't work for you any longer."

"Stop jesting, Sullivan. This is serious."

"I know it is. That's why I've been telling you to leave before you get tangled up in it any more than you already are."

"What if you confess, and tell the magistrate *why* you stole the paintings?" she went on, as if he hadn't been trying to make her see reason. "Might they not transport you, instead of . . . hanging you?" A tear rolled down her cheek.

It tore a hole in his chest to not wipe that tear away. He dug his fingers into the bars. "That is a possibility," he acknowledged.

The sudden light that leapt into her eyes as he spoke frightened him. Abruptly he realized why she'd asked the question. *God, he loved this woman.*

"You are not going to Australia with me," he stated flatly, putting every ounce of conviction he possessed into the sentence. "I would rather hang than put you through that."

"Sulli—"

"No."

"Your five minutes is up, *Mr. Smith,*" the guard said, approaching them and making it clear that he didn't believe the name Lord Darshear had apparently given him.

Isabel grabbed his shirt harder, as though she were trying to pull him through the bars. "What can I do to help?" she asked, desperation making her voice shrill. "Anything, Sullivan."

"Stay away from me," he returned, bracing himself against the metal. "In everything. Stay away from me."

"Come, my dear," her father said, putting a hand on her arm. "We must leave."

"No! I want to stay."

"Please, Isabel," Sullivan whispered. "Please go."

"I love you."

"I love you," he returned. "And I'm so sorry. I would give you everything, if I could. But we both know that I can't. So all I can give you is a chance to recover your reputation. Let me do that, at least."

A sob broke from her throat. It felt as though it had ripped from his own chest. With a last look at him she turned and buried her face against her father's chest. For a long moment Lord Darshear looked at him. Sullivan met his gaze, trying to say with his expression what he couldn't with words — that he loved Isabel, and that this was the best and only way he could show it.

Finally with a small nod the marquis turned and left, Isabel still clutched against his side. Sullivan leaned against the bars, watching for as long as they remained in his sight. When the door down the corridor creaked open and then slammed shut again, it felt like the crack of doom.

"Tibby, come down to breakfast."

Isabel remained seated beneath the window of her bedchamber. The sun had risen, then. She hadn't noticed.

Douglas left the doorway and walked into the room. "You've been sitting there all night, haven't you?"

It hadn't actually been that long, she didn't think. They hadn't left the Old Bailey until after two o'clock. Time had become a very odd thing. And she didn't care for it any longer. Time could go to the devil.

Her brother knelt beside her chair. "Come and get something to eat. We can go riding after, if you like. You looked grand yesterday, riding Zephyr. We'll have you jumping fences by the end of the week."

We. Douglas and who else? Not Sullivan, because she would never see him again. And she didn't feel like jumping, anyway. She didn't feel like anything.

"Is she coming down?" Phillip leaned into the room.

Douglas glanced back at their older brother. "I think she's broken."

"I wouldn't doubt it. You might have told one of us, Douglas."

"What, that Sullivan was the thief? Most of the damned paintings that went missing were done by his mother."

"No, the other thing."

"That Tibby was in love with Waring? No one told me that. I just noticed. And I haven't even kissed a chit yet. What does that say for you?"

They had it wrong. They'd used the past tense. As if she didn't love him any longer. As if he were already dead. Perhaps they were merely getting used to saying it that way.

"Don't say his name," Phillip grunted. "You'll only make it worse."

"Worse than what? I'm not even certain she's breathing."

Phillip squatted in front of her. "Tibby, get up. Don't be difficult."

"That's not very nice."

She wasn't being difficult. Not on purpose. It was only that she didn't want to be there. She didn't want to be anywhere, really. But she didn't want to worry them, either. "Yes, let's go have breakfast," she said aloud.

Her brothers exchanged glances, then each one took an arm and lifted her to her feet. She felt stiff; evidently she *had* been sitting for quite a while. They guided her to the door, and then they were abruptly in the breakfast room. That seemed odd. When had they descended the stairs? She couldn't remember doing so.

Someone pulled out a chair for her, and she sat again. Had she dressed for breakfast? Oh, well. She supposed if she were naked, someone would have said something. Or she'd be cold.

"I told you boys to leave her be," her father said from somewhere off to her right.

"But she was just sitting there. I was ready to poke her to see if she would do anything," Douglas returned, setting a plate full of strawberries and toast in front of her.

"And where's Penny? She's still in her evening clothes, for Lucifer's sake." Phillip placed a cup of what looked like tea beside the plate.

Warm arms wrapped around her from behind. "Never you mind what she's wearing," her mother's voice came. "We'll see to

423

it after she eats something."

Douglas's face came into view beside hers. "She's not eating."

Yes, eating. That was why she'd come downstairs. So they wouldn't worry about her. "I'll change clothes after I eat," she said, and picked up a strawberry.

"Put it in your mouth," Douglas instructed.

"Douglas, leave her be."

"She's been holding that bloody thing for five min—"

"Language!"

"Apologies, Father. But it's been a very long time."

Isabel blinked. "It has not been five minutes."

"Yes, it has," Douglas countered. "You need to eat, Tibby."

There was that blasted time again. It hurried here, and stopped there. The next time she blinked, Sullivan would probably be dead. "What time is it?" she asked, fright tightening her chest. That much time couldn't have passed.

"It's nearly noon," her mother said in a soothing voice.

"On what day?" Isabel pushed to her feet. "We have to do something."

"First you eat. Then we'll talk."

Oh, she needed to get out of her head. Nothing in there made sense. But it would hurt outside. Then again, Sullivan was outside, and there had to be something she could do. Something to save him. "They're going to hang Sullivan."

"I think she's coming back to life," Douglas observed.

"Stop talking about me like I'm not here," she snapped. "Papa, do you know the people he took the paintings from?"

"Some of them, yes. But —"

"We — you — should go talk to them. If you can convince them not to press charges, then the magistrate will have to let Sullivan go free."

"That's our Isabel. She's back."

"Douglas, stop it! Don't you understand? Sullivan's been arrested for multiple thefts of property belonging to the aristocracy. They will hang him if we don't do something." Her voice shook. Everything seemed to be shaking, and she didn't protest when Phillip helped her back into her chair.

"The thing is," her older brother said evenly, "we've been at this since dawn."

She looked at him. "You've . . ." She finally looked around the room. Really looked. He, and everyone else who'd taken seats at the breakfast table, looked tired and worried, though she knew it had to be more about her than about Sullivan. But he was part of her, however hard he tried to push her away.

"I don't condone his actions," her father said after a moment. "But I do understand them. And I have to say that Dunston and Tilden both deserve a sound thrashing."

"I don't care about them."

"I know. The problem is, no one else knows the details, and a trial these days takes place as much among the gossips as it does in the courts."

"So we tell everyone."

"The problem, Tibby," Phillip took up, "is that we — and you, especially — aren't going to be believed. You've sided with a commoner."

"Sullivan is not —"

"Please, let's not argue amongst ourselves," her mother interrupted. "We can't indulge in flights of fancy. We must deal in facts."

"And the fact is," Isabel said, nodding, "I'm ruined. I knew it would happen, and I went on anyway. I'm sorry about that. I should have told you everything so much sooner. I didn't even want to like him, you know. I only hired him so I could get evidence and expose him as the thief."

"If I weren't so tired," the marquis growled, "I would be very angry. If he'd been less of a . . . a gentleman, you might have been killed."

Her father considered Sullivan to be a gentleman. For a moment she let that sink into her tired, wounded soul. Small compensation for his current predicament, but it was still something. And the only thing she had to grasp at today. "So you haven't found a solution, then," she finally said. Her eyes felt tired and dry; she didn't seem to have any tears left at all. Otherwise she would have been weeping yet again.

"Not yet. According to today's *London Times,* he's being held but no evidence has yet been recovered."

Of course it hadn't been. Lord Bram had hidden it somewhere. And thank goodness for that, and for the Duke of Levonzy's younger son. She'd never expected to be grateful to Bramwell Lowry Johns for anything except not choosing her for one of his notorious flirtations.

"Even if they never find anything, it will still be Sullivan's word against Oliver's. And if the thefts have stopped, that will speak against Sullivan, as well."

The knocker on the front door distantly clanged. A moment later Alders appeared in the breakfast room doorway. "Begging your pardon, my lord, but Lady Barbara Stanley is here, and urgently wishes to speak with Lady Isabel."

"I don't want to see anyone today," Isabel said. It wasn't quite true that the snubs and cuts of last night hadn't bothered her; if everyone had simply ignored her presence it would have been bearable. It was the snide sideways glances and the half-audible mutterings that had her wanting to scream and pull out her hair.

The butler bowed. "I shall inform her."

A minute later feet pounded down the hallway, and Barbara half stumbled into the room. "Apologies, everyone," she said breathlessly, batting at Alders as the butler rumbled up behind her and tried to block her advance, "but you must hear this."

Phillip stood. "What is it, Barbara?"

"There's been" — she took a breath — "another theft."

Chapter 24

"What?"

Evidently sensing that Isabel was about to suffer an apoplexy, Barbara rushed around the butler and helped her back — again — into her blasted chair. "I was walking in the park with my sister Julia, and everyone was talking about it."

Phillip moved out from his chair and gestured for Barbara to take his place. "Please tell us what you know."

With a nod, Barbara seated herself. "The first thing we heard was that Lord and Lady McGowan's estate in York had been burgled. But then someone told us it was their home on Curzon Street."

"Prentiss House," Phillip supplied.

"Yes."

Isabel clutched her friend's hand. Her very good friend, she was fast realizing. At any other time she would have been happy to see Phillip's growing esteem for Barbara.

Today, though, her friend had brought a candle into a very dark cave, and she couldn't think of anything else. "Is it just rumors?" she asked, hoping fervently that it wasn't. For heaven's sake, what a change a few weeks had made. Now she was hoping — praying, even — for news of robberies. Of course, it eased her conscience a little that Lily Prentiss had been one of the first to begin snubbing her.

"No," Barbara returned. "It's not just rumor. We actually ran across Lily with her cousins in their barouche. They awoke this morning to find a half dozen paintings gone from their walls, including one by Francesca W. Perris."

"Oh, thank goodness," Isabel breathed, feeling faint.

On her other side Douglas waved a napkin, fanning her. "This family has gone mad," he muttered, "because I'm ready to cheer, myself."

"You should have heard all the talk, Tibby," Barbara continued, grinning. "Everyone — or practically everyone on horseback, anyway — was saying what a fool Lord Tilden had made of himself yesterday, accusing Mr. Waring of being the Mayfair Marauder. They're saying it was because Mr. Waring refused to sell him a horse. Your horse, Lord Chalsey."

"Ulysses? I'll be damned." He cleared his throat. "I mean, bless me."

"Whoever the thief is, he certainly did Mr. Waring a favor," Isabel's father said distinctly.

She'd nearly forgotten that Barbara didn't know who the culprit was. "Will they release Sullivan now?" she asked, hope biting at her, almost painful after the cacophony of emotions wrung through her since yesterday.

"I would assume so," her father answered. "Unless they can prove that he is the thief and has an accomplice."

The problem with that was that if they looked hard enough, they would discover it to be the truth. She needed to know he was safe. If he'd been set free, then at least he could flee before they decided to arrest him again. *They* could flee. If he wanted her to go with him, she would. But did he? He'd certainly made a large noise about getting her away from him last night.

"I want to go to the Old Bailey and see what's happened," she stated.

"Absolutely not."

This time her father's expression showed no sympathy at all. Last night she'd pushed harder than she ever had before, and her family had given in. If she attempted it again, she'd likely be risking losing their support. And this morning their support and love had been . . . vital to the continued beating of her heart. "I need to know," she said more evenly.

"Phillip, perhaps you might take a ride in that direction," the marquis suggested.

"Of course." Her brother started out, then paused. "Lady Barbara, are you here alone?"

"No. My maid is with me."

"Then perhaps I could persuade you to take a curricle ride with me."

Barbara blushed. "That would certainly raise less suspicion. Yes. I would be pleased to go driving with you." With a swift kiss on Isabel's cheek, her friend rose and hurried over to take Phillip's arm.

Isabel watched them out of the room. She disliked being removed from the equation. Sullivan was . . . he was *hers*, after all, and now she wasn't supposed to go see that he wouldn't be hanged? Over the past day, though, she'd learned something important: Her parents, whom she'd always known loved her, were also willing to risk their own reputations on her behalf. As were her brothers. She had an obligation to them as much as to herself.

"We were thinking, Tibby," her father said

into the silence, "that we might return to Burling before the end of the Season."

"Because I'm ruined. I apolo—"

"We know you apologize. You were reckless, my dear, but believe it or not, there are worse things than being ruined."

"I —"

"It might have been you put under arrest alongside Mr. Waring," her mother took up. "And your actions reflect on all of us."

"He may behave in a gentlemanly manner," her father continued, before she could slide a single word in, "but he's a horse breeder. And a man without a father in the eyes of the law. There is no reason for you even to have conversed with him, much less for . . . whatever happened between the two of you."

She'd never outright said that she and Sullivan had been intimate, but she'd already known that at least her mother suspected — especially after her own behavior last night. "Am I being selfish to care for him?" she asked, not certain she'd even spoken aloud.

"You're being unwise," her mother returned.

She pushed to her feet, hopefully for the last time that morning. "Then I am still unwise. Douglas, I would like to go riding with you." She sent another glance at her parents. "In the park only. I won't make things any worse."

"You'll very likely be given the cut direct again, as you were last night," the marchioness pointed out.

"I suppose I should get accustomed to it, then." Isabel took a breath. "I shall have to learn not to follow my heart. I'm not certain I still have one beating in my chest after last night, anyway. Perhaps it'll be a simple thing to do."

"Isabel."

"I'm not being dramatic," she returned, heading for the door. "It terrified me to think that he might hang. But now I'm realizing that I've lost him, live or die. Either him or you. And I can't stand the thought of that."

As she left the room, her parents sat in silence. "This isn't over with, is it?" Lady Darshear asked after a moment.

"It took her eleven years to ride a horse," the marquis observed, "but she still managed it. No, I don't think she's given up. And frankly, I'm not certain what to do about it."

"We take her away to Burling before Sullivan Waring manages to set eyes on her again. If he's to be released from gaol at all."

"Yes, you're correct, of course. It's just that . . . as a man, I admire Waring. Last night, his concern was for Isabel and her reputation. I can't accuse Lord Tilden of having the same concerns. It's his actions that have hurt Tibby this time. Not Waring's."

"But you know that she and he must have . . . must have . . . been together," his wife stuttered, blushing.

"Yes. And the part of me that's a father wants to castrate Waring for touching my daughter. If he merely meant to ruin her, though, he could have accomplished it easily. That wasn't his goal."

The marchioness stood. "Well, while we're deciphering his motives, I'm going to summon the servants and begin packing."

Her husband pushed away from the table as well. "I'll help."

Sullivan shaded his eyes as he walked down the front steps of the Old Bailey. Even overcast, the sky seemed bright after a day in the dim, smelly cellar. He took a deep breath.

"You look thinner," Bram drawled from the far side of the street where he sat on horseback, Paris's reins tied off to his saddle. "I think gaol has disagreed with you."

"Very amusing," he returned, accepting the reins as Bram tossed them to him and then swinging up on his gelding. "I suppose I have you to thank for me tasting daylight again?" he went on in a lower voice.

"Have no idea what you're talking about. You know I never help anyone."

"I stand corrected, then. I owe you nothing."

"Wait, I've changed my mind. I do like taking credit. It was me. And I recovered another painting for you, by the by."

Sullivan eyed him. So that was how he'd done it. "Then I offer my thanks again."

They rode in silence for a moment. "It's a bit addictive, isn't it?"

"What?" Sullivan asked. Every muscle in his body wanted to turn toward Bruton Street and ride up the drive to Chalsey House.

"Theft."

"I didn't look at it that way."

Bram eyed him. "No, you wouldn't. At any rate, you're a free man. Shall we to Jezebel's for a drink and a whore? Two whores. I don't share, either."

"No. Home, I think."

"Are you certain?"

"Yes."

"There's not somewhere else you'd rather go?"

Sullivan pulled Paris up. "Is there some information you'd care to impart?"

"Not a thing. Except I received word that you'd been arrested from some hay-covered fellow named Phipps, and then by the time I arrived with wagons at your cottage I found it already being ransacked by Lady Isabel and Lord Douglas Chalsey."

His hunch had been correct. She'd gone herself to attempt to rescue him. Even more telling, she'd sent Phipps for help and ridden home on her own. Seeing Bram still looking at him, he cleared his throat. "She came to see me last night."

This was one of the few times since he'd met Bram that he looked surprised. Shocked, even. "Beg pardon?"

"I told her to go home before she made things worse for herself. I told her to stay away from me." He forced a laugh. "She seemed practically ready to be transported to Australia with me."

"Hm. Silly chit. All this because of that one kiss. She sounds dim and desperate."

Now Bram wasn't even bothering to be subtle with his baiting. "She's neither, and you know it."

"Well, you certainly did nothing to encourage her attentions. We both know that you'd never entangle yourself with a proper young thing."

"A proper young thing of superior birth and bloodline," Sullivan added. He drew a slow breath. He trusted Bram with his life, but hearts were another matter. His friend had long been rumored to have sold his in a game of cards. "I'm a fellow who sees something, makes a decision, and takes action."

"I know you are."

"I'm at a loss, Bram," he finally offered, starting Paris off at a walk toward home again. "I sat in that damned cell last night, and all I could think was that I'd made her cry. Not that they were going to hang me."

"Don't do anything, then," his friend returned, urging his own mount, Titan, to fall in beside Paris. "Oliver's being ridiculed at this very moment for jealousy over you not selling him a horse, and —"

"More of your doing?"

Bram shrugged. "Who can say? I'm a genius. Anyway, Lady Isabel's got enough friends that eventually the stigma of being *your* friend will go away."

"So what do I do, sell her another horse and train it? How many can she purchase before people become suspicious again?"

"Don't let anyone know that you're keeping company with her."

"God, you don't have any morals, do you?" Sullivan retorted, ignoring the fact that he'd already been contemplating exactly that.

"None whatsoever."

"So I suppose I encourage her to marry some old baron or other to keep anyone from suspecting our affair, and I keep climbing in through her window at night?"

"That's how you did it, then," Bram murmured, lifting an eyebrow when Sullivan glared at him. "Yes. Everyone gets to have what they want."

"What if I want more than that?"

"Well, in an ideal world she would be independently wealthy and could avoid marriage while hiring you to run her stables. But —"

"I want to marry her."

Bram stopped again. "You can't," he exclaimed, his usual jaded drawl missing.

Sullivan drew Paris in a short circle around the duke's son. "I know that. I can't help that I want it, though."

"Christ, Sullivan. She's not carrying your child, is she?"

"No. I would not father a bastard. Ever."

"Then what —"

"I love her, dammit all. I love her."

For a flash he saw it in Bram's eyes — the aristocratic dismay. There were some lines even Bram wouldn't cross, and condoning a marriage between an aristocrat and the natural son of a painter was one of them. Then the usual smooth cynicism covered it over. "Your options are limited, my boy," was all he said aloud.

"My options are nonexistent," Sullivan retorted. "Don't trouble yourself."

"Sulli—"

"Thank you again for your help. I have some appointments — if I still have clients. Good day."

He left Bram in the street. The situation wasn't his friend's fault, and neither were the obstacles, but a lie or two would have been appreciated. A faux-offer of support. Anything but that look of affronted horror.

So he'd been proven innocent — even though he was guilty. Oliver looked foolish — even though his accusations had been correct. Isabel had been snubbed just for giving him a hug of gratitude and continuing to employ him afterward — not for the sin they'd actually committed together.

If he'd ever needed a reminder that he was a heathen and didn't belong among the exalted, yesterday had provided it. And he couldn't go on as he had been with Isabel. It wasn't fair to either of them. What, then, was he going to do? Go back to his business as if they'd never met? Read the gossip pages to see who and when she would marry?

It had been easier being a soldier and then a thief. At least he knew what he risked, and what the rewards and consequences could be. In this game, there didn't seem to be any rules — and the only prize he'd earned thus far had been a night in prison and the frustration of realizing that nothing he could do could ever make him good enough to deserve her.

Cursing low and long, he reached his cottage. He half expected the door to be flung open and the stable burned to the ground, but from the outside everything looked the same as it ever did. Riding up to the stable, he dismounted and pulled Paris's reins over the gelding's head.

"Mr. Waring! Thank God!" Samuel strode out of the building and grabbed him bodily around the shoulders. "I knew them magistrates would come to their senses and set you free!"

"Samuel," Sullivan returned, shrugging out of the man's grip as swiftly as he could.

As his other employees emerged, all of them looking relieved, he put Paris between them and himself and went to work unsaddling the gelding. "I'm here and, I hope, finished with that idiocy," he said tightly. Of course they were pleased to see him; without him, they would be out looking for other employment. "There's likely been some damage to my reputation, so let's pull every horse from the auction, and —"

" 'Every horse'?" his head man, McCray repeated, frowning. "But that's half a dozen mares and the two —"

"Instead of the usual lot, I'm going to offer up Hector. Vincent, you'll need to go to Lord Esquille and recover him. We're a week short of the time we contracted him out for stud, but I'll make good on the difference plus five percent of Hector's sale price."

Vincent nodded and headed into the stable. "On my way, Mr. Waring."

"Hector?" McCray's frown had deepened. "He's worth more to you as a stud animal than you could ever sell him for at one go."

"I know that, John. But he's also going to stir up a great deal of interest. I want everyone clamoring after him, and I want whoever doesn't win the bidding to be bloody jealous. Then at the next auction we'll see who thinks they're too good to deal with me."

McCray nodded. "Aye. I'll write up a new docket and get it out to Tattersall's."

"Do that. Halliwell, see to Paris, will you? I need a wash and a change of clothes." And he wanted to see the inside of his house, but the less his employees knew about the actual dealings, the better for them.

"Mrs. Howard near fell down dead when she saw what Bow Street did to your things, Mr. Waring," Halliwell said as he took Paris's reins to lead him inside the stable. "It didn't help when Lord Bramwell Johns came by first thing this morning and told her to stop messing about and go home."

"Is she here now?"

"Aye. She came back a short time ago. She was sweeping up buckets of broken dishes when last I saw her."

"Thank you."

As Sullivan made his way into the small cottage, what he wanted most was a few moments alone to think — or not to think, as imagining Isabel's face and Isabel's kisses and Isabel's voice did nothing but make his chest ache and his throat tighten. Inside the front room, he stopped. Bits and pieces of his life lay scattered and broken across the floor. The walls were mostly bare, and seat cushions were torn open, feathers and cotton spread across the floor like snow.

"Oh, Mr. Waring," Mrs. Howard wailed as she turned from dusting feathers off his end table, "you're alive! I thought they might have hanged you straightaway, and then what good would it be finding out you'd been wronged by that dratted Lord Tilden?"

"Thank you, Mrs. Howard." He brushed off the plump woman, then stopped as he reached the foot of the stairs. "Mrs. Howard, I'll see to this. Take the remainder of the day off. And tomorrow as well. With full pay."

"But there's such a mess here, Mr. Waring. How will you —"

"I'll see to it."

Slowly she set down her duster. "Very well, then, sir. I've a roast baking in the oven in the hope that you'd be alive and returned to us in time to eat it."

"That's very kind of you. I'll see you day after next."

"Yes, Mr. Waring."

He listened from his small bedchamber upstairs until he heard her leave. Thank God. Another person telling him how awful people were to accuse him of theft, and he'd begin pummeling someone.

As he stood there, he was very aware that he stank. He smelled of prison, indescribable scents that couldn't possibly be mistaken for anything else. Scowling, he stripped out of his shirt and waistcoat and boots, then returned downstairs and went outside to fill a water bucket. Standing by the well, he dumped it over his head. Christ, it was cold. He did it again. And once more.

As he straightened, tossing his head to clear his wet hair from his eyes, he abruptly forgot about the wet and the cold. She sat there on horseback, looking at him from across the yard. Isabel.

CHAPTER 25

"Douglas, go talk to the grooms," Isabel said, her gaze still on Sullivan.

Water was running down his bare chest in slow rivulets. Wet and slick and delicious. Her mouth went dry.

"I'm not going anywhere," her brother exclaimed.

She'd already forgotten he was there. Sullivan had filled her thoughts before. But now, after she'd so nearly lost him, she could scarcely remember to breathe at the sight of him.

"I say, Tibby!"

She jumped, uncertain whether that was the first or the fifth time Douglas had said her name. "What is it? For heaven's sake."

"I said we need to go." Her brother frowned at her. "Don't you realize how much trouble we'll be in if Father finds out we came here? Not to mention Mother."

"Yes, I know. A great deal of trouble. Go

away, Douglas."

Her brother sighed, then swung out of the saddle. "When I fall in love with a chit," he said, helping her down from Zephyr, "I'm going to be much more sensible about it." He lowered his voice. "This is a bad idea, Tibby."

"So you've been saying for the past twenty minutes," she muttered back. "I can't explain it to you. I *need* to talk with him."

Douglas nodded as she released his hand. "I saw you this morning. I *do* understand."

She leaned closer. "Then go away."

"Lucifer's balls," he grumbled. "And don't you tell Father I said that. Because I suppose I can say anything I like as long as I'm keeping your secrets."

"Yes, I suppose you can."

He wandered off to the stable, and she watched as he became engaged in conversation with one of the grooms. When she turned to find Sullivan again, all that remained by the well was a large puddle and the bucket. No sign of the man himself.

For a moment she froze. He'd actually gone into the house without even bothering to say hello. She *knew* he'd seen her. Eyes narrowing and her heart clenching, she stomped up to the front door and shoved it open.

"I told you to stay away from me," he growled from just beyond the doorway.

"How am I supposed to do that? Yesterday I thought —"

Sullivan grabbed her shoulder and pushed her back outside. "You do it like this. I don't want you here."

He shut the door on her.

Isabel glared at the heavy oak. He had actually just thrown her out of his home. After what she'd felt this morning, dying would have been easy. And now he didn't even want to look at her. People she'd known all her life had turned their backs on her and gossiped about her last night, and all she'd been able to think about was going to see him, touching him.

She turned the handle. The door didn't budge. *He'd locked her out.* She was the daughter of a marquis, and he was a damned . . . something, and he thought he could dictate everything. She would see about that.

Isabel strode back into the yard, grabbed the empty water bucket, and returned to the door. Then she hurled the bucket at it. It rebounded with a loud thud. "Open this door!"

Silence.

She picked up the bucket and threw it

again. This time it broke with a satisfying crack. "Let me in!"

Again nothing.

The planks of the bucket were a nice size to grasp in her fist. She selected one and began beating on the door. "If you're trying to avoid a scene," she shouted, "you're doing very badly at it!"

"Go away."

"I am a noblewoman, and you are a blasted commoner. I demand that you open this door at once!"

"No."

She continued hammering. One of the grooms emerged from the stable, and then another. Then her brother reappeared. She kept beating on the door. "You think you're being so damned noble, don't you? You're a coward! You're a damned cowar— Ouch!" A splinter dug into her palm.

The door opened. "You've hurt yourself," he said, and took her arm to pull her inside. "What did you do?"

He still wore nothing but his trousers, and those clung damply to his thighs. "It's nothing. A splinter."

Sullivan shut the door behind her. Well, at least she'd made it inside. "Let me look." He guided her toward the window, holding her hand, palm up, in his long fingers.

Artist's fingers, she realized, even with the calluses. "It's deep. Hold still."

"I — Ouch!"

She tried to jerk free, but he held her hand steady, plucking the long spur of wood out from the base of her thumb. A drop of blood welled out, and he brought her palm to his lips, sucking gently. Her knees buckled.

"Isabel." Sullivan caught her, lowering her gently to the floor and kneeling beside her. "Are you well?"

"No, I'm not, you idiot." She shoved at his bare shoulder, trying to ignore the warmth of his skin beneath her hand. "You threw me out of your house."

"And once again, I told you to stay away from me."

Despite his words, he hadn't let go of her injured hand. And his own fingers trembled a little. "We both know what the correct thing to do is," she said, on a hunch running her fingers up his bare shoulder. "But yesterday — this morning — I thought you were going to hang. I apologize if I'm unable to . . . to stop feeling anything because you say I shouldn't."

Ice-green eyes lifted to meet hers. And then he lunged, taking her to the floor, his mouth seeking hers hungrily. With a smothered gasp Isabel kissed him back. She dug her fingers into the hard muscles of his back, trying to pull him closer against her.

"You are so stubborn," he muttered, kissing what seemed like every inch of bare skin she possessed. He unbuttoned the front of her hunter-green riding gown down the front, his mouth trailing after. As his lips grazed her breasts, she gasped again. "So stubborn," he continued.

Isabel kept silent, afraid that if she spoke aloud he would realize what he was doing and stop. Instead she kissed him back, wanting more but letting him direct the moment. When he abruptly pulled away from her, though, sinking back on his haunches, she sat up. "Don't stop."

"Not on the bloody floor." He slid an arm beneath her knees and another around her back, and lifted her up. With his free fingers he bolted the front door and then strode across the floor and up the stairs.

She kissed his throat, feeling the deep rumble of satisfaction and arousal in his chest where he pressed against her side. Her parents knew of her fondness for him now, but she still didn't think they understood it. Even she wasn't certain she could put it into words. He'd helped her face the greatest fear in her life, but not only because he'd shown her how to ride. Because of him she'd realized that other things had more significance than a childhood terror. She might have lost him. She still might lose him, but that was something she could at least fight against.

Sullivan set her down on his large blue bed in his dark, masculine room. He surrounded her here, inside and out. As he settled over her again, she reached up to undo the fastenings of his trousers.

"This is a mistake," he murmured, taking her mouth again, sliding his tongue between her lips. In the next second he grabbed her lapels and pulled them apart, baring her breasts to his very capable hands and mouth.

Of course it was a mistake. Everything between them had been a mistake. That was why it seemed so . . . precious. None of it should ever have happened. Isabel shoved his pants down, and he kicked out of the damp things. In almost the same motion he slid her gown up past her thighs, using one hand and his knees to bare her legs. She helped him, pulling the heavy material of her riding dress up over her hips.

"I want you," he continued in the same desperate tone, and pushed forward, sliding deeply inside her.

Isabel moaned at the filling sensation.

Tossing her head back, she clung to his shoulders with her fingers and wrapped her ankles around his thighs as he pumped hard against her. This, this was what he'd taught her. That two very different and yet not-so-different people could, for a scattering of breathless moments, be one.

"Isabel," he breathed, in time with his motions, his gaze holding hers as she tightened and then shattered with a shaking groan.

At the last moment he yanked free from her grip and rolled away. Breathless, Isabel watched him climax. She understood why he did that, why he left her each time, why that made him a better man than his father. But the deepest part of her heart wished that he wouldn't leave, that he would find his release in her.

"Is that what you wanted?" he finally asked, returning to her and lying on his back so she could rest against him, her head on his shoulder. The shoulder with the two nearly identical scars only inches apart. Two more times luck had kept him alive, two more times they might never have met.

"Part of it," she admitted, running her fingers along his skin.

"It's only partly what I want from you, too, Tibby."

"Take everything, then."

"You would marry me?"

Her heart pounded against her chest, reckless and much less cautious than her mind. "I would if you asked me to."

"I can't do that."

"Sullivan, stop deciding what I do and don't want of my own life. I've thought things through, you know."

"I don't think you have. I'm nine years older than you are, Isabel, and I've seen a great deal of how spiteful and hard the world can be to someone like me. And if you're with me, you will suffer the same fate. Even worse, because you willingly descended to it from a great height."

"I don't care."

"Yes, you do. Or you will. What would you do, live here with me? Take care of my household? That's a task that would keep you occupied for five minutes or so. Cook and clean for me? I have a housekeeper. I don't want you to be my maid, for God's sake."

"You're making decisions for me again." A tear ran down her cheek to land on his hard chest.

"I am not. I want to make certain you understand that in exchange for sleeping by my side you would lose everything — *everything* — that rightfully belongs to you. And even if you're willing to make that sacrifice of yourself, I am not."

No, no, no. She wasn't going to make it that easy for him to pretend he could just say this was ended and have it go away. "Then we just continue with this as we have been. No one need know."

"So you would stay a spinster forever? No children, no husband? Would you live with your parents? Or perhaps take work as some old woman's companion, in a shabby bedchamber with one window always open so I could climb in during the night and do a bit of rutting, then leave before dawn?"

Sullivan watched the anger and frustration growing in her eyes as he forced her to look ahead, to see what lay before her if she remained on this path. He hated himself for doing it, but that was nothing compared to how he would feel if he gave in to what both of them absolutely wanted. He didn't blame her for wanting more of herself than his small life could give her — he wanted more for her just as badly.

"You should go," he said quietly, kissing her forehead and then sitting up.

"How the devil am I supposed to stay away from you?"

"I'm asking myself how *I'm* to stay away from *you.* You're my beating heart, Isabel."

She shook her head, her pretty brown eyes hurt and furious. Whether it was with him or with the situation he didn't know, but he preferred her anger to her tears.

"No," she snapped. "Don't say nice things to me any longer. It's not fair, and it's selfish of you." Swiftly she scrambled off the bed, straightened her skirts, and rebuttoned the front of her gown. "And you're a fool. You make me so . . . angry, Sullivan."

Not looking at him, she left the room and thudded down the stairs. Cursing, Sullivan dragged his damp, unwieldy trousers back on and strode after her. "Isabel."

She whipped around, facing him from just inside his front doorway. "What? I can't love you, and I won't hate you, so what? What do you want of me?"

Everything. "Nothing," he said aloud. "You looked very fine riding Zephyr."

She looked down for a moment, then lifted her gaze again. This time he couldn't even read her expression. "Is that your way of saying our agreement is finished? No more lessons for horse or rider?"

Doom closed over him again, for the second time in a single day. "Yes."

"You . . ." Her sweet mouth closed over whatever it was she'd been about to say. Then she left his home and shut the door softly behind her.

He wished she'd slammed the door, knocked it off its hinges. Sinking onto the bottom step of his stairs, he rubbed at his face. He didn't smell like the Old Bailey any longer, but he did smell like her. Her citrus scent clung to his hair, his skin, his hands. Already he wanted to go after her, to tell her that he'd been wrong and that of course he would be content to climb through her window every night for the remainder of their lives.

He felt torn in half. With every hard beat of his heart the idea of going after her became more reasonable. "Damnation," he muttered, pounding his fist into his thigh.

His house was a wreck, his life was a wreck, and he could think of nothing but plunging forward headlong to make it worse. Why not drag her down into hell? At least they would be there together.

"No, no, no." He shoved to his feet. First he would set his house, and then his life, back in order. It would get easier to forget that she lived and slept only twenty minutes' distance from him.

As he reached the kitchen, he slowed. Small piles of broken dishes lay at regular intervals; he could only imagine what it had looked like before Mrs. Howard had begun cleaning. Why Bow Street would think he'd hidden paintings in a teapot he didn't know, though he imagined some of the carnage had been due to their frustration at not finding what they sought.

Picking his way barefooted through the carnage, he pushed open the door to his secret room and went inside. Bram and his men had returned the paintings, leaving them stacked along the back wall. The other items he'd liberated in an apparently successful effort to turn suspicion away from himself lay in a half dozen boxes on either side of the door.

And a new painting had joined the others. He squatted in front of the small rectangle and picked up the note set against it. Bram's dark, elegant hand greeted him — as if he had known he wouldn't be there to say whatever it was in person.

"Bloody mind-reader," Sullivan muttered, unfolding the missive.

"One more for the collection," he read to himself. *"If you've lost interest in continuing the hunt, perhaps I'll do it myself. B."*

Sullivan picked up the painting and angled it so he could look at it in the candlelight. One of his mother's last works, after he'd left for the Peninsula. In fact, he'd never seen it before. A young girl and boy played along a stream bank, the girl gathering flowers and the boy stacking stones. The lad had the same brown and gold hair as he did; in his mother's paintings, the boys always seemed to look like him. She'd never let go of that image — him as an adventurous youth with a world of possibilities ahead of him.

He wasn't that lad any longer. He'd found his life, and for the most part, he enjoyed it. There was only one thing he'd ever wanted that he couldn't have, and that was a future with Isabel Chalsey. Once he'd met her, everything else had stopped: Revenge, justice, whatever it had been, all became secondary.

Seeing the thirteen paintings there stacked against the wall made something clear. Having them back hadn't gained him anything. Yes, he'd annoyed Dunston, but so did flies and mosquitoes. And that's all the significance that his actions had had, except for himself. They'd nearly gotten him killed.

Perhaps now, though, they could finally be useful. His mother had told him that the paintings were his heritage. Were they? Or were they images of a life he'd never had and would never know? A lie in rainbow hues.

But they weren't useless. If they were his

inheritance, he would do what he needed to with them in order to gain himself a future. Because staying here and brooding over things about which he had no control would get him nothing but madness.

He pushed upright, then headed upstairs to shave and put on some suitable clothes. He needed to do something he'd sworn never to do in his life. He needed to go see the Marquis of Dunston.

CHAPTER 26

"Do you have any idea how poorly this makes you — us — appear?" George Sullivan, the Marquis of Dunston, strode the length of his office and back again to his desk beneath the garden window. "You were damned irresponsible, Oliver."

"What I know," his eldest son Oliver, Viscount Tilden, returned, "is that his name is connected to ours whether we attempt to ignore that fact or not. Simply because no one discusses him to your face doesn't mean they don't talk. I won't have a damned thief going about to dirty our good name."

"So instead we have rumors flying about Mayfair of a false arrest and your jealousy over a horse."

"The arrest wasn't false," Oliver retorted. "One of his damned shifty friends burgled McGowan, and you know that. The truth will come out."

"I don't want the truth to come out. And

what I *know* doesn't signify, Oliver. It's what the rest of London *thinks* that concerns me. And they think you used your high station and influence to have someone arrested for no discernible reason other than your jealousy. And you've managed to make a private matter public. Now the Sullivan and Waring names are irretrievably linked in everyone's mind and on everyone's tongue."

"I —"

"Even worse, you've made him a sympathetic character."

"Then we'll allow it to be known that he's taken up with Lady Isabel Chalsey. That should take care of him."

The marquis rounded on his son. "What would be known is that she favored a nothing over you, a viscount. You would all be ostracized. And I will not have my heir spoken of in the same manner as that . . . upstart."

"This is ridiculous. I've done nothing wrong."

"You've done everything wrong. And the moment you suspected that Lady Isabel preferred Waring, you should have distanced yourself. Obviously the chit has no sense of propriety."

"Obviously," Oliver repeated. "I've remedied that error now."

"Now everyone believes her to be the innocent party in this. Avoiding her will reflect poorly on you."

"I never want to set eyes on that doxy again."

"You will dance with her at the next opportunity. Then you may avoid her."

The viscount clenched his jaw. "This is a damned cartload of horse shit."

"All of it begun by you, so you will set it right. We will not be sneered at or gossiped about. Is that clear?"

"As glass," Oliver commented darkly. "What of Waring and his thievery?"

"He's earned a reprieve. If he begins it again, you will leave it to me to deal with him. It is none of your affair."

"No, it was your affair that began this."

Dunston reddened. "None of that, boy!" he roared. "Now get out and try to prove yourself worthy of my regard again."

Oliver stalked out of the room. A moment later the front door opened and slammed closed. Bah. Oliver could pout all he wanted, so long as he did it in private. Which was where this entire debacle should have stayed — in private.

Because his oldest boy was correct. Whether his friends and acquaintances dared make mention of it to his face, the family had been delivered a blow. Sullivan Waring might have begun the insulting behavior, but Oliver had allowed himself to be drawn into it. And now the Sullivan family, a bastion of propriety, had suffered a blackened eye. It would take some work to recover from the injury.

The butler appeared in the open office doorway. "My lord, you have a caller."

"I'm not in."

His servant hesitated. "I understand, my lord, but . . ."

"What is it, Milken? For God's sake, speak up."

"Your caller, my lord. It's Mr. Sullivan Waring."

For a second Dunston stared at the butler. Clearly he'd heard the man wrong. But Milken's expression remained tense, his body angled as though he were ready to flee the room. Waring. At Sullivan House. "Where is he?"

"On the front steps, my lord."

Outside, where anyone passing by could see? "Show him to the morning room. I'll be there in a moment."

With a quick bow the butler hurried out of the doorway and back down the hall. Dunston paced back and forth in the small office for five minutes. No sense giving the impression that he was anxious.

What could it be, anyway? A threat of blackmail? Assurances that Oliver would no longer make accusations against him? Swiftly he ran all the possible reasons for the unprecedented visit through his mind, and came up with responses to all of them. Only then did he walk down the hallway.

Sullivan stood in the middle of the morning room. Dunston's morning room. He could have seated himself, he supposed, but just walking through the door had been difficult enough. Making himself comfortable — that was both impossible and out of the question.

Dunston took his damned time, but finally he opened the door and walked into the room. "What are you doing here?" he asked without preamble.

The marquis drew out the word "you," making it sound as though he would sooner have expected to see Bonaparte on his doorstep. Since Sullivan would rather have been in France, in all likelihood it equaled out.

"I wish to discuss something with you," Sullivan returned, keeping his voice low and even. There were two other Sullivan offspring and the spouse in residence here, and he didn't want to see any of them.

"You have brought rumor and disgrace to my doorstep. I have nothing to say to you."

"I want to leave London." He'd thought the words over and over during his ride to Mayfair, but saying them aloud felt . . . final. That was what he wanted, though. A stop. A different direction for the remainder of his life.

Dunston started to answer, then closed his mouth, already pinched in perpetual disapproval. "Good. Go, then."

"I have a successful stable here. Relocating my stock and employees and expanding my business will take funds."

The marquis' brow lowered. "You want money? From me? I will not be blackmailed or threatened into any —"

"You took some things that rightfully belonged to me," Sullivan interrupted. "I am prepared to give them to you, in exchange for a fair price."

"You stole them!"

"I only took them back. Now I will sell them to you, as should have been my right in the first place."

"And what would I do with them? They're considered to be in the possession of the Mayfair Marauder."

"I don't care what you do with them. Tell

everyone that after my arrest the thief realized he would be caught sooner or later, and you were able to step in and negotiate their return."

"No."

With effort Sullivan kept his stance relaxed and his fists from clenching. This was the plan. Dunston *would* go along with it, because staying on in London, knowing how close he was to Isabel and being able to do nothing to change the circumstances of his birth, would be impossible. "Yes, you will. I can make the rumors Oliver's roused seem like nothing. And I will do so."

"Blackmail. I despise it. And you."

"Then you shouldn't have made me."

"I should have had you drowned at birth."

"You've already told me that."

"It's still true."

Sullivan looked at him. "You know, I wondered why my mother lived as your tenant even after you refused to acknowledge me. I've figured it out. You loved her. And she cared for you, even after she married William Perris."

"I don't —"

"That's why you did nothing where I was concerned. Your damned obsession with propriety wouldn't let you acknowledge me, but drowning me or sending me off to be raised elsewhere would have angered my mother. And then you would have lost her." He took a slow step closer. "And her memory is why I am going to give you the thirteen paintings I've recovered, along with the other items from the homes I visited. In exchange, you are going to give me ten thousand pounds."

"Ten th—"

"I'm not asking you to acknowledge me, because I know you never would. I'm not asking for an apology, because I know you would never admit to being wrong about anything. This is not an inheritance or a gift. You are paying me what you owe me for the items you took and that I am now making into a legal, private exchange."

For a long moment Dunston glared at him. If the marquis refused to make the bargain, Sullivan would do exactly as he threatened. He wouldn't like it; he'd found that love had dulled his taste for vengeance. His so-called father could thank Isabel for all of this, not that either of them would ever know it.

"Ten thousand pounds, and you will sell a horse to Oliver."

"No."

"I imagine you want all rumors regarding you and that bit of muslin you've been mooning af—"

"Do not insult her. I won't warn you again."

"You want the rumors gone," Dunston revised. "Sell him a horse and they will be."

Damnation. It had to be done, he told himself. And it would help Isabel. "My Hector is going up for auction at Tattersall's day after tomorrow. He's the best stud stallion I own. Tilden can bid for him."

"A private sale would be more effective."

The marquis was correct. "Very well. I'll sell him my bay gelding, Paris. My private mount, in a private sale. As long as I don't have to see him or speak to him. And the amount is one hundred fifty pounds. No negotiation."

"Done."

He was fond of Paris. This was supposed to be painful, though, he decided. More painful. "I'll send the horse and the items here tomorrow, separately. You have the cash money here for my man McCray at noon."

Dunston nodded. "Anything else?" he asked, his tone trying to be sarcastic and not quite succeeding.

The pain went both ways, then. Good. Whether Dunston's came from being forced to part with money or from knowing to whom he had to give the funds, or even from something deeper, Sullivan didn't know. Neither did he care. "No. Yes. There is to be no further snubbing of or gossip about Lady Isabel Chalsey. Anything you can do to help recover her reputation, you will do."

"She does seem to be a mostly innocent party in this." The marquis drew a breath in through his nose. "It will be done."

"Thank you for that. The rest makes us even. Good day." Sullivan turned on his heel and headed for the door.

He expected a parting insult, steeled himself against it. The sound of silence from the morning room behind him seemed almost like a . . . victory. A very small one, but he would take what he could get.

And that left only one more thing to do.

If Isabel had any doubts that her parents truly meant to leave Town before the end of the Season, the fact that they'd packed the entire household in three days proved it. She loved Cornwall, and she loved Burling, the way the breeze from the ocean came up in the afternoons, salted and wild. But leaving London meant leaving every possibility of a life with Sullivan behind. That made their imminent departure almost too painful to consider.

She didn't argue or balk at any of the whirlwind around her — after all, this was for her benefit. Even so, she couldn't help glancing out her bedchamber window every few minutes to see whether Sullivan would appear on the drive.

His things had mysteriously vanished from the tack room. Her younger brother said nothing about it to her, and she hadn't quite felt up to asking. Now, though, she'd begun to debate whether her imaginings were better or worse than hearing that yes, Sullivan had sent over a note, and yes, he'd mentioned that he didn't want her to know anything about it. Or worse, he hadn't mentioned her at all.

"Tibby?"

"I'm upstairs, Mama," she called back, stirring from her seat by the window to pretend that she'd been assisting Penny with packing up her clothes.

The marchioness practically floated through the open door. Something had lifted her spirits. Isabel stopped rifling through her hair ribbons to watch.

"Tibby, look at this. We've been invited to a dinner party at Lord and Lady Clements's home tomorrow."

Isabel frowned. "They're good friends of Lady Dunston."

"Yes, they are. I think this bodes very well."

"Does this mean we're delaying our departure?"

Her mother looked from her to the invitation. "I would like to, but neither do I want anything to happen that might . . . cause more damage."

"I've already done enough of that," Isabel returned feelingly. She knew other families who would have banished or disowned a daughter for the chaos she'd caused. But bereft as this had left her, she still felt their warmth and caring and concern wrapped around her. "I'll do my utmost to be charming and innocent."

With a smile, the marchioness kissed her on the cheek. "We'll decide on our plans after the weekend, then. Who knows? This may signal the end of the nonsense."

Uncertain whether her mother meant the rumors Oliver had raised or her own behavior, Isabel smiled back. "I do hope so."

The dinner party did go well, and so did the soiree after that, and the ball on the following Tuesday. Isabel didn't understand quite what had happened, since no new other scandals had erupted to take everyone's attention, but her so-called indiscretions had apparently been forgiven and forgotten.

So the family unpacked again, and she pretended that she didn't still look for Sullivan on the face of every rider who passed the house or who rode by while she exercised Zephyr in Hyde Park.

"Did you see the bonnet that Fiona Meston was wearing?" her friend Barbara asked as they stepped down from the barouche they'd taken shopping.

"Someone should tell her mother that freckles are endearing, not something to be hidden away." Isabel lifted a hatbox and stepped back as Tom the footman came to unload the remainder of her purchases. She wouldn't say anything more about Fiona; it would feel like gossip, and she avoided that with a passion.

Barbara glanced around them, then took Isabel's arm. "I'm not supposed to tell you this," she whispered, "but Phillip took me to Tattersall's yesterday morning."

Isabel's heartbeat quickened. *Oh, for heaven's sake.* Now she couldn't hear mention even of the horse auctions, because Sullivan frequented them. *Stop it, you silly chit.* "I'm so glad that Phillip has finally realized how wonderful you are," she said aloud, knowing that was not what her family was trying to keep from her.

"Yes, he's quite wonderful himself." Barbara blushed prettily. "But the thing is, we saw . . . *him* there. His prime stallion, Hector, was up for auction. It sold for four hundred and eighty pounds."

He'd sold Hector? Why would he sell the most sought-after stud in the country? She realized that Barbara was looking at her expectantly. "That's odd," she offered.

"And there's something el . . ." Barbara trailed off as she looked beyond Isabel's shoulder.

"Good afternoon," the cool drawl of Oliver Sullivan came from above and behind her.

Squaring her shoulders, Isabel turned to face him. "Good —" She stopped, staring at the horse he rode. "What are you doing with Paris?" she demanded.

"I purchased him. He's a fine boy, too, aren't you, fellow?" He patted the gelding on the neck.

"But —"

"I wondered if I might speak with you for a moment," Lord Tilden continued, dismounting.

"Are we speaking now?" she retorted.

"I hope that we might be." A muscle in his cheek jumped. "I — My father, that is, recently acquired the paintings and other items taken throughout Mayfair. Apparently the Marauder grew worried that the authorities would catch up to him, and so he contacted Dunston. So I asked if I might return your family's pieces to you, and apologize at the same time for any . . . trouble I might have brought to you."

She watched him speaking. He knew who the thief was, just as he had to have realized that she did. This tale, then, wasn't for her benefit. "Thank you," she heard herself say. "Will you bring them inside?"

"Of course." He pulled a flat package from the back of his saddle.

"Tibby, I'm to have tea with Mama and Julia," Barbara said, looking from her to Oliver. "Unless you —"

"I forgot. Thank you, Barbara. I'll see you tonight, yes?"

Barbara kissed her on the cheek. "You shall."

Once Barbara climbed back into the barouche and the vehicle rolled onto the street again, Isabel motioned for Oliver to follow her up the shallow steps and inside the house. "I'm surprised to see you," she said. "We didn't part well."

"And my behavior was unforgivable. By way of explanation," Oliver continued, nodding as Phillip, accompanied by Douglas, trotted down the stairs to join them, "I'd badly wanted Paris from Mr. Waring, and he'd refused to sell the animal. I had no idea what would come of everything. Thankfully we've made amends, and as you just saw, he did agree to part with Paris."

"Yes, and why is that, again?" she returned, taking the Francesca Perris painting from him and handing it to Douglas. "Please spare me the nonsense."

His jaw clenched. "The details are exactly as I said. Anything else, Isabel, is none of your affair." He pulled the porcelain dove, small crystal bowl, and silver salver from another satchel and placed them on the hall table. "I assume this is everything."

"Yes, it is," Phillip said when she declined to answer.

"Very well. Good day, then." He turned around and left the house.

"Well, that's interesting," her older brother mused. "Apparently the Sullivans and Mr. Waring have had some dealings."

"Shh," Douglas muttered. "Don't mention his name."

Isabel glanced from them to the pile of returned goods, then headed back out the front door. "Oliver!" she called.

He pulled Paris to a halt halfway down

the drive. "What is it?" he asked brusquely.

"Why did Sullivan sell Paris to you?"

For a long moment he glared at her. "So that the difficulties would appear to be between him and me, and that you were in no way involved."

Sullivan had done it for her. "That's why you and your family have gone out of your way to be civil to me, as well, isn't it?"

"It was part of the agreement." He looked away down the street, then drew in a breath as he returned his gaze to her. "You could have had me, you know," he said slowly. "Now I won't have his castoff, and he has his blunt to leave London. Permanently." He paused. "At least I got a horse out of the deal."

With that, he kicked Paris in the ribs and trotted off down the street.

Isabel sank down on the step. Sullivan was leaving London. None of the things Oliver had said mattered in the slightest, except for that. He'd meant it, then. He wouldn't allow her to be a part of his life, however much she might be ready to accept it.

"Tibby?" Douglas sat beside her.

She lay her head on his shoulder. "Did you know he was leaving London?"

"I knew that one of the big stables was in the process of relocating," her younger brother answered. "I figured it was him."

"Why didn't you say anything?"

"What good would it have done?"

She thought about that for a moment. "None."

"Then I don't know whether you want to go inside or not."

Isabel lifted her head to look at him. "What?"

He nodded his chin toward the street. "Someone's here to retrieve Molly. And this time you can't say I didn't tell you what was going on."

For the space of a heartbeat, Isabel closed her eyes, the remainder of her brother's prattling fading into nothing. Then she looked in the direction Douglas indicated. Sullivan rode up the drive on his black Achilles, his ice-green gaze steady on her. "I think I'll stay out here," she murmured.

Sullivan drew up Achilles at the foot of Chalsey House's front steps. He'd spent the morning rehearsing what he would say and how he would go about it. He needed to say goodbye to Isabel. She'd walked out of his house and shut the door on him. For her sake he should probably have made that their last encounter. For his sake, though, he wanted to see her one last time, and to make her understand that this was the best, most logical way to end things. Still, seeing Isabel sitting there as though she were waiting for him threw off the balance he'd carefully assumed.

"Good morning," he said, swinging down from Achilles.

She remained seated. "Good morning. Douglas, would you fetch Molly for Mr. Waring?"

So he was back to being Mr. Waring again. Stifling a frown, he tied off Achilles and sat on the step as Douglas nodded and hurried around the side of the house. "I saw Tilden up the street. He didn't look happy. I presume he was here?"

"Yes, he returned the items that were stolen from the house."

Sullivan nodded. One of the clips in her pretty blonde hair had come loose. He worked his fingers, fighting the urge to touch her. They could be seen from the street, after all, and he had no intention of setting her reputation back on its heels again. Not when she seemed to be returning to Society's good graces.

"Interestingly enough," she said abruptly, "Oliver was riding Paris."

"I do sell horses," he countered smoothly. "It's how I maintain my business."

"Is that why you sold Hector, too?"

"I sold Hector because people want him. My business has been a bit . . . flat over the past few weeks. I wanted the attention."

"It seems odd, then, that you would choose to leave London now."

He blew out his breath. "You are very well informed."

"I discovered it all just a few moments ago," she returned, finally looking at him. "You should stay."

"I can't, Isabel."

"Because of me?"

"Honestly?"

"Yes, if you please."

His Isabel had changed since they'd met. She seemed less changeable, and more serious. She appealed to him even more now than she had before. And that was dangerous. Keeping that in mind, he edged an inch or two farther away from her. "Honestly, then. I can't stop thinking about you. You're in my mind, in my heart, every moment of every day. And I can't have you wi—"

"You *can* have me. That's what I keep trying to tell you."

"I would ask for your hand in a second if I thought I could give you what you deserve. But we both know that I can't do that. And whatever you say now, you would resent me once you realized that having me in exchange for everything else you have now wouldn't be worth it."

Tears hovered at the corners of her eyes. "You should let me decide that."

"I want to. And that's why I'm leaving. I sold those damned paintings to Dunston for a very good price. I bought a small estate in Sussex. I'll have ten times the land I had here in London."

Isabel stood, brushing off her skirts. "I thought I was the proud one, Sullivan, but I was wrong. I'm sorry you think so little of your life that you don't wish anyone to share it with you. And I hope your business does well in Sussex. Now, if you'll excuse me, I need to go change for luncheon."

"Isabel." He stood up as she topped the stairs and the butler pulled the door open to admit her. "Tibby."

"You're already the man that I want, Sullivan," she said, turning in the doorway to face him. "If you ever realize that it's you and not your standing in Society that I fell in love with, you know where you can find me. But I'm tired of fighting you for something we both want. If you're happier being miserable, then do it without me. I suppose you would have to, though."

With that, she went inside. The butler sent

him a startled, affronted look, and then closed the door.

Sullivan looked for a moment at that door. She still didn't understand. He couldn't even have followed her inside, because he wasn't allowed through the front doors of fine houses. And she wouldn't be, either, if he married her.

"As you wish," he whispered.

CHAPTER 27

Three months later

"Mr. Waring, someone left open the conservatory window last night, and the rain has ruined the burgundy chairs."

Sullivan looked up from his accounts book to eye Dudley. "Then throw them out," he returned.

"But it's only the material, sir. The rest can be sal—"

"Then do that, Dudley."

The butler gave an audible sigh. "Yes, sir. I only needed your permission first."

With another glance down at his expense accounts, Sullivan forced a smile. "Then you have it. Eventually you'll have me trained in all this. Bear with me."

The butler nodded. "Of course, sir. And Mrs. Howard wishes to know your choice for the evening's menu."

Mrs. Howard never used to ask what he cared to eat. He supposed having a kitchen thrice the size of the old one and a cottage for her and her husband to live in had made her more conscious of her new role. And his. "Tell her to cook whatever she wishes. She knows I'll eat it."

A muscle jumping in his cheek, the butler sketched a bow and left the room. Sullivan went back to work on figuring his monthly expenditures, then tossed the pencil onto his desk and sat back.

Out his window he could see Halliwell exercising Achilles on the path beside the stream. Closer by, in the main stable yard, Vincent and the new fellow were unloading sacks of feed grain from a wagon while Samuel led one of the new brood mares out to the nearest enclosed pasture.

Most men probably would have selected a room with a more scenic view of their property to be their office, but the stable yard was the most vital part of his property. He wanted to keep an eye on it. Actually, he wanted to be out in it, but lately he seemed to be spending more time closed behind doors than out of them.

He should have expected that, he supposed, going from owning a small stable and employing five people to owning an estate with a name and employing nearly two dozen. It kept him busy, and left him mentally and physically tired — and that had been the best part of all of this. No time to think of other things.

Except that she still managed to keep her place, in that corner of his heart that she'd taken over, on the fringes of his mind where an image of her could arise at every unexpected moment of the day or night. Especially of the night. Isabel. His Isabel.

He shook himself, pushing to his feet. So now he had the trappings of nobility. However wealthy he might become, in the eyes of her world he remained a nonentity. None of the nobles on the estates neighboring his ever came to visit, not that he'd yet asked them over. They came on occasion for business, but with his new philosophy of trying not to hate every aristocrat, he didn't want to ask them to stay for meals and have them refuse. And he hadn't been invited to their homes except to see and compliment their stables.

It would have been enough. Before he'd met Isabel, this life would have made him ecstatic — except for the complications of trying to run a household and the amount of time he had to spend bent over his books. The price of being successful, he supposed. And he had a great many more people relying on him now.

He walked down the hallway to his small library. It was odd, having more rooms than he knew what to do with. Next he'd be ordering a billiards table — a nobleman in everything but actuality.

Once Bram had learned that he was putting together a library, the blackguard had begun sending him books of Far Eastern erotic art, and another small stack of them lay spread across a chair. Hm. Dudley had been at them again, then.

As for himself, whatever the joke Bram thought he was playing, nothing stirred him any longer. It was probably odd that he would remain faithful to a woman he would in all likelihood never see again, especially after the life he'd lived, but he would have her or no one.

Wandering to the window, he looked outside. The view from the library was of the front of the house and the side pasture, the latter being used by half a dozen mares he'd acquired since the move to Sussex. The former was empty — and then it wasn't.

A single black coach turned up the long, winding drive toward the house. A yellow coat of arms adorned both doors, but it was too far away to make out. Sullivan frowned. He didn't have any appointments scheduled until tomorrow afternoon. And it couldn't be Bram, because he refused to travel in a coach bearing his father's family crest.

Returning to his office, he shrugged into his coat. He refused to contemplate who the occupants might be, because he knew whom he wanted it to be. And that was ridiculous.

She wouldn't come after him, anyway. She'd made that very clear. It was up to him, she'd said, and he wasn't going anywhere. He wasn't that selfish. Or so he told himself.

"Mr. Waring," Dudley said, as he topped the stairs, "you have a caller."

"Who is it?"

The butler held out a silver tray. Belatedly Sullivan reached out and took the calling card. Damned pretension. Then his breath stopped. "Did you let him in?" he asked, clenching his fist around the card and rendering it into an unrecognizable wad.

"He is in the morning room, sir."

"Very well." Making himself breathe again, he headed down to the ground floor.

"Shall I bring tea, sir?"

"Tea? No. He can get his own refreshment somewhere else."

The butler cleared his throat. "Very good, sir."

Outside the morning room Sullivan

squared his shoulders. Then he opened the door and walked inside. "Lord Dunston," he said.

The marquis turned from gazing out the far window to face him. "Well, you *look* like a gentleman."

"You've come quite a distance," Sullivan returned coolly, easier now that he knew the tone of the meeting. "I would have hoped you had a better insult to hand."

"You made a muck of things for me this Season," Dunston continued, remaining on his feet. Either he didn't want to soil himself by sitting on his bastard's furniture or he wasn't comfortable there. It was an interesting thing to realize.

"You began it." Sullivan deliberately took the seat closest to the hallway door.

"Yes, I suppose I did."

Sullivan opened his mouth, ready to continue the argument. Then he closed it again. Well, that was a surprise.

"You didn't expect to hear me admit that, did you?" the marquis went on. "You are not without fault, certainly, but it was my actions that precipitated yours. While you acted wrongly, I expected more of myself. And of my son."

"I'll assume you're speaking of Tilden."

Dunston flipped a hand in dismissal. "I've

sent Oliver to tend one of my properties in York." He paused for a moment. "And I'm wondering whether your sale of that horse to him was intentional on your part."

Sullivan frowned. "Beg pardon? Of course I knew I was selling him a horse. A damned fine one."

"In everyone's eyes he bullied you into it, to try to recover his own reputation."

This time Sullivan snorted. "Can't say I'm too troubled by that."

"No, I didn't imagine you would be." Finally Dunston came around the front of the chair and sat opposite Sullivan. "The problem being that I won't have us being seen as cruel or overly arrogant in picking on a social inferior. Especially a respected one. And a talented one."

"Then you probably shouldn't have done it. Don't expect me to come out and correct everyone's impressions. I doubt they would listen to me, even if I were so inclined."

He only half paid attention to what he was saying. Instead, his thoughts caught on what Dunston had said. Not that he was a social inferior — he knew that well enough. But that the marquis knew him to be respected. The way Dunston had said the words, it almost sounded as though he shared in the feeling.

Isabel had told him the same thing. Not in the same way, since she wasn't concerned about Society's perception of either of them. But that *she* respected him. As a man.

And he'd walked away from her. He'd made the decision that she wouldn't like his life, that she wouldn't be able to hold her head up when her old friends snubbed her. But they'd been snubbing her since a fortnight after he and Isabel had met, and she'd never faltered. She'd tried to tell him that, as well, but he hadn't listened.

He closed his eyes. *Good God. What had he done?*

"I've decided to acknowledge you."

Sullivan shot to his feet. "Excuse me. I need to be somewhere."

"Didn't you hear me?" Dunston called, following him into the hallway. "I said I mean to acknowledge you."

"Yes, do whatever you want," Sullivan said absently, heading up the stairs. "Dudley! Have Halliwell saddle Achilles. And send Gerald up to see me. I need to pack some things."

She would be at Burling at this time of year. It would take him two days to get to Cornwall on Achilles, if he rode hard enough. And he would.

"I am making you respectable!" Dunston bellowed up the stairs. "Show some bloody gratitude!"

"I'm already respectable," Sullivan returned, pausing at the top of the stairs. "You want to help your family. That's fine. Do what you will."

"This will put an end to the feud between us."

"I ended it three months ago, my lord."

"I'm prepared to give you a yearly stipend."

Sullivan lowered his brow. "I don't require anything of you. This is about what you feel is necessary. Now, if you'll excuse me, I need to go see whether I can mend the largest mistake I've ever made in my life."

Dunston looked up at him for a long moment while Sullivan tried not to fidget. Finally the marquis nodded. "You are not mine," he said.

With a scowl, Sullivan took a step back toward Dunston. Not that damned business again. "I'm not your son? Then why are you —"

"No! No. You are not my largest mistake. You . . . you have courage, and a greater sense of honor than others of my blood."

"Thank you. See yourself out, will you?"

The marquis blinked. "You won't —"

"Good day, my lord."

If Dunston expected to be called father or some such thing, he was in for a disappointment. Still, being acknowledged would make him more acceptable in the eyes of the *ton*. There would still be places he couldn't go, not that he cared. No, he'd discovered something else, thanks to George Sullivan: Even with his birth and the thefts — or perhaps because of them — he was a good *man*. The other things didn't matter.

And now he needed to go convince someone else that he'd learned his lesson, and hope that she was more forgiving toward him than he seemed to be toward his own flesh and blood.

"I am not going to teach you to jump," Douglas stated.

Isabel urged Zephyr around her brother and his mount. "Why not?"

"First of all, Father would break my skull whether or not you broke yours. And secondly, no."

She grimaced at him. "I'll ask Phillip, then."

"He'll say the same thing."

Yes, he probably would. In truth, she didn't feel secure enough in the saddle to attempt leaving the ground. But it would be something she could strive for. Something to keep her occupied. She'd nearly run out of things to embroider and books to read. And the village women would begin throwing rocks at her if she went down to bring food and clothes and help them plant their gardens more frequently than the thrice a week she'd already managed.

"Come along. We still have another mile around the lake, and I'm getting hungry."

"You're always hungry."

He flashed her a grin. "I'm a growing boy." With a kick he sent his gelding, Thunderous, into a gallop. "Try to match this," he called over his shoulder. "Then we'll talk about jumping. And I'll wait for you at the bridge!"

"Men." Isabel sighed. "Walk on, Zephyr."

Once she centered herself on her seat, she flicked the reins again. "Trot, girl."

Her brothers both directed their mounts with their heels and the reins, but she felt more comfortable stating what she wanted. Apparently Zephyr's trainer had realized that, because the mare responded most readily to verbal commands.

With the ever-watchful groom falling in behind her, she continued along the lake path at Burling. Though she'd traveled on it since she'd been a child, this was the first autumn she'd seen it from horseback. And she loved it. Every day, weather permitting, she dragged Douglas or Phillip or her father along the lake. When they had business elsewhere, she went out with just Otto the groom.

Sullivan had broken her heart, but he'd given her some freedom. The trade didn't seem quite fair, but at least she could feel the sun on her face and pretend that the tears in her eyes were from the crisp sea breeze.

"Don't wind the reins around your left hand," a low voice drawled from behind her and to the left. "Let them hang down along your side."

Oh, my God. She flinched at the familiar voice, and Zephyr tossed her head, nickering. "Whoa, girl," she said, her voice shaking a little. "That's a good girl."

Before the mare even came to a stop, a strong arm reached over to hold on to the bridle. Isabel drew a sharp breath and looked over. Sullivan sat close enough to touch, his ice-green gaze on her face. "I didn't mean to startle you," he muttered.

His tawny hair was windblown, his cheeks and chin dark with beard stubble. Aside from tired shadows beneath his eyes, he looked exactly the same as the last time she'd seen him. He hadn't wasted away, pining for her. For the briefest of seconds she felt torn between disappointment and keen, painful joy at seeing him again.

"Help me down," she ordered Otto, who hovered on horseback several feet away.

Before the groom could dismount, Sullivan beat him to it. "Go back to the house," he countered. "I'll see to Lady Isabel."

So he was still ordering her grooms about. "Do as he says, Otto," she added, seeing the groom hesitate. Obviously Otto didn't know the famous Sullivan Waring by sight. "I'll be in momentarily."

The groom tugged on the brim of his hat. "Very good, my lady."

Once the groom was out of sight through the thin scattering of trees, Sullivan lifted his arms. Not certain yet what she would say even if she could keep her voice steady, Isabel pursed her lips and allowed him to put his hands around her waist and lift her to the ground.

As soon as her feet touched the path, she pulled free of him. "Now. What the devil are you doing here?"

He tilted his head, a lock of hair obscuring one eye. "I thought about what you said."

Joy pushed up through her heart again, and her mind pushed back just as fiercely. She was *not* going to go through that hopeless helplessness again. "Hm," she said noncommittally.

" 'Hm'?" he repeated, his brow lowering.

"You said you'd thought about what I said. You didn't say what you'd decided about it."

Brief, exasperated humor touched his gaze. Good. Now he knew how she'd been feeling for the past . . . forever, it seemed. Since the night they'd met.

"Very well. I decided that you were correct. I shouldn't have been making your decisions for you."

She blinked. "*That's* what you decided? That *you* don't know how *I* feel about *my* life?"

"That's not everything I decided," he retorted. "I just began with that so I could get the apologizing over and done with."

"Just like that?" Perhaps she was snapping too hard, but if she could control the conversation, then he wouldn't be able to hurt her. She couldn't stand it if he simply apologized and left again.

"Isabel, please. I've ridden for two days. I just finished speaking with your father. I don't —"

"What?"

"I'm attempting to do this corr—"

She coiled up her fists and shoved. With a surprised *whumph,* Sullivan staggered backward — and landed on his backside in the lake.

"Isabel!" he roared, shooting back to his feet.

For a stunned second she just stared at him. "Oh! I didn't mean for —"

Sullivan strode out of the water, swept her up in his arms, and dove back in. Cold water closed over her head. Sputtering, Isabel scrambled back to her feet.

"How dare —"

"I love you, damn it all!" he broke in. "Will you let me finish what I'm trying to say?"

Knee-deep in water, a fish, she was certain, nibbling at her ankle, Isabel folded her arms over her chest and tried to remember to breathe. "Very well," she said with as much dignity and calm as she could muster. "You did come all this way."

"Yes, I did. Dunston came to see me."

She searched his eyes. That couldn't have been pleasant, but all she could see was the same slightly amused expression deep in his gaze. "Are you well?" she asked.

He nodded. "He said something that

struck me on my thick skull. Apparently Oliver and the family have found recovery from the scandal of my arrest difficult because they look like bullies, and I am well respected." A slow smile touched his mouth. "He respects me."

"It's about time he realized that. And you, as well."

"I know, I know. You told me the same thing." He took a breath. "I suppose, much as I hate to admit it, that I wanted to hear it from him. But that's not the point, is it?"

"You tell me."

"I have an estate now," he went on. "Amberglen. And I hired a butler so I wouldn't have to keep running down the stairs when someone came calling."

She smiled. "I'm happy for you. Truly."

"Thank you." He reached out, unfolding her arms and taking both of her hands in his. "I have aristocratic neighbors, but I cannot guarantee that they will ever come calling, or send out an invitation for a social visit."

"Sullivan."

"I know, you don't care about that. But are you certain? Absolutely certain?"

Goodness. This time when joy pushed at her heart, she let it in. *Finally.* "I —"

"And I nearly forgot," he interrupted with

498

the worst timing ever. "As I was running out the door to come after you, Dunston decided that the only way for his family to recover their reputation is for him to acknowledge me as his son."

Her mouth gaped open. "You left that until now?" she managed.

"It didn't signify. But I thought it might be a point in my favor when I spoke with your father. Which is why I spoke with him first. So he wouldn't shoot me when I returned to the house with you."

"He wouldn't dare," she breathed, tears gathering in her eyes and tumbling down her cheeks.

Sullivan sank to his knees in the water. "Isabel," he murmured, still holding her hands in his, "you set my life upside down, and you've made me happier than I ever would have dreamed I could be. I thought I needed to be someone I wasn't in order to win you. But you liked who I was. I love you. . . . I love you with everything in me. Isabel, will you marry me?"

She gulped air, tears obscuring her eyes. "Yes," she quavered, throwing herself into his arms. An estate, a life without total ruination — she still didn't care. He'd asked as the man he was, and she loved him for that. Everything else was secondary. "Yes,

I'll marry you."

He kissed her, pulling her hard into his arms. "Thank God," he murmured thickly, kissing her again and again. "Thank God."

"I love you, Sullivan," she whispered against his mouth, the cold water beginning to make her shiver despite the warmth welling up inside her.

"I love you, Tibby. So much."

She wrapped her arms around his shoulders, holding him tightly. "May we please get out of the water now?"

With a chuckle he lifted her in his arms and slogged to shore, where Achilles and Zephyr stood calmly nibbling at the grass. "As you wish, my lady. As you wish."

EPILOGUE

Isabel stood on the front steps of Amberglen and waved into the morning sunlight. The coach bearing the Darshear coat of arms rolled down the curving road and out of sight behind the hill. With a sigh, she lowered her arm again.

"Please tell me there's no one else."

Sullivan took her hand. "That, my dear, was the very last of our guests. With the exception of twenty-seven employees and eighty-one horses, we are alone."

She smiled. "You make it sound crowded."

"Then perhaps we should find somewhere more private."

Before she could respond, he swept her up in his arms and carried her back inside the manor. The butler saw them going up the stairs, laughing, and so did a footman and two maids. It still seemed odd, that people could know she loved Sullivan, that they touched and kissed, and no one so

501

much as batted an eye.

No one here at Amberglen, anyway. And considering that they'd already been invited to three house parties by neighbors, their acceptance seemed likely to spread as far as the borders of Sussex, if not beyond.

"What is it?" he asked, looking down as he shouldered open the door of the master bedchamber.

"I'm married to you," she whispered, curving her hand along his lean face.

Sullivan leaned back, closing the door behind them. "In a church and in front of witnesses, so don't try to escape me now." He chuckled as he set her down gently on the wide bed. "Bram said I made a beautiful groom."

"No, he said you made a passable groom. Only a fortnight, and you're already exaggerating the tale." She reached up to push his jacket off his shoulders and down to the floor.

Kicking out of his boots, Sullivan slipped onto the bed beside her. "It'll be different now, with your friends and family gone. Not everyone will be all smiles to see us together."

She tangled her fingers into his hair and pulled him over for a deep, slow kiss. "For the last blasted time, Sullivan James Waring, I don't care who smiles at us or who doesn't."

He smiled against her mouth. "Yes, yes. I believe you." With a hug he rolled them so that she was straddling his hips. Sitting up with her, he reached around her back to slowly unbutton her gown. "I think you should wear fewer clothes," he murmured, kissing her shoulder as he lowered her dress to her waist.

"That might make people talk."

As his mouth closed over one breast she gasped, arching her back. Sullivan's warm hands trailed down her stomach and then lower, and she shivered deliciously. All hers. He belonged to her now, much more so than when she'd attempted to blackmail him.

She sat back to yank his shirt free, and he pulled it off over his head. Then she went to work unbuttoning his trousers, her fingers eager and stumbling over the fastenings.

"No one's going to interrupt us, you know," he murmured, kissing her again. "Take your time."

"This is the amount of time I want to take," she returned, standing up to shrug out of her gown. "And you don't appear to wish to wait, either," she observed with a breathless grin.

"If it had been up to me, once we left the church we wouldn't have set foot outside this room except to eat."

He pulled her to the bed again, putting her on her back to kiss her once more. His warmth surrounded her, heating her from the inside out. And to think, once she'd believed that being Society's darling provided her with everything she wanted. Being his darling, however, meant so much more.

Slowly he entered her, the slide exquisite and breathless. "Sullivan," she moaned, digging her fingers into his shoulders.

Sullivan kissed her again, his pace slow and deep and steady, driving her closer and closer to the edge with every thrust. "I love you," he murmured.

She shattered, clinging to him helplessly as the world spun wildly around. This was him; this was her Sullivan, and she couldn't imagine ever wanting to be anywhere else than with him.

His pace increased, his head lowering to her shoulder. Isabel moaned again, holding as close to him as she could, waiting for the moment she'd come to love above all others. "I love you," she returned breathlessly.

He lifted his face to gaze at her, his ice-green eyes deep and glittering. Then he found his release inside her, groaning as he came. "Isabel. My Isabel," he breathed, settling beside her to wrap his arms around her.

"Always," she whispered back, sinking into his embrace. "Always."

ABOUT THE AUTHOR

Suzanne Enoch once dreamed of becoming a zoologist and writing books about her adventures in Africa. But those dreams were crushed after she viewed a *National Geographic* special on the world's most poisonous snakes — of which 99% seemed to be native to Africa. She decided to turn to the much less dangerous activity of writing fiction.

Now a *New York Times* and *USA Today* bestselling author of historical and contemporary romance, the most hazardous wildlife Suzanne encounters are the dust bunnies under the sofa.

To see pictures of those dust bunnies, please visit *www.suzanneenoch.com*.

Suzanne loves to hear from her readers, and may be reached at:

P.O. Box 17463
Anaheim, CA 92817-7463

Or you can send her an email at *suzie@suzanneenoch.com.*

The employees of Thorndike Press hope you have enjoyed this Large Print book. All our Thorndike and Wheeler Large Print titles are designed for easy reading, and all our books are made to last. Other Thorndike Press Large Print books are available at your library, through selected bookstores, or directly from us.

For information about titles, please call:
(800) 223-1244

or visit our Web site at:
http://gale.cengage.com/thorndike

To share your comments, please write:
Publisher
Thorndike Press
295 Kennedy Memorial Drive
Waterville, ME 04901